DARKNESS COMES AGAIN

THE SIRIANS SERIES
BOOK ONE

K.M. DAVIDSON

Cover and Interior Map Design by Brian Andersen
Edited by Wonder and Wander Editing Co.

First Edition April 2024

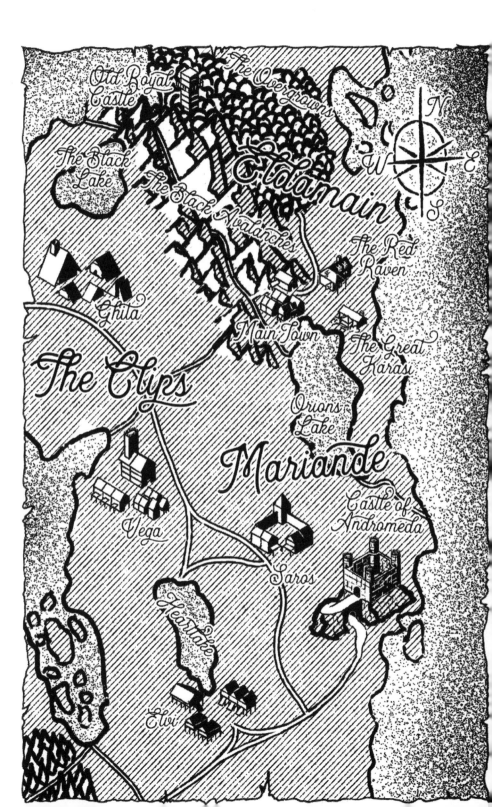

Content Warning

This adult fantasy novel contains mature themes and content that may not be suitable for all readers. Readers are advised that the story includes depictions of violence, graphic imagery, explicit language, and scenes of a sexual nature. Additionally, the narrative explores challenging subject matters, including but not limited to death, betrayal, and psychological distress. Please exercise discretion and know that the content may trigger or be unsettling for some audiences.

★★★

This book is dedicated to the wide-eyed child within,
To the dreams we cherish, forever untamed.
May these words rekindle the spark that once gleamed.

I know they did for me.

PROLOGUE

The King walked down the private wing of the castle, the hard soles of his leather boots thumping in a steady, sure rhythm that mimicked the beat of his heart. His velvet maroon cloak flowed behind him, slithering along the rug that stretched out across the floor.

Once in front of the wooden door, he rapped on it swiftly. A single heartbeat later, the door swung open in response. The maiden stood before him, blocking his view into the room.

"I am here to see my daughter," he announced. "Step aside."

With a simple curtsy, the maiden stepped to the side, her back flush against the wall. She stared straight ahead, her face a stone mask of indifference.

Sitting on the cushioned ledge, The Princess rested the side of her face against the cool glass window, nothing but an air of longing shrouding her. The King narrowed his eyes, the Mark on her forehead stark against her pale skin.

"Daughter," he snapped, tapping his foot. The Princess whipped her head, allowing him the full view of the six-pointed Mark and ruby necklace, which glittered in the faint light coming through the windows. Her eyes filled with apprehension and fear the moment they locked with The King's.

"Father," she barely breathed, lurching from her spot. She quickly gathered her skirts in her hands, bowing in a curtsey. She held it there, just as her father had taught.

"Rise, child," he drawled, flicking his wrist. She stood at attention, her hands clasped tightly in front of her. She pressed her shoulder blades together, holding her chin up. "How many times have I told you to leave your hair unpinned to guard your face?"

"I'm sorry, father." The Princess quickly removed the gold pins from the sides of her hair, allowing her bangs to fall over the Mark like a curtain. She added, "The summer causes them to stick against my skin, and it itches."

"I did not ask," he lectured, earning a flinch from her. "You are to do as you are told. You do not question your King. Understood?"

"Yes, Your Highness," she whispered, keeping her face impassive despite the tears burning her eyes. The King narrowed his eyes at her once again.

"I came to inform you that your brother, Prince Sorin, is to be married to The Princess of Teslin," The King announced, not bothering to see the rare flicker of joy across the young Princess's face, "We will be leaving in a few short days. Brand will be responsible for your care—"

"Will Brand and I be traveling together, then?" The Princess inquired, unable to contain her excitement as her hands flew to grip the necklace at her neck.

"Do not interrupt me, child," he barked as he approached her desk. He tilted his head to observe the drawing on The Princess's desk.

The figure of a girl stood out in the middle of the parchment, painted in maroon ink while an amorphous black surrounded her. The King cleared his throat, facing where The Princess stood—anticipation overwhelming her so much that the Mark glowed through her bangs like the morning sun.

"But, no," The King remarked, "You and Brand will be staying. You will not attend the wedding."

Her hands dropped from her necklace, slowly and painfully falling to her sides as her shoulders slouched forward. She frowned and asked, "Why? Am I not old enough? I have been doing brilliantly in my studies, I've kept quiet in my room... Surely I have shown the proper decorum to attend a Royal wedding, Father. Please, it is all I wish to see."

"I forbid it," he declared, his voice bouncing off the bare stone walls. He took two steps towards her, and the air shifted, thickening like the humidity before a storm. It fogged his mind and burned his throat like smoke, yet there were no flames he could see.

He cleared his throat. "You are cursed, child. The Mark you bear on your forehead and the power that runs rampant in your veins keep you from enjoying the ways of the court. Your Mark will taint the legacy I have spent decades rebuilding. I will not have some measly *girl* crumple all of that just because she wants to attend a party. You were not made for the Korbin legacy. It's why I have twelve other sons."

"Father, please," she begged, her fists tightening beside her, shadowed by her skirts.

"I will hear no more of it, Daughter," The King sneered, turning on his heel. "Gather yourself. Your Mark is glowing, which only further proves to me you have no control—"

The scream that tore through The Princess in that moment would haunt The King until the day he died and beyond; it followed him into the afterlife. It rang out, high-pitched and animalistic as though it were ripped from her chest.

He instantly whirled to face her again, and the anger, pain, betrayal, confusion, and rage radiated off her. It morphed her facial features, blackness consuming her once robin egg blue eyes so they melted with her pupils. Strange, vein-like, black tendrils stretched from the corners of her eyes, reaching for her temples and cheekbones, barely brushing the Mark in the middle of her forehead. Black mist surrounded her and vines of inky black began to slither on the floor beneath her.

The lilies on the night table withered and dried instantaneously as it approached.

The King's heart nearly gave out at the sight. He had never seen power in such a Dark form from his Sirian parents or siblings.

The tendrils stopped just in front of him.

"Why, Father?" The Princess whimpered, the black mist pulsing around her. The King could not speak, only stare in horror at what stood before him. With another gut-wrenching scream, the room plunged into complete Darkness.

CHAPTER 1

T he glug of beer flowing from the barrel and the low chatter of patrons fill the bar tonight.

Once both glasses in my hands are full, I venture over to the table of regulars cackling in the corner. Dahlia smirks from the other side of the bar, and I glare with a curled lip.

"Two full glasses for the boys," I announce to the table. Willem and Remy acknowledge me with a small smile and nod, despite the shadows concealed in their eyes, and I already know tonight will end in them fighting each other to silence their inner demons. "Are we all doing okay otherwise?"

"Yeah." Willem accepts both glasses from me. "Thanks, Reva."

I pat his shoulder before stalking over to where Dahlia still stands with her arms crossed, mouth quirked up, and brick-red eyes glittering with amusement.

"I just started my shift," I sigh, fiddling with the stack of liquor bottles. "What could you possibly have to tease me about?"

Dahlia gasps, feigning shock. "You think so little of me."

I peer at her from the corner of my eye.

She chuckles under her breath, an evil little sound. "I heard from Rol that a drunken lass was singing and dancing on tables last night." She leans back against the bar top and crosses her ankles in front of her. "Rol also said the same lass took a rather dashing traveler to the stock room for a few minutes."

I suck in a harsh breath of air and gawk at Dahlia. She continues to smirk, those eerie-colored eyes burning with delight.

I grab her wrist, yanking her closer. "We don't need to talk about that last part to anyone who didn't see it," I hiss.

"Oh, Reva." Dahlia laughs, tugging on my ponytail. "Come on. You provide us with the entertainment some have been craving for decades in this ghost town. Don't be so shy. You certainly didn't seem to be last—"

I stalk away, jaw clenched, to Willem and Remy's table as her cackling echoes behind me.

Willem is too absorbed in a deep conversation with another regular at their table to notice me, but Remy smiles as I stand beside his chair.

"Dahlia giving you a hard time about last night?" He winks with a half-smile that reveals a sharpened canine. "You know we all mean no harm."

"I'm glad I can be the butt of the jokes that spice up your mundane, monotonous lives," I reply with a tight smile. "You can't tell me you lot never took advantage of the travelers."

Shadows pass momentarily over his eyes, and guilt clenches in my chest.

I should know better than to reference his past, especially

when their moods suggest they're not in the spirit to reminisce with me tonight. These mood swings come with the territory of Magics who live decades longer than humans; the longer they live in a world that isolates them, the more pain and trauma they endure.

"Indeed," he laments, his eyes darting over my shoulder to where Dahlia stands as he fiddles with his now-empty glass. I twist around, and she's bent over the bar top, talking to another regular on a stool.

"Another beer, friend?" I ask, placing my hand on his shoulder. He leans into my embrace, warming my heart.

"Make it a sharp one this time," he answers with a nod of his head. "A glass of that fine stuff you and Karasi have been cooking up. I might be cashing in early tonight. I need a peaceful sleep."

"Whatever you need."

As I walk around to the back of the bar, Dahlia flashes me a tense smile that tells me she's preoccupied with the local on the stool in front of her.

I grab the amethyst-colored carafe from the back of the shelf on the wall. Pouring a new glass for Remy, I tune into Dahlia's conversation.

"It just doesn't feel right," the man whispers quietly. "You noticed it, too?"

"I can't deny that it's strange," Dahlia agrees, shifting on her feet behind me. "The darkness of the Black Avalanches is normal, but this just doesn't feel like the shadow. It's getting darker and thicker."

"That's the Abyss, child," he hisses under his breath.

The Black Avalanches. The mountains that tower before Eldamain shield us from the rest of our continent. They are associated with many religious and superstitious myths that date back to Creation.

Known for an unexplainable shadow that lives within their peaks, there has been a strangeness about them that's grown over the last decade or two, but particularly in the last three years.

Dahlia described it best. The shadows have thickened to a black smoke, yet it's thicker than smoke. All those who have some sort of power can feel a heaviness in the air that presses against your body whenever you are near. The older locals call it the Abyss.

"I've never been religious," the patron sighs heavily. "But, we cannot continue to deny what this means. Kuk is returning."

"You lot and your superstitions," Dahlia chuckles, but the rustling behind me indicates she's walked away from the conversation.

I stop stalling and head back over to Remy's table, catching the tired eyes of the patron and giving him the smallest smile. He nods once before tipping back the rest of his drink in one gulp.

"What's that talk of Kuk going on over there?" Remy glares towards where Dahlia now stands at the opposite end of the pub as he accepts the glass from me without looking. "I didn't know she was one to entertain Abyss and god-talk."

"Why do you think she walked away?" I whisper before meeting Dahlia at the table she's cleaning off. I help her gather the glasses and dinnerware, following her towards the wash basin.

"These townspeople," she says in a hushed tone. "They need more things to do around here. They're going off the rails."

"I don't blame them," I admit with a shrug as we place the dirty dishes into the bucket. "Despite being a damn melting pot of every tale and religious practice, the Abyss is the only consistency that brings them together. To have it playing out and potentially growing right in front of them? There will be more talk of the Gods."

Dahlia rolls her eyes, grumbling, "They think Kuk is coming back? The Gods abandoned us a long time ago. The Korbins made sure of that."

She glances up at the ceiling, drawing her finger across her throat. I chuckle, yanking the hand towel off my shoulder and playfully whipping it across the back of her leg just as the bell at the door of The Red Raven jingles.

The pub falls into a deafening silence, an odd tension growing in the air. I lift my eyes to Dahlia, but hers are trained curiously on the door with a crease between her eyebrows. I follow her line of sight to the front door.

A rather handsome man stands stiffly at the entrance, hands clasped behind his back. He can't be much older than me, if not my age, wearing wool slacks with a brown cloak, thick ivory scarf, and dark gray cap.

As he drifts toward the bar, he removes his hat to reveal deep auburn hair that matches the stubble along his jaw. He runs a hand through it before sitting down on the stool directly in front of me. He smiles at me, kind and gentle.

He doesn't belong here, and probably shouldn't be here alone.

"What can I do for you, stranger?" Dahlia questions from behind me with nothing but excitement in her voice. She maneuvers to stand beside me, drying a glass with a cloth.

The stranger meets both of our gazes and I swoon. His eyes are the color of two perfectly polished emeralds, shimmering beneath heavy eyelashes.

Definitely doesn't belong here.

"I hope it's not too much to bother you for a hot drink," he asks in a northern Etherean accent, one side of his mouth turning up to reveal a small dimple peeking out from underneath that reddish stubble. "I know this is a pub but a man can hope—"

"Coffee or mulled wine?" I blurt. Dahlia instantly picks up on that and simpers with an eye roll. She leaves me with the stranger, strolling through the pub towards Remy and Willem.

They're watching the encounter like wolves.

"A coffee will do for now." He unwraps the scarf from around his neck. I force a tight-lipped grin onto my face.

Scanning the room, I latch onto Dahlia. I raise an eyebrow in request and her shoulders slump. She glares at me before shuffling towards the fire to throw the coffee kettle on.

"She'll get that started for you," I assure. "Is there anything else we can help you with tonight?"

Those glowing eyes study me, scanning my face. I

shift in my boots from their intensity and inquisition. My forehead tingles faintly, but I push the anxiety down.

The last thing I need today is a slip-up with a handsome stranger. That would not end well for him, and I'm sure it wouldn't improve Willem and Remy's moods.

"I actually came here on an errand, and I am trying to decide how to ask what I need to without causing a problem." He leans in towards me. My gaze darts over to where the boys sit—who are pretending to be busy with whatever card game they've started.

I drag my eyes back to the man, whose eyebrow is now risen. "Are those the innkeepers?"

"Not per se," I shrug, nonchalantly. "The Red Raven isn't an inn. Besides, they're not the owners. Just a few regular eavesdroppers."

"There seem to be a few of those here," he murmurs, and it's evident this makes him uncomfortable.

"Don't worry." I gently place my hand on top of his. His head shoots down. "No one here means harm as long as you don't."

He slowly looks back up at me through his thick lashes, that eyebrow still raised.

Gods, I could devour him.

"I can assure you I come here with no mal intent," he smirks. I tenderly remove my hand, fold it within my other, and stretch out my arms on the bar top.

"Well, then, ask away. You've got no better audience than me." He fixes his gaze on me, his face relaxing until he almost appears bored.

"I come here searching for someone of great importance in Eldamain," he recites like a line in a play. "I have been told that there is a red raven that sings of where to find them."

My mouth goes dry.

The sound of chairs scraping against the floor draws my attention toward the table where Willem and Remy are. Both of the men are standing beside Dahlia now, all three of them facing this stranger and me.

He's talking about Karasi, and no one has asked for her in quite some time.

Karasi has been known throughout the world as the most powerful sorceress; a title that has placed her beyond others. As long as anyone can remember, she has remained hidden in Eldamain.

Most people seeking her out just want to see her for entertainment, like her ability to offer them a glimpse into the future is a circus act. Those who come seeking her with the code—the one this man just used—need something dire from her: healing a family member, medicine to aid an illness, their fortune foretold before making a drastic life decision, assistance in a difficult birth.

"What do you want with her," I utter, barely above a whisper. I drop my hands to my sides to try and control the wave building within me.

He must sense the opposing shift in the pub because he straightens on the stool and drops his hands into his lap. Uncertainty simmers in those green eyes.

"It's on behalf of someone very dear and important to me," he explains cautiously. "A matter of life or death."

For a minute, I don't answer. Behind him, the Magics continue to listen.

While wary, Dahlia is still intrigued. Willem stands wide-legged with his cigar burning between his fingers, ready to pounce. I look at Remy in silent question.

He nods once.

"Follow Orion on the path that leads you to the land of brilliance," I recite. "You will find who you seek."

Dahlia slams the mug beside him on the bar top with a tightlipped grin.

But he doesn't flinch. Instead, he holds my attention with nothing but kindness emanating from him.

I leave him, walking back to Willem and Remy's table while Dahlia takes my place behind the bar to start washing some of the dirty dishes. I stand between the two men who have since sat back down, placing my hands on their shoulders.

Remy flinches, glancing at where my hand rests before glaring at me in a warning. "Those hands are a little toasty, huh?"

"I've got it under control," I insist, removing my hands and wiping them on my apron as if that would cool them off. "You boys doing okay, though?"

"I feel like we should be asking you that question." Willem peers around me to get another glimpse of the stranger at the bar. "Looks like he could be a royal pet. The way he holds himself is too stiff to be a wealthy merchant's kid." Willem turns back to Remy. "When was the last time we heard those words from someone?"

"If I had to guess," Remy mumbles. "I would say a little over a decade ago."

We all turn back to the bar, regarding the man leaving coins on the counter as he layers back up. I know he only had a few sips of that coffee.

He glances over his shoulder just before reaching the door, making eye contact with me.

"And I have a bad feeling," Remy continues in a whisper. "That this might have to do with what happened back then."

★★★

I hastily unlock the front door of our hut, a gust of wind nearly ripping the wood off its hinges. Once I'm through the doorway, that same force of wind yanks the door shut behind me.

I rip off the hood of my coat, the fur edges clinging to the frozen strands of my raven-black hair that managed to escape my cap and the cold lingering on my coat as I hang it on the rack. I summon my own internal, personal furnace to warm my body.

"I bet that comes in handy for ya'," Karasi grumbles from where she nests on her sofa. Her head is the only exposed part of her, the rest of her pudgy body cocooned in a giant quilt.

"It does," I smirk, all lips and no teeth.

The fire I kindled earlier is dim, meaning she hasn't left that spot for a few hours, which has my chest clenching in concern. I focus on the embers, my forehead creasing. After a brief moment, the flames roar back to life.

She murmurs a muffled thanks.

"Dahlia sent me back with treats." I lift the sack dangling from my elbow. "Where do you want me to put them?"

"Set them on the table for now," she sighs, closing her eyes against the fire's heat and subtle, orange glow.

I shake my head as I toss the sack onto our wooden table. The loud thunk echoes off the quiet walls. I peek at Karasi from the corner of my eye.

She cracks one eye open, scowling. "There seems to be a problem stirring within you, child. Don't hold back on my account."

"I know you're ill, Karasi," I explain, shoving the stranger from my mind. "But, getting up and moving around the home could help you. Like, for instance, getting up to at least kindle a fire. I wonder sometimes how you managed the bad winters before I existed."

An unintelligible, cat-like hiss is all I get from her.

I narrow my eyes into thin slits.

She throws the quilt off, the couch protesting underneath her before she slowly hobbles towards me with the help of her cane. Her wrinkled eyes meet mine, those marigold-yellow irises and vertically slit pupils burning into me.

"That may be, but that is not what stirs inside you," she pushes.

"We may have a guest coming." I pull my cap off and rub at the salve on my forehead with a cloth from the table. Her eyes flash to the Mark on my forehead before meeting my eyes again. "Someone came asking for you today at The Red Raven. Willem and Remy agreed to run the errands I was supposed to do for you tomorrow so I can stay with you—"

"Who asked," Karasi interrupts, carefully placing herself in one of the kitchen chairs.

I follow suit, gauging her reaction while I sit beside her. She looks thinner, regardless of her pudgy body. The braids gathered on top of her head are gray now, which have only completely grayed like this in the last decade.

"I couldn't tell you," I admit, fiddling with my necklace. "He had to be around my age, most likely mortal. Auburn hair, green eyes—"

Karasi chuckles darkly. "Another beautiful stranger, Reva."

"He asked in code, Karasi," I retort, exasperated. "Not by name."

I swear her deep brown skin pales slightly, but it happens so quickly that I second-guess myself and chalk it up to the shadows produced by the fire.

She clears her throat, asserting, "Well, that hasn't happened in quite some time."

"Remy said it's been a little over a decade." I fold my arms. "He also believes they're related."

"Remy sticks himself into places he does not belong." Karasi slouches deeper into the seat. "We shall see what the winds have brought us when this stranger is ready."

"Okay, Karasi," I drawl, boosting myself from the chair. We fall into silence as I unpack the bag from Dahlia.

I try to rack my memory for the last stranger that visited.

Remy isn't wrong that it has to be over a decade since Karasi had anyone asking for her in code.

When I was younger, I vaguely remember visitors coming and asking for the Great Karasi to help them, and I know our home was revealed to them only when they used the exact code the stranger recited at The Red Raven. And while I am old enough to remember the last person who came, I can't place who that was or what they needed help for.

"I'm going to bathe," I announce, irritated. I count some of the vials and jars I pull from the bag. "Also, this is a lot of supplies from Dahlia. Are you sure you weren't expecting someone?"

"Don't test the Fates, Reva," she warns. She inspects the supplies I didn't finish putting into our cabinet, waving me away without looking at me.

I roll my eyes, stomp into the small bathroom, and lock the door behind me.

I use the pails of water I'd gathered this morning from the lake to fill the tub. I stick my hand in the water, using my powers to warm it to near-scolding.

I start to peel off layer after layer, but I glimpse myself in the old mirror on the back of the door. My golden, hazel eyes glisten back and the six-pointed star on my forehead stands out, an indent that is a few shades lighter than the rest of my olive-toned skin, like a scar.

My Sirian Mark.

The Mark that could get me killed if it weren't for a simple magic salve Karasi created long ago that camouflages it against the rest of my skin. I push my finger against it, a tingling sensation spreading across my forehead.

After lowering myself into the tub, I try to clear my mind as the hot water continues to thaw my stress and tension. I sigh, closing my eyes and sinking further into the tub until the water rests below my nostrils.

Being a Magic is not an easy occupation in our time. Long ago, they were able to live amongst mortals without question. Now, a Magic would be lucky to walk the streets of any town outside of Eldamain and make it back unscathed both mentally and physically. If you happen to be employed by royals, they shove you in a coat closet and pretend like you don't exist.

So, instead, many opt to live in outsider-land known as Eldamain, a country ruled by another and all but forgotten. The mortals seek you out only if they need you.

I heat the tub more, the warmth soaking into every cell of my body.

Despite facing harsh prejudice, being a Magic still allows you to live a relatively honest existence, performing healing magic and living with the small physical differences your House has passed down to you, like sharp canines, strange eye colors, or other odd features.

Unlike me, who pretends to be any normal Magic. I have to conceal the evidence that I'm anything else with a salve or a hat and suppress the powers that run in my veins.

I instinctively place a wet, dripping hand over my forehead, touching the skin just beside my Mark.

Born with the Sirian Mark, I am wanted in no kingdom,

which is why I have to hide.

Because I should be dead.

CHAPTER 2

I hunch over the lakefront, scooping up the final bucket of water and placing it onto the cart. Yanking it toward our home, boots crunching in the snow, I peek through the glaring sunlight reflecting off the white ground.

Remy strolls towards me with one hand in his pocket, the other gloved one gripping a strap over his shoulder. As he gets closer, I recognize the big sack slung across his back.

"I appreciate you offering to grab these last night," I greet as he gently lays it onto the cart. "Karasi was very nonchalant about the whole stranger thing, but I still didn't feel right leaving her alone with the chance of that stranger coming by."

"Let me pull this," Remy requests.

"I've got it. You already ran the errand for me." I try to tug on the handle but—I have to admit—the weight has doubled.

A big grin spreads across his cheeks, revealing both of his sharpened canines. "I was watching you struggle with the water, and I know this bag has made the cart a hell of a lot heavier. I'm shocked you even thought you could bring this from town by yourself."

"I would've brought the cart," I mutter. He snatches the handle from my grip.

He purses his lips as if to say he doubts that would've helped, trailing the cart behind him like it weighs nothing.

"Did you find out anything about the man?" I ask after trotting to catch up with him.

"You and your humans, Reva." He squints ahead, shaking his head.

"It's not often we get humans, especially looking for Karasi."

"Sure, that's the reason." He side-eyes me, continuing, "But, no sign of him directly in town. There was a carriage and three tents spotted not far from The Red Raven. We're thinking that could be his party."

"A carriage?" I question. "So, he didn't come alone?"

"Whatever he needs help with is probably inside that carriage," Remy says more to himself than to me. "It's nothing we can't handle."

"You don't know that." I stop him with an arm on his bicep. He tilts his head to look down at me, a good foot taller—which is saying something since I've usually got an inch or two over the average woman. His deep purple eyes flicker with concern.

I narrow my eyes. "There is something you're not telling me."

"You know it's not for me to tell, Reva." He sighs, twisting his head back towards the house. "I have a gut feeling. And, you know us Magics can't ignore those."

"I know that more than most." I let out a small chuckle.

"Karasi being prophetic and all."

He chuffs, his shoulders loosening a bit. "You've got me there."

"I guess I could attribute her aloofness to that." I shrug. "She could've seen this coming. But *my* gut tells me there's more to this, too."

"That's my girl," Remy smiles again, giving my shoulder a light shove before resuming our walk. "Follow that gut, even if it does involve Karasi."

I beam, watching my boots in the snow.

When I met Remy for the first time, I had to have been around five or six years old. He came to Karasi's, flustered, with wind-burned cheeks. As a kid, I thought maybe he was a bat and that he had flown here. His height combined with his lean frame, strange purple eyes, and canine teeth, I was fascinated by him. He was the first Magic I'd encountered other than Karasi that couldn't truly pass for a mortal.

He took one look between Karasi and me and uttered: *What have you done?*

Since then, Remy, Willem, and Dahlia have gone from adults who helped care for me to my mentors when Karasi would be too vague about life lessons, to some of my only friends in this world. And, like all Magics, they've barely aged since then.

"Do you remember when you met me for the first time," I blurt as we hit the porch. I grab two buckets of water, gauging his reaction from the corners of my eyes.

He pauses over the cart, and as he slowly stands back up he has the same haunted look in his eyes as he did last night.

"What made you think of that?"

"Just reminiscing," I say with a shrug. "It'd been a winter like this."

"How could I ever forget." He lets out a single, dry laugh, more like an exhale. He stares at the door, saying, "She had been silent for years, but five years to Magics is so minimal we just thought she was on another adventure of hers. When word got to town that she had been here all this time raising a *child*, let alone a…"

He lets *Sirian* hang silently in the air between us. I look away from him and follow the trail our footprints left from the start of the porch and out to the lakefront. The lake stretches on for miles without any land in sight. Beyond the lake, the country known as Mariande thrives.

The land of brilliance.

"But you didn't turn out to be so bad," Remy says, resting a hand on my shoulder. "Besides, it's been cool to watch you grow into the woman you are today without a single gray hair on my head. Even if you've almost set me on fire multiple times."

I laugh, and Remy's face lights up, full of admiration.

I've always wondered what it was like to live the life of a Magic, not aging like normal mortals do, and not knowing exactly how long you'll live. Some age at half the speed of a normal mortal, while there are others like Karasi who are hundreds—maybe a thousand—years old.

Because of this, relationships are different for them. While I might consider Remy family, what am I to *him*?

Sure, he's known me since I was young, but now we

look like we're the same age, if not a few years apart. It's hard to differentiate the sentiment towards him from friend to brother to father figure.

"Let me help you bring these in," Remy insists, hoisting up the sack before grabbing a bucket in his other hand. "I need to chat with Karasi before heading back into Main Town."

"Good luck with that," I chuckle.

Remy and I bring all the buckets in before he acknowledges Karasi's presence on the couch. She glares at both of us for a short moment from underneath her blanket. With a creak of the couch, she reaches for her cane and uses it to hoist herself up.

"I never thought I'd see the day the Great Karasi needed a wooden stick to walk across her hut." Remy folds his arm, a playful glitter flashing in his eyes.

"Watch your tongue, boy." Karasi wags her cane at him. "I have much more time on you; more than you'll ever know."

"And how long is that?" Remy simpers. Even at nearly 60 years old, Remy is still a child to Karasi. She has never admitted her age to anyone, and I doubt she ever will.

I roll my eyes, leaving the two of them to play the same game: Remy pokes the bear and Karasi mutters obscene things at him.

I unpack the bag, noticing again that there are many more supplies in this bag than normal.

"Karasi," I interrupt them, holding two identical jars of healing salve, my stomach dropping like dead weight. We already have one in the cabinet, which is plenty for our work with the town. What has Karasi seen? "Why have you ordered so many supplies? First from Dahlia, now from town?"

Remy's smile falls instantly, but Karasi's is completely unreadable. I pay attention to Remy because I know he'll give it away before she does.

As predicted, Remy falters, a muscle flexing in his clenched jaw.

"I think it's time for you to go," Karasi says sternly. "We don't need someone arriving to an audience."

Remy inhales, pressing his hands against his temples. He nods to Karasi or himself, I can't tell. I regard him as he turns around with painful speed, marching the short distance to the door. He reaches for the doorknob but stops himself before he turns it. His grip tightens, creaking under his strength.

"Reva," Remy says, his back stiff and those eyes endless, purple depths. My heart stops in my chest and my stomach twists in a knot.

"Remy," Karasi warns, her tone deep and threatening. He whips his head over his shoulder. His eyes flicker between Karasi and me before settling on her.

"It's happening, isn't it?" Remy asks her, sending my heart into an unhealthy rhythm.

Karasi doesn't answer him, her face still stoic. She blinks those bright, eerie eyes at him once.

"It wasn't enough time," he confesses. My heart tightens in my chest when his gaze finds me, confusion and pain latching onto me.

"It never is," she answers. I turn to Karasi, and those hard eyes are focused on me now.

Remy throws the door open with a crack of wood, storming down the front steps.

"Remy," I exclaim, rushing to the threshold and stopping to stand under it.

He pauses a few feet away from the porch, turning to me. A small, sad smile takes his face as he says, "I know it's been a while. But remember to keep a leash on that power, kid."

"I don't understand—" I start to move onto the porch, but he holds up a hand between us.

"Prove the world wrong."

Without another word, he walks through the powdery snow in the opposite direction of Orion's Lake. I stand there in the doorway until he is a small figure bobbing in the bright glare reflecting off the snow.

I shut the door with my back, and Karasi stares at me with the same intensity she scrutinized Remy with, but there is still no emotion to read.

"What is going on?" I whisper, a small panic rising and burning in my chest. Karasi studies me before taking hold of her cane and rising from the chair without a word.

Because, if I had to guess, Remy knows something is coming, and it felt an awful lot like goodbye. And even though I don't plan on going anywhere anytime soon, Karasi presumes otherwise.

"No." I rush across the space between us, squeezing myself between her and the couch. "No Great Karasi antics.

You have to give me some sort of answers here."

"You will know soon enough, child," Karasi says, eyes glowing. "I can't be the one to show you the things of this world. Not anymore."

I flinch. "What is that supposed to mean?" Tears threaten to escape. "You're dying, aren't you?"

"We are all dying, *aster.*" Karasi leans against her cane as I roll my eyes with a deep, frustrated breath.

"No more riddles," I plead. "Don't talk to me like another Magic. Talk to me like your..."

Daughter hangs between us in the air like a question, and I wait for her to answer it.

Since my real father placed me in the hands of Karasi to protect me, she's all I have ever known. I don't know what my parents looked like, let alone who they were. Just as Karasi has one name and no last name, so do I. I am just Reva.

In my twenty-two years of life, Karasi has never referred to me as her daughter, even if she adopted me, in a way. I am just Reva, an unclaimed orphan.

"Go clean yourself up," Karasi says instead, my heart deflating. "We need to be ready for our guests."

Even though I'm one of the only people in the world she's ever let get close to her, sometime's she's as distant from me as any other stranger.

Despite being one of the only people in the world, and her entire life, she ever let get close to her, sometimes she's as distant from me as any other stranger.

I stalk to my room, slamming the door behind me, as childish as it may be. I've lived my entire life a mystery, dancing around Karasi's prophecies and having to suppress my heritage.

And I know she does it for a reason. Sharing what she knows could alter it into a less favorable future. It doesn't mean I have to like it, nor does it make living in that world easier.

***

The knock on the door startles both Karasi and me. I stop sorting through the payments from the last few days' work, making eye contact with her from across the room. She tilts her head towards the cabinet. After shoveling the money into it, I quickly grab the nearest cap and position it on my head, over my Mark. Heart thumping wildly in my chest, I steadily open the door.

The sun bounces off the snow gathered on the porch, momentarily obscuring the figure in front of me and blocking my view of the lake where Remy and I had been hours prior.

"Hello?" I greet the stranger, my vision adjusting.

The stranger from The Red Raven last night stands straight, his feet together and arms at his side, flanked by two other men dressed in formal suits rather than the casual attire I'm used to. Snug, black pants hug their legs, swords sheathed at their sides, and thick, maroon tunics embroidered with gold designs and buttons across each of their broad chests.

"We meet again," I say, peering up at him.

"Wait." The stranger furrows his brow. "*You're* Karasi?"

"For the sake of both of our troubles." I chuckle darkly, shaking my head. "I wish I was. Please come in."

"My apologies." The stranger bows in front of me, smirking at me from beneath his heavy eyelashes. The small dimple peeks from underneath his stubble, and I steady my breath.

I side-step away from the entry, waving my hand to welcome them in. All three step in one at a time, crouching under the doorframe, their hands poised on their swords. Their eyes scan every crevice of our small home as if looking for threats.

"What do you need, boy?" Karasi demands, ceasing all movement in the house as she hobbles across the living room, cane in tow.

"Madam." My stranger dips his head. "My name is Sir Finley Wardson, and I come from the royal family of Mariande with—"

"From where?" I interrupt. The uniform, the weapons, running an errand for the royal family...

They're Knights of Mariande. A Knight of Mariande was at The Red Raven last night, undercover, asking for Karasi.

And we told him where to find her.

Karasi levels me with a glare before cutting in. "Oh, no. You can get the hell out of my house. I will not play any games with—"

"I promise, ma'am," Sir Finley stutters, his hands splayed out in front of him. "Please. The family wouldn't send us on a childish game. If it weren't the King's son, I wouldn't be here.

"I understand you assisted with his birth, and that you were able to give a remedy for him. Unfortunately, those remedies are no longer helping him. We were hoping that if you were to come to the castle, you'd be able to help."

"In exchange for," Karasi says, her voice flat. A distant look I've never seen before clouds her eyes, muting their brightness.

"A generous salary, of course." He grins half-heartedly. "The King and Queen of Mariande want to offer a permanent position as The Royal Healer. We don't know what sort of treatment the Prince needs. He may need round-the-clock care from a witch for the rest of his life, but we're not sure. Which is why the King wants to offer the position in good faith."

She leans on her cane, eyes narrowing to stripes of gold. "Will I be shacked against my will as I work, hidden in a broom closet to be called only when my skills are needed? It may not seem like much here in Old Eldamain, but here, at least I'm free."

Her cane offers a groan in protest. I want to reach out to her and insist she sits, but I'm too stunned to move.

The royal family of *Mariande* wants a witch permanently under their roof to help the young prince. I knew Karasi had helped in the prince's birth, but Remy, Willem, and Dahlia have always made it clear that other kingdoms don't want to acknowledge Magics.

"There are no consequences for performing magic underneath King Darius and within Mariande borders." Sir Finley regains some color to his face and adds, "The King ensures your protection."

"How can King Darius ensure my protection?" Karasi scoffs. "There is no protection for Magics."

He shakes his head, explaining, "You would be protected in Mariande. Magics live free."

"Free?" I echo. Karasi side-eyes me.

Karasi points her cane at him. "And what will the King do when other kingdoms find out they've employed a witch as their Royal Healer?"

"There will be no need to respond," the other knight, with broad shoulders, says instead.

Sir Finley's jaw ticks. "There are already witches working with the prince now."

My breath hitches in my chest. Having witches openly employed in a royal castle is unheard of. Typically, Magics are shoved in a corner—or in a desolate country—until someone needs them.

Sir Finley glances over his shoulder at the bigger knight that spoke, leveling him with his head tilted slightly down. The knight responds with a stiff nod.

"Well, that sounds like a generous offer." Her eyes widen, and she blinks at Sir Finley before going into a fit of coughing that rises like a wave from her chest.

"A dream, really," I add, allowing her to collect herself.

She wipes her mouth with a handkerchief, talking around it, "How long did your King give you to fetch me?"

"We have another night's rest before we head back to Mariande," he confirms.

A heavy, uncomfortable silence falls over us all gathered

in this odd circle in the middle of our small hut, my gaze bouncing between Sir Finley and Karasi.

Her body is stiff and tilted away from him, wary, but there is still this all-knowing air around her that has my stomach twisting and flipping. She tips her head back, and even though he has inches on her, she manages to look down on him.

"Unfortunately, I won't be going," she finally announces. The stranger startles in protest, but she picks up her cane and points it directly at me. "But, she will."

I straighten, my fingers suddenly tingling with my powers threatening to reveal themselves.

Me?

Remy's words from yesterday come to mind. *Remember to keep a leash on that power.*

With the three knights staring at me, all I manage to stumble out is, "What?"

"I mean no offense." Sir Finley chuckles nervously, ignoring me. "The King requests someone of your skill level. Is she as good as you?"

"She's better," Karasi admits, and I open my mouth to try and protest, but she continues, "I am ill. Frankly, I've seen much better days and I can't endure a trip to Mariande. She's been my trained apprentice since birth, and I have full confidence in her abilities."

"We need the night to discuss this before we take someone back that is not you," Sir Finley demands, fingers pressed against his temples. "I don't want to bring a woman back just to send her home."

"Take your time." Karasi gestures to the door, swinging her arms up. "If you wish, you could camp on my plot. There's room for you out there, I'm sure. You came prepared with tents for the cold, yes?"

"More than prepared, I'd say," mutters one of the knights. Sir Finley shoots him a stern look; he is clearly the leader in this dynamic. They shuffle to the door, nodding their heads goodnight. I follow behind them.

"Pardon my manners," Sir Finley blurts suddenly, pressing his hand against the doorframe beside my head. "But I haven't caught your name."

In this proximity, his bright emerald eyes practically glow like a true gemstone, streaks of a lighter tone breaking up the pure color. I have to force the words out of me, shoving them to the surface.

"Reva," I breathe. I clear my throat. "And you are Sir Finley?"

"The proper term, I suppose, is Sir Finley." He nods once, a small smile twitching at the corners of his lips. "But, since we might be colleagues, you can call me Fin."

I nod once before he turns on his heel and walks down the porch. I shut the door, pausing momentarily with my hand on the wood. I check the boarding on the front window to verify it's latched.

Hands flexing and burning at my sides, I reel on Karasi, my powers rising with my anger.

"Are you out of your damn mind?" I hiss, power surging through my veins and emanating a white glow throughout the hut.

Karasi ignores me per usual, completing her journey back to her favorite spot on the couch. She leans her cane against the wall behind the sofa, but she doesn't sit.

Pressing her lips together, she regards me as if it's just another ordinary day and she's waiting for me to cook supper. My mouth hangs open in disbelief.

"Truly, Karasi. What have you done?" I ask again.

"As I always do." Karasi frowns, head tilting to the side. She points her knobby finger at the door. Her wrinkled hand trembles, and I can't tell if it's from weakness, cold, or some other rare emotion. "Before you were ever put on my doorstep, I knew it would be my responsibility to give you a chance at life. The Stars called you home, orphaned by parents who tried to fight for you instead of turning you over. The Fates and your father gave you to me to guide you down the right path. Thus, I have. And I continue to do so, even now."

"By putting me under the roof of one of the most powerful royal families in all the kingdoms?" I ask in disbelief, ripping my hat off and throwing it to the ground so my Mark glows in our dimly lit home. "With *this*? This life in hiding was safer than being killed if someone saw this. They may be accepting of Magics, but that does not mean *my* kind. If they find out—"

"I've taught you how to control yourself and how to hide it." Karasi coughs again, each hack a blow to her body and mine.

She falls back against the couch, sighing in relief when the coughing finally ceases. I walk the short distance across the room and sit beside her, rubbing my clammy hands on my legs.

"I can't trust myself that much," I whisper, twirling my hand to kindle the fire a little. "And, how am I supposed to leave you? You can barely keep a fire going when I'm gone for a few hours. What are you going to do when I'm not here?"

"I took care of myself for a long, long time before you came into my life." Karasi wraps her arm around my shoulder with a frail hand, muttering into my hair, "I will manage after you are gone. I know I don't have much longer left in this life, *aster*. The Fates demand it of me. You are meant for much more than this, Reva. So much more. And it starts with taking this position."

"Remy knew I was leaving." I choke against the pain burning in the back of my throat.

Karasi frowns, her eyes glowing from the flame in the fire. "I can only reveal so much to you, *aster*. There is a prophecy far greater than any other I have ever received in my life. It brought me to my knees the first time I saw it. The events were put into motion long ago, but it grows stronger now."

"You mean to tell me that accepting this position will fulfill a prophecy," I question, scrunching up my face. "Why me?"

Karasi chuckles, her body jiggling beside me. She pats my shoulder, sighing with what I hope is bliss. "Oh, child. You still have so much more to learn. You're going to need every last swell of knowledge that I and the others have taught you. Just know there are Dark things happening in those kingdoms that even I don't have the answers to."

"Dark things," I repeat, turning my head towards the direction where I know the Black Avalanches loom. "The Abyss. It has something to do with this?"

"Use what resources you can." Karasi shrugs beside me. She gazes in the opposite direction, towards the door that leads to Sir Finley and the other knights outside. "The Abyss is strong. I feel it deep in my bones. Something Dark is rising, Reva, but always remember your Light."

CHAPTER 3

I give the knights until sunset before extending my hospitality, waiting for them to set themselves up in private and have their closed discussions. I grab the basket on the table and shove fresh, warm bread and cheese soup in it to carry out to them.

Only a few yards from our plot, closer to the border of our property, three small tents surround a fire in the snow. Karasi won't be happy about the attention it could draw, but what did she expect them to do when it's cold enough for snow to stick?

Their tents are made with thick material meant to withstand as much of the cold as possible. Two horses huddle behind me against our house and a carriage sits off the snow-covered road that leads travelers from the main route.

I shuffle through the snow, carrying the basket in one hand and a bottle of spirits in the other.

"Hope you boys are ready for a cold night," I announce to avoid startling them. Sir Finley looks up first from their discussion and offers a small smile. The other two give me wary glances. I clear my throat. "I bring food and spirits to help keep you warm."

"Do you wish to poison us?" The broad-shoulder knight chuckles to himself, elbowing the one with the scar on his eyebrow beside him.

I narrow my eyes, halting in front of the fire. I imagine how fun it would be to jump-scare them with an unexpected burst of flames—

"Quit it," Sir Finley snaps, pinning his eyes on them under the glow of the flames. The casual way he sits or even stands wouldn't give off a typical figure of authority, but the stringency he levels them with reveals otherwise.

"No harm done," I smirk, handing out the bread and bowls of soup. "But you all will feel real guilty for being rude once this food hits your stomach."

Unable to contain themselves, Sir Finley and the knight with the scar dig right in. The broad knight eyes me skeptically, sniffing the bread.

I pass the spirits to them, which they each take a swig from before passing it to the next. The scarred knight actually looks up to the heavens and whispers a silent prayer to himself.

"This is incredible," Sir Finley says around the food, trying to cover his mouth with the back of his hand. "We appreciate the hospitality. We didn't bring anything but dried meat, nuts, and water, so this will help with the warmth."

"Don't mention it." I smile softly. "If you give me this job, I'll make you guys my special bread and cheese soup whenever you want."

"What is this spirit?" The broad knight interrupts. "A

special witch recipe?"

"You could say that."

He continues to scarf down the food in his hands, hogging the drink.

"On that topic," Sir Finley says after swallowing. "I would say pack anything you might need to bring with you. We believe the King will be satisfied with any witch capable of Karasi's abilities, as long as they can prove trustworthy and successful. You won't need a lot of clothes. I'm sure the King will send for a seamstress once you arrive to provide clothing that suits your position."

Not that I have much anyway... "Thank you. As surprising and sudden as this all is, I do appreciate the opportunity. I've only been to the border of Mariande a few times, and I've surely never been in the castle."

"You're in for a treat," Sir Finley comments, pausing to slurp the soup. "I like to say its weather is more tolerable than all its sisters across the country."

"Isn't that what they all say about themselves?" I smile back. Sir Finley stares at me, not unkindly. I fidget under my coat. "I better get going. You guys should rest."

"As should you." The other two knights mumble their agreements without looking at me. "Thank you, again."

"My pleasure, Sir Finley." I bend at the waist before strolling back towards the house, but not before catching his blush in the fire's glow.

"Please, call me Fin," he calls out behind me.

I smile to myself as I trudge back through the snow.

Once inside the house, I lean my back against the shut

door with the basket hanging in my hand. Karasi clears her throat, sipping on her soup obnoxiously.

"What?" I blurt.

"You might as well join him in his tent tonight," she mumbles under her breath.

I aim my firepower precisely at her spoon, warming the contents even more. She takes another sip and winces before swearing at me under her breath.

I chuckle, tossing the basket onto the table. I try to fix myself a bowl but pause at the sudden sadness that rushes into me.

I peek over my shoulder at Karasi hunched over her soup at the table, staring absently at the bowl, dipping the spoon in and passing it to her lips before repeating the motion. Her every move is gentle and cautious, as though it takes quite a bit of effort to do such monotonous tasks.

These are some of my last moments with Karasi. They may be some of my last ever again.

***

To my surprise, Karasi and I are up before our knights in not-so-shining armor the next morning. It's not until we've finished breakfast and gathered my things by the door that the rustling of their tents. Karasi hobbles over to me while I peek out the cracked door.

They pile their packs and crates onto the back and top of the carriage. Fin points at something towards the horizon in the direction of Mariande, his mouth moving in some sort of discussion. The two knights only nod.

The thump of Karasi's cane reaches me before the thump of her feet. Her delicate hand caresses my long braid. I close my eyes against the tender touch, my throat clogged with burning sadness. My chest tightens as my breath starts to come quickly.

"Time flew by much faster than I'm used to," she whispers, her breath tickling my neck as she gives the end of my braid a light tug. I exhale a quivering breath and try to blink away the tears prickling the corners of my eyes. My heart clenches as she adds, "You will be extraordinary, *aster*."

Aster, or star in the old Etherean language. For once, the nickname feels more like a brand than a term of endearment.

"I'm not worried about my success, Karasi," I reply, turning to face her. Silver lines the edges of those eerie, marigold cat eyes of hers. I stifle a sob, which sounds too much like I'm choking.

And maybe I am. I can't take a deep enough breath to keep my vision from swimming. Her face softens uncharacteristically. She sets her cane up against the wall beside me before her coarse hands cup both of my cheeks.

"I saw you, *aster*, before your parents even walked this earth," she whispers, her thumb tracing a path along my cheekbone. Dampness trails behind her thumbpad. "I saw you as I see you now, and I saw you when I'm gone."

I swallow any other rogue tears, shaking my head gently against her hands.

I'm shocked. She's speaking of her visions, or maybe a very specific vision. Why would she have a vision of me before she met me, let alone before my parents were even born?

"Fate will demand sacrifice, Reva," Karasi continues, her eyes pleading for me to understand what she's telling me. "The Abyss does not lie, and you have a role to play."

"How could I have a role to play in something I'm not entirely aware of?" I ask, searching her face for any more emotion, but she's a blank slate.

"Trust me," she insists, pulling her hands back from my face to grab her cane. "Whether you know enough now, you have a strong destiny. You will be glorious, and I will always be there with you."

One of the knights whistles at the horses from outside and there's an answering snort from the animal. I grab my hat, sliding it over my head as an added layer of protection on top of my salve.

Karasi smiles up at me. She takes a deep, unwavering breath before gently grazing her hand across the middle of my forehead where the star-shaped Mark rests underneath the cap.

"I've lived many years and many lives, *aster*," she whispers, her hand gripping my shoulder. "But, you have been my greatest journey. You'll always know where to find me if you need me."

My lip quivers, and I can't help but launch myself at her. I throw my arms around her neck and bury my face against her. I commit her smell to memory, her distinct musk and lavender calming my racing heart. I squeeze my eyes shut as her arms wrap around me in return, the cane bouncing against the back of my leg.

I can count on one hand the number of times Karasi has held me like this, and I can't ignore the resolve in this hug as she braces her free hand against my shoulder. She presses her cheek against my head.

It takes all my strength and willpower to peel myself away from her. She takes two steps from me, and two knocks at the front door echo those steps. I turn my head over my shoulder in time to catch Fin peeking through the crack in the thick door frame.

"Do you need more time?" He asks, eyes glowing in the morning light. I open my mouth, but Karasi beats me to it.

"We're ready. Those two trunks are her things," Karasi orders him. Fin frowns at my two trunks before picking one up. The broad knight follows his lead, picking up the other.

My two trunks: one full of my personal items, the other full of those extra potions and supplies the castle will not have instant access to.

Realization dawns on me. *The extra supplies.*

She had ordered extra supplies that both Dahlia and Remy had delivered, all planned before I had told her about the visitor. What really worries me is why she believes I need all of this.

I spin my head to face Karasi, braid whipping my shoulder. I prop my mouth open to ask her more about this prophecy, but other thoughts cloud my brain.

Instead, all I can think about is how she's been everything to me. How her hard-ass attitude and no-nonsense glares could never cover up the admiration and awe that always shone in her eyes. How my love for her could never be enough to repay her for what she did for me, taking me in when I could've been left to the wolves.

Despite all of that, I say nothing.

She stands in front of me, contented and all-knowing. She nods once, aware of everything I haven't said. She whispers, "Go now. It's your time."

My mouth snaps shut. I back away and out the door, until I'm standing on the snow-covered porch. With finality, Karasi clicks the door shut, effectively ending our life together after twenty-two years.

I don't know how long I stand there, wondering if she still stands on the other side or if she's moved to the couch. Will I hear her move across the floor like she might hear me move down the deck?

"Are you sure you're ready?" Fin asks. I startle, twisting my head over my shoulder to stare at him. "If you need the time—"

"Now or never," is all I can manage. I quickly wipe any tears before heading for the carriage.

Fin follows behind me, quietly trailing me in the snow. Once we get close enough to the carriage, he walks ahead to open the door, his hand extended towards me. I jolt back from it.

He chuckles, a small smirk lifting a corner of his lips. "I'm *helping* you in the carriage."

"I know what it's meant for," I mutter under my breath. I reluctantly accept his hand, using it to boost myself into the dim carriage.

He comes in after me, carefully maneuvering into the seat across from me. I swipe the fabric in front of the window away, peering out as the carriage lurches forward. My home grows smaller and smaller as we move forward, the crack inside me growing by the minute.

I arrived in a wooden basket, and now I'm being carried out of here in an even bigger one.

"I hope you're comfortable," Fin offers. I release the curtain, letting it sway back before meeting his gaze from the corner of my eyes. "It's about a 20-hour trip. The men will be taking turns driving."

I fold my arms over my chest. "Will we be stopping for breaks?"

He relaxes back and closes his eyes. "We will camp for one night to let the horses rest."

I tighten my grip on my arms and sway with the bumps along the road. The faint chatter of the two men leading the horses drifts in through the window with a gust of brisk air.

I tuck my hands under my armpits, carefully warming my body with a spark of power and heat underneath my skin. Fin shivers once and a force of habit has me almost reaching out to warm him, too. We can't let that happen, or they'd probably execute me on the spot.

I take the silence to piece together some of the strange things Karasi has said over the last couple of days.

You are meant for much more than this, Reva . . . And it starts with taking this position.

If Karasi's great prophecy involves my role in this—the events unfolding right now—does that mean she knows her role?

The Fates demand it of me…Fate will demand sacrifice.

Sudden panic rises from my stomach, hot and acidic, before making its way up to settle in my chest. My heart pounds against my ribcage uncomfortably at the magnitude of that statement.

"So." Fin clears his throat, interrupting my spiraling thoughts and rubbing his hands together to warm them. "Is Karasi your mother?"

I hesitate before answering and contemplate how much I should share with him. How do I even begin to describe my relationship with Karasi, especially without revealing what I am? He waits patiently, his emerald eyes bright.

"You don't need to be suspicious around me," he comments. "We'll be colleagues the moment you meet the King."

"I've never met a King," I respond, mostly as a reminder to myself. I unfold my arms and interlock my hands together in front of me. "I honestly don't know much about the other countries, not in the ways that matter. Karasi never divulged and I never cared enough to ask. What's it like out there in the world?"

Something akin to a suppressed anger flashes in his eyes. What else must be going on with the mainland, and how much of that Remy and Dahlia even know about?

Fin looks at me, but it's more like he's looking through me, and shakes his head.

"It's true what they say about Eldamain being a sanctuary for escape," he grins half-heartedly. "Battle for power is the simple way to explain it. Mariande has become more progressive by taking a stance for Magics. It's shaking things up a bit."

"Is that why the King is openly bringing a witch under his roof?" I inquire, tilting my head to the side. His silence is enough of an answer. "Is the King's boy *actually* sick?"

"Ironically enough, yes."

I frown. "Ironically?

He shrugs. "Things seem to always work out perfectly for the King's plans. I'm not saying he is an unkind or horrible King. Quite the opposite, but sometimes I question his luck."

I guess it'd be a good idea to learn as much as I can or need to before getting to Mariande.

"Some people have it, some people create it," I mutter to myself, "So, the youngest prince? I'm guessing that means he has siblings. Like I said, I don't know much."

"Well, there's the eldest twins, Prince Tariq and Princess Eloise, who are twenty-four," he says, a familiarity in the way he says their names I wouldn't expect a normal knight to have. "Then, the youngest, Prince Clint."

"Which is who I'll be working on. And what of the other two?" I wonder aloud. I have no expectations about how this family might react towards me coming into their home. The questions still remain: how *progressive* is Mariande and who are the *progressives*?

"Princess Eloise is quite vocal and involved with anything happening inside the castle, so I'm sure you'll meet her rather quickly," Fin laughs to himself. "She is fascinated by all things abnormal. So, she'll take a liking to you."

"Thanks," I glare, folding my arms across my chest. He smirks.

"Prince Tariq is actually in Riddling meeting with the royal family on some important political business," Fin explains. "He's very involved within the army and country. You know about the Queen, right?"

"I know about the Queen," I quietly repeat, remembering the first time I'd ever asked about the royal family of Mariande.

That also happened to be the last time, after Karasi went into grueling detail about her assistance after the delivery of who I now suspect is the youngest prince. It was right after she had returned from that trip. I vaguely remember her returning after leaving me with Remy. I had to say I was about nine years old, which puts the memory... Thirteen years ago.

Over a decade. My vision tunnels.

Remy seemed to have an inkling of understanding about what was going on. Something that happened with Karasi when she went to Mariande for this prince led her to believe they would come back for her.

Or maybe she always knew I would have to go in her place.

Or maybe it had to do with this grand prophecy of hers, and she took the job in the first place to put these events into motion.

The silence in this carriage is too much for these thoughts reeling in my mind. I start to ask Fin, "What is your duty? What could you have possibly done to have the task of retrieving the Great Karasi—"

The carriage hits a rough part of the road, lifting it off the ground. I lose my seat, my knees hitting the floor of the carriage as my torso falls into Fin's lap. My hands grip rather generously onto his thighs for stability, muscles flexing under my touch.

I look up at him, baring my teeth in a sheepish grin. His deep emerald eyes have darkened in hue and the blush in his cheeks even has the heat rising to my face. After a too-long moment, he grabs my biceps and helps me back into my seat across from him.

"It's not what I did," Fin says, clearing his throat. "It's my position within the army. I'm just a knight given the job of acquiring very important people when I'm not needed at the castle."

I hum, straightening my back and suppressing the thoughts of his muscled thighs in my hands. "So, what position are you then? General?"

"How much do you really know about the roles within an army," he chuckles, reaching into a pocket hanging from his belt. He hands me a gold badge. Above the crest of Mariande, it reads: Lieutenant Colonel.

"I know nothing about rankings," I admit, handing him back his badge. "But, it sounds important."

"After the General, which is the King, I'm one of the 4th highest ranks," he tries to explain. It falls flat for me since I'm not well-versed with Mariande, let alone its army.

He catches on, diverting the subject. "You never

answered my question, by the way."

I frown, trying to recall what he asked. "Oh. About Karasi being my mother?" He nods, blinking. "She's like a guardian, I suppose."

"How long has she been your guardian?" I search his face, trying to find a hint that there's some sort of malicious intent behind his question, but he's just open and curious.

"My entire life." I shrug like it doesn't leave a hollow corner in my heart. "I was left on her doorstep when I was just an infant, and she raised me and taught me everything I know." His eyes soften, but I hold up my hand with my palm facing him. "I don't want pity. It is what it is."

He presses his lips together, his gaze searing into me.

I sigh, sinking into the carriage seat and crossing my arms over my chest. "What about you? Does the King surround himself with orphans?"

"Unfortunately, no—" Fin stops himself, tilting his head to the side. He sputters, "I mean, it's not unfortunate that I'm *not* an orphan, at least not for me… Not that you being an orphan is unfortunate…" He trails off as a weak, breathy laugh flutters off my lips.

"Calm down, Sir." I urge him, "Why don't you start that over?"

He chuckles, rubbing the back of his neck. "Both of my parents are alive. I grew up in Saros, the capital of Mariande."

"Only child?" I close my eyes to the rhythmic thumping of the horse hooves along the road, leaning my head back against the frame of the carriage.

"Yeah. Just me." Even with my eyes shut, I know Fin is

watching me.

We slip into a comfortable silence again, and soon enough, I'm lulled to sleep in the carriage.

CHAPTER 4

I jostle awake in the carriage, instantly aware I'm alone in a dimly lit cabin. I peer out the window, catching Fin's groomed auburn hair in the setting sun as he talks to the other guards over a fire, cooking game meat.

I tap my feet in the carriage to alert them that I'm awake, but they continue their conversation undisturbed. I reach for the door and stick my head out to look at the men. Fin glances briefly over his shoulder, giving a small wave.

"Hope I'm not intruding," I say. Fin pats the boulder beside him, wagging a piece of meat at me from his other hand.

"You're just in time. We were talking about the route and timing, where we'll stop for the night based on the map," Fin explains. "We'll be camping, if that's okay with you. You can stay in the carriage for the night if you prefer."

I grimace at the thought of sleeping in a headband or cap, but I can't trust the salve to stay on all night while I sleep. I pray to the Gods I get my own room at the castle and not a shared quarter.

"Thank you," I whisper, taking the meat from the outstretched stick. I sit on the rock, waiting for someone to initiate another conversation. The other two avert their gazes as they chew. I turn to Fin who's been more willing to talk. I clear my throat. "Tell me more about Mariande."

Fin nods, resting his roasting stick on his lap. He holds out a hand, asking, "Would you prefer politics or the family first?"

"Probably the family," I grumble, completely aware of how off-the-wall we could get with a high-ranking military official discussing politics.

Fin clears his throat before taking a swig of water. "We can start with Prince Clint," he begins, "He's thirteen, and he may be sick, but he's got a sense of humor about him. I'm not sure how your interactions will be with the twins, based on the Prince's health."

"How does that work when the oldest are twins?" I jump in. "How will they settle that one when it comes time to take over the throne? Or is it just automatically the male?"

"Simple," one of the knights mumbles around his food. "Princess Eloise gave it up when they first ever sat the two down to have the discussion. She told King Darius that she didn't want it, under the condition she got to choose exactly how she would be involved with the kingdom."

"She handed it over," I repeat to myself, an image forming in my head. "What did she want to do instead? Organize balls?"

"No," Fin snaps, rather sharply. "She wanted to be educated in history and geology. Elly actually has a fascination with the history of Aveesh as far back as we can go. Including—"

"Lieutenant, Sir," the knight with the scar cuts him off. "It's not best here. We're still in uncharted Eldamain."

Fin clears his throat, nodding his head against his own slip-up. The informal reference to the Princess does not go unnoticed.

"You seem familiar with the royal family," I connect. "More than those two are. Not just because you referred to the Princess without her title and by what sounds like a nickname, but I can tell by how you talk about them."

Fin presses his lips together, briefly shutting his eyes. I chuckle to myself, taking another bite of food. For a high-ranking official, I know Fin has to be young. Young, and still a little clumsy.

Fin half-grins to himself and turns those emerald green eyes to me, explaining, "My entire life has practically been spent within the castle walls. I grew up alongside Elly and Tariq, learning with them where it was deemed appropriate and spending any free time with them that I could. As improper as it might be, they are some of my best friends."

I softly smile at him, raising an eyebrow in fascination. I never truly knew what to expect when I met royalty, particularly knights of a powerful country, but Fin makes it seem like I could also befriend the people I'm soon to be employed with.

Starting with Fin. Something about how he can hold himself like a General, or whatever he is, and somehow still be humble and act like he's no different from a lowly, hidden Sirian like me.

The thought of making friends brings that burning

sensation to the back of my throat. I may have gotten a sort of goodbye from Remy, but I didn't get to say anything to Dahlia, Willem, or even Rol, who's put up with my antics for the last four years I've worked for him at The Red Raven. And I'll never see all the regulars again.

I clear my throat, rubbing my hand against the back of my neck. "So, what of these politics?" I question, looking at each knight. "You said earlier that Mariande has been making some noise accepting Magics?"

"There are a few countries on the Main Continent that are not happy with some of the choices the King has been making," Fin answers, the other two playing with their food. "Especially some of the more progressive ones. No war, but there are threats from them."

From what I understand, there are three leading countries: Mariande, Riddling, and Etherea. I'm not sure what Mariande's relationship is like with Riddling since they share the sea between them, but if their Crown Prince is visiting with them, it has to be somewhat positive. I mean, I didn't even know the names of the family members until Fin told me.

The other powerhouse would be Etherea, but I've never heard anything good about them.

"We should probably get back on the road, Sir," the broader knight interrupts. With a nod of approval, we all start to clean up the small stop.

Helping me into the carriage, Fin whispers, "You know, for a Magic, you aren't so scary."

"For a Knight," I wheel my head to him. "You aren't so

pretentious."

Noses practically touching, playful glee brightens his eyes. He flares his nostrils, taking a step back while shaking his head. He clears his throat. "It is my turn to take the reins, ma'am, so I will see you at our next stop. One of these lovely gentlemen will be resting with you until we make it to camp."

"Reva," I correct, determined to have the final word. "Just call me Reva."

"Reva," he repeats, bowing his head. The broader knight slips into the cabin after me, taking a seat where Fin had been before. He gives me a tight-lipped grin, a clear signal he will not be as chatty as Fin.

***

After one short night of sleeping in a carriage and another long day of travel, I wake up to Fin gently shaking my shoulder awake. I startle, almost smacking him in the head with my own skull as I jolt forward. I touch my head, relieved that my hat is still in place.

Fin gapes at me with his eyebrows halfway up his forehead, still alarmed.

I smile sheepishly. "Sorry. I'm guessing we're here?"

"Yes, we are," he responds, ducking down as he jumps out the door.

From where I sit, there's a glimpse of light from various torches reflecting off different shades of square, gray stones on the ground. A few different doors surround us, each with one or two guards stationed at them.

How many of them are like Fin, who doesn't appear to be bothered by a Magic, versus the bigger knight who instantly was skeptical of me?

Or potentially worse.

Fin holds out a hand, but I hesitate. "Hey. Don't worry. Everyone's readying for the night, so you won't have to worry about introductions until the morning."

"Not exactly all that's on my mind," I whisper to myself, my forehead pulsing. I breathe sharply through my nose, accepting his warm hand.

It is still a chilly winter night, but nowhere near as cold as Eldamain. The air is even heavier, not as sharp as the icy winds off the lake.

After stepping out of the carriage, I slowly turn around in a circle, asking, "Are we in the middle of the castle?"

Pale gray stones cover the entirety of this courtyard, from one entry to the other. The expanse has to be the size of a sporting arena.

The stone castle slices through the setting sun, casting shadows in what's left of the remaining light. Candles flicker in windows and various torches illuminate the stoneway.

I'm surrounded by different levels of towers, some ranging from two stories to six. The stone walls are also pale gray, except for some spots with soot or smudge marks from fires, battles, weather, or time. Balconies jut out sporadically with intricate stone railings.

The towers extend into the dusky sky, broken apart occasionally by what I can only assume is a post for protection where knights are currently stationed for the night.

"Yes," he nods, following my trailing gaze. "Once you pass through the arches of the gate, you land in this courtyard here. You should see it in the morning. There's a lot more of the detailed work in the windows. For now, it probably just looks like a bunch of rocks."

"You forget Eldamain's former castle is a literal pile of rocks somewhere in The Overgrowns," I remind him, my feet tapping against the stone as I walk in a small circle. "This is astonishing, even in the faint lighting. You can hardly believe that this castle has been standing for Gods know how long. It looks like it's a decade old."

After I'm only met with silence, I peer at Fin from the corner of my eye. He's no longer following my gaze, but instead, his eyes are locked on me. I narrow my eyes at him with a small smirk, raising an eyebrow. Color rises to his cheeks, and I catch a guard walking toward us with a torch.

"Good evening, Sir Finley," the guard greets. "Before Their Highnesses went to bed, they informed us to escort the Healer to her room. They will meet with her after breakfast in the morning to further discuss the young prince's condition and her stay here."

"Thank you, Sir," Fin nods once. "You may return to your post. I will escort her to her room."

"I am right here, you know," I remind them.

The guard frowns underneath the glow of the torch, but Fin is beaming.

He holds out his arm in a gentleman-like manner. I rest

one hand in the crook of his elbow and the other on his forearm. His bicep flexes as he guides me towards the same door the other two soldiers went through earlier.

Once we step through the threshold, I take the opportunity to really absorb every detail of my surroundings. The walls are all lined with candles lit and encased in glass that leaves them dim in the night.

The walls are all covered in a dark maroon wallpaper—the color of the old families that ruled these lands for hundreds and hundreds of years. Paintings of people who are long gone line the walls we walk beside, occasionally interrupted by the door of some room or closet.

Based on the number of windows I saw from the outside and the number of doors we've already passed—closet or not—I've never experienced a place so grand with so many places to explore.

Being within fortified, thick stone walls, knights, paintings of older rulers, and every reminder that I *am* under the roof of royalty, there's an oppressing weight that sits deeper on my chest. I'm already overwhelmed, and I haven't even met the King yet.

"I can tell by your face you're trying to take it all in," Fin chuckles under his breath. "I told you I've spent my entire life here, and I still can't get used to everything in this castle. There's a lot to discover."

"That's extremely intriguing." I raise an eyebrow at him. "Will I be allowed to roam?"

His smile morphs, no longer reaching his eyes, and quickly becomes a grimace. "I'm not sure."

I don't expect him to have all the answers. He was sent to retrieve Karasi, and he's returned with *me*. I empathize with his uncertainty more than anything because my acceptance and the benevolence of the King and Queen all lie on my shoulders, as well as the success I'll have with their son.

Not to mention my ability to keep my true identity and my Mark a secret.

"Well, Reva," Fin sighs, stopping in front of a dark, wooden door. "This will be where your room is."

I let go of his arm, taking a deep, steadying breath before shoving open the small frame of the door. I expected a small cupboard of a room, but instead, it opens up into a bedroom and living space that is as big as the shack Karasi and I lived in. My hand flies to my mouth as I step deeper in.

The ceiling has to be around nine feet high, made of deep wooden slats and beams. To my left is a bed frame made from bronze with intricate floral designs and a rather large mattress adorned with powder blue bedding.

To my right is a grand fireplace with a mantle made of pure white marble. Two plush chairs sit in front of it with a table resting between them. Directly across from the door is a small window, which has me whispering a thanks to the Gods.

On the right side of the room, on the other side of the fireplace, is a privacy veil and a bathing tub to the likes I've never seen. The water basin is beside it with a hand pump already equipped in the room.

There is a large chaise that matches the chairs below the small window, and to the right of that is a desk and what appears to be a kitchen-like area with empty containers to store herbs and ingredients.

"I think this is just as big as your other home," Fin vocalizes. "No offense."

"That was my first thought," I agree, walking to the center of the room. "I'm worried about the expectations of the King and Queen."

"Well, they were prepared for the Great Karasi," Fin nervously mutters. "Hopefully, I don't lose my rank for that decision."

"Blame it on Karasi," I chuckle. "She was the one who decided not to come and forced me in her place. And, no force on earth can move the Great Karasi when her mind is set, so don't take it personally."

"I'll keep that in mind if they doubt your abilities," Fin scoffs, shoving his hands in his pockets. "I have a feeling you'll fit in great here. You're already getting along with me."

"Something tells me that's the least of my worries." I nod once towards the door, ready for some privacy. And a bath. "In the morning right?"

"Yes, ma'am," he bows, backing towards the door. "I'm sure either I or one of the servants will retrieve you. Until tomorrow, Reva."

"Goodnight, Fin," I whisper, waiting until he shuts the door between us. I turn back around on my heel to face the rest of the room.

My trunks sit against the foot of the bed, the only evidence that I lived anywhere else. Instead of unpacking, I continue to scope the layout of my room.

The one window faces into the courtyard, but there is a single piece of fabric to cover it for privacy that is currently swept to the side with a bronze tie-back. After moving it in front of the window, I walk back over to my door, clicking the lock in place before ripping the knit hat from my head.

The fresh air on my head is a sweet relief. Two days of traveling with the hat on has left red indents on my skin from the fabric and the hair on top of my head is a bird's nest. I rub the Mark on my head, the strange tingle from the contact spreading across my forehead in response. I pull my hand away, staring as it starts to glow faintly in the muted light of the room.

I call the firepower forward, drawing it up from where I've shoved it down while traveling. I hold my hand, palm out, towards the fireplace. I shoot an orange and red spark into the fireplace, the wood instantly igniting.

After a much-needed bath, I work on organizing all of my potions, herbs, and elixirs into the cabinets in a way that is familiar to home. Every time I pull out a bottle or vial, I have a memory from my childhood and teachings pop into my head—Karasi instructing me on all the various purposes.

Once both my trunks are emptied, I lay in the bed and let my body sink into the soft mattress. I've never laid on a mattress like this before, just the scrap hand-me-downs Karasi would get from Gods-know-where.

My heart tugs towards the window, guilt overwhelming me again. While she appeared relieved and at peace with the decision she made to let me go, her words still linger in my mind as I drift to sleep.

I will manage after you are gone. I know I don't have much longer left in this life.

CHAPTER 5

M y internal clock awakens me just before a hard knock
echoes in the cold room. The mornings still hint at
winter, a thin coating of frost climbing across the window.
Hand outstretched, I call my power forward and the fire
slowly kindles into a dull source of heat.

"Miss?" A small, squeaky voice intrudes, "I'm here to
fetch you for breakfast. You are due in 30 minutes with the
King and Queen, and you should eat before your meeting."

"I'm up," I call back, "Just give me a few and I'll be
presentable."

"I suggest you wear something," she pauses and I sense
her mulling over her words. "Neutral."

"Knickers it is," I grumble back. I head to the water basin,
swirling my heated hands in the bucket.

After I've washed my face and rebraided my hair, I choose
to don a simple, rust-colored skirt that sits on my waist and
a white, long-sleeved blouse with pillow sleeves. I shrug on a
black, velvet vest over the top and secure my necklace around
my neck.

I apply a generous amount of my salve and blend it until
there isn't even a blink of a scar there. Slipping on some flats,

I unlock the door, and the maid startles, cocking her head to the side.

"You," she swallows, hand against her chest. "You're younger than I expected."

"Magic, right?" I wink. Her face pales, but she nods.

I'm not so used to talking about magic with someone other than another Magic, let alone within castle walls. But Fin did mention the King has no intentions of keeping me a secret.

"Follow me, Miss," she whispers. I smirk to myself, tagging along behind her, down the opposite corridor from where Fin and I had entered last night.

The corridor is identical to the one that led to my room, give or take a few of the portraits eyeballing me. We head to the northern tip of the castle, and I catch a glimpse of tall, stained-glass windows before they disappear out of view.

I follow the girl down a short set of stairs where we emerge in the kitchen. A large stone wall houses various fires with pots resting above them, and the chef works at a wooden table scattered with various vegetables and fresh loaves of bread.

The maid gestures towards a small table tucked around the corner from the entrance. As I lower to the seat, the chef murmurs to himself under his breath.

He cuts two slices off a loaf, then slathers each with a deep purple jam before wobbling over to me with a plate in one hand and a cup of tea in the other. He places them in front of me on the table without so much as a glance my way.

I try not to scarf down the warm bread and fresh jelly, but

my decorum has the chef chuckling to himself as he places some of the used kitchenware into a large tin tub.

"Is there something amusing?" I question as I finish off the final piece of bread.

The chef eyes me from the corner of his hooded eyes. When he speaks, it's a rich, deep accent that I know only comes from The Northern Pizi.

"I have seen quite many things before and during my employment for royals of Mariande," he explains, amused. "Never a pretty witch eating like an orphan of the mountains."

"You should see my party trick," I call out, but I direct my sly glance at the girl.

She jumps back against the wall, startled. I roll my eyes and sip my tea as the chef lets out a laugh that shakes his burly shoulders.

"Do not mind Charity," he says over the clashing pans.

"What about you?" I ask from my seat. He stops, smiling over his shoulder. "Should I mind you?"

"Chef B needs no minding." He continues with his work as Charity cautiously treads closer to me.

"Miss," she mutters. "It's time for your meeting with the King and Queen."

"It was nice meeting you, witch girl," Chef B hollers from the wash basin. I can't help the twitch at the corner of my mouth.

I follow Charity back out the way we came and down the same corridor as my room. At the end of my hallway, there is another set of stairs, larger and grander than the ones that led to the kitchen. We climb up a couple of flights in silence. The next hallway we walk down has completely bare walls except for a few unlit sconces.

With nothing to look at, I start to check every part of my body, rolling my shoulders and forcing them down and back to keep them from slouching forward. I lighten my steps so I'm not dragging them, as if I'm walking to the gallows, and fiddle with my hands, not sure if they should be in front of me clasped, behind me, or straight at my sides.

After a silent, heart-pounding walk down the hall, Charity stops in front of two large, mahogany doors carved with the old Etherean language that has evolved over the years. I tried to learn it a long time ago, but I didn't have enough books or resources to have someone teach me or for me to teach myself. I only recognize the word *Magic*, which has me tilting my head, squinting to try and read more.

"Are you ready," a familiar voice whispers beside me. I jump, turning around and instinctively smacking Fin on the shoulder. He chuckles, rubbing where I hit him. "I'll take that as a no."

"How do I prepare for a meeting I know none of us were expecting," I mutter under my breath so only Fin can hear. "Are you coming in?"

"Yes," he laughs, resting his hand briefly against the small of my back. "Look at me if you get nervous."

I nod as both mahogany doors open. Fin jerks to attention instantly before he walks in. I quickly fall in step with him, unable to tear my eyes away until we are in the middle of the dome-shaped room.

All the walls are splattered with colorful scenes of what can only be a cohesive story. I catch a few images that represent the different Houses of the Magics, and I swear there may even be an image of a humanoid figure with a 6-pointed star on its forehead.

In front of me are the King and Queen of Mariande, poised on their grand thrones, flanked on either side by half a dozen guards.

"King Darius, Queen Lucia," one of the guards introduces. "I present Reva…"

"Just Reva," I interject. The Queen tilts her head to the side and the corner of the King's lip twitches.

"I present Reva, escorted by Sir Finley Wardson," the guard finishes.

Fin bows out of the corner of my eye, so I drop into a curtsy. When we rise, the Queen and King stare at me with intrigue.

"Reva." King Darius scratches his short, graying beard, turning his attention to Fin. "I mean no offense, Wardson, but did I not ask you to bring the Great Karasi? Unless this is an elaborate presentation by the old witch, I believe you owe me an explanation."

"Your Majesty, if I may," Fin asks, waving his hand before him. The King nods, beckoning him forward. Fin takes two steps, regains his posture, and clears his throat. "As you requested, we arrived at Karasi's plot and spoke with her about your request, but she was rather ill when we arrived. She expressed her desire to go, but feared she wouldn't last the trip or the stress of Prince Clint's condition."

"Then, who—or *what*—is this?" King Darius' voice rises as he points at me. "Is this young woman going to save my son?"

"Your Majesty," Fin continues with a steady voice, fully composed. "The Great Karasi chose this woman as her successor. She has lived with Karasi and trained her entire life as a Magic. Karasi alluded that the girl is more capable than her."

King Darius turns his head to me, piercing amber eyes resembling autumn leaves. He rises from his chair and takes long, slow strides down the dais before stopping on the final step, towering above me. His fair skin creases as he narrows his eyes.

"Karasi is a—" he pauses, tilting his head to the side. "A familiar of mine. We've done business together in the past. I trust her judgment if she says you're better than her. Karasi may be many things, but humble isn't one of them."

"Your Highness," I begin. "I've been trained in everything Karasi knows. I hope I can bring something a little different to the table—"

"My son isn't a project to test new experiments on," King Darius interrupts, barely masking the panic behind his eyes. "I want you to fix him."

"I'm going to do what I can," I insist. "But, I need to see what sort of treatments he's been getting so far. We may need to experiment to determine what's going on and what will work moving forward. If I can guarantee anything, it's that."

"We shall see," King Darius mutters, dipping his head at

me before returning to his throne. The silence presses against my skin until he takes a seat. "As for your duties, Miss Reva, your work starts tomorrow. The Queen and I have urgent matters that have a tendency to pull our attention away from our son, but I will be expecting a weekly briefing on your progress with him.

"You'll be meeting with his previous nurse in the morning before she is sent on her way," King Darius explains, his hand reaching out for his wife's. "You will primarily be his personal healer, but you'll also be the Royal Healer for the entire castle, which means we'll turn to you for urgent matters. We expect you may know health techniques beyond those we have hired before, which could be beneficial for our knights."

"You'll be with our son every day," the Queen adds, her hand resting on her chest. "We want you to stay nearby at all times in case of an episode. As far as we are concerned, you can expect to be here for the foreseeable future."

The silence returns, blanketing the room as the echo of her voice fades. I clear my throat awkwardly, speaking, "And, pardon my asking, but what sort of freedoms will I have here?"

"Shall an emergency arrive, perhaps regarding Karasi," King Darius eyes me cautiously. "We would gladly send you on your way to handle private matters. Otherwise, we prefer it if you stay where you are near Clint as often as possible, but you won't need to be by his bedside every single moment. We also encourage occasional days off to recuperate. As for the castle—"

"We don't wish to imprison you by any means," the Queen says softly, shaking her head, her platinum blond hair grazing her bony shoulder. "You've trusted us enough to take you in knowingly as a witch to care for our son. We wouldn't hold that against you, especially if it means saving Clint. You can go into town for personal matters and explore the castle. Anything you need you can find at Castle Andromeda and within Mariande."

My heart squeezes in my chest. While it all sounds like a dream job, I can't help but recall Charity and her apprehension. If there are those who, like her, fear me, that means there are plenty of others who aren't as cautious in their fear. Instead, I consider those who may retaliate against me.

How much would they protect me then?

If our world is in turmoil over power, Mariande is about to appeal to any Magic or progressive thinker out there. They could win the world over if they play it right and play it strategically.

Despite my anxiety, excitement bubbles up inside me, mingling with it.

A royal library means an abundance of history.

"Any other questions, Reva?" King Darius asks. I shake my head, remembering my manners.

"No, sir," I bow my head. "Thank you for your time, and I will do everything I can to help."

King Darius nods toward Fin. "It seems you and Sir Finley have become somewhat familiar with each other already so he will be at your disposal unless he's needed for military matters. We want you to be at ease here, so having a guide you're comfortable with will surely help. Will you have any conflicts with that, Sir Finley?"

"Not at all, Your Highness," he nods. "I would be happy to help Reva."

"Well, then we are settled, Reva." King Darius rises, stepping towards me until he is directly in front of me again. Compared to a Magic, he is not that tall, but his power radiates from him like an entity in itself. "I have no doubt you will also meet my daughter, Princess Eloise, in due time." A smirk twitches at the corners of his lip. "You are dismissed, Miss Reva. Sir Finley, just a word?"

I curtsy before glancing over my shoulder at Fin as he mouths: *Wait for me outside the door.*

Once out of the room, my eyes briefly connect with the King's, and he dips his head just as the door shuts.

The guards stand tall and strong on my side of the doors, not regarding me but not ignoring me, either. An eternity passes before Fin exits the room with an exasperated grimace.

After the door shuts behind him, he faces me with a beaming smile that illuminates his eyes. My heart flutters momentarily.

"That went a lot better than I expected it to go," I explain, falling in step with him as he heads down the hallway. "Unless I completely missed the King and Queen lecturing you."

"No, nothing that exciting," he chuckles, glancing down briefly. "That was more of military business, news from

Tariq. Those sorts of things."

"Do I get to know 'those sorts of things' yet?" I hint with a shove of his shoulder. He glares down at me with an eyebrow raised. I don't push that one. "Why *didn't* you get yelled at?"

"Sometimes I believe it has to do with my relationship with the royal family," Fin admits, a nostalgic peace sweeping over his features. "Aside from being close to Eloise and Tariq, my father was a very close friend of the King's for a long time. One would say they were like brothers."

"So, you're like a nephew to the King?" I ask, realizing that I'm suddenly working very closely with people the King deeply cares about. First Fin, and soon his youngest son. I hold out hope something doesn't go wrong in terms of a particular Mark.

"You could say that," Fin mulls, stopping in front of another set of double doors."But, that means he can be disappointed in me easier than if I was just any other one of his Lieutenant Colonels. Look," he nods toward another set of double doors. "We're here."

"Where?" The double doors offer little clue as to what lies behind them.

"The first stop on your tour." Fin waits, expectantly.

The old Etherean language is carved into the frame here, too. This time, though, I don't recognize any of the words. These wooden doors are thicker than the last—older. No one guards this room, but a lock below one of the door handles suggests it's an important room.

"The library." Fin hovers his head over my shoulder,

directly next to my head.

Behind these heavy doors could be answers to the questions I've asked my entire life about my heritage. Maybe even the answers to my future. "Can I go in there?"

"Not alone, unfortunately," Fin sighs, motioning for me to follow him down the hall. "This library belongs to Eloise, now. You'll have to really warm up to her if you want to go in there by yourself."

"So, you're telling me that so few people use this library that she can just schedule her busy life around those who need something?" I glance behind me at the doors, and one creaks shut.

"No one ever goes in there or really wants to besides Eloise, honestly. All military journals and books of importance are in a strategy room, which is where Tariq prefers to hide out when he's studying."

I continue to trail behind him down the stairs to the bottom floor. I bite my lip, wondering aloud, "Do you think the princess and prince will accept me as you have?"

Or will I have to fight a daily battle of glares, harassment, and insults?

Fin pauses too long for comfort. "Not from Eloise or the young prince. They are the two friendliest and most harmless people in the world. If you misbehave, Eloise may get on you about it like a mother hen.

"You never know with Tariq. It depends on how things go by the time he gets back from his sabbatical. Hell, he could be a new man. As for some others around the royal court..."

"Some are still not as progressive as others," I finish, our arms brushing against each other softly. He offers a sad, side smile in return. I peer up at Fin, his defined jaw striking in the dim light of the hallway.

It'd be foolish not to find more allies here. The last thing I need is to isolate myself from others who could have an influence over not only my current role within the castle but maybe even the Abyss gathering in the Black Avalanches down the line.

If I can win him over at least as a Magic, maybe someday I can as a Sirian.

I internally laugh at myself and the naive hope.

Fin stops abruptly, grabbing my wrist to keep me from continuing down the hall we're going down. He twists me to face him.

"This is one of those people who are not as progressive as others," he whispers, his jaw ticking. "I would just say very little for now. Pick your fights with him when you have more solid ground here."

"Okay." I nod as my nerves creep up on me. I stare up at Fin, hoping the offer still stands to look at him if I'm nervous. He stares ahead at the approaching figure with an air of professionalism until the footsteps come to a halt in front of us.

"Sir Pax," Fin greets, "As you may have heard, the Great Karasi was unavailable so we had to take her prodigy in her place, who you will find—"

"Let me guess," a deep, rumbling voice interjects. "She's pleasant, despite being a Magic."

I take slight offense, whipping my full body to face this Pax guy, "I—"

I stop myself short, startled. I can't lie and say this man isn't beautiful, and I want to know what is in the water in Mariande.

Pax is not just taller than Fin. He's grossly more intimidating, filling out his similar but more intricate uniform with bigger arms and broader shoulders, his sleeves dipping with every muscle. His wide shoulders are set back, hands clasped behind his back, as he peers down his nose at me with brown eyes that match his rich, chocolate skin. His cropped black hair fades as it approaches his ears, and a tamed beard hugs his sharp cheekbones.

"Reva is our new Royal Healer," Fin announces. Pax's facial features are nothing but straight lines and tight muscles, but he tilts his head to the side, scrutinizing. "Reva, this is Pax Forde, Lieutenant General of the Mariande Army."

"*Sir* Pax Forde," Pax corrects, that deep voice rattling my bones. "You would be smart to refer to any knight by their formal name, but since Sir Finley has a soft spot for trashy Magics, I suspect you're already disregarding such formalities."

"I beg your pardon," I snap, my body instinctively taking a step closer to his wall of muscle as my finger stabs his stiff pec, prepared to tell him exactly what he can do with his formalities.

Fin curses under his breath.

This is probably not what he meant by saying *very little*. It doesn't even make me appear tougher, especially since

I have to crane my neck up further to try and make eye contact.

"I hope you will behave during your time within the borders of Mariande," Pax continues, ignoring the fact he blatantly insulted me without knowing anything about me. "If I suspect any treacherous behavior from you, I will not hesitate to report to the King. I have little tolerance for your kind."

I flinch, even though this is what I initially expected. These were the attitudes Remy, Willem, and Dahlia spoke of, the scorn and disgust people would not hesitate to show you when they knew what or who you were.

Sir Pax nods his head once at Fin before stalking past with the swagger of someone I would expect is a Lieutenant General or whatever that meant.

"He's higher ranked than you, huh?" I manage to finally say after we clear the next hall, still unable to meet Fin's gaze quite yet, heat flushing my neck and cheeks from Sir Pax's insults.

Fin clears his throat, delicately placing his hand on my lower waist to usher me forward. I quickly glance at him from the corners of my eyes, and his calm expression almost masks the angry glint in his eyes.

"Yes," he confirms, his answer clipped. "Tariq is also a Lieutenant General. It's the next step below the King."

"Well, damn," I breathe. "I'll do my best not to piss him off."

Fin quietly chuckles, and my anxiety softens a bit.

"That was a pretty sassy move, by the way," Fin mutters,

leaning into me as we stroll. I sigh through puckered lips.

"Not my best moment," I admit. "I guess you could say I have a bit of a temper when it comes to disrespecting me or the people I care about."

"Good to know you'll have my back when Elly calls me a thick-headed ninny for eating in the library." Fin beams wildly, and he must know what his easy smile is doing to me because his gaze flicks to the pink rising in my cheeks. I narrow my eyes but can't help the grin that escapes me.

"You think I care about you?"

He stops walking again, but this time by stepping in front of my path. I almost slam into his chest with barely an inch between us.

"I think you have taken a preference to me. At least enough to hang out with me and watch me when you're nervous." Fin shrugs, but he's still got an anything-but-innocent smirk plastered on his face. Those damn dimples also peak through his stubble, which is one of the most enduring things.

I bite my lower lip and those emerald eyes darken again like the carriage ride.

"So, what's the excitement around this courtyard I only saw in the dark?" I cut through this new, building tension before doing something stupid.

Fin blinks momentarily, but in an instant, he grabs my hand. "I'll show you."

CHAPTER 6

I finish applying the salve to my Mark, my eyes flickering between the window and the mirror, still unsure about how much I trust the thin fabric in front after I swore I saw my window on my tour yesterday.

In the daytime, the courtyard had been bustling with people compared to the emptiness on the night we arrived. The castle stood like a barrier around it, shaped in a circle with only two entrances or exits on opposite sides. From the walls of the castle to the ground of the enclosure, it was constructed from an array of gray stones.

Almost every window looking into the courtyard was made of stained glass depicting colorful illustrations of what could be historical or mythical stories. I spotted the sequence of windows that I had caught a glimpse of when following Charity to the kitchen. I couldn't depict what scenes they portrayed, but I saw enough 6-pointed stars that, now, I'm determined to find out.

After Fin showed me the courtyard, he finished giving me the high-level tour of the castle on places he thought would be useful to me in the next week—before he was called away to some official military business. I took the night to eat dinner alone, unpack more of my supplies before my first day, and consider what I'd learned thus far and what was expected of me.

A knock on the door echoes through the room, followed by Fin's voice, "Are you ready for your first day?"

"One second!" I straighten my pleated maroon skirt before grabbing my black bag jammed with a few elixirs that can aid with pain or sleep. Without knowing what to expect, the young prince could find some sort of relief with at least one of these.

I walk up to the door and swing it open. Fin stands with his arm outstretched.

"As ready as one can be, I suppose." I shrug, tucking a stray hair behind my ear.

He raises an eyebrow, holding his elbow closer for me to take. I roll my eyes but accept his offer anyway. I wrap my hand around his bicep, my stomach flipping a bit at the muscle underneath.

"Alright," Fin says, guiding me down the hall. "I'll help introduce you to Clint, and his old nurse is going to be there to give you a rundown of his situation, state of health, treatments she's used… All that information that goes over my head."

"That's how I feel about the military things you say," I tease, which earns me a small jerk of his elbow. I glare at him. "I'm sure it took you a while to understand everything. Hell, it took me a long time to remember what herbs and mixes fixed what problems. Like how the use of cinnamon for so many ailments and mixes is just…"

I trail off, my mind wandering to Karasi sitting at the dinner table with me and about 12 different vials, trying to review each use of cinnamon. She kept redoing her braided bun over and over every time I mixed them up—an anxious tick that would come out when she was losing her patience with me, frustrated because she was trying to teach me. Teach me all she knew, as fast as she could—

"Reva?" Fin's voice breaks through my memories. I turn my face towards him and he eyes me skeptically. "Where'd you go?"

"I was just remembering something from when I was a kid," I whisper, softly. Small memories click together like puzzle pieces connecting.

Fin stops in front of a single wooden door, staring at it as if he can see through what lies beyond the threshold. A small smile briefly appears on his lips accompanied by a sad glint in his eyes.

"A lot has been changing," Fin sighs, those eyes on me now. "I know what you're feeling. Questioning everything that's led you to the place you're at right now, the exact moment you're living. Too many things seem coincidental, too…"

"Like it was predetermined," I finish, nodding once. "And, not in a 'by the Gods' way. By a 'someone on earth' way."

Fin's mouth downturns as he shrugs. I shake my head, placing my hand on the doorknob.

But I don't turn it.

"Don't start questioning yourself, now," Fin whispers,

leaning in. I take a deep breath, trying to ground myself but inhaling him unintentionally.

Citrus and ocean air, like the summers when Remy would take me to the beaches on the eastern coast of Eldamain.

I stand a little taller, the serenity calming me enough to coax out my courage.

Fin whispers again, "The Great Reva."

I frown, giving the door a shove. "You're gonna need to work on that." Fin's laugh follows me into the bedroom.

I walk through the doorway, and the sight of the child on the bed makes my heart drop and my shoulders slouch forward.

No. It's not a child. It's a teenager. And that pains me more.

Even with blankets draped over his legs and clothes hanging on his body, the white nightshirt reveals his thin, malnourished body. Shoulder bones hold the shirt on him, his cheeks sunken. Dark, purple circles rim underneath his eyes as if he hasn't slept since birth. His too-pale skin, nearly the same color as his shirt, resembles a corpse. Pale blond hair swoops across his forehead, just over his eyes.

Those eyes, which are the same shade of amber as his father, hold all the life of him. Golden yellow melts into an orange-red hue as the irises meet the pupil.

They remind me of changing leaves in the fall.

But, while he has the same eyes as his father, he has the same facial features as the Queen, even as skinny as he is.

"Fin!" The boy cracks a smile, those eyes shining more.

Fin side-steps away from me to sit in the chair at the side of his bed. He carefully places his hand on the boy's shoulder, offering him a genuine smile that reflects the same joy as the boy.

Despite the wide grin taking up half of Fin's face, his eyes are dim, not quite reflecting the same emotions he's trying to portray. "How you feeling today, Clint?" Fin asks.

I take a few steps forward and there is a small, petite woman with her hair pulled into the tightest bun gathering some vials in the corner of the room.

"I think I'm okay today," Clint answers, frowning down at his body as if he'd find an answer. "The pain medicine is doing well for the most part, but I still can't keep any food down."

"We're working on it, Prince," the woman says, turning to face me. She presses her lips together in acknowledgment. "Is this the new nurse? A young girl?"

"I'm flattered," I grumble, curling my lip.

Clint's smile returns after he lays those eyes on me. I can't help the warmth that spreads through my chest at his reaction. Even with an obviously critical condition, he smiles just like any other teenage boy.

I offer a single wave of my hand. A very evident blush breaks out across his nose and cheeks before engulfing his entire face.

"She's beautiful, isn't she?" Fin mumbles to Clint from out the side of his mouth. He raises his eyes to me, which twinkle playfully.

My pulse increases and my heart pounds against my

ribcage. I clear my throat and lower my head to hide my own blushing.

Gods, *blushing*?

"Definitely prettier than Nurse Isla," Clint agrees. I assume Isla is the middle-aged nurse standing beside him, who rolls her eyes in distaste.

Joking. The boy is joking and taking typical teenage jabs at a woman who's cared for him probably his entire life thus far.

"I've got a few things to do," Fin announces to Clint and me, rising. "But I will check in on you later to make sure Reva hasn't stunned you with her beauty. Reva…"

I narrow my eyes at him as he walks over to where I stand. He gently tugs my wrist, leaning in to whisper, "Please. Do what you can for him, however you can. Even if it's just treating him like a normal boy."

I nod once in understanding before Fin leaves me with Isla and Clint. After shutting the door behind him, Isla continues moving about the room, tidying up various tools and vials.

"Well, Clint," I sigh, moving to the chair Fin had been sitting in. "I'm Reva, and I'll be your Royal Healer if we want to be technical here. But, more importantly, I want you to know I don't mean to harm you. Whether that's with questions about you or your treatment."

I don't care about why Fate or Karasi brought me here. This kid deserves a fighting chance, and I'll do everything I can to save him. "We're going to get through this, you and me."

"I know you're only trying to help in whatever ways you can," he reassures, side-eying Isla. "We've had to go through a lot to be where we are."

"Things were working perfectly fine for nearly thirteen years," Isla interrupts, throwing the cloths she was gathering onto the floor. She braces her hands on the workbench, her shoulders slumping forward. I can't imagine the pain she's feeling at being unable to help Clint anymore. "Everything was working fine. Until it just stopped. A few weeks ago, everything stopped cold."

"None of what you'd been doing works anymore?" I question, furrowing my brow. I had never heard of remedies just... stopping. It doesn't make sense. Natural herbs don't create immunity.

"The only thing that works on occasion is the pain medicine. The remedy that helps him keep food in his system doesn't work anymore, either."

I regard Clint, concerned we're talking about all of this directly in front of him, but he is entirely unphased by it. He's old enough now to know what it means when medicine stops doing its job. He can feel it and explain it better than a younger child.

"Do you have all of the formulas and mixes recorded?" I ask, standing from the chair. Isla points to a notebook on a table set up against one of the walls on the other side of the room. I wander over to it.

Unraveling the string, I open it only to find these are all loose pieces of parchment stuffed into binding. I quickly scan a few pages as I flip through it, noting aloud, "These are dated—"

"Since I was employed," she cuts in. "Karasi referred me to the family shortly after she left. She told me I should record every single medicine administered. The date and time, the measurement, the reaction from Clint. You'll find that the records support the claims. Each page is a damn-near identical copy of the day before until we hit a growth period. Then we pivot, and it works. That cycle continued. Until now."

I flip to a section a few weeks ago, skimming the pages as quickly as I can. She wasn't lying or misspeaking. Up until about three weeks ago, the days were identical. Then, it hit the three-week mark and things just got chaotic.

She tried to pivot every few days, and nothing worked like it used to, even with a little more wormwood here and a bit of coriander there. But it was like his body stopped accepting all treatment.

"I appreciate you keeping tabs," I voice. "But, you said Karasi referred you? And told you?"

"She was the one who gave me the original formula." Isla stands beside me in front of the table. I glance into her wrinkled, sad eyes, still holding the notes in my hand. "I know of Karasi and her gifts. She predicted this day would come, and warned me about it, but I thought maybe she misread it. She believes you must know something either I don't, or she doesn't, or both."

The knowing and understanding are in the intensity of her gaze. Somehow, I know she knows what I am.

I lower my voice to barely above a whisper, "I don't know

how the things I know could possibly help or change the course of treatment."

"There's a way," she nods once, starting to back away. "You must figure it out."

Clint glances between Isla and me, his eyes darting back and forth. I try not to let him see my own confusion and anxiety toward the task at hand. I'm starting to sense Karasi had a little more faith in me than she should've, or I even have in myself.

"Prince Clint," Isla's voice cracks as she starts, tears welling in her eyes. "It has been a pleasure serving you these thirteen years. I wish you nothing but a swift recovery and a long life of good health. I hope to see you walking the streets of Mariande in no time, and you will be so kind as to acknowledge your old Nursemaid."

"You'll always have a home here, Nurse Isla," Clint says softly, nothing but love and admiration in those stunning eyes. "I will never act unkindly to you, no matter how old I get."

Isla swiftly wipes a rogue tear away, bowing briefly before heading straight for the door. She hesitates in the doorway. "Good luck, Miss Reva."

I straighten as she leaves the prince in my care. His words to her echo through me.

I will never act unkindly to you.

A witch by his bedside his entire life, and he never treated her unkindly and had nothing but love for her. Whether that was a product of being in her care his whole life and her—or someone—teaching him this compassion, it is something that helps alleviate the giant weight that has been placed on my shoulders.

"So, Clint." I clear my throat and stop at the edge of his bed. "How are we feeling today?"

"My body is sore," he explains, looking down at himself. "And, like I said, I can't keep food down."

"How long has that been going on?" I ask, scanning him.

Too thin. He is way too thin for thirteen, which could be contributing to his achy bones. He should be growing and going through puberty right now.

"The throwing up was the first thing that started happening when we realized something was wrong."

I turn through the notes again, flipping back over the last month until I find the nausea. I read over each day for the last few weeks before striding over to my bag, searching for the one ingredient I know will help. I only have access to this thanks to Dahlia.

"I think I can make a difference in that department." I pull out the vial and twirl it in front of me. I get to work, narrating to Clint, "Now, your body aches could be due to lack of nutrition over the last month. It could also be contributing to the weakness and lethargy I saw in Isla's notes."

"That's what she said, too." He swallows. I peek over my shoulder, noticing he's gone a shade paler, if that's even possible.

He suddenly jerks, leaning over the side of the bed where a bedpan sits. His gagging, followed by vomit hitting the pan, fills the room. My chest tightens.

"You hanging in there?" I ask, mixing the powder to allow him a moment to collect himself. As the thought crosses my mind that the powder without food might agitate his stomach, I spot a piece of bread on the desk. "I know this might not sound appealing, but I'm going to need you to take this medicine and try and eat this bread."

I walk over to the opposite side of the bed as the pan, sitting beside him on the mattress. I pass him a small cup of the liquid and powder mixture, followed by a slice of bread. His eyes go dull at the sight of it.

"I know you think it'll come up." I reassure him, "I promise you, it won't with this."

He takes a deep, long, unsteady breath before he nods once. One hand reaches out to grasp the cup, the other for the bread, quivering. He takes another breath before tossing the liquid back.

He pauses, waiting for it to instantly come back up, I suppose. He lifts the bread to his mouth, sniffs it, and shuts his eyes. He keeps them closed as he takes a small bite, waiting again. He takes another bite and waits.

After repeating this two more times, his eyes finally shoot open. The light returns to them, a grin slowly climbing his hollow cheeks. My heart warms at the excitement and I let out a breath that is a cross between a chuckle and a sigh of relief.

Suddenly, he starts to devour the bread. I hold out my hand, gently grabbing his forearm. "Hey, hey, kiddo. Calm it down. I need you to do exactly what you were doing. Take a bite, then wait a minute before another. Otherwise, you're going to agitate your stomach."

His cheeks redden as he restrains himself. I wait until he's finished the piece of bread before moving back to the notes to make my own.

"Now, most likely," I explain to him, hand on my hip. "Your nausea started because of something involving your original illness. I'm worried it's an internal issue that I can't see, so we may need to do a lot of experiments in order to figure it out. Some will be bearable." I grimace. "Some might not be. I want to do some research first, though. For now, we've got you all squared away on the nausea so maybe we can try packing some meat on those bones again."

"This is more than amazing." He sighs, sinking into the pillow. "I know I'm going to have to eat light with stew and bread until we know for sure I'm good, but the fact that maybe I can have cake again…"

I laugh at that, patting his leg. "If you can keep some lunch and dinner down, *maybe* I'll let them give you a small slice of sweet bread. No crazy amounts of sugar like cake just yet, but if things go right the next few days, I don't see why not, Prince Clint."

"Just Clint," he says, blushing again just as red as earlier. "You can just call me Clint."

"And you can just call me Reva," I say, a deep tenderness settling into my bones.

***

Walking through the dimly lit halls with Clint's health

notebook in hand, I try to recall where the library is. I need to research more about his condition, but that means I need to get into the library and hopefully find some sort of librarian.

"Are you lost?" A honeyed voice asks from the end of the hall. I twirl on my heel, facing the owner.

Her long, dark blond hair catches my eye, flowing below her chest, but her soft waves are all I can make out from this distance. A steel blue dress hugs her waist, accenting her hourglass figure, made curvier by the ballooned sleeves.

"I'm trying to find my way to the library," I call from down the hall, waving my notebook as if that explains anything. "I have research to do."

"Oh, yes!" She gestures for me to come closer. "You're off by a whole floor. Go up these stairs and turn down the hall." She must glimpse the disorientation on my face because she chuckles and says, "I can take you up there."

"Thank you." I sigh in relief, grasping my skirt in my free hand to meet up with her. "I was worried I'd wander for hours before finding it."

"You're the new Royal Healer, right?" she asks. I finally get close enough to make out her facial features: wide, deep-set eyes and a curved jawline.

"Correct," I reply, sticking my hand out as I approach just a few feet in front of her. "I'm Reva…"

She smiles warmly, a small glint of amusement in her eyes that reveals exactly who she is. Heavy lashes frame all-too-familiar amber eyes.

"Princess Eloise," she confirms.

"I should probably bow," I realize, announcing aloud

with my hand gripping hers still. She giggles, shaking her head.

"There's no need." She releases my hand to take hold of the stairwell railing. I fall in step beside her, her hair bouncing around her shoulders. "I don't see the necessity to be called 'Princess' on a daily basis. Takes up way too much time when you can just call me Eloise. I like to reserve my nickname for my friends."

She winks, which has me relaxing a bit in relief, releasing the tension in my shoulders I didn't realize I'd been holding. I clear my throat. "I appreciate the kindness. Also, I appreciate any help regarding the library. I have a feeling I'm going to spend a lot of my free time there."

"For Clint?" She turns her head, her eyebrows raising as she fiddles with the cuffs of her sleeves. That weight returns to my shoulders, again, rubbing the back of my neck right at the base of my head where the growing headache threatens to put me to bed early.

"Yes." I nod, exiting the stairwell after her. If what Fin says is true and the Princess has adopted the library, she may be able to point me in the right direction if I share my progress. "I was able to help his nausea. He kept down his lunch and dinner, in which, of course, I negotiated banana bread with the kitchen for him to have with breakfast in the morning."

Eloise chuckles, keeping just a step or two in front of me. "Only day one and it sounds like you've already made a difference."

"As long as it stays that way. I'm worried, based on the last few weeks, that this is only temporary. I want to read more about his condition and any internal complications that may arise. I'm worried that there is something happening inside him we can't see…" I trail off, hoping not to scare her or appear inexperienced.

We stop in front of the big, mahogany doors that seal the library. "First off—" she points at me. "I can keep up with what you're talking about. You need someone to bounce ideas off of to figure out what's happening to my brother? I am all ears, Reva. Second, I may know just where to start."

She shoves one of the doors and holds it open for me.

I have never been in a library before, least of all a royal one. The ceilings soar up three stories high and the bookshelves line every inch of wall space on every level. Shorter shelves create aisles on the main one.

Eloise leads me to a desk, scattered with books, on the right close to the door, along with a few seats and a chaise. Beneath the desk, maroon carpet stretches far beyond my view, dropping two stories before continuing down a darker path in the library.

"If you need to figure something out or learn something," Eloise whispers as if she'd disturb the texts sleeping deep in the back. "There is definitely a book for it. From medical to historical to geographical, it's all here."

"I don't know where to begin." I sigh, my head fanning from wall to wall. "Is there a system here to figure it out?"

"Lucky for you," she wags a finger at me. "There is. But, as you can see, we have much going on here. I have a select few trusted assistants recruited from Saros to help with these sorts of things. There's at least one or two a day until the early afternoon. If you want to make a few notes, I can have them go looking for you first thing in the morning."

"That would be great," I say, grabbing Clint's notebook for a piece of paper. I use a pile of books on the desk to write on. "Do you come in here often?"

"I try to make an appearance at least once a day," Eloise answers, inspecting one of the books on the desk. "If you need to come in here at any point, you can go ahead and make notes for the assistants. It's always unlocked as long as someone is here."

I narrow my eyes at her over my writing. "Fin made it seem like it would take me a while to get you to give me that privilege?"

"Oh, Fin." She laughs, her face softening the same way he does when he talks about the royal family. "He's just bitter that I won't let him in here alone. I trust none of the boys. They just make a mess of things."

As if any indication, she gestures to the books piled sporadically on the desk. I chuckle, handing her the slip of paper in my hand. She studies me before gently taking it and scanning it over.

"I really appreciate the help," I pause. "And kindness. It means more than you realize to have kind people around for a change."

"I don't believe in treating anyone otherwise unless they ask for it." She shrugs nonchalantly, moving around the other side of the desk. "And, like I said, a day in and you're helping my brother. Which is all I could ever ask for."

I let out a breath of relief. "Again, thank you."

"If you ever need anything at all," Eloise adds, staring at me with those glowing eyes. "I want you to know you can come to me. There haven't been a lot of girls around. The ratio has been pretty uneven my entire life. It's nice to have another female in the ranks. Not that I'm trying to force your hand in friendship, but you know… If you ever need a friend or a girl."

My heart swells, but I can't thank her enough. I nod once in acknowledgment, pressing my lips together tightly. I get the sense that Eloise and I won't need to force anything.

CHAPTER 7

E loise's assistants kindly dropped off the various medical, herbal, and healing books I asked for at my door the day after my visit to the library. I spent my next few dinners hanging out in the kitchen with Chef B, using one of the small tables to read in private.

I've taken notes on every type of illness that could affect Clint's stomach or lower intestines. So far, I've found a few different options that don't make me feel any better, from food allergies to blood disease and masses.

After two dinners trapped with Chef B, I traveled through the hall where my bedroom is and stumbled upon a public study room equipped with a few plush chairs and mahogany-lined walls. A grand fireplace made from different colored red brick took up most of the back wall, with a large painting of a man in military uniform above it.

Now, I sit on the ground in front of the fireplace, hunched over my notes splayed across the coffee table between the chairs. I write out a few potions with adjustments to the formulas to test with Clint, adding herbs with anti-inflammatory or numbing properties to make things less painful for him while still being able to reveal any signs of the possible illnesses I've recorded.

"I wondered where you might plant a flag," Fin says. I snap my head up from my work.

He leans casually against the chair on the opposite side of the coffee table, an auburn eyebrow raised and his emerald eyes glowing in the light of the fire. He presses his elbow further into the chair, his muscles flexing underneath a simple black tunic.

"The sound of fire crackling helps me focus," I admit, wishing I could explain to him that it's my firepower that lulls my thoughts. I wave my hands over the papers spread across the table and gather my thoughts, an idea forming. "In Eldamain, we need fire most months of the year, so it kind of becomes an extension of you."

"No judgment here," he assures, bending over the chair and using a long arm to pick up a paper teetering on the edge of the table. He gives it a brief glance, wincing. "What is this? *If the subject vomits a green substance, there is a bacterial infection.*"

"Science experiments for our poor Clint, I'm afraid." I sigh, nibbling my lip. "I'm trying to find experiments that cause him the least amount of distress to help figure out what's going on, but I can't avoid everything because sometimes, his negative reaction or pain can be a clue."

"Clint is a pretty tough kid," he answers, shrugging. He gently sets the paper back down, maneuvering around the chair to sit. "He can handle anything you throw at him."

He sinks into the chair directly in front of me, rubbing the palms of his hands against his dark gray slacks. He relaxes his head back, blowing out a deep breath between his lips. His dark auburn stubble travels down his neck and his bare chest peaks out from the collar of his tunic…

Nope. I stop my mind from wandering to places it doesn't belong. I clear my throat quietly, straightening my back and focusing on my notes again.

"So, where have you been?" I don't look up, masking my tone so it doesn't sound like I've been waiting around for him. I add, "I haven't seen you since I met Clint a few days ago."

"I got called about a disturbance in Saros." He groans, rubbing a spot on his shoulder, his lip twitching in discomfort. "Seems like some men from Etherea have been spying around where they don't belong, and the people of Mariande have been trying to take matters into their own hands."

"The citizens?" I ask. He nods, meeting my eyes. I shift uncomfortably, adjusting my position on the floor.

"It's mostly the taverns in town, which are all run by a burly lot of men and women who, and I quote, 'don't need no help from some knights in shining armor'," he mocks, but with an amused smirk on those smooth lips.

I try to imagine a town that doesn't just shut the windows at the first sign of trouble but defends its fellow neighbors.

Fin continues to massage the same area on his shoulder again to no avail.

"Do you have a sore spot?" I say, placing my work on the coffee table and pushing off the floor.

"One of the fights we broke up. They got me from behind with a chair leg and hit this spot I always have trouble with," he grumbles, waving a hand at me as I walk around the table to him. "It's just agitated now. Nothing that time won't fix."

"I'm the Royal Healer," I lecture, folding my arms across my chest. "This is my *job*. I'm here to heal you from these things so you don't further injure it. I'd venture to guess you won't let up in training and it'll become something worse."

He stares me down for a moment, squinting. Part of me wonders if he doesn't trust me deep down, despite any flirting or hint of a budding friendship.

After a full minute of gazing at each other in silence, he gestures behind the chair, leaning forward and resting his elbows on his knees.

"Don't hunch forward," I correct as I walk to the back of the chair. I place a gentle hand on his shoulder and tug at it so he leans back again.

He obeys, resting carefully.

I examine the muscles and tendons of his shoulders, searching for any tough spots that make his muscles stiffen. I find a few key points, marking them with my fingers positioned above them.

He mumbles in discomfort, "Is this supposed to be helping, because I can't imagine—oh."

I suppress the urge to laugh, pressing my lips together, at his attitude shift as I knead the muscles and tendons with my knuckles. He releases a deep, content moan that shoots through me, a blush rising to my cheeks. His head lolls back, eyes shut.

Every part of his face is relaxed, his jaw unclenched, the lines in his forehead smoothed, and his pale pink lips slightly parted.

I take a steadying breath. "You know." My voice comes out hoarser than I'd care for it to be. "I have a salve that can help relieve this tension. All you have to do is apply it to the spot I'm working on at night, which should help relax it."

"Incredible. Truly magic," Fin murmurs, his voice a rumble. I can't fight against the giggle that escapes my lips.

His eyes flutter open, staring at me and nailing me to the spot. My breath catches in my throat as I stop kneading.

He breathes softly as if I'm a frightened animal that's easily scared. He blinks a few times, whispering again, "Truly incredible."

Instinctively, I brush a stray strand of hair off his forehead. I pause with my hand lightly grazing his temple.

His eyes are incredibly bright, like jewels melted into a pool of green. All I see is him, completely oblivious to anyone passing by or entering the study. Neither of us move for too long.

A log falling into the pile startles both of us, sending me back a step from the chair. My arms are still bent perpendicular to my body, my hands limp at the wrists.

I throw my shoulders back as he quickly lurches from the chair. He faces me head-on and stands at attention, eyes wide in just a bit of surprise but also pleasant shock.

"Thank you, Reva." He clears his throat, adjusting his tunic. "I can walk you back to your room and grab that salve from you if you don't mind?"

"Not at all." I shake my head, gathering my skirt as I move through two chairs to gather my papers off the coffee table.

Fin starts to help, collecting some of my notes into his own pile. The silence between us is thick, so I ramble, "I probably shouldn't be up much later. I find that Clint has a way of getting me to make promises and deals if he can improve his well-being. He kept the actual chicken down today, seasoning and all, so I promised if that happened, I would take him on a walk through the castle grounds in his wheelchair."

"Solid foods now?" Fin asks, eyes brightening as he hands me the papers. I shovel them into a book to keep them secure, holding the small stack in my hands. "That's Clint for you. He uses that sweet, teenage boy charm on everyone around him and gets them to do things for him."

Fin shakes his head, snatching the small stack of papers and books from me before I can protest.

I purse my lips. "I don't mind," I admit, following him out of the study. "To see the joy on that face is worth it. I feel like I'm already a little attached to him in just these first few days."

"His spirit and resilience are contagious," Fin tells me, smirking. "It's amazing, really. He's such a strong kid and he has been through so much. I'm constantly impressed by him. I think that sort of attitude can pull people in. That kind of light becomes a beacon."

"So poetic, Sir Finley," I tease, shrugging into him. He

dips his head to examine the papers in his hands, even if he's not actually reading them.

"Have you had any other troubles around here?" Fin peeks at me from the corner of his eyes. I stare straight ahead down the long hall.

"I find that there are definitely some service women and men that look at me like I'm going to sprout wings and fly," I reveal with a sigh. "Then, there are the knights who sneer at me and make some vulgar comments under their breath as I pass by them. Other than that, I've had no trouble."

"I'm sorry you're having trouble." He frowns. "I can say something to the King, if you want."

"I don't want to cause trouble." I wince, imagining provoking those particular individuals. "As long as it stays verbal, the words I can take."

"If you're worried about people attacking you," Fin says with knitted brows. "I can teach you some self-defense moves that will at least incapacitate them until you can run or seek assistance."

I pause before my door, head tilted to the side. "I actually might take you up on that. I appreciate the offer."

Learning a few moves probably wouldn't be the worst thing in the world. I learned some basic maneuvers from Remy and Willem when I started working at The Red Raven, but to learn from a Knight of Mariande would be even more beneficial.

Fin grins, handing me my stack of papers and books. "I mean it when I say if you need any help, anything at all, you can come to me."

My fingers brush against his, and he clears his throat.

"Oh!" I yelp. "The salve."

I quickly shovel into my room, Fin's footsteps echoing not too far behind me. I place my things onto the worktable, scanning the shelf for where the salves are. I reach for a few of the small tins, reading labels written on a small parchment sealed to the top of the container with wax.

"I saw you wearing this the day we came to Karasi's," Fin says, peering over my shoulder at my necklace hanging on a nail beside my workbench. "A gift?"

My heart tightens. I slowly place the salves back, keeping the one for Fin.

The circular, hematite stone reflects the light in a silver strip across its depthless black, enclosed with a gold circle and attached to a dainty gold chain.

I spin on my heel, holding out the silver tin. "We think it's a family heirloom. My father left it with me when he dropped me on Karasi's doorstep. It might have been my mother's."

Fin accepts the tin, examines the small container, and waits for me to continue. I press my lips together, signaling the end of this conversation.

I can't quite get past the need to keep Fin at a distance, concealing personal information. Apart from that, the details of my heritage and who I am are so vague that I don't know how I'm supposed to explain that to someone who not only has a complete family but also belongs to the royal one.

"I'm a good listener, whenever you're ready," Fin assures with a smile, backing towards the door. "No matter how long that will take. You'll find I'm pretty patient."

I let out a huff of a laugh from my nose, shaking my head. "We'll see how patient you are after working with me for a few months."

"Try all you want to break me." Fin grabs the door handle, pausing. "I have an iron will."

"Get out." I laugh, shoving his shoulder. I call out to him as I close the door. "And, goodnight."

"Goodnight, Reva." Fin grins wildly, spinning around and stalking down the hallway without a final look behind him. I click the door shut, pressing my forehead against the door frame.

My iron will to avoid complicating things with Fin is not as strong as I thought.

***

I push Clint's wheelchair around the garden on the brick path, mindful of any uneven pieces that threaten to launch him out of the seat. Both of us are bundled in our coats, the air still sharp and chilled for the end of winter in Mariande.

Compared to how Eldamain is fairing right now, the temperature here is bearable as long as the wind from the coast doesn't pick up. Regardless, Clint has his eyes shut against the fresh air with a subtle smile on his face in bliss.

"Feeling good?" I ask, leaning down closer to his head. A nod is his answer, eyes still closed. "Great. It's good to get some fresh air. Good for the soul."

"I don't think I've been outside since my condition has

plummeted," he muses, eyes opening to take in the garden. "We'll open the window every now and again, but it's been too cold. And, when I have cold sweats, warm or cool air won't relieve them."

"Those are the worst," I agree. "I've got something that might be able to help with that. It's a cloth made of special material that stays cool, but the weight of it helps calm the chills that run through your body."

My eyes roam over the various plants, bushes, and trees that make up the garden. Since it's winter, many of them are covered with tarps to protect them against the cold. I'm sure at the peak of winter it protected them against the snow, too.

How is Karasi fairing in her home, considering the storm we got right before I left? It doesn't ease my mind remembering how I'd found her after my shift with a dying fire, and I only hope Remy or Dahlia are checking in on her.

"You remind me of my sister a bit." Clint tilts his head back to try and look at me. "You're kind to me, you make me laugh. You're also very smart for someone like yourself."

I laugh, feigning offense. "Someone like me?"

"I mean," he stutters, cheeks turning a deeper pink than what the cold has done to them. "Because you're young. You're not like Isla."

"No, I'm not," I confirm, steering around the curve of the garden. "But I should let you in on a little secret. Witches and warlocks don't age like normal folks. They can be sixty years old and still look like they're my age. I could be eighty for all you know. Never think you know how old they are."

"How old can they live to?" He asks, his eyes wide.

"Well, I have a friend that's over one hundred years old. And, you know the Great Karasi?"

"That's who my dad sent for, isn't it? My mom said she helped me after I was born and Fin says she's like your mom."

A sharp, swift pinch of my heart has tears burning the back of my eyes. I take a deep, steadying breath before continuing the conversation. "No one knows how old she really is. I don't even know. Some say hundreds and hundreds of years old. Some say she may even be a thousand years old."

Clint whips his head around, almost turned entirely sideways in the wheelchair. His face is utterly priceless, all color leached from it and those eyes bugging out of their sockets. It pulls a full laugh from my lips, so much so that I hold my hand against my stomach.

"You can't be serious," he whispers, as if talking about her would conjure her. I resume our walk down the path.

"Oh, but I am," I whisper back, leaning close to his ear. "She has seen every continent and met many Kings and Queens. Dead and alive. Some say she was alive when the famous Korbin brothers took to every throne in Aveesh."

"That's just nonsense and fairytale talk," Clint answers, crossing his arms, but I can tell he's not entirely convinced that it's just that.

I chuckle under my breath, standing up straight again.

As we near the castle, a few guards stand by the door we have to walk through. Quite a few more than before, actually.

"What's going on?" I voice. Clint stiffens at the sight of

them.

"I don't know," he responds. "But I don't like the feeling in my gut."

"Word of advice," I muse as we cautiously approach the door. "Always listen to that feeling—hello, gentlemen."

Each one of the knights guarding the castle entrance stares me down with menacing glares. I meet each one of their gazes and narrow my eyes. The one standing just beside the arch of the door smirks before spitting at my feet.

"Now, that was entirely uncalled—" I'm cut off by a man clearing his throat.

Taking up the entire doorway, Pax glowers at me from his towering height. One hand lays limp against the long sword at his side. I raise an eyebrow in challenge.

"Strange weather for a stroll through the gardens," Pax observes, not even glancing at Clint. Those deep brown eyes just stare into my soul. If looks could kill, I'd be a pile of ash. "What was the purpose?"

"Reva promised me fresh air," Clint answers quietly, head bowed. "I asked her to."

"No offense, Young Prince, but I was asking your Magic," Pax responds, still no flicker of movement to acknowledge Clint, despite addressing him. I straighten, throwing my shoulders back.

"Not that I need to answer to you, Sir *Pax*," I sneer. "But the Prince has been showing incredible improvements and energy these last few days, and as a reward, I promised him a stroll through the garden. I found it fitting since the boy hasn't been out of his room since his health declined a month ago. Now, the sun has peaked, and it's time to go inside for lunch."

Pax doesn't appear to breathe as he stands like a brick wall blocking the doorway. A small smirk crawls up his cheeks during my spiel, the other knights around us snickering. I take a deep breath through my nose.

"Unless you would like to explain to King Darius why his son catches the flu from sitting out in the cold far past the time he should." I tilt my head to the side. "You let me know. I am only here to serve."

"Yeah, you are," a knight snickers under his breath, eliciting dark chuckles from some of the others. Their hungry gazes roam my body, and it takes every bit of strength to keep myself from shivering.

"That's inappropriate," Clint blurts, eyes locking with every single knight surrounding us. His hands are fisted on top of the armrests of the chair, and I swear his body tenses.

As if he were trying to stand up.

But the young prince holds an air of authority about him, even at the age of thirteen and confined to a wheelchair. I glimpse the royal he may be one day, or maybe even the royal his older brother is.

The knights stand at attention, no longer looking at me but out into the garden for any threats lurking in the bushes. Pax's face is a perfect, neutral mask again.

He steps out and to the side so we can get past. I push the wheelchair on. Just as we are inside the doorway, I peer over my shoulder, meeting Pax's burning glare, and simper.

"By the way," I whisper loud enough for him and his

posse to hear. "I am *the* Royal Healer, Sir Pax. If you insist on formalities, it's only fair."

"I don't extend formalities to those who don't deserve it," he responds, anger setting his eyes ablaze. "Those with ugly hearts do not deserve formalities."

"At least we're in agreement on that, *Pax.*"

Before he can respond, I whip back around and push Clint down the hallway, shushing him as he tries with all his might to keep his snickering hushed. I manage to suppress my smile, but not too hard.

Only because his gaze sears into my back from down the hall, trying to set me on fire.

Too bad only one of us has the power to actually do that, but we're not going to let him in on that secret.

CHAPTER 8

I open the big library doors, peeking around the doorway for one of Eloise's assistants. Instead, I catch the Princess sitting at the desk with her dirty blond hair pinned in a bun at the top of her head. She lifts her head from the book she's reading, meeting my gaze, her eyes lighting up.

"I was wondering when our paths would cross again." Eloise beams, sitting up. "I thought maybe my offer of friendship scared you away."

"No, not quite," I respond, stepping into the library and walking over to her desk. "I got the books from your assistants and I've been spending my dinners alone reading through them, making notes, adjusting the formulas... Magic things."

"I'm glad you got them," she says. "And, I hope you've found the things you need?"

"Enough to work with for the next week or so." I lean my hip against the desk, catching the title of her book.

The Truth to the Myths of Ancient Aveesh.

I frown. "Are you casually reading about ancient history or is this for some greater purpose?"

"The purpose of understanding our world, I suppose. I've

been fascinated with the lost tales of our religions that people refuse to talk about anymore. The old versions, not the new, twisted ones."

"Can't say I'm very knowledgeable on the Gods," I admit. "But, I feel like they've been coming up quite a bit in the last few months. Some Magics say there is something brewing in the air that pertains to Kuk."

Eloise stares through me, her eyes distant, biting the inner part of her lip like she's mulling over a thought. She leans over the desk, her bun just inches from my waist. I raise an eyebrow as she inspects the doors, then twists her head towards the rows of books on our right.

When she deems it safe or clear, she folds her arms against the desk. "There has to be something happening, Reva," Eloise exclaims in a hushed voice. "You can't say as a Magic you haven't felt it?"

"Is this something we should be talking about?" I warn, but she waves her hand at me as though she could wave away my doubt and concern like a speckle of dust.

"There's no place safer than here," she insists. "No one comes in here except me, and now you. The assistants are gone for the day."

I can't deny the skepticism and reservations I have about discussing the Black Avalanches with the Princess of Mariande.

But there are plenty of benefits to outweigh those feelings.

Not only does she have access to an infinite number of books that talk about these things, but she's also openly reading a book on ancient Gods that created the Magics and Sirians, the religions, and the mythologies of our old world.

I'm reminded of the patron at The Red Raven on my last night of work and what he'd been rambling about with Dahlia.

I also consider some of the things Karasi said to me and her ominous message about something dark coming.

I grab the chair from the side of the desk and sit across from her.

"Fin said you know geography pretty well," I ask, leaning my elbows on the edge of the desk. "So, you know the Black Avalanches?"

Her eyes brighten as she inches closer to me, folding her hands underneath her armpits. She bobs her head, pressing her lips together.

"Something is going on," I begin cautiously. "A lot of Magics in Eldamain were getting chatty about them acting up."

"Mountains acting up," Eloise repeats, placing her head in her hand as she pauses. "In what way?"

"I don't know if non-Magics notice this, but the Black Avalanches have an otherworldly shadow about them. It's different now."

"From our end of the mountains, I can't say that I know what you're referring to," Eloise muses. "But that could be a possible theory. The Magics versus non-Magics being able to see it."

"I'll try to explain it as best as I can," I clarify, holding my hands out. "It's like there are always clouds shadowing the sun from touching them. Or like there's some invisible tree always covering it in a shadow.

"But, in the last few months, it's changed. It's not shadowed anymore. It's more like thick, oily smoke, or ink."

"Have you gone there to know it's *oily*," Eloise asks in disbelief, lip curled.

I laugh, shaking my head. "That's a journey I don't enjoy taking. But I have been there before. Not since the strange phenomenon, but the people who live closer to them explain it that way. I also used to have a straight view of the peaks bordering the corner of Mariande, Eldamain, and The Clips."

"Is that where you and Karasi lived?" Eloise stands from her desk and walks towards a cart with books.

I hesitate, realizing I broke a cardinal rule of Karasi's. I shouldn't be advertising where she is to people. Otherwise, they could appear at her doorstep unannounced and harass her, which is the last thing she needs.

But not only do I want to trust the Princess wouldn't do that, I also don't know if Karasi stayed with me gone.

"Yes, that's where our home was," I pause, considering."Well, I guess it still is. It's just not my home, now."

Eloise stops shuffling through the books on the wooden cart, glancing over her shoulder at me with a softened face. "I'm sorry, Reva."

While I normally would shy away from it, I sense genuine care radiating off of her. Care about me, my story, or my well-being I can't exactly identify.

"It's okay," I respond, smoothing out my blouse.

She walks back over with two books in her hands. She places them on the desk, standing on the opposite side again. Her hand grasps the top of mine, giving it a squeeze.

"I can't imagine what it's like to leave home," Eloise says quietly. "Especially if what Fin has said about Karasi's health is true. If that's the case, I am truly sorry that you had to leave your only family."

I swallow the tight knot in my throat, fighting against tears in hopes of forcing them back into their places behind my eyes.

I clear my throat, scanning the titles of the books she's placed before me. "What are these?"

"Well." Eloise removes her hand from mine, holding the books out to me. "I know that you don't have a lot of time on your hands, but I figured if you were curious about the history of the Black Avalanches or maybe some other tales of them, these books might help. It gets a little mystical with the Gods and demi-gods in one of them, while the other talks about facts like relics or items that have been found there on expeditions."

"I'm actually intrigued now," I chuckle darkly, accepting the books. "I'm curious to see if there is anything that's happened to the mountains like this before. With the inky shadows."

"I definitely think it's worth a read," Eloise nods, sitting back in her chair.

I hold the books, staring at the title of the top one: *The Mystery of The Black Avalanches*. Straightforward enough.

"You said that you feel something, too," I inquire, narrowing my eyes. "What have you experienced?"

Eloise stares over my shoulder towards the back of the library. She shakes her head ever so slightly, letting out a deep sigh she's been holding in.

"Things are strange," Eloise starts, meeting my gaze. "Our Magic communities have been a little restless, moving around town, asking questions about the Darkness or the Abyss."

"Magic communities," I mull over. "You have a Magic community here?"

"A small one, but it's grown in the last few years as Father's support for the Magics has grown, and they've put their trust in him," Eloise explains with a sheepish smile. "We're hopeful you accepting this job here will encourage more to come."

I recline all the way back in my chair, crossing my arms over my chest.

A whole Magic community within Mariande, particularly the capital city, is monumental. Multiple Magics trust an entire kingdom to vouch for and protect them as people.

And Eloise is right. When word gets out that I'm here working in the castle as The Royal Healer, more Magics may flood this city in search of a normal life.

"Fin hinted maybe there's a motive behind it," I challenge, tilting my head to the side. "You seem pretty intelligent. What do you say?"

Eloise smirks, mischief setting those orange hues in her

eyes ablaze. "I would agree. A King does nothing without a motive when it involves his kingdom."

I roll my eyes, but I recall what she said about the Magic communities. My mind starts spinning as I startle in the chair, sitting straight up. "Did you say the Abyss?"

"Yes," Eloise drawls, eyeing me suspiciously. "We weren't sure exactly what that meant... But you know?"

"Possibly," I mutter, but her eyebrows raise expectantly. "The Abyss is what some of the older Magics are calling this. It's come up in conversation, and some say it involves the Sirians."

"Something to do with *them*, that you've just heard in conversation?" Eloise questions not unkindly but with more credulousness.

"When the elder Magics have their superstitions, it's always linked to the Sirians." I shrug.

I happen to know *exactly* how the Abyss is linked to them, but I'm not about to have this conversation with the Princess of Mariande.

The Abyss is what Magics have been using to describe the strange substance that has claimed the Black Avalanches. It's linked to the Darkness, which Eloise mentioned in conjunction with the Abyss.

The Darkness is said to be an infection of the Sirian power.

That power—the Light—is exactly what it sounds like: a type of kinetic energy. On the other hand, the Darkness manifests like black tendrils or vines.

The way Karasi described it to me a few years ago, she

said it was like an entity, a parasite. It can be twice as powerful as the Light of the Sirian, and a hell of a lot more dangerous. It can infect and, when wielded effectively, can cause its victims to choke on it like tar and invade the mind.

The Darkness rises within a Sirian child when there is fear surrounding them and their powers during development, particularly when it's directed toward the child. That fear causes the Light to morph.

Where the kinetic energy of the Light can allow them to glow, light things up, and energize them, the Darkness just turns things...well, *dark*.

I have never experienced another Sirian before, let alone one that could wield the Darkness. Thankfully, Karasi raised me around those who did not fear me or my Mark.

Alas, in a world where some are allowed to survive as I have but live in fear of themselves, one would consider that the Abyss of the Black Avalanches would react to a host of hidden Sirians that wield the Darkness.

***

Clint and I sit quietly in his room reading our respective books. While I study the pages of another rare medical conditions book, Clint reads through *The Mystery of The Black Avalanches,* which he managed to snatch from my bag when I hugged him this morning.

He hasn't taken his eyes off it, even while I'd done my examinations. He blindly accepted whatever vials or food I handed him. I chuckle every time he grumbles something under his breath with awe.

"Reva," Clint blurts, still focusing on the page he has open. "It says here that expeditions have found strange carcasses that are unlike any animals that roam anywhere in Aveesh. What does that mean?"

"Some Magics believe they come from the beings their Houses represent," I shrug, flipping a page without looking up, "When the demi-gods created the Houses, it was because they had turned those beings into more mortal forms."

"Do you really think the Gods roamed amongst us?" He asks.

"Where I come from, Clint," I explain, bookmarking my page. "We have to believe *in* the Gods. Like I said, how else do Magics vary so differently in physical form? The Gods roaming among us explains the existence of the Magics and their abilities, even the Sirians. How else do they have super strength or speed? How would the Sirians have such power as they did? It doesn't mean I think I should honor them."

"I wish I knew more about the Sirians," Clint muses, whispering *that* word. "What happened to them, what it was like when they existed and ruled the kingdoms… I feel like it's a curse to even speak about them, but I don't understand why."

My heart tightens in my chest, and at the same time, the contents of my stomach stir restlessly.

Listening to a young prince discuss the Sirians at all is an enigma, but the fact that he is trying to wrap his head around the transgressions regarding their disappearance is enlightening. As far as anyone in this world is concerned, they no longer exist, so there's no need for anyone to bother about them.

That would explain why he doesn't know much about them to begin with. Whether his agitation stems from a lack of historical reference or true empathy, it makes me want to take any chance I can to influence this young boy to see the good.

"You and me both, kid," I say evenly. "I'm sure your parents would behead me for letting you read about the Black Avalanches, let alone the Sirians, though."

"They're the ones that have the books in their library, aren't they?" he challenges, sticking a piece of parchment in between the pages to hold his place. "They could easily be like the Queen and King of Etherea and forbid free access to the library."

"They do that?" I question, but I'm not surprised.

Etherea, the country neighboring Mariande's southern borders, is known for being very conservative in its views of anything related to Magics and Sirians. Many in Eldamain described Ethera as stepping into a different time, trapped in the era when the Korbin brothers ran rampant through Aveesh trying to wipe out anything that posed a threat to their reign and legacy.

"I'm sure people in Eldamain know the state of that country," Clint echoes my thoughts, curling his lip. Once again, I contemplate how much his older brother, the Crown Prince, has influenced his mannerisms and thoughts.

"Well, as much as I would like to continue these historical and rather philosophical questions with you all day." I slap my hand on my book. "I have something I would like to try if you are down for it. I want to see you all healed up so that I can make sure your kind heart can rule properly one day and change the world."

Clint sets his book aside, sitting himself upright without so much as a wince. I move towards my box of herbs that I brought up today, all of the contents chosen based on a quick glance at some of the potions I saw in the book I'd been reading.

As I sort through the vials, the click of the door handle opening has both Clint and I exchange wide eyes in relief.

Whoever is walking in had perfect timing.

Clint quickly slips his Black Avalanches book underneath his pillow just as King Darius walks through the doorway before Fin.

"Good afternoon, Miss Reva," King Darius greets with a nod of his head. "Someone reported to me that there had been laughter coming from this end of the hall, and I had to investigate personally because that was a rare occurrence when Clint had a Healer in his room previously."

Fin is beaming as I bow. "Thank you, Your Highness. Clint has been on the mend."

"I have read the reports you've given to my guard." The King folds his hands behind his back, walking towards where I stand by my supplies. Fin purses his lips at me, his eyebrows shooting up his forehead, as he struts over to Clint's bedside. The King adds, "Tell me, Miss Reva, how do you *feel* about Clint's progress? Not the official report."

"I have stated most of my findings and opinions within

the report," I assure, placing the few vials I'd picked up on top of the chair beside me.

I move to fold my arms across my chest but realize how casual that is. After an awkward fidget, I settle them beside me. An amused snort comes from the King of Mariande.

"You don't need to keep up a formal front for my sake, Reva. I find them boring." King Darius chuckles, peering into my box.

I press my lips together briefly before explaining, "As I said, he is making progress. He's able to hold food down, his strength is restoring daily, he has the ability to concentrate on tasks, and he is awake far more than he is asleep."

"I hear a 'but' coming," he mumbles, inspecting a vial of kava.

"But," I confirm, interlacing my fingers in front of me. "I'm concerned about the longevity of these remedies. Most of the ones I've found have been for temporary relief. I'm concerned that these will not last us as long as Karasi's initial remedy."

"Treating, not curing," King Darius mutters quietly. He places the kava back in its empty space, facing me fully. His voice is a little clearer when he asks, "And Karasi can be of no help?"

"She insisted only I could help," I sigh heavily, pressing my fingers to my throbbing temple. "Whether that means she is on a quest to help me in my learnings as a Healer or genuinely does not know what to do is beyond me."

King Darius releases a long breath, glancing over his shoulder at his son. "I know you've been doing incredible work, Miss Reva. Seeing my son full of life is something I thought I'd lost. Do what you can and use the library at your disposal. Have you been able to meet with Eloise?"

"I have," I confirm, motioning my head to the books next to my box. "She's giving me more than enough for the next week."

King Darius smiles affectionately. "She's had her head in books since she could identify illustrations. The first thing she ever picked up was a map."

From the conversations I've had with Eloise, I'm not shocked in the slightest. My lip twitches up briefly, catching the King's attention.

He raises an eyebrow.

I elaborate, "I'm not shocked to hear that. I've already grown a little fond of your daughter. And your son for that matter."

"I can tell they've grown fond of you." King Darius' eyes fall on Clint.

Clint and Fin are huddled close together, heads nearly touching. They are both staring at the King and me, whispering to each other.

I raise an eyebrow at them.

Clint instantly breaks into a blush across his cheeks, but Fin fights his smirk with a wink.

"Is that for me, Sir Finley?" King Darius asks with no hint of amusement in his voice.

Fin shoots up from the chair, straightening at attention as it clatters to the ground. Clint snickers at him, trying to mask it with a cough. A grin breaks out across my own face, the tension in my chest lightening.

"If you wish it to be, Your Highness." Fin straightens, saluting. The King narrows his eyes at him, but there's a faint upward pull at the corner of his lips.

"Miss Reva," King Darius turns his attention to me. "You can take leave early today. I have found some time in my schedule and would love to see personally how my son is doing. It's been a while since I've been able to sit by his side."

"Absolutely," I agree with a bow. "If you ever find that you have some time for your son to join you in your office or anywhere else in the castle, as his Healer, he's well enough to travel to you by wheelchair. We've been taking strolls through the grounds, so I don't see why he couldn't join you and your wife. A change of scenery is helpful to him."

"That's good to know, and better to hear." King Darius walks over to his son, switching spots with Fin.

I start to gather my belongings in a pile. Fin quickly appears, joining in the cleanup.

"You don't have to do that," I say under my breath. Fin lets out an unintelligible sound that tells me, *But I want to.*

I shoot him a glare and he ignores it as he picks up my box of potions and vials with a toothy smile. I grab my books, placing them on top of the box with an even cheesier smirk.

His face falters momentarily at the added weight but he doesn't complain as we step into the hall and begin the journey back to my room.

"I would ask how Clint is coming along, but truly, I have never seen him better," Fin compliments, bumping my shoulder with his own. "I also heard what you said about all of your work being a temporary solution?"

I sigh, the statement settling on my shoulders and into my bones.

"The remedy I'm giving him every day is just an altered version of what he was getting before. It had only curbed the symptoms and eventually stopped working, just like I suspect these will." I imagine Clint returning to the ghost he'd been when I arrived, and my fists ball at my sides. "I was hired to find a cure, not to mask the current problems. What ails him isn't normal, and that is never what a Magic or Healer wants."

"Is there no way to find out?" Fin inquires, a slight panic radiating from him as a deep crease works its way between his brow.

"Other than unnecessarily cutting him open," I half laugh in disbelief, mostly at the situation we're in. "But even then, if I felt like it would help, I don't know what I'm dealing with and that could potentially harm him further."

Fin and I continue our walk to my room in comfortable silence. I mull over what Karasi could possibly have been thinking, that I would be able to help this boy more than she could.

Growing close to the kid hasn't helped my situation in the slightest, because now I could not just be failing the Royal family—a daunting fact in itself—but I could also be failing this child I've come to care for.

My knowledge surely cannot expand beyond Karasi's.

I unlock the door to my room, holding it open and

allowing Fin to go in ahead of me. He heads for the small kitchen-like area he knows I use to store my vials, placing the box on the wooden top.

I take the books off the top to place them on the table beside my bed. I skim the titles before mumbling, "Godsdamnit."

"Something wrong?" Fin inquires, coming to inspect them with me.

"I forgot a book I was letting Clint read, and I just remembered it's currently under his pillow," I groan, rubbing my temple with my right hand, a dull ache forming behind my Mark.

I know I'm going to need to expel power soon, but I can't begin to determine how or when. Using a small bit of firepower to light and dim the fire isn't cutting it.

"A book he probably shouldn't be reading, but you let him?" Fin guesses, grinning mischievously at me.

I whip my head, narrowing my eyes. "If the King sees I let his son read about the Black Avalanches, I'm sure I'll never be left alone with the kid again," I groan, sitting at the edge of my bed.

Fin chuckles to himself, clearly finding my problems amusing. He takes a seat beside me slowly, our legs brushing against each other.

"If the King lets his daughter have free reign of one of the largest libraries in the continent," Fin explains, hands rubbing his knees. "I highly doubt that he's concerned his son is reading about some mystical mountains."

I blow a breath of relief, laying my head gently against

his shoulder.

Being around these royals is such a drastic difference from what I anticipated. I was ready to work around strict rules and tight leashes, but in reality, the Hespers seem to have the freedom to do as they wish and educate themselves with more progressive literature.

The Princess was allowed to deny being the first in line to the throne because she didn't *want* to.

"You'll get the hang of this country soon," Fin encourages, speaking softly as he nearly reads my mind. "I'm sure growing up in Eldamain really didn't allow you to learn a lot about the goings-on of the world. People who don't actually live within these walls barely know or understand the inner workings of the Hespers either. You're already getting access to a unique point of view that most Saros doesn't see, let alone Mariande."

I nod against his shoulder, the fabric of his uniform stiff against my cheek. My eyes start to drift closed…

Not before I remember that we are not only in my private room, but the door is still wide open.

I jerk upright, putting a small distance between where our legs had been touching. Fin's eyes flash disappointment momentarily before softening.

"Sorry about that," I clear my throat. "I'm just a little drained is all."

But Fin doesn't respond. Not verbally, at least.

Instead, his hand reaches out, brushing my hair off my cheek where it had gotten stuck from leaning on his shoulder. He tucks it behind my ear, his hand trailing a line down the back of my neck.

His fingers pause and my breath stops in my chest, my pulse quickening. My eyelashes flutter against my cheeks and his eyes darken to a forest green.

The bed creaks underneath him as he shifts closer to me. I don't even resist as he tugs ever so lightly at my neck, my head tilting back to angle my face up to him more.

"You are incredible, you know that?" Fin whispers, our faces close enough that his breath tickles. He searches my face, shifting from my eyes to my lips, which only sends the butterflies in my stomach on a wild chase.

"You don't know me well enough to be the judge of that yet," I whisper back, lost in the jewel depths of his beautiful, gleaming eyes.

He inches even closer, our noses brushing against each other. I softly inhale, every part of me heating up, and I hope to the Gods I'm not actually warming up.

"I doubt there is anything you could say or do to change that, Reva." My heart pounds against my ribcage as his words repeat over and over in my head. There is no way he could possibly know what I really am, let alone if those words would still be true if he really knew.

But right now, that doesn't matter to me. I'd done plenty with numerous men who would never know who I really was.

And this could be the same.

I finally close my eyes and start to lean in when someone clears their throat near my door.

Fin and I fling ourselves across opposite ends. I pin

myself beside the table at my bed with my knees backed up against the mattress, and Fin somehow ends up near the fireplace. We both snap our attention to the door, and I relax a little when I recognize Eloise, standing there with two books in her arms.

"Son of a…" Fin trails off, hand clutched to his chest. "You about gave me a heart attack, Elly."

"Good," she nods stiffly at him. She swivels her head back and forth between us. "I would presume you are both old enough by now to know how to close a door. If not, here is the memo: close the door if you're about to make out."

"We were not—" I start but Eloise simply raises an eyebrow at me. The muscles twitch at the corners of her mouth.

"Oh, please." Eloise steps into the room, placing the two books in her hand on the coffee table by the fireplace where Fin is rigid. "Don't insult me, Reva. I thought we would be past that by now."

All I can do is stand there with my mouth propped slightly open as she waggles her eyebrows before strutting out of my room without another word.

Fin and I finally look at each other, and I can only imagine the blush that spreads across his cheeks mirrors mine.

"I better go to—" Fin pauses, gesturing towards the door and waving his hand in a small circle.

I bite my lips down, agreeing with a tight nod. He opens his mouth to say something but decides against it as he closes it again before bowing to me. I wait for him to leave the room, frozen in place with my door still wide open.

I can hear Karasi's *tsk tsk* in my head, just like I can see her twinkling cat-like eyes.

CHAPTER 9

A few days after the moment with Fin, I find myself wondering if he's avoiding me. It's my first true day off since I arrived about a month ago, and I instantly contemplated if he would be available to spend time with me touring the castle more or venturing into Saros, the town the Castle of Andromeda resides in.

Once I realize what I'm fantasizing about, I splash my face with cold water.

Not that fantasizing about his lips moving against mine and other parts of me is a bad thing. In fact, I welcome those thoughts with open arms.

But, fantasizing about *dating* Fin? That is something I've never allowed myself to do with any guy, and I'm not about to start now.

Just as I finish tying my skirt, a knock echoes through my room. I quickly scurry across the room and reach for the handle, yanking it open. I'm instantly agitated at my traitor heart when it deflates as I meet Eloise's amber eyes.

"Oh, Reva, don't look so disappointed," she scoffs, pushing through my door. I say a blessing to the Gods that I put my salve on this morning before getting dressed.

"I am not disappointed," I exclaim, looping my bag over my head.

"I know who you thought would be at the door." She eyes me with a smirk. "A certain knight that you've spent a lot of time with since your arrival would be my first guess, and I am rarely wrong."

"Okay." I chuckle, crossing my arms over my chest. "You're not wrong, but that doesn't mean I'm disappointed to be graced by the princess."

She curls her lip at me, running her finger over the back of the chair by my fireplace. "If you're going to call me that, we can't be friends."

"Are we friends?" I question, taunting her.

She narrows her eyes at me before plopping herself into the chair dramatically. "I would like to think us discussing scandalous matters like Magic, mountains, and the Sirians would make us friends."

I nearly choke on my own breath, startled. "When did we discuss the Sirians?" I move closer to where she sits in my room. "I feel like I'd remember that."

"Not in depth," she snorts, rolling her eyes. "But you mentioned it briefly. If you are going to be my friend, Reva, the first thing you need to know about me is that when I hear something that is unfamiliar to me, I look for the answer."

"The Abyss," I remember, nodding to myself. "And what did you find?"

"Just some books. Someone long ago ensured that not all records and books on Sirians were entirely erased from existence." She stands suddenly, brushing off her maroon wool skirt and straightening her patterned vest. "But, that is not why I'm here today. I figured that on your day off, you'd like to be somewhere other than sequestered in your rooms or Clint's. Fin mentioned he gave you a tour of the outside of the castle, but not really the inside. Who better than the one who has lived here her entire life?"

She holds her hands out wide, using her right hand to gesture to herself.

I narrow my eyes. "Fin sent you to babysit me?"

"Oh, for the love of the Gods, Reva," Eloise laughs, walking to me. She loops my arm through hers and heads directly for my door, dragging me along. "Have you never had friends before? This is what we do. We hang out and look out for each other. We don't need you dying of boredom."

"Thank you, Eloise," I say, my heart warming. I bump my shoulder against hers. "I appreciate you taking the time to actually hang out with me."

"First things first," she begins, leading me down the hallway towards the central part of the castle. "Elly. When we're alone or with Fin and Clint, just call me Elly."

She's not joking about this friend thing. "I'm honored."

She leads me through the castle, passing the entryway I'd come through when I first arrived. We turn down one of the many hallways and head toward where I know the stained glass murals are.

The first casts a multitude of colors onto the floor as we pass the kitchen entryway and enter a massive foyer with a grand staircase.

"Do these tell the story of Mariande?" I inquire, my eyes snagging on different details I did not catch before.

There is repeated imagery in every mural. On top of the 6-pointed star, there are lilies, dark maroon and gold pieces, and ravens. I swear some of the stars are the identical shape of the Sirian Mark.

"Pre-Korbin legacy, yes," Elly confirms, stopping to observe them with me. "While eventually every kingdom was ruled by a Korbin son, adopting some of the symbols you might notice, they all didn't belong to the Korbins. They belonged to the many families of Mariande before them."

"So the lilies, ravens, maroon—" I give her a pointed look. "And stars?"

She nods slowly, returning a wry expression. "We know who the stars really belong to."

The Sirians.

I don't respond, but I take a moment to study each of the eight murals that line the wall from left to right. Elly follows my line of sight, pointing to each as she explains.

"The first one is the Creation Story, where Kuk and Khonsa fought and produced Aveesh and the Gods that rule our world."

The beings I can only assume are Kuk and Khonsa are depicted as small, human silhouettes, one made of black glass with tiny pieces of blue and purple and the other made of purple glass with an aura of orange and yellow glass.

Below them are four small figures, each a different color: opaque white, vibrant blue, gold, and champagne. The final has the Sirian Mark on what I assume is its forehead.

I may not be able to distinguish the other three, but I know that one is Danica, the Goddess of Nature, Energy of All Things, the Morning and Evening Star, and the Creator of the Sirians.

Elly moves on to the next. "This second one tells the story of the First King of Men, a demi-god, Enki. He was said to be the son of the God of Humanity, Rod, and a human."

This mural depicts a humanoid kneeling before another, whose glass glimmers like it's made of pure gold, a halo encircling its head. Eight ravens, each with one red eye in the shape of the Sirian Mark, fly around them.

"This third one is Bodhi, demi-god and another descendent of Rod, sharing the story of Creation with humankind."

This portrays a figure in maroon, hands outstretched. At his feet is a plain book, but I can make out the Sirian Mark on the corner of the page. A raven sits on his left shoulder and there is a lily hanging in the figure's right hand.

"This fourth one is the creation of the Sirians." Her voice quiets on the last word, but my Mark itches underneath the salve.

Similar to the crowning of Enki, Danica stands with her finger pointed at a bowed figure—specifically at his forehead—where his Mark sits. Again, eight ravens are flying around them and there are lilies scattered at their feet.

Elly moves on to the others, explaining that the last four are the crowning of various Kings who did incredible things for the continent before the Korbin brothers and their father, King Alrik, single-handedly made the Sirians something to fear.

I cannot take my eyes away from the stained-glass version of Danica before me, though.

It's a simple piece of glass, but the longer I stare, every detail of her becomes clearer, as if the artist was able to capture them with the stained glass.

Glowing white eyes, iridescent strips of fabric hanging around her body in a revealing fashion, and her bald head.

"Reva?" Elly interrupts. I startle, the tingling in my Mark fading. I shake my head to clear it, blinking. "You okay? You look…"

"I'm fine." I wave away her concern and stretch my hand out to loop it back into the crook of her arm. She takes it hesitantly but regards me with concern and another emotion I can't quite decipher. I shrug. "Just deep in thought."

Elly shows me around the castle before our stomachs alert us that we need food. When my mouth drops at the size of the formal dining room, Elly insists that we take lunch here and have ourselves a good time instead of my usual table with Chef B.

She leaves me seated at one of the many available chairs at the table and disappears into the entrance that leads to the kitchens. Her voice carries as she converses with who I can guess is Chef B by the sounds of his baritone, and it sounds like he's not happy with her.

"What are you doing in here?" A deep voice I unfortunately recognize interrupts my thoughts. I shut my eyes momentarily before pivoting my head towards the door Elly and I entered.

Pax stands at the doorway, his hands clasped behind his back. The distrust seeps out of every pore on his body.

"It's lunchtime," I say, my hands folded in my lap. "And this is the dining room. I'm sure even someone as ignorant as you could answer your question."

"The dining room is reserved for the Hesper family," he explains, strutting towards me. The click of his boots echoes off the marble floor, like a clock ticking toward disaster. He places his hand on the table in front of me, leaning in. "While you may be the Royal Healer, that does not grant you permission to flaunt about as you please."

"I am not *flaunting about.*" I lift my chest and push my shoulders back. "Besides, I was asked to accompany the Princess of Mariande."

"By who?" He searches the massive space, sweeping across the row of empty velvet chairs on the opposite side of the table. He leans back down until his dark eyes align with mine, promising nothing less than blood. "I see no princess."

Not a moment too soon, Elly bursts from the kitchen in a fit of giggles. Bottle of what appears to be wine in one hand and two glasses in the other, she ungracefully scurries towards me. "Sorry for the delay, but Chef B was trying to insist it's too early for wine, so I practically had to fight my way—"

The bottle nearly slips from her hand when she catches Pax's massive outline hovering over me. He uncurls beside me, his hands returning to their usual place behind his back. His shoulders and chest relax and his face softens, making him a little more handsome.

Okay, he's actually gorgeous.

Pax bows at the waist. "Princess." Elly conceals her earlier shock with a small smile, avoiding my eyes. His gaze slides from Elly to me. "I was not aware you and Miss Reva were acquainted already."

Miss Reva? I'd roll my eyes if not for the palpable tension radiating from them. Pax may be relaxed, but his forearms are flexing from how tight his grip is on his own wrist. Elly sways imperceptibly as if she might suddenly launch herself at him.

"Reva and I have been doing research to help Clint," Elly explains, placing the glasses carefully on the table in front of me. She hands me the open wine bottle, so I get cracking pouring our glasses, eavesdropping. "It just so happens a beautiful friendship has blossomed, so I thought I'd treat her to lunch."

"Treat me?" I question, but she kicks me in the ankle under the table.

What the Kuk is happening?

"Yes, the usual lunch and wine date." Pax nods once, his eyes shifting briefly to me, hands flexing at his side. "Do you need…"

"I have alerted the kitchen already." Elly clarifies, her eyes dropping to his lips timidly, and it all comes crashing into me at once.

Sexual tension. That is what hangs like humidity in the air between these two. I have to fight my body to keep the shock and amusement from taking over my facial features.

Part of me wants to laugh, while the other part of me

wants to just vocalize my realization and establish I'm not conjuring something that isn't real because of my own debacle.

Elly's eyes briefly dart my way with all the promise to throttle me if I make a sound, which doesn't help my internal battle.

"If you are secure, I will leave you to it," Pax states, standing fully to attention again with his normal composure restored.

He shoots me one final glare, pinning me to my seat before exiting the room. Neither Elly nor I dare a single sound until the door shuts behind him.

I burst at the seams. "Okay, now that—"

Elly snatches the wine glass from my hand, holding one finger to me as she downs the wine straight from the bottle.

"For the love of the Gods, do not say anything," Elly whispers in a prayer.

But I am not a God.

"Elly!" I squeal, "I have so much to say and I don't know where to begin. First of all, I thought I was going to be privy to you and Pax—"

"Ay!" She yells, jabbing her finger at me with a glare as she sits beside me.

"Second of all," I continue, glad she understands what I could *feel* in this room. "Pax? Of all the incredibly fine-ass men here, you pick him?"

"He is *beautiful*." Elly snatches her glass, and by the size of her gulp, she knows exactly where I'm about to go with this.

"Okay, I can't argue with that," I agree, twirling the wine in my own glass. "I don't expect you to have any loyalty towards me so soon. But Pax has been anything but kind to me since I arrived. That was the first time I've ever heard him call me 'Miss'. And, when some of the other knights start to harass me, he's not necessarily stopping them."

"Loyalty or not, Reva," Elly says softly, placing her hand over my forearm. "No one deserves to be treated poorly because of who or what they are. And you've done nothing but good since you've been here, so I agree with you that his behavior is unacceptable."

"So, is the sex incredible?"

Elly spits her wine across the table, sputtering. "Dear Gods, I forgot you're from Eldamain."

She and I sop up the wine in silence. I wait, not wanting to push her to talk. After a few minutes, she sits back in her seat as I collect the soiled napkins, handing them to one of the staff members, who brings out a soup, salad, and sandwich for both of us.

"He's not always been like this," Elly explains quietly, circling her spoon in the soup. "All of us grew up together: Tariq, Fin, Pax, and me. We ran these halls and received schooling together. It was Tariq who appointed Pax and Fin to their stations.

"But, as my father started to change some of the rules and laws around Magics and made things more public, it changed something in Pax." She takes another large gulp of wine and continues, "I know this is not who Pax is. It's his father fueling his head with nonsense and prejudice because he's an Etherean. They don't think like we do, but he never seemed bothered by Pax's upbringing with us until my father changed things. That's when Pax started to become distant. Fin has been getting the brunt of him because he's more vocal to Pax about his behavior recently. I've just kept my distance, and Tariq has been gone."

"Pax is a grown man, though, and has been since the King changed things," I challenge, shaking my head. "Does his father speak for him?"

"It's complicated," she softly shrugs. "It's not my story to share, but I'm just hoping you get a chance to see the real him and that he tells you himself."

I place my own hand on top of Elly's, stopping her from twirling the spoon. She looks up at me, and the depth of her sadness steals my breath, but also the love that is still there for him.

"It is not your job to fix him," I insist, squeezing her hand before returning to my food.

"It's not fixing him," she replies with a thin smile. "It's leading him back from the dark."

CHAPTER 10

I sit on one of the chairs in front of my room's fireplace, a book propped open in my lap about yet another tale of an internal illness that could not be fixed, even with Magic.

I try to expel some pent-up energy, playing with flames in the fireplace, morphing them into shapes and tendrils that dance with one another up the chimney without allowing it to lose control. My hand glows a faint orange as my fingers and wrist twirl around.

My control over the firepower and flames has been anything but that.

Remy was responsible for training me with it. The little control I do have over it allows me to ignite fires, alter existing ones, and warm body temperatures, but those abilities only came after I'd burned down a few old, abandoned houses and trees and gave Remy a gnarly burn on his arm.

Healed by Karasi, of course.

I felt some relief when I was able to manage it enough that I wouldn't risk my own exposure. Taming and wielding the Light had been somewhat easier than the firepower, but forget about weaponizing either of them.

It wasn't like I had any other Sirian in my life to teach me, and a Magics' abilities are nothing like the Sirians'.

Beyond their ability to create helpful medications and potions with their blood, all Magics have are enhanced abilities like senses, stamina, strength, and the few characteristics and—occasionally—powers they get from the Houses they come from.

Sirians, on the other hand, can manipulate, generate, and utilize energy to accomplish different tasks from the most mundane to combat.

When one can manipulate energy, how do you teach them when you don't know how to yourself? I was lucky to learn how to wield it enough to expel the unbearable build-up that happens when you don't.

I quit playing with the flames and call to the Light. I open the door of energy that lies within me just a crack, feeling its force as I allow some of it to come forward.

The energy glows in my hand like a bright, white ball, the veins in my hand mirroring the color, but a tinge of yellow-gold. It hovers above my palm with small, vine-like streams connecting it to my fingertips, the energy pulsing.

I raise my other hand, turning the ball into a tunnel that connects to the palm. The energy vibrates subtly, my fingers tingling in response to the rarely used power and energy gathering in front of me.

A knock at my door startles me, the Light vanishing as it snaps back into my body. The force of it has me bending over at the waist, clutching my abdomen. The flames in the fireplace flare in response.

Another knock sounds.

"One second," I answer, flipping the book face-down on the coffee table and checking my Mark in the mirror. Luckily, none of the salve burned off from the subtle power usage I'd been doing for the last hour.

I pull the door open, and it's Fin. I can't help as the corners of my lips curl up my cheeks.

The tightly drawn focus on his face and his hands gripped together send a jolt of worry through me, but the moment I start smiling, Fin returns it with a slight sag of his shoulders as he unclasps his hands.

"Well, look who decided to show his face around these parts of the castle," I greet, placing a hand on my hip with the other resting against the doorframe.

Delight lights up those emerald green eyes. "I didn't know you had been waiting up for me." He leans against the doorframe and I find myself, once again, mere inches from him. He smirks. "If I had known that, I would've completely disregarded any requests from the King and Crown Prince."

"Oh," I feign shock, moving my hand from my hip to my chest. "The Crown Prince? All the way from his sabbatical?"

"I am important enough to receive special correspondence from Riddling." He straightens, flattening his shirt against his stomach.

I don't miss the flex of muscles underneath.

But, at the same time, I realize he's wearing a simple shirt and slacks. "No knight uniform today? That seems like a very rare occasion."

"Elly informed me that you had yesterday and today free. And, since Elly had you all to herself yesterday, I figured today was my turn." He holds out a hand in front of me in invitation.

I want to say the same retort about being babysat but him donning normal street clothes makes me want to do a lot more than that.

Instead, I slip my hand into his, letting my smile spring free. I snag my key before he yanks me out of the room and down the hall. "Where are you taking me?"

He places my hand in the crook of his elbow, holding his head high. "You have been sequestered in this castle for the last month."

The mischievous side-eye coupled with his broad, side smirk puts a skip in my step. His playfulness and joy radiate from him and seep into me, making me lighter than I've felt in a long time. "While this castle is grand and beautiful, I know it can easily feel like you're trapped on an island. And something tells me that you have been trapped on a threadbare island your whole life."

The statement startles me.

I stop walking, my hand slipping from his elbow as he continues. I stare at him, a strange sense of truth settling into the pit in my stomach.

He turns around, regret swirling in his wide eyes and arched eyebrows. He stutters, "Reva, I didn't mean—"

"No." I straighten the patterned vest over my blouse. "You're not wrong. In all my life, I've never left Eldamain."

He trudges back to me until I'm face-to-face with the

unbuttoned collar of his shirt. He places both hands on either shoulder, giving them a comforting rub. He asks, "Would an evening in Saros be something you're comfortable with?"

All I can do is nod, because the amount of excitement I have is met with equal apprehension. "I have never been around so many people before, let alone as an open Magic around humans."

"That's why I am not in my knight uniform." He gestures to the soft, white cotton over his broad chest, leading us toward the door to the courtyard. "Tonight, we are Fin and Reva. Just two normal citizens enjoying an evening of food, drinks, and debauchery."

"Extra of the debauchery," I laugh, the weight that had settled into my stomach lifting and floating away.

As the carriage pulls out of the castle grounds, fields pass by in golden waves of wheat and grass, an occasional farmhouse encroaching upon a plot every few minutes

We pull up to Saros after a fifteen-minute ride, and my breath catches in my throat.

Dozens upon dozens of buildings stand behind a short stone wall, carriages flowing in and out of various gaps and openings along it. People weave in and out of alleyways with baskets and carts, some dragging horses or donkeys behind them.

Stepping out of the carriage, I'm greeted with talking, music, people, and colors, so different from Main Town in Eldamain. This is a city, bustling and moving; postmen with parcels, carts pulling boulders and piles of logs, kids chasing each other in laps around a fountain, adults embracing each other and toting baskets of food.

There are rows and rows of wooden and brick buildings ranging from apartments to storefronts and restaurants. Lamps line the streets, young boys illuminating them as the sun starts to set.

"This is like a dream," I whisper in awe, using Fin's outstretched hand to ease out of the carriage. Once my foot is on the ground, I take a few steps away to spin in a slow circle, taking in the surroundings.

"You've barely left the carriage," Fin laughs, motioning for me to follow him. I scurry to catch up beside him.

It doesn't take us long in our walk for me to notice the attention we're getting. Women huddle together in groups, laughing to themselves and casting glances at Fin as we walk up and down, block after block.

"You seem to be quite a popular man," I mutter, leaning into him. "All the ladies are looking at you as we pass."

One woman shoves another gently, causing her to stumble into our path. Fin holds out his arms to steady her, but he is stiff as he nods once and continues walking.

I scoff. "They're literally throwing themselves at you for your attention."

"How unfortunate." He tilts his head, speaking low beside my ear, "My attention has been otherwise occupied. I've barely noticed."

He grins down at me like a fool, mouth agape. I roll my eyes, but I can't contain the one I return.

His chuckle vibrates through me, "Can you say you empathize with them? Have you ever been so swooned by the appearance of another man that you did anything to get his attention?"

"I can't say I have," I sigh, dramatically. Fin eyes me, the ghost of his smile still there.

I follow close beside him, taking in my surroundings. The air is still chilly, but I appreciate the fresh air and the spices of food wafting through the streets.

Fin takes us through the doorway of a pub, the music blaring loud enough that others are yelling to communicate with each other. Memories of The Red Raven instantly barrel down on me, my heart clenching as Remy, Willem, and Dahlia cross my mind.

I swallow the lump in my throat, refusing to let my homesickness ruin this moment.

Fin guides us to two empty spaces at the bar, flagging down one of the two bartenders.

A girl in a black skirt and corset throws a bar towel over her shoulder. "What will you be having?"

"Two house ales," Fin orders, and I nod when she raises her eyebrow to confirm with me. The bartender grabs two glasses to fill up and Fin turns to me. "What I would give to have a bottle of that stuff you gave us the night we came to collect you."

I bust out laughing, resting my hand on Fin's shoulder. He chuckles, his eyes twinkling.

I gather myself, still sputtering as I say, "Collect me? What a choice of words, Sir Finley. Besides, I can make you that brew myself if you'd like. As a thank you gift for taking me out to Saros."

"That would be amazing," Fin groans, throwing his head back. The bartender hands us our glasses, and Fin places money on the bar. We swirl around in our chairs to a table where a pair of drunken patrons argue about a stack of cards. "So, how does this fare to your place back in Eldamain?"

"I mean, Saros is unbeatable," I say over the music. "The town is just incredible. This pub, though, is a little more laid back than The Red Raven, even if there seems to be more people here right now."

"You say that now, Reva." Fin sips his ale. "Wait until the music picks up and you finish that glass. Things will kick up a notch or two and you'll see what Mariande is really about."

"So, you all *do* know how to hold your liquor," I exclaim.

Fin holds up a finger, leaning in. "I never said we could hold our liquor."

I cackle at that, watching all the patrons interact and mingle with one another. A knight sits at a table with a lady in a beautiful gown on his lap, laughing at something he's said.

"Don't worry," Fin whispers, leaning in. "Those are some of the good ones. In fact, that woman sitting on his lap is a Magic."

As if summoned, the woman turns her head, meeting my gaze. She could be around my age, with dark skin, charcoal-gray dreadlocks, and piercing, ice-blue eyes—almost silver.

She nods her head once.

"Are we in a Magic-owned pub?" I ask Fin, meeting his gaze. He just smiles, knowingly. "How many other shops are

Magic-owned?"

"I would say some of the most successful storefronts in Saros are owned by Magics." Fin shrugs. "We told you things have changed here."

Being in this pub, owned by and surrounded by Magics, I can only imagine how Remy, Willem, and Dahlia would react. Gods, I wish I could see how Karasi would react.

I don't know if I'll ever know exactly how old she is, but did she know a world where Magics lived amongst mortals like this?

If she does remember, what would it be like to see this again? If she doesn't, what would it be like to witness it after all this time?

The second I finish my beer, Fin grabs my empty glass and places it beside his own on the bar. The music picks up, and nearly everyone makes their way to an open area in the back of the pub. Fin jumps from his seat, holding out his hand.

"Do you dance, Reva?" He asks, locking eyes with mine. My heart flutters in my chest.

"Not very well," I admit, but I accept his hand. "Doesn't stop me, though."

Fin pulls me close behind him to the back of the bar as we stick to the outside of the main circle that's formed in the middle. We find a good spot, even if people are occasionally brushing against us.

I sway to the music, still surveying those around me. I catch a glimpse here and there of people I know are Magics based on their characteristics: cat-like eyes that remind me of Karasi, strange colored irises that are still noticeable in the dim lighting like Dahlia, sharp canines like Remy, and even speckles of iridescent skin that resemble scales along someone's neck.

"I thought you'd be used to Magics," Fin teases, leaning in and having to shout in my ear being this close to the band.

Perching on the balls of my feet, I place my hand against his bicep to steady myself. "Oh, I'm used to them. I'm just more in awe that there are this many outside of Eldamain."

"This isn't even half of it," Fin grins wildly, excitement brightening his eyes. My heart melts, still in awe at how Fin reacts to Magics. His admiration is clear as he watches on with a proud glint in his eye.

Those who venture into Eldamain to find a Magic pouring their ale are always full of fear or disgust, so seeing this is quite the change. It's like wiping cobwebs out of the corner of Karasi's after a long winter and opening the windows to let in the fresh air.

But, just like Karasi's, we can't always have those windows open. Winter always returns, and where does his acceptance draw a line?

"And, this is truly the King's doing?" I ask, raising an eyebrow. Fin nods, his eyes wandering around the group of people dancing. "Why?"

"I think you should talk to him about it," Fin suggests, glancing knowingly. "I feel like you would have a lot of good information to give him on how to speak to the Magics and show them we want to repair our relationship with them."

I frown up at him, tilting my head to the side. His

attention has moved away from me, though, and he's aimlessly glancing around the crowd. I purse my lips with the full intention of bringing this conversation up again.

I can barely get time to discuss Clint with the King. When would I get time to tell him about a rather large initiative that affects not just Saros, but the whole country and even the continent? How Mariande conducts themselves will affect the other countries, how they respond, and what they'll do in either support or retaliation.

Fin pulls me away from my thoughts by wrapping my hands around his neck. I narrow my eyes at him as I lace my fingers between each other, inching my body closer so we're pressing against one another.

The music is a little fast-paced, but we still sway and shimmy to the beat without space between us, aware of his hands gripping tightly to my hips.

The intimacy between us as we dance together, moving back and forth amongst the crowd, is something I've never had with another man. Despite the countless one-night stands with men I don't care to remember, nothing is more intimate than the intensity with which Fin stares down at me.

He leans his head down closer to mine, my heart frantically fluttering in my chest. Pressing our foreheads together, the tips of our noses brush together. I send thanks to the Gods that my arms are wrapped around him.

I close my eyes against the warmth radiating from him and within me. I search for his heartbeat against my chest which is just as frantic as my own. His hands scale up my back, putting pressure against the middle and pressing my body further into his.

He pulls his head back enough to stare into me with that piercing gaze. A question.

In my room, there was an opportunity to stop things before they spiraled, but now, dancing with him, the moment to reject anything building between us has passed. I should shake my head and tell him that taking this extra step makes us something more than friends.

Because I don't know if I'm ready for something more than that. I don't know if I have the time or the effort for something more than that, not with a sick boy to care for and an impending Darkness following me wherever I go.

Fin is everything a girl could want in a man. Kind, compassionate, affectionate, funny, protective… Finding a guy like that is a gift. I'm not sure I know what to do with a gift like this—a gift like Fin.

But I never say no to a gift.

I keep one hand on the back of his neck, the other reaching into his hair. I pull his face into mine, our lips pressing together, hesitantly at first.

His mouth moves leisurely against mine, deepening the kiss. I forget about the rest of the world around us as it falls away, becoming just us at this moment.

I intend to savor it.

Our hands start roaming, his moving to hold my face between his and mine resting just below his pecs on his hard stomach.

I have not been kissed like this in a long time, so

thoroughly and so intentionally. It's like the fire that runs through my veins is manifesting to life before me. It's familiar and reassuring, and I relax into him, letting his strength and mass absorb all the feelings running through me right now.

I focus on kissing this beautiful, mortal knight.

Fin is the first to pull away, both of our chests rising and falling with our rapid breath. I straighten, biting my bottom lip in hesitation. Fin's eyes darken nearly two shades at that, his thumb softly caressing my cheekbone.

"We should probably make our way back to the castle," he whispers, barely audible above the music but I hear him since we're still pressed together.

All I can do is nod in response, letting him take my hand and lead me out of the bar. My other hand timidly presses against my lips.

And I can't even blame it on being drunk.

CHAPTER 11

I traipse through rows and shelves of books, passing various medical books. Some I recognize, whether I've read them in my time here or in Karasi's small collection.

The scent of parchment and binding is particularly strong in the books with technical recordings and the private diaries of past Healers. At this rate, I've gone so far back that the medicine and methods we practice nowadays have surpassed what any of these books can give me.

Nonetheless, I continue the dirty work of double and triple-checking because I can't afford to miss something, no matter how small.

As I follow my path back toward the pile that's growing on the table in the middle of the library, a random row of books catches my eye.

There is a particularly worn-down book shoved between the end of the bookshelf and the large encyclopedia in front of it. Bending at my waist, I carefully slip it from what appears to be its permanent resting place.

I wipe some of the dust off the top and scan the exterior, but there is no title. It's a simple, leather-bound journal with cracks spreading across it.

At a glance, I'm concerned about the fragility of the pages inside. Holding my breath, I slowly unravel the string binding it closed, simultaneously walking back to the table.

After gently placing it on the table and pulling back the cover, I have to stop myself from slamming it shut again.

On the inside of the cover, pressed into the leather, is a small stamp of the Sirian Mark. Across the bottom of the page, in faded ink, it reads: *Kraden Hexas, Royal Healer of the Mariande Kingdom.*

All of the air leaves my lungs in a sound mimicking a whimper.

This journal is hundreds and *hundreds* of years old.

I hesitantly turn the brittle page, and based on the date in the top right corner, this book predates King Alrik Korbin's reign by about a generation or two.

So make that a thousand years old.

I can't imagine it having anything worthwhile, but something in my gut lurches at the thought of putting it back. Instead, I rewrap the book with its string and delicately place it in my satchel just in case I run into anyone on the way back to Clint.

The last thing I need is for someone to catch me with a journal written by a Sirian.

I check the clock and decide now is probably the time to head back.

"Lacey?" I call one of Elly's assistants sitting at the front desk. "Could you have somebody deliver this pile of books up to my room? I have to head back to the prince, so as long as it's there by this evening."

"Of course, Miss Reva," she acknowledges before returning to the task in front of her.

I sling my satchel over my head and onto my shoulder, leaving the pile behind with the book burning a hole in my bag. Exiting the library, I nearly collide with a few knights on shift, startling them.

"Sorry about that," I mutter, quickly maneuvering around them when I recognize some from the surly group that harasses me every chance they get.

"Where are you off to in such a rush?" A few of them snicker, but I don't turn around. I keep my head held up, walking towards the stairwell that will take me to Clint's wing.

One reaches for my arm. "I'm talking to you—"

"Gentleman," a familiar, relieving voice booms, emerging from an adjacent hall.

I whip my head over my shoulder as Fin faces the group with his back to me. He stands at attention with his hands clasped behind his back. "Did the clock not just chime moments ago? Are you at the shifts you've been assigned?"

"Yes, Sir." One of them salutes as they all clack their heels together.

Fin shifts so one hand rests on his hip and the other on the hilt of his sword. I have to suppress my smile.

This is the first time since I met him that I've seen Fin authoritative, and it's unbearably hot. Granted I can only see his body language and not his face.

"Well, then why do I hear you *playing*," he hisses with a snarl at the end.

This has them all stiffening, their attention looking past Fin and me to the end of the hall.

Fin's voice returns to normal as he says, "Let us not forget the activity we've seen in Saros. A castle is not fortified if every watch is not prepared at all times."

"Yes, Sir," they say in unison.

Fin nods his head once before turning on his heel to face me head-on. "Allow me to escort you to Prince Clint's quarters, Miss Reva," Fin orders in the same tone, but he throws in a wink now that he's not facing them.

It takes every ounce of power within me to keep my face a neutral mask, despite the silent squeal inside. He doesn't wait for my response, stalking past me towards where I was headed. I follow behind him like another obedient comrade.

Once we are in the stairwell, it only takes us a single flight of stairs before he pins me to the wall. My palms flatten against his solid chest in front of me, ripping a small gasp from my lips.

"Hear anyone coming?" Fin whispers, looking up the stairs.

I try to peer down around his body pressing into me. "I don't think—"

He cuts me off, planting a kiss directly on my lips.

I softly moan against his mouth, and it doesn't take me long to melt into the stone wall as his lips move around mine.

My mind flies away, all senses hyper-fixating on the brush of my breasts against his chest.

"Sorry," he apologizes between pulling away and giving me quick pecks. "I don't usually escort people this way."

"Well," I place my hand on his chest, grinning like a cat. "While I would love to stay in this stairwell with you, I do have a young prince to attend to."

Fin sighs, an immovable wall against my hand. I narrow my eyes at him. "I feel that the Prince would be a little lenient if I explained the circumstances."

"Oh, no," I shove harder and he backs away. I lecture, "We are not involving the royal family in this. I am still too new to be galivanting about with a knight of the royal army. I have a reputation to fix."

"To fix?" He questions, taking the lead as we resume the journey back up to Clint's room. "What do you mean?"

"I've told you there are people that give me a hard time for what I am," I explain, holding my skirts in my hand. "This includes insinuating that I'm some sort of whore that slept my way around Eldamain and now I am taking my antics into the halls of this castle."

"You mean to tell me they call you that to your face?" He says, lip curled.

"I mean, not directly using the word all the time…" I trail off, pausing as we stand before Clint's door. I swivel to face him, frowning. "What do you mean *to my face?*"

Fin's face flushes and his eyes are downcast at Clint's door, purposely avoiding my gaze. I breathe through my rising temper, dampening the power that's trying to bubble to the surface.

He clears his throat uncomfortably. "I know the knights talk to each other, and I reprimand them when I can… I didn't think they were saying the same things to you directly."

"What are they saying, Fin?" I glare, narrowing my eyes. He looks over my shoulder down the way we came from.

That definitely doesn't help my control. I stomp my heel on the ground, growling. "Damnit, Fin. What do they say?"

"Nothing different from what you're hearing." His gaze meets my own. "But I can't disclose those exact statements from official meetings—"

"They are discussing me during *meetings*?" I half-yell incredulously.

"Reva." His hand flies out to grab my wrist but I yank it back. I hold my finger up in front of him.

"No," I whisper, wagging my finger at him. "They continue to talk because they don't think there are consequences for doing so. They believe it's okay to continue to talk about me and act like that toward me, and there are people like Pax who aren't correcting them. Apparently, people of your rank aren't correcting them, either."

"Reva," Fin pleads, trying to reach for me again.

"The last thing the young Prince needs is to see people harassing me. Even he has had the gall to correct knights." I turn the knob, cracking the door open to signal the end of this conversation. "And directing them just to continue the work they should already be doing isn't standing up for anything."

With that, I turn my back on him, my heart fluttering frantically as my entire chest cavity clenches. I shut the door behind me without looking back, leaning my back against the hard wood with a heavy sigh.

Fin might be kind with his actions but there's a side to him that can't—or won't—stand up to others. I can't fathom how he doesn't correct knights who are supposed to protect people like me when, instead, they're treating them poorly both to their faces and behind closed doors.

And, with someone like the King on his side, how could he not use that to his advantage? Even if Pax were to retaliate being a rank above Fin, all he would have to do is tell the King what's going on.

The bed creaking pulls me out of my thoughts.

Clint sits upright, his legs crossed in front of him with a book resting open on top of them. A single eyebrow is raised, scrutinizing me.

"You know," Clint says, dog-earing the page without looking at it. "Isla never exposed her personal life to me."

I angle my head, pressing my lips tighter together and widening my eyes at him in a warning not to push it.

A bright grin breaks out across his face.

Suddenly, all that happened before this doesn't even matter because this kid eases any grief I'm battling.

His skin looks normal. There is no gray hue, and it helps me recognize just how many features he and Elly share.

"We aren't even 10 years apart," he pleads, resting an elbow on his knee and placing his chin in his hand. "I have nothing but time."

"I'm glad you said that," I grin wickedly, walking towards the edge of his bed and placing both of my hands on the frame. "I could put you to work, you know? You love reading so much and I have a lot of books for us to get through."

"Only if they're interesting and teach me the things I shouldn't be told about," he counters, narrowing his eyes at me. He's still smiling though, and there's a glimmer of hope that we can really fix this ailment of his.

"Black Avalanches, Magic," I count aloud, sitting at the edge of the bed. "What else could I possibly give you at this rate that you haven't already dabbled with?"

"I read something…" He trails off, the smile slipping away. I frown, studying him. He leans back into his pillows, stretching out his legs in front of him. "I don't want you to tell my dad."

"Clint," I drone, my frown deepening. "What did you take?"

"I didn't take anything," he insists. "It was something I read in the other Black Avalanches book. The one that was a lot more mythology and lore than the expeditions."

"Something that's going to help you?" I question, standing from the bed. I head over to where I'd left my vials to mix together the new blend we've been trying, which seems to be contributing to the coloring in his skin. "You know I'm all ears, Clint, and my sole priority in life right now is to get you healthy so you can be a normal thirteen-year-old prince."

I don't turn around to look at him, but the tension thickens in the room. I wait, giving him his space and time.

As I add the final ingredient to the glass, he blurts, "Have you ever met a Sirian?"

My vision goes black as the glass with the extra ingredient clatters to the floor, shattering and spilling the contents all over the floor. I swear under my breath, bending down to pick up the small pieces.

Clint sputters, "I'm sorry, Reva, I didn't mean to startle you. I just know that Eldamain is a safe place for Magics, so I just wondered if maybe you've met a few Sirians in hiding or…"

I steadily rise with the shards of glass gathered in one hand and the vial with the mix in the other. I twist to face him at the same time he lowers his head in embarrassment or shame, I cannot tell.

I take a deep breath, settling the frantic energy threatening to gather around me, not to mention the tingling in my Mark.

This is not my day.

"I need to know why you're asking," I say softly, almost a whisper, as I walk over to his bedside.

I hand him the vial, throwing the broken pieces of the other into the waste bin. I sit beside him on the bed, scooting close enough to his outstretched legs so I'm directly in his point of view.

I place my hand on his shoulder. "I'm not mad, Clint," I explain. "I just didn't expect that. Talk of the Sirians isn't exactly a casual dinner topic."

"I know," he nods, meeting my eyes with his bright amber ones. I sigh heavily, waiting.

He continues, "I just don't understand why we don't know more about the Sirians and how they used to exist among us just like you or me. They used to run the countries and then it's like they vanished from the history books."

"I don't know if it's my responsibility to tell you about this," I admit, shaking my head. He opens his mouth to say something, but I stop him, "I'm not saying that I won't help you learn, though. It's important that you understand the history of the Sirians and their relation to the country you could possibly run one day."

"I don't think I'll ever run a country," he scoffs. "I'm the youngest of three."

"From my understanding, your sister doesn't seem to want to run one." I shrug. "You'll have to marry someone to strengthen relationships, right? It might not be this country, but it could be another."

"No one will want a sick husband or King," he admits softly, his face falling in defeat and angry tears welling.

I lean forward, both of my hands framing his face. "You are an incredibly kind and compassionate prince. You care about those who do not have a voice, and you help give one. That is what this country and this world need.

"I'm also convinced we will heal you permanently from whatever has ailed you since you were born. I told you it's going to be my sole priority to do so, and I'm not going anywhere until I do."

Suddenly, Clint lurches forward in his bed, hugging my neck tightly. Tears prickle at the corner of my eyes, and I blink quickly to send them away.

I return his bony, if not warming, embrace, pressing both my hands against his shoulder blades.

"I'm really glad you came when you did, Reva," Clint whispers against my shoulder.

I close my eyes with a serene smile. "Me too, kid."

★★★

I walk beside Elly through the streets of Saros, her arm looped through the crook of my elbow. I'm entirely aware of the knights following closely behind us, their faces a mask of indifference, even if their eyes occasionally dart towards the townfolk lingering in alleyways.

"How do you live with knights following you everywhere you go," I mutter quietly, glancing briefly over our shoulders.

"I could ask you the same thing," Elly counters, raising her eyebrow at me with a sly smirk. "There is one knight in particular that seems to be wherever you are."

My face instantly flushes, heat rising to my cheeks.

Elly chuckles to herself, clearly proud of her comment as her focus falls back in front of her. I recall a previous night walking down another street of Saros with said knight and kissing him in the bar.

"He kissed me," I find myself blurting, albeit quietly, to keep away the attention of the knights trailing us.

Elly's head whips towards me, her eyes wide, but there is some other emotion clouded behind her shock that I can't read.

Something that makes me lean away.

"Are you not used to kissing beautiful men?" Elly inquires, turning her head forward but still looking at me from the corner of her eyes.

"I've done more than that," I mumble. Elly snorts, shaking her head. "That's beside the point. We work together, and I am trying to figure things out with Clint—"

"It was a kiss, Reva." Elly laughs, eyes crinkling. She turns us down another street crowded with more people. I catch a few signs that indicate a fashion district of sorts. "No one is asking you to commit to the boy."

"But do you really think Fin would be the type that if I went around kissing whoever, that it wouldn't bother him? You know him better than I do, Elly."

Elly chews on the inside of her cheek, tilting her head to the side as she considers my words. "You're not wrong there." She sighs "Fin isn't the type to flounce around and typically doesn't aim for the girls that do."

"I am usually the flouncing type," I admit, catching a few people staring as we pass by slowly. There are some that even bow.

"I would argue that because you only spend time with Fin, myself, and Clint, you are—in fact—not the flouncing type."

I scoff loudly, poking roughly into her ribs. She winces, but not without a playful glint in her eyes. "If more people didn't look at me like I would require their firstborn, maybe I would be."

"Alas, you don't go around kissing me." Elly shrugs, narrowing her eyes. "Yet."

I roll my eyes so hard they might get stuck back there, which only elicits a snicker from Elly. I window gaze, but I contemplate what she said.

There were plenty of individuals that I messed around with when I lived in Eldamain, some that would be considered regulars. What we did was never considered a relationship. It was more like some sort of pleasure-for-pleasure business transaction.

Then again, I was never friends with the people I made out with.

Elly steers us into the entryway of what appears to be a jewelry store. We unlatch our arms to fit through the narrow entrance, followed by the sound of bells tinkling.

I crane my neck back to look up at some string that we may have triggered, but there are only the bells dangling from the ceiling.

"An enchantment spell," I breathe, letting my eyes trail down with my head.

I scan some of the nearest shelves, recognizing different rare gems and jewels. There are even gems mixed together that I have never seen before, which is saying a lot, considering Eldamain is a country that experiences a lot of trade across its borders—both legal and illegal varieties.

"The owner is a Magic," Elly clarifies, walking down the first short aisle of shelves lined with various raw gems. "I would say most aren't as observant as you are to the sound of bells."

"Someone has come across my bells," a deep, regal voice interrupts as a figure appears just at the end of the aisle. The knights stand by the front door, one facing inside the shop and the other focused outside. They aren't alarmed by the stranger.

"Jorah," Elly greets, reaching for him and grasping his hands.

I assume this is the Magic, and not by way of greeting, but by the fact that it's quite clear he reigns from the House of Argo.

A spattering of blue scales climbs down one side of his neck and disappears below the hem of his collar. The tunic under his deep purple suit jacket has an open neck, but there are no scales under the black-gray chest hair peeking out. His slicked-back hair is mostly black, save for a few natural gray highlights scattered throughout. He towers over both Elly and me, but he hunches close to her with both of her hands drawn towards him.

"Princess," he greets, that voice even more regal than King Darius. "I feel it has been far too long since you've graced my presence."

"I've been a little busy with Father and Clint," she explains, shrugging nonchalantly. "Our new Royal Healer also has me running rampant in the library for information."

I clear my throat, gaining both of their attention. I raise an unamused eyebrow at Elly.

The Magic, Jorah, peers around her head, narrowing his eyes as he studies me. Elly releases his hands from her grasp, turns sideways, and flourishes a hand in my direction.

"Jorah," she says again, "This is Reva, our newest Royal Healer."

Jorah steps forward, extending his manicured hand out between us. His face is still studious, scanning not just me but around me as if reading my aura. He speaks first, "A young Magic, I presume?"

"I was raised and trained by the Great Karasi," I admit, accepting his outstretched hand.

When our skin contacts, his narrowed eyes fly open. They briefly flicker between our hands and my face.

"*Raised* by Karasi," he repeats, his hand tightening on mine. "I heard the rumors down here, but I thought it was another elaborate tale whipped up by Karasi herself."

"No rumor," I awkwardly shrug, trying to pull my hand back. His grip tightens more, putting an uncomfortable amount of pressure on my fingers.

Elly notices, her eyes flitting to where our hands are clasped before cautiously eyeing Jorah.

"We are all connected by the waters, child," Jorah says, lowering his deep voice to a rumble. "The waters speak to me."

"You're prophetic like Karasi?" I question. I've never met another Magic that had the abilities she does.

He shakes his head, a quick movement. "Not prophetic, precisely." One side of his mouth twists up. He pats the top off my hand with his free one, now grasping it between both of his. His finger gently tickles my palm. "Do you know the blood of the body contains water, child? It speaks of things some do not know."

I frown and tilt my head in confusion.

I try to recall the bit of knowledge I have on the House of Argo, but it's difficult to remember everything about each house when Magics have been thinly spread worldwide in hiding; they like to keep everything about themselves secret.

It's why powers vary so drastically from one member to the next.

"Sometimes things we do not wish others to know," he whispers, almost too quietly that I barely hear him.

My attention pulls back to where he's deepened the pressure on my palm, drawing the same symbol twice. I meet his eyes, which are such a beautiful, deep blue with splashes of silver-white within. They remind me of the churning ocean against a beach.

"Jorah," Elly finally interrupts, distracting him enough so I can yank my hand from his grasp.

I cradle the hand he held in my other, pressing my thumb into my palm where he had been insistently tracing over and over again.

"Apologies, child," Jorah collects himself, turning to face Elly fully. He motions for us to follow him toward the back of the shop where there is a wooden workman's table scattered with various tools and shards of jewels.

"Have you repaired it?" she asks, anxiously. Her hand flies to her neck, fingertips lightly grazing her collarbone.

Jorah walks around the back of the table as Elly and I stand on the opposite end, shoulder-to-shoulder. He holds up a finger, searching the table.

She stiffens, and her frustration radiates from her. "Do you mean to tell me you have it lying around on this mess of a table?"

Jorah pauses briefly, ignoring her. His hand reaches down, plucking a chain off of the table.

At the end of the silver chain is a small pendant shaped

like the head of a raven. On either side of its head are two rubies in the shape of stars.

"The size and placement of the rubies made it difficult to shape," Jorah explains, studying the pendant with his hand hovering below it. "Alas, I was able to replace both the rubies."

"Gods," Elly breathes, taking it from him and cradling it to the same spot on her collar she had briefly touched. "You won't say anything to anyone?"

"My dear," Jorah grins proudly. "I value your friendship far too much to compromise it over a silly heirloom that has probably been repaired many times over since its creation. I will tell not a soul."

At the last statement, Jorah's ocean-blue eyes briefly flicker over to me, so fleeting I don't think Elly catches it.

That, or she assumes it's a warning from him to keep my mouth shut about this necklace, too.

"Thank you, Jorah," she breathes, pulling out a small pouch from her satchel.

I help her clasp the necklace back on around her neck before we leave. Just as we approach the door, Jorah calls out to us. We both look over our shoulders.

"Come back whenever you please." Jorah winks. "The pendant on your hematite necklace looks like it may be loose, child. Be mindful of that."

My hand tingles where he had been tracing, but I raise it to my neck where my own necklace hangs.

Elly leaves first through the door, the knights maneuvering so we can get out. We walk silently for a block before it gets the best of me.

"What happened to your necklace?" I ask her, fidgeting with my own.

She sighs, shaking her head in shame. "I wear it too much," she admits. "I know I do. It's a family heirloom, passed down through the female line of the Royal Family of Mariande from generation to generation since before the Korbin brothers took the throne. I know Jorah isn't wrong to assume it's been broken and repaired before, but it's precious nonetheless."

"The gems fell out," I guess.

She nods, smoothing her skirts. "I didn't notice you have a hematite necklace. You know the mythology behind them, don't you?"

"I can't say I do," I answer, finally letting my hands fall to my sides. "But I'm guessing you know."

Elly glares at me, continuing, "They say that Magics who carry an item of hematite have the blood of the deities in them. The hematite was given to the demi-gods and their families to ground them in the mortal realm and keep them from yearning for more power that would cause them to dabble in the beyond."

"It's just a myth," I assure, but even that weighs like a lie on my tongue.

"What if that's what Jorah was talking about," Elly ponders. "About not knowing what's in your blood? What if your real parents were descended from a demi-god like Bodhi or Enke?"

"That would be interesting," I admit because that could

be possible.

I wouldn't know where to find that out, though, since many of the tales of demi-gods have been lost to old texts and history.

I also know what Jorah was more than likely talking about. The weight in the pit of my stomach plants itself there and I have to fight my powers from rising to the threat.

I press my thumb against my palm one more time, where he had traced the shape of the Sirian Mark over and over.

CHAPTER 12

I shut Clint's door behind me, pressing the back of my head against the wood with a deep sigh.

Watching his body try to fight the treatment again is devastating and heartbreaking, even more so as he tries to smile after vomiting his dinner.

There's another version of the remedy that we've been using, but I know deep in my gut that it's only going to be another temporary solution just like the one we've been working with for a little over a month now.

I head towards the direction of the study I've claimed, hoping the lull of the fireplace will help me concentrate on the books weighing down my satchel.

I turn the corner of the hall, nearly slamming into a wall of knights.

"My apologies," I blurt, my hand flying to my chest in shock.

Unfortunately, the sneer that flies to the one knight's lips is anything but forgiving. I fight to keep from rolling my eyes.

I do not have the patience to deal with this group today.

"I will never understand why they let you roam about

the castle alone," one of them grumbles to the rest, bending towards his companions while still staring me down.

"I am treating the prince," I snap, narrowing my eyes. "I can't wait for knights to appear to escort me where I need to go so that I can continue to save him."

"You really think *you* could save Prince Clint when the previous Magic in your place couldn't?" He crosses his arms in front of his chest, scowling. "What makes you believe you're any different than that old witch?"

"I don't have to justify myself to you." I straighten my shoulders and tighten my grip on the strap of my bag to keep from shaking.

The power inside of me is bubbling with anxiety from his words clanging in my head. I try to move past him, but his hand thrusts out and grabs my wrist, yanking my body against his.

"And do you have to justify yourself to Sir Finley?" He chuckles darkly, his gaze roaming from my lips and down my chest. "It seems like you spend an awful lot of time with him."

"Excuse me," I scoff, flames burning the back of my throat. My eyes fall to where his hand still clenches my arm before meeting his glower. "I fail to see how that concerns you in the slightest."

"I'll make it my business," he snarls low under his breath. "I will make anything about you my business if I wish."

Anger and fear rage against my self-control, trying to escape from my body and demonstrate to the arrogant knight exactly what fear tastes like. A small headache starts wrapping around my head, pulsing from the Mark that's hopefully still hidden under the salve I wear.

"What do you say, men?" He twitches his head to the pack, who have crept closer during our conversation. "Shall we show the Magic Healer how we induct them into the castle workforce?"

One looks a little wary, but the other two snicker in agreement.

My heart pounds in my chest, my power prickling underneath my skin. I close my eyes against the sting, trying to wrench my arm from his grasp, which only makes him angrier. He jerks me closer to him, tearing a gasp from me.

The overwhelming sensation of being trapped causes my vision to wobble. I struggle against the knight, but he's physically stronger than me.

He's a Knight of Mariande, for the Gods' sake.

As his hold tightens, I realize my powers are the only way out of this. The fact that I may have to expose myself as protection against these knights settles deep into my bones, and a wave of sadness envelopes me.

I have to sacrifice what I've built thus far.

Another knight snakes his hand onto my waist, but Clint's smile flashes, bright in my mind like the Light I wield.

Saving the prince, my friendship with Elly, and whatever has been building between Fin and me—do I just let the abuse escalate and risk Clint's life or do I sacrifice what I have gained to defend myself?

Just as I'm about to make my decision, a deep voice

interrupts. "What is the meaning of this?"

The knights jump away from me, except the one holding my arm. He and I turn our heads towards the other end of the hallway.

My heart sinks momentarily at the sight of Sir Pax before my eyes meet the shocked emerald ones beside him.

I let out a deep sigh of relief that relaxes every part of me, including my rising Light.

"Lieutenant," the knight acknowledges. The other three bow before standing at attention again. The one holding my arm uses his free hand to point at me. "We found the Magic Healer wandering about the hall suspiciously, so we were apprehending her."

Sir Pax blinks at the knight before turning his attention to me. He calmly asks, "Can you confirm this, Magic?"

Anger blazes in Fin's eyes as he pins them on the knight.

"What happened to 'Miss Reva'," I grumble.

Pax raises an eyebrow expectantly, so I sigh. "But, no I cannot confirm. I was simply headed toward the study from my day with Prince Clint. I was accosted by your knights on the way."

"Accosted," Sir Pax nods, folding his hands behind his back. I want to rip his arms off. "In what way were you acting that caused you to be accosted? And what did you plan on doing in the study?"

"Sir Pax—" Fin begins, but Pax holds up his hand. Fin snaps his lips shut.

My annoyance must be blatantly obvious because Fin's face softens, surveying me.

"I do *not* answer to you," I snarl, the Light pulsing in my veins.

I catch one of my hands starting to glow faintly, and it draws Fin's attention. Just as it winks out, Fin blinks rapidly, frowning.

I take the distraction as an opportunity to yank my arm from the knight with all the strength I can muster. Once free, I cross my arms over my chest and tuck my hands under my armpits to hide any more glowing until I have full control over myself.

I wheel my gaze on every single knight here. "I do not answer to any single one of you."

"When a knight apprehends you, you should find it in your best interest to obey any orders if you plan to be part of this staff," Sir Pax threatens, one of his hands coming to rest on the sword strapped to his belt.

"Sir Pax," Fin mutters under his breath again.

Pax rolls his eyes before turning to face him. "Is there something you would like to say, *Colonel*?" Pax sneers the last word, narrowing his eyes at him.

Fin's gaze flicks to mine briefly before submitting to Pax with a shake of his head. My heart drops to my stomach.

"My best interest is none of your concern," I say to Pax, but I keep my eyes fastened on Fin.

Hurt and shock flash across his face, but there's a fleeting flash of regret.

Knowing my point has been made, I fix my attention back to Pax, meeting the endless dark depths. "If you have a problem with the liberties I've been given to help treat the prince, take them up with the King. In fact, take them up with the princess since she's been assisting me with my research. She can tell you how I spend my time."

Pax's eyes darken even further, but the rest of his face stays stoic.

I turn on my heel and march back to my room without taking a second glance back.

By the time I make it to my door, my hands are shaking as I battle the all-out war I am having with my powers to keep them at bay. I unlock the door handle and shove my way in, flinging my bag to the side.

Instead of the fire, my veins glow a bright white from the Light of the Sirians. I take deep breaths in and out, counting to four each time just like Remy taught me.

I hold my hands out in front of me, the kinetic energy swirling in my palms. I rarely use the Light, and it's been longer since I've almost lost control. The strong undercurrent races through my body, which is starkly different and unfamiliar from how it usually feels.

It's as if the ability has intensified, which I didn't think could be possible at this point.

A knock on my door startles me, my power snuffing out like a candle being blown out. I briefly glance at my reflection in the mirror, my eyes returning to their normal golden-hazel color as the white-gold fades. My Mark still remains hidden under the salve.

"Reva," Fin's voice travels from the other side of the door.

I don't answer, silently standing and staring at the door.

The soft tap of what's probably his head against the wood

echoes quietly. "Please. I just want to talk." The soft plea in his voice softens me, and I already know that those green eyes are downturned in guilt.

I groan, frustrated, stalking across my room. I reach for the door and then fling it open, the force of it blowing stray strands of my hair back.

I glare at him through slitted eyes, one hand on my hip and the other holding the door open. His eyes widen in shock, hair disheveled. He's distraught, which does nothing for my will to be angry with him.

I want to reach out and slap him, ask him why he didn't say anything, but the other part of me wants to feel his arms wrap around me.

I sigh, waving him in. I look over his shoulder to make sure there is no one to witness him enter before shutting and locking it behind us. I lean my back against it, my head falling back.

"Please let me apologize," Fin breathes, pacing the space in front of my fireplace. "I didn't mean to offend you in any way."

"I thought you were in my corner, Fin," I explain, closing my eyes briefly. "I *need* people in my corner. You said if I needed anything, I could rely on you. I need people who stand up for others."

"I know," he pleads, stopping beside one of my chairs.

I push myself off the door, moving to stand in front of him. "You may not outrank Pax, but I'm sure you outranked those other guys. King Darius clearly favors you. You've said as much yourself. I'm sure if you ended up in a pissing contest with Pax, he'd take your side, especially considering the King is the one who hired me."

"I *know*," Fins groans, his hands gripping my shoulders. "I think I was shocked that it's been this bad, or that they'd get that aggressive about it. I am truly sorry, Reva. I know I should've said something back there. I tried, and I know that's not good enough. Not with how they're treating you."

"It's a difficult life, Fin," I explain, shaking my head. "I know that I have been relatively sheltered from the anger people have for my kind, living in Eldamain my entire life. But, I knew this would be difficult, being in a kingdom that has just started to accept Magics."

"I should've guessed that. You are so normal that I forget you've been secluded from the rest of the world. I wanted to show you that there are people who accept you for exactly what and who you are, and I feel like I'm failing you with that."

"Normal," I whisper, fixating on the fire flickering in the fireplace. My own guilt creeps in, not just at the fact that I know he's been trying, but that he believes that he is simply defending a Magic. "It's not your responsibility to prove those things to me."

"It's not about responsibility. It's about caring enough about you that you should know what that feels like."

His hand tenderly grips my chin, turning so I meet his eyes glowing by the light of the fire. He smiles softly, taking a step into me so I have to crane my neck to look at him.

He holds everything in his eyes, the complete trust and admiration he has placed upon me, making my heart clench in my chest.

Fin's one of the first people I've let get close to me who hasn't known me since I was a child. Not only that but he wasn't forced into getting to know me.

He has willingly gone out of his way to be my friend, so much so that he has defended me before. And now, it's clear his feelings have developed on a deeper level.

"Reva," he softly mutters, breath tickling my cheeks. My knees weaken.

There have been so many times that I've considered just how far his compassion would go. Sharing the burden of my identity with at least one person here entices me.

His thumb caresses my jawline. "You've come into my life in the most unexpected way possible. And, when you did, I didn't care that you were a Magic. All I could see was this strong, selfless woman leaving her safe life to work for a foreign kingdom and save their son—a kingdom she owed nothing to.

"And, to top it off, you're the most beautiful woman I've ever met. I don't know if you've noticed, but you've had me wrapped around your finger since day one. I would do anything to make you happy. And I promise I will do everything to make you feel safe."

"Fin," I plead, my heart cracking in my chest.

I had let him see too much, let him in too fast. Sure, I care about the prince, but I can't hide that the deeper reason I came was to discover more about the Abyss and the Mark hidden between us by a simple salve.

"I know my actions today didn't demonstrate that," he

admits. "Maybe I haven't been doing the best job, but you have to know who you are in your heart… That's what I care about. I don't care about that you're a Magic."

The truth is I was about to sacrifice the prince's life to protect myself from the knights. If I had used my power and shown myself, I would've had to flee.

"You need to understand," I whisper, barely audible.

I take two steps back from his embrace, his hand floating mid-air where he grasped my chin. I tremble, fighting against everything Karasi has ever taught me. She'd kill now to stop me, but something inside me is at peace with any consequences of my decision.

Maybe it's not peace, but that guiding influence of Fate that's followed me my whole life.

"I'm not exactly what you think I am," I continue, wiping the perspiration on my hands against my skirt. "I can count on one hand the people alive that know what I am. You trust me so much and care for me, and I know your heart is right. You came to apologize for something that really isn't your responsibility, but you've made it so. I need you to trust me, and I need you to swear to secrecy."

"Anything," Fin whispers, too concerned or shocked to move or utter any other word.

My heart sits heavily in my stomach, a sharp sting in the back of my throat as I swallow.

This could be making a terrible mistake or lapse in judgment, but something inside me is telling me that—while terrifying—this choice is entirely correct.

I reach for that spot in the middle of my forehead, slowly

wiping away the salve with the back of my hand.

Fin frowns, opening his mouth. Whatever he was about to say falls on silent lips, his face twisting into shock as the salve comes off, revealing my deepest darkest secret lying underneath.

I can't stop trembling as my hand gradually lowers to my side. I call to that place where my power sits inside me, creating a ball of energy that swirls in my hand.

"This is the safest way to tell you my secret, Fin," I admit quietly. "I never know who's listening, but I have this. I've had it my entire life. This is why Karasi sent me. She knew I could learn more about my people, help the prince in a way other Magics can't, and somehow she believes I can save the world…"

I try to break this impending silence, but my mouth dries up. It stays open, but nothing comes out.

Fin continues to stare at me frozen in place.

Tears burn in the corner of my eyes. I call my power back into me, my empty, dull hand still hovering between us.

In a blink, Fin is directly in front of me, slipping his hand over my wrist.

"Forgive my silence," he whispers inches from my face. His eyes flicker to my forehead, then back to my eyes. "Seeing you wipe away what I thought was skin was more of a shock than what you just admitted, honestly."

I let out something between a sigh of relief and a chuckle, relaxing under his soft admiration. Instinctively resting my head against his shoulder, I take a deep breath as his hands wrap around my back and the weight begins to lift from my shoulders.

I shrink back to study his face, clarifying, "So, that's it? No other reaction?"

"Just a lot of questions," he says, tucking a loose strand of hair behind my ear. "A lot of questions, but it's hard to be inconspicuous with these questions, so I will save them another time when we have more privacy.

"Otherwise, Reva, I want you to know this changes nothing. I told you I will only ever care about who you are." He uses his hand that tucked my hair back to cup my cheek. His thumb grazes my cheekbone, then slides down my face and jawline. He tips my chin up gently, leaning in.

I allow gravity to pull us together, his lips pressing softly against mine. My hand grips his forearm fiercely as his tongue runs along the seam of my lips before tangling with my own.

This. I could have this.

I melt into him as a soft moan escapes me, causing him to pull back.

"In the hall," he begins, his voice raspy. "Your hands... I thought I had seen something, or that my eyes were playing tricks on me."

"You did see something," I sigh, brushing my hand along the veins on his forearm. "I was losing control. It can rise sometimes when I'm in danger or really anxious."

Fin scans my face, his eyes lingering on my exposed Mark. He uses his grip on my chin to tilt my head side to side

"You are absolutely gorgeous," he admires. "And, you're

safe with me."

I search for him for comfort and ease, and I know he would protect me if anything ever happened, whether it be knights or some other unforeseen, dark force.

I launch into his arms, meeting his lips again with more force and heat. He responds immediately, bending his knees enough to grip the backs of my legs over my skirt, lifting me against him. I wrap my legs around his waist and plunge my hands into his hair.

He moves against me, taking us toward my bed. The soft mattress flattens against my back as Fin tenderly presses his body against mine. His hips line up with mine and his arousal presses against me through his pants. He trails kisses down my face, my jawline, my neck.

I arch into him, rolling my hips. The moan that rumbles through his body heats my core.

His hand starts to roam over my blouse, trailing a path from my waist to my breast where he cups it in his hand. His thumb swipes over the peak, the friction against my nipple sending lightning sensations through my body.

I breathe against his lips, the realization dawning on me that it has been a long time since someone has touched me this way.

Too suddenly, he disconnects his lips from mine and hovers above me, eyelids drooping. I raise an eyebrow at him.

"It takes a lot for me to say this," he says, his voice rough. "And, I can't believe I'm actually saying this, but I want to prove to you that I care for you. Every last part of you."

"You don't realize how much you already have," I

chuckle in disbelief, shifting underneath him. But he's not wrong. I have a tendency to jump the bones of random men, but never a man who has known me for me, let alone openly cared for me. "But since I just showed you this part of me now, for myself, I should let you prove that."

He skims his finger across my forehead, unable to break his gaze away from my Mark. I dissolve at the tenderness there, embracing it.

He peels away, falling beside me in my bed. I mirror his position, twisting to face him. I place my hand flat on his chest and lay my head in the crook of his shoulder. His hand starts to sweep up and down my arm.

"So, what do we do now," he asks, quietly.

I shake my head against him. "I have been wondering that since the moment I got here."

Despite knowing Fin's acceptance, I'm still apprehensive, my chest tight. More than anything, I'm exposed without the salve as my Mark sits entirely on display.

"We'll figure it all out," Fin reassures, his other hand coming up to cover my own that is resting on his chest.

And, for the first time since leaving Eldamain, I have someone I can believe in.

CHAPTER 13

I fidget with the hematite necklace around my neck, pulling it back and forth on the gold chain. I simultaneously pace back and forth in front of the double doors where I met the King and Queen when I first arrived in Mariande.

My power is thrumming with my pulse like a slow, steady simmer. With Fin's help, I'm hoping to find somewhere to release this built-up power that hasn't had a decent outlet in nearly two months.

"Miss Reva," the knight at the door interrupts. I stop mid-stride, gaping between him and the cracked door. "The King is ready for you."

"Thank you." I walk through the open door underneath the threshold.

Like the first time, King Darius sits on his throne underneath the domed ceiling, but the one meant for the Queen is empty this time. He slopes forward with his elbow resting on his knee and his hand framing the side of his face. His graying hair is disheveled, and his cloak hangs over the arm of his Queen's throne.

"It is good to see that you are well, Miss Reva," King

Darius announces, reclining against his throne. "Though I wish it were under different circumstances, of course."

"I understand that Sir Finley spoke to you about the incident in the hallway the other day," I admit, recalling the conversation we had where he warned me he had said something.

"That is correct," King Darius nods once, deeply sighing through his nose. He pats his hand on the armrest. "I don't know how to begin to apologize for my men's actions. They are supposed to represent Mariande and an extension of the royal family. It reflects poorly on my values and goals as a king."

"For what it's worth," I say carefully. "It is the same few men that have given me a problem from the beginning. Otherwise, the rest of your staff and military has been manageable."

"Manageable?" King Darius' eyebrow curves upward. He rises from his throne, walking down the few steps of the dais to stand in front of me, hands clasped behind his back. A vision of Pax standing that same way has me nearly flinching. "Do tell."

"There are those who are kind and compassionate towards me." Clint, Elly, and Fin all flash in my head. Even Chef B makes an appearance. "There are those who see me simply as a coworker, and there are those who see me as a Magic. They're not cruel or rude, but I can tell they are cautious, if not skeptical. I can sense their wariness about me holding such a high position."

"I understand that progress takes time," he mulls, pacing

before me. "You know about the Magic communities I've put up not just here in Saros, but also across the Mariande Kingdom."

A statement, not a question. "I will say I was startled when I found out."

"It's unfortunate that was your initial reaction, but I can't blame you. Your people have faced terrible prejudice for hundreds, if not thousands, of years. Why would a kingdom suddenly switch its stance on how it views the non-human community?"

"That is a question I've thought about more than once, Your Highness." I follow him to the other side of the room where he gazes upon one of the murals. "With all due respect."

He observes in silence, contemplating or trying to put some emphasis on our situation. I glance between him and the mural depicting the creation of the Magic bloodline.

The Goddess Morana stands in a field with a mountainous range soaring ominously behind her. At her feet, the Creatures of Old are scattered. Serpents and dragon-like creatures represent the House of Echidna, bird-like beings and large wolves for the House of Nemea, and a ball of water containing mythical creatures of the House of Argo.

"I believe it was never meant to be this way," he quietly admits, and suddenly, I'm reminded of a young prince who wants a better world for all his people.

I am no longer shocked to know where two of his children come from, at least.

"We fear what we cannot control, Reva. My father was a cruel king, not unlike those before him or those who may sit on other thrones. I rose to my kingship at a young, unexpected age due to the untimely death of my parents, but I always knew I was going to change things in this world."

I absorb all he's saying, but I can't wrap my head around whether or not he's just talking about Magics.

There have always been some kingdoms that push and pull when it comes to the prejudice the Magics face, but it is a fact that there is no kingdom that has accepted Sirians since their downfall nearly a thousand years ago.

"I do apologize, Miss Reva, and know that I have told my son, Prince Tariq, about the altercation," he says as he turns to face me.

I furrow my brow in confusion.

He chuckles. "To prepare my son for his role as king one day, I allow him to run our royal army as he sees fit. In his absence and in the case of an emergency, he placed Sir Pax in charge of the regular operations. Since Sir Pax seems to have wrapped himself up in this nonsense, I felt that it was a situation Tariq needed to make a decision on. Myself and Sir Finley drafted the letter."

I clear my throat. "I appreciate all you've done."

With a letter postponing any decisions about the men, including Pax, I know the target on my back is dim for now.

The minute punishments—if any—are dealt, I don't know I'll be as safe as everyone affirms.

"I know bringing you into this castle and putting you in as the Royal Healer to represent your people is a cross to bear," King Darius affirms, strolling back to the dais and his throne. "But, I like to believe we can bear it together. You're still young, especially for such a high-ranking member of the staff in the kingdom, and I want you to know that whenever I can, I want to help.

"As I said previously, my children are at your disposal, as is Sir Finley. I hope you take advantage of all our resources and ask for those we don't have."

"It's a cross I'm willing to bear, Your Highness," I answer honestly. "I can't thank you enough for standing beside me and other Magics. It's inspiring, and I hope it can initiate change throughout the kingdom and the world."

If I can help represent a marginalized group of people full of those I care about like Remy, Dahlia, Willem, and even Karasi, it's nothing compared to the true group I represent.

That would be an entirely different conversation.

★★★

"How busy are you?" Fin interrupts, bearing on the back of my chair.

I narrow my eyes, my legs dangling over the side with my book and notebook placed perfectly on each thigh.

He grins triumphantly, and I already know this means he's found something or has something for me.

"That depends," I drawl, folding my quill into my notebook as a marker. "Why is there a mischievous glint in your eyes?"

He frowns, still leaning over me. "There is not."

"Fin," I chuckle, dryly. "You are terrible at hiding your emotions, at least with me. It's written all over your face that you have something up your sleeve."

"Okay," he scoffs, the smile returning to his face. "It's nothing mischievous by most standards. I just figured that maybe we could... talk." *About me being Sirian* is what he leaves hanging in the air.

I bite my lower lip, gently rolling it between my teeth. His eyes momentarily flash to my lips before meeting my eyes again, awaiting my answer.

I take a deep breath, a lead ball settling in the pit of my stomach. "Are you sure?" I stack my books on top of one another and slide my things into my bag, careful of any loose papers.

"I promise, Reva," Fin insists, his voice soft. The chair groans as he moves away from it.

He struts around the front of it to meet me, grabbing my bag out of my hands to sling over his shoulder. He doesn't wear his normal knight's uniform, but rather a simple tunic and slacks like he had when we explored Saros.

"Lead the way, Sir." I wave in front of us. Without hesitation, he grips my hand in his, leading me out of the study and down the hallway. "How did you come across this place?"

"There are very few people that know about it," he explains, the clicking of our shoes bouncing off of the stone floor. "One of them is me, another is the Crown Prince—who is not here—and the other is Elly."

"We risk Elly walking in on us, then." I stop walking,

planting my feet in the middle of the hallway. Fin's arm pulls taut against my hand.

He twists his head to glare at me instantly. "Reva," he sighs, exasperated. He squeezes my hand reassuringly, tugging gently. "I promise you Elly is occupied at the moment. She's with the king, but she won't be there all day."

I press my lips together, waiting a heartbeat before I continue with him. I pick up my speed to catch up, peering from the corner of my eyes. "You are insufferable, you know that?"

"I've been told as much," he laughs, those eyes gleaming with mischief again. I can't fight the small smile that creeps up my face. Those eyes shift to pure glee. "There she is."

"What do you mean?" We take the stairs, and something tells me we're headed for the library.

"You've just seemed troubled lately, and I know that it has a lot to do with, well, everything," he hints, glancing at me briefly before resuming, "I feel like I haven't seen that beautiful smile enough lately."

"Finley," I warn, shaking my head.

Having him talk about me this way as we walk down the open halls twists my stomach into a knot.

"You never tell me to stop." That dimple peeks out from under his auburn-tinted stubble.

We approach the library door, stopping in front of it. "You know she has assistants that work and the door is mostly locked—"

Fin cuts me off by producing a key from his pocket. He places it in the lock, shoving the door with his shoulder.

The library is shadowy with a few torches lit to keep it from being pitch black. Fin waits for the door to close behind him before locking it. I wait in the entryway, my gaze trailing where he goes.

Instead of taking one of the main tables in the front, he turns down the first main aisle that leads to the back of the library. I follow after him.

"I figured this would be the safest place to discuss anything," Fin begins, veering down another aisle that opens into a space where there are two hidden tables and some chairs. "The only people that come in here when the door has been locked are Elly and the assistants, who are all gone for now."

I loom at the end of the aisle as he takes a seat at the opposite side of a table. He plops down into the wooden chair with a dramatic sigh, settling back with his hands behind his head.

His gaze pierces into my soul. "Well, Reva," Fin clears his throat. "I am ready whenever you are."

My hands tingle, as though just the admission of my powers brings them to the surface to try and play with whomever dares to challenge them.

I twist my fingers together in front of me, breathing through it.

Revealing what I am to Fin was one task; diving into detail on any questions he may have about me is another feat.

One that will twist him deeper into my life and the secret people have died and risked their lives to keep.

"You have to understand what you're asking," I admit, stepping closer to his chosen table. "Once you know this, there is no going back. This is not a fairytale that you get to hear and continue on with your life with a new lesson learned. This is real life, and I am just one Sirian life."

"I know what I'm getting into." Fin sits upright and folds his hands on the table. "I have always questioned the lives the Sirians were subjected to, and there is no doubt in my mind that you are worth it."

I sigh heavily, the breath reverberating through my body. I plop into the chair across from Fin, sitting before him. I place my interlaced fingers on the table. "What do you want to know?"

"Karasi isn't your mother," Fin begins, studying me. "So where did you come from?"

"I don't know the entire story around that, actually." I shrug, my heart clenching in my chest. "All I know is that my father left me on Karasi's doorstep when I was an infant and that he had been running from people who were hunting him because of me. She said if he never came back, he was dead. So he's dead. Whether by someone's hands or he abandoned me entirely has yet to be seen."

"I don't want either option for you," Fin sadly says, his head tilting to the side. "So you really don't have a last name?"

"I'm sure I do." I furrow my brow. "But, if I do, I don't know it. Karasi probably knows it or has an idea, but she would never tell me."

"You said she mentioned that you could save the world?"

Fin asks, studying my face. "What do you mean?"

"Fin," I chuckle darkly. "So much of my life is a Godsdamn mystery. So, again, I don't know a lot of the specifics. It has something to do with what's happening to the Black Avalanches. Karasi was vague, but she says it's a sign that something dark is brewing in this world..."

"And you need the Sirian Light to battle it," Fin finishes, his face contemplative. "The Magic communities have been talking about the Abyss. I didn't know what it was, but I brought it up to Elly and she said you and she had talked about it, too. It can't be a coincidence that Magics from Eldamain to Mariande are talking about it."

"I brushed it off when I was in Eldamain." I shake my head, trying to gather my thoughts. "But I have to agree. I don't think it's a singular account anymore. There is not a soul alive that remembers when the Abyss manifested for the first time. I learned about it from Karasi and other Magic legends, but I never thought I'd be able to recognize what the Abyss would feel like."

"It has to do with the Korbin Brothers' Legacy, doesn't it?" Fin asks, leaning forward a little. "The changes King Alrik initiated that led to all the brothers' conquests? I know the king sought to end the Sirians."

I breathe sharply through my nose.

"King Alrik was successful." So much history told by those who won. So much of it wrong... "Karasi always insisted that there is more to the history of King Alrik, his sons, and his motivations to eradicate the Sirians. He was so thorough in wiping them from existence that any of their history is practically non-existent. Anyone who knew the truth of the Sirians went into hiding."

"So, what do you know about this Abyss?" Fin questions, leaning back in his seat and crossing his arms over his chest.

"The Sirians have two types of power: the Light and the Darkness," I start, holding my hands before me and calling my power into my hand. "Thankfully, I have the Light.

"It's an energy, a power that allows me to do a lot of different things. I can generate energy like I'm doing with this ball in my hand or I can conjure it to use it like a visible force, which allows me to throw or move objects. I can also use it to charge objects which could make them explode."

The ball of white-gold Light reflects off the yellower green in his eyes as he stares at it, mesmerized. I put it out by closing my fist.

He shifts his eyes to me again. "And the Darkness?"

I pause, considering telling him about my firepower, but that may be a conversation for another day.

It has nothing to do with the Sirians. If Karasi knew where that came from, she never said. That is a mystery to me still, and it's also something I don't have complete control over to the extent that I do with the Light.

"The Darkness is everything the Light isn't," I explain, resting my palms against the table. "Karasi believed that it forms in a Sirian when there is fear around the child's power if they are forced to withhold what they are and suppress their powers.

"Somehow, it tends to be more powerful than the Light. Karasi believed it was because there is always more Darkness out in the universe than there is Light. Some of the more religious believe it originated from Kuk."

"One of the deities?" Fin clarifies, frowning.

"Kuk is the Deity of Darkness, so many people have associated the Abyss with him, but it's not. It's the work of a Dark Sirian. The power they wield is the Darkness, while the Abyss is the phenomenon that happens in the Black Avalanches. So, the Abyss is Darkness manifested."

I stare at the rows of books extending beyond us, drawing my hands together. "I have never met another Sirian, let alone one that wields Darkness. Karasi and other Magics describe the Darkness as a living ink, spreading like a disease. It slithers over your body like a snake, and it fills you like pouring tar down your mouth."

"I think I can live without imagining what that feels like." Fin winces, rubbing the back of his neck. "So, why the Black Avalanches?"

"The tales, myths, and beliefs of the Magic community say that if the Abyss of the Black Avalanches lives, Darkness has risen again. In a world where some Sirians have survived, like myself, it's not shocking there are some who live in fear of themselves." I pick at my nail, mulling over my next thought. "But what's concerning is that if the Abyss is responding like it is, that means there is a host of Sirians alive wielding the Darkness somewhere, running rampant with their power."

"If the Darkness is everything the Light is not," Fin muses. "And if a Dark Sirian is twice as powerful as one that wields the Light, humanity doesn't stand a chance."

He's right.

And that's the most terrifying revelation.

I pull my hands into my lap, staring down at them, where a faint tingle of power lingers in my hands, surging through my veins.

To wield the Light at any time is a risk, but to wield the Darkness is to declare war.

I can't imagine where to begin searching for them, and beyond that, what does it mean if I find them? Have they been so corrupted by evil that they're beyond saving?

How am I vital to a cause when I barely know how to use my own powers?

"The Darkness is really what King Alrik feared. It's what the world fears," I say quietly, regarding Fin through my eyelashes. "What if there aren't enough hidden Light Sirians in the world to stop what is coming? The Dark Sirians cannot be the ones to seek retribution for centuries of pain. They will paint *all* Sirians as everything the world thought we were."

"And Karasi insists the answer lies with you?" Fin chuckles in disbelief.

I can't even bother to be offended because I share his incredulity.

"She said I can find answers here." I wave around the library. "There must be books on the Sirians that can help me understand my powers better."

"And that you can single-handedly defeat whoever is wielding the Darkness?" Fin shakes his head. "You said so yourself: there are multiple people doing it, not just one individual. You have never trained your power for combat, let alone to its full extent."

"Karasi is different from most Magics," I explain, tilting my head to the side. "She has very unique prophetic powers. I can't begin to see why she thinks I could help save the world, but I'm sure there's more to it than me taking it all on alone. There has to be."

"Whatever you need, Reva," Fin urges, reaching across the table. "You have my support. I will help you in whatever way I can to figure this out."

I swallow against the lump in my throat, avoiding his gaze because I fear what's there. "I don't want you lying for me, Fin. This is risky getting you involved. If someone finds out you're searching for this information, you could probably lose your position—"

"I don't want you to worry about me," he insists, standing from his chair. "I can handle myself."

"This isn't a game," I exclaim, standing to mirror him. "My existence is basically against the law, and digging into things that you shouldn't be—"

"Reva," he interrupts again, smiling playfully. He walks around the table towards me.

My irritation bubbles, wishing I could smack some sense into him.

I rotate to face him, and he grabs my shoulders. "We'll figure this out. Trust me."

Trust was what got us here in the first place.

CHAPTER 14

I hand Clint his medicine, waiting for him to toss it back. After a quick flick of his neck and a wince, he hands me back the empty vial. I chuckle at his shiver from the not-so-pleasant taste, taking notes on how many days this potion has been working and the outcome so far.

"What is Karasi like?" Clint asks, swinging his leg over the edge of the bed.

I start some of his workouts that we've been practicing, having him lift his leg up and down by the knee and hip, hoping to restore muscle and strength to them.

I bend down to stretch his calf muscle. "What made you think of her?"

He shrugs, tilting his head to the side. "You just never talk about her," Clint explains nonchalantly. "She's your mom."

"I don't know if that's the right word for her," I sigh, remembering the last conversation we had before I left. "I've told you she is an obscenely old woman. She never considered herself a mother. At least I don't think she did."

"She had you since you were a baby," Clint winces as I roll his leg in his hip. "She raised you! She taught you Magic, she taught you potions, she probably taught you how to walk and talk. You can't get much more motherly than that."

I gesture for him to lie on his back. I take his leg in my arms, trying to stretch it out more for him.

I inhale, fighting the pressure in my chest. "Everyone has a different idea of what a mother is, Clint. Some think that you have to birth the child to be its mother. Some believe you don't have to share blood. Karasi was more of a guardian or mentor. I had other people that helped raise me. It was a much-needed, combined effort."

"Well, if she was your guardian," he huffs, closing his eyes as I extend his leg in and out. "Who are these other people that raised you?"

"So many questions today," I chuckle, humming around my pressed lips. "What about you, kid? What's it like being a prince in a castle?"

Clint peeks out of one eye, expectantly.

This kid...

I purse my lips, letting out a huff of a laugh as I switch to the other leg. "They're all Magics," I tell him, following the same movements as before. "Eldamain is full of them. While it's owned by The Clips, they leave it alone other than collecting taxes. With the open land and the protection of The Overgrowns, it makes a perfect home for anyone that doesn't have one."

"But they have a home here, now," Clint frowns, both eyes wide open. "Magics can live in Saros, Vega, and Elvi."

"No one in Eldamain knows that." I shrug, patting his leg as I rest it against the bed. I stay beside him, folding my hands together in my lap. "When Fin came to get Karasi, that was the first we'd heard about Magic communities. Word doesn't travel fast to Eldamain so we don't know much at all about the goings-on of the world, let alone one specific country."

"Don't the other Magics talk to each other? Wouldn't they share with their friends that there is somewhere for them to live?"

"It's a little more complicated than that," I sigh, my gaze wandering to the cracked window.

"I want to understand," Clint pleads, shifting his weight on his pillow with a wince. "I don't receive the same teachings in modern politics as Elly or Tariq. When they were my age, they were learning all sorts of things and preparing for their future. I want to pretend at least I could have a future running a kingdom, just like you said."

I roll my lips together, blinking back the burning in my eyes. I clear the sharp tickle at the back of my throat, nodding. "It has much to do with safety, intentions, and resources. Magics want to make sure that—before they invite more of their kind—it is actually safe to be here. Linked to that would be gauging if your family's intentions are true and not a way to get their people killed.

"But most important are the resources available to go around. While Magics occasionally rally together in Eldamain, they're very private people. They don't trust easily, even if it is someone like them. Naturally, that means they're not going to share. If there isn't a lot of space for them in a town already bustling with mortals, they won't want others taking their business or living."

"Saros is getting crowded," Clint admits, biting the inner

corner of his lip. He rests one hand on his stomach, rubbing gently. "Elly, Isla, and Fin have told me about it. And, the other towns are still so new."

"See, you're getting it!" I stand from the bed, smoothing out my skirt. "I told you, kid, you've got a knack for this. The best advice I could ever give you is empathy. Always think like the people you're trying to talk to. Learn as much as possible to understand their points of view better."

"Tariq says that," Clint muses, narrowing his eyes at me. "He even says that about your enemies. Is that why you don't try to hurt people who are scared of you or treat you like you're less than?"

"It's part of it, yes," I admit, folding my hands over my chest. "But sometimes, there is no amount of empathy in the world that can help me understand why people go to such lengths to mistreat others."

"I consider the ways some of the knights have treated you. I can understand why some people are scared and avoid you, but I don't understand why they have to be so mean to you."

"Some people respond to fear with anger, and they lash out. It all depends on who they are, how they were raised, their egos… Those sort of things." I move back to the worktable where the notebook rests, reaching for the quill to jot down the exercises we did and Clint's response to them.

Even turned away, I swear I can hear his brain still working overtime behind me.

"Like Pax?" Clint voices, catching me off-guard. I pause mid-scribble, frowning down at my hand. "Elly says it's because of his dad that he's angry. She also says it's because he's sad and doesn't want to be hurt."

I set the quill down, folding the pages. I twist around and rest my hands behind me on the edge of the table.

If Elly, Fin, and even the Crown Prince are or were close with Pax, I can only imagine he had some sort of relationship with the young prince, too.

"How did Pax react to Isla if she's been your nurse your whole life?" I ask, frowning. "Elly made it seem like Pax hasn't always been the way he is."

"Pax never cared much." Clint shrugs, swallowing. "He started acting weirder as the Magic community grew, and when my dad said they were going to hire Karasi to be the Royal Healer, he freaked out and hasn't been the same since. He started keeping his distance from everyone. It happened to be about the same time Tariq left. He told Pax he hoped he could pull himself together by the time he came back."

"How do you know this?" I ask, letting out a breath of laughter through my nose and shaking my head. "Does your brother tell you?"

"Tariq tells me everything," Clint says, but the color drains from his face.

"Clint, are you—"

Clint interrupts by lurching to a seating position, one hand covering his mouth and the other hand pressed against his stomach.

I lunge for the waste bin next to the bed, shoving it underneath him just in time for a brown and black liquid to spew from his lips. My stomach instantly bottoms out, and my heart rate spikes.

"Oh, Clint," I groan, reaching my hand across his forehead.

I push back his hair, and while there are beads of sweat forming from exertion, there isn't a fever. After depositing one more cup of liquid, he flops onto his back, eyes glazed.

I hand him a clean rag off the side table to wipe his mouth. Once he's finished, I exchange the cloth for a glass of water.

"I'm sorry, Clint," I whisper, sitting on the edge of the bed with him.

"You have nothing to be sorry for," Clint reassures, clearing his throat. "I should be sorry you had to watch me puke. I'm sure that's your least favorite part of the job."

"How often has it been this color?" I ask, frowning at the bin on the floor.

He shrugs. "Sometimes it's that, sometimes it's more like blood, and other times it's a normal yellow like that one time." He sighs heavily, his one hand still hovering over his stomach.

He had been doing that minutes before he vomited.

"Does your stomach hurt?" I press gently, gauging his reaction.

"It did right before," he frowns, wincing but not enough that I'm concerned he's in pain anymore.

What I am concerned about is the hard quadrant in his lower abdomen. I press on it harder, eliciting a hard inhale of air through his clenched teeth.

"Sorry," I apologize again, pulling my hand away. "Does

it hurt more when I press on it or when I'm pulling away?"

"When you press on it," he answers.

I draw my eyebrows together. "Have you always had that hard lump in there?" I try to recall any mention of it in his medical journal from Isla.

"I started to notice it right before you came," he concedes. "I didn't tell Isla because I didn't think it mattered. I thought maybe it was nothing and I was crazy. Then you came, and I started feeling better, and I thought maybe it went away."

I let out a deep, frustrated sigh, pinching the bridge of my nose. "Clint. Anytime you notice something about your body, I need you to tell me. We don't know what we're dealing with and anything can be helpful, okay?"

"Okay," he agrees, nodding.

He rests his head against the headboard, his eyelids heavy. I pat his hand before getting up to gather some supplies and give him a dose of medicine for his pain and nausea. I can't tell from the color of his vomit if the treatment stayed down, but I don't want to risk giving him another, so this will have to do.

If he has some sort of mass in his stomach, I'm not sure how much longer this treatment I have been giving him will work.

We've only been treating the symptoms, not the actual problem, just as I suspected.

And I feel like I may be working against a clock.

★★★

I told Chef B and Charity I planned to have dinner in my room.

I need to focus on finding information that will be able to help me figure out what is going on with Clint. If not with my powers, at least with some sort of medicine.

The soft knock on the door echoes quietly through my room. I place a piece of parchment in my book, stretching my arms above me before walking to the door. I pull my robe a little tighter around my nightgown.

"Thanks, Char—" I pause, realizing the person at my door isn't Charity. "Fin? Is that my dinner?"

"Yeah," he grins, eyes glittering. "I intercepted Charity on the way over and thought I'd deliver it myself and see how you are doing today."

"I'm okay," I sigh, gesturing for him to come in. "You can put it on the coffee table there."

I shut the door behind us, my gaze flickering between him and the open books on my coffee table. He places the tray of food carefully beside my notes, turning his head to the side to observe them. He reaches for one of them and I recognize it's my report for Clint.

Fin's face instantly falls. "Is Clint okay?" He asks, holding out the paper in front of him. The fireplace shadows his face, making him more severe than he probably intended.

"For the most part," I answer, crossing my arms in front of my chest. I walk over to one of my seats, slowly lowering myself to it. "He was fine, besides vomiting today. The mass has been there a while and I'm not sure if it's grown since he first noticed, but now I can keep an eye on it. I'm concerned that he has a cluster of cells in his stomach that are growing."

"Cells?" He frowns, looking down at me. "Aren't our bodies supposed to have cells?"

There's a small tug at the corner of my lips. "Yes, but sometimes they grow too much and create a mass. It can be the size of a gem or as big as a ball. It just depends on how aggressive it is."

"And you're not sure how to fix it?" Fin sits in the chair opposite of me on the other side of the coffee table. He rests his elbows on his knees, clasping them between his spread legs.

"It's only a hunch right now," I reassure, but even I can't fight the nagging feeling that I'm onto something. "And not yet. It seems I can treat the symptoms, regardless of what is going on, but not eliminate what's truly ailing him. Which is exactly what I was worried about."

Fin presses his lips together tightly, nodding.

He starts arranging my dinner, pouring tea into a teacup, and glances up from beneath his eyelashes. "How do you take your tea?"

"Fin," I sigh, reaching out my hand to grab a piece of bread. I rip off a chunk and plop it into my mouth. "You don't have to do that."

"I know." He shrugs. "I want to, though."

"That's what I'm worried about," I mumble under my breath.

He hears me, though, causing him to frown so deeply that his eyebrows almost meet in the middle.

"Why are you worried about that?" He questions, resting

the tea back on the table.

I briefly shut my eyes.

First Clint, now Fin. I can only deal with so many puzzles at once.

I knew from my talk with Elly that the moment would come when Fin might insinuate we're dating or something more than friends. I don't know where to begin with dating, and now that things have become even more complicated with Clint, I don't know if I can spare any time to try.

"I have lived my life a certain way for a very long time," I explain, placing the bread back on the small plate. "I've been mostly secluded from the world. I've had a very small group of people I've kept close to me. Any man who's ever been romantic in my life is not meant to last. I don't do long-term relationships or dates. I could never risk someone getting close enough to understand and accept what I am."

"I understand and accept who you are, Reva," Fin admits with a kind smile peeking through his stubble. He runs a hand through his auburn hair, tousling it.

"I know," I insist. "It's just... I've never had that before. I don't know how to do this. I don't know if I *can*. You know Clint is my priority and I can't be distracted by that. If something else is going to require my attention, like learning how to use my powers better and whatever it is Karasi thinks I'm made to do, I don't know if I can give myself away to someone else."

"I'm not going to ask you to do something you're not comfortable with," he says softly, leaning forward. "I know we come from different worlds, but I'm not naive, Reva. I know the various natures of relationships and how they exist. I'm not foreign to them. I would like to believe, though, that something about us could be different than that. Something more."

Guilt bleeds from my cracked heart, my chest tightening to keep it from seeping out.

I would like to think we could be something different—Gods, do I want that.

I don't want to hurt him more than I already will, but I only have room in my life for one guy right now, and that's Clint.

"I can't promise you that. I don't want to lead you on or hurt you. I value how much you care about me, but I might not be good for you."

I let that statement sink in, that maybe I'm not meant to have someone of my own. I live a risky existence and now I could be jeopardizing that.

My dad, who disappeared—or was killed—because he had a Sirian daughter, crosses my mind. Now, I could be risking someone I've come to care for. Whether that be as my friend or a lover.

"You're worth finding out," Fin admits, getting up from his seat. He moves the coffee table back to maneuver around it.

Kneeling in front of me between my legs, he places both hands on my thighs and gently traces circles with his left hand. "I am in no rush here, and Clint is my priority, too. He's like a little brother to me. I wouldn't do anything that would get in the way of that. I wouldn't ask too much of you. Just exactly what we're doing as long as I don't have to share you with anyone else besides him."

"I don't want to promise you anything," I remind him quietly, lowering my head to stare at his hands on my legs. They move up to my face, cupping it. "All I can give is what I have right now."

"Okay," he nods, leaning closer to me.

He places a gentle kiss against my lips, a whisper of others we've shared. It's so tender, I worry that he already expects something of me that I can't give.

CHAPTER 15

C hef B shouts something at me as I slip out of the kitchen with a whole pastry in hand. I chuckle to myself on the servant's stairs back to the main hallway, biting a chunk out of the crust.

I turn towards the direction of the study, passing an adjacent hallway when a blurred figure falls into step beside me.

I take another bite, side-eyeing Fin.

"You busy?" He asks, shoving his hands into the pockets of his black knight uniform.

"Why," I mutter around the pastry mash still in my mouth, squinting.

"You mentioned needing some training," Fin peeks nervously over our shoulders. He grips my elbow in his hand, tugging me towards the direction of the courtyard entrance door. "I have some time that's freed up today and I have the perfect exercise."

I wrinkle my nose and curl my lip, scoffing, "What are you talking about?"

"Remember," Fin urges stiffly, still dragging me along. "You said you needed someplace to let loose a little, and I said I could teach you some moves."

I rack my brain, trying to figure out what he's talking about as he tugs me into the courtyard.

There are two horses standing side-by-side, their tails twitching back and forth. As we approach them, Fin is examining me expectantly.

I shake my head slowly.

"You know what I'm talking about," he nearly pleads, his gaze flickering from my Mark back to meet my eyes.

It clicks.

I had told him I needed to expel power.

"Right!" I yelp, throwing the pastry over my shoulder. One of the horses eyes me suspiciously. "Totally forgot!"

"Gods, Reva," Fin laughs, shaking his head, "For a Magic—"

I point my finger at his face. "You'd benefit greatly from not finishing that thought."

Mischief glitters in his eyes as he hoists me onto the horse, double-checking my stirrup length before mounting his own.

"So, where is this place that you presume is good for some hand-to-hand combat?" I inquire, catching a few knights eyeing us from their posts.

"The place we train others," Fin says, and then with a quick flick of the reins and a kick of his heels, his horse starts trotting.

I ride behind Fin on my horse on a path going east towards the coast that I know stretches north towards Eldamain, if you go far enough. If we were to follow the coast, we'd end up at The Red Raven.

My heart clenches in my chest, tears brimming my eyes and a sting tickling the back of my nostrils.

Fin glances back, frowning. He slows his horse to let mine catch up.

"Is everything alright?" He scans my face.

I offer a small smile. "I was just thinking about Eldamain." I shake my head, trying to clear the image of Dahlia and me laughing, her eerie, brick-red eyes gleaming. I swallow back the homesickness that rises. "The Red Raven is pretty close to the coast."

"So I recall," Fin smirks, his gaze now straight ahead as we near a beach.

It isn't as sandy as I thought it'd be, rather a beach made entirely of small pebbles. A rowboat rests halfway up the rocky beach, its back end bobbing with the waves.

Fin's eyes turn back on me, a contemplative cast to them as if he's trying to read me. "You know it's okay to miss them."

"I know it is." I furrow my brow, gripping the reins tighter.

"I mean, it's okay to openly miss them," Fin clarifies, sympathetic. "You keep it all inside you. Sometimes sharing the stories with them helps."

I release a single, breathy chuckle.

The horses move slower as the grass melds into the beach, picking up their legs dramatically. I try to imagine how irritated Willem and Dahlia would get knowing I'm talking about them. Remy, on the other hand, would probably not care in the slightest.

"I was—" I pause, clearing my throat and pulling back on the reins as Fin stops his horse beside the boat. "I was thinking about... I guess you'd call them my friends? Family?"

"They don't have to be blood-related to be your family," Fin chuckles to himself, hopping off his horse. He grabs a long, forked stake from the pack on the horse's saddle, using his boot to stomp it into the ground. "I have no siblings, but I grew up with the Hespers. They're like my brothers and sister."

"I've noticed." After securing the reins to the stake and tugging to test the knot, he repeats the process for my horse. "You could say they were my family. They've all been in my life since I was about 5 years old."

"I thought Karasi had you since you were an infant?" Fin casually asks. He walks around to the opposite side of my horse, holding his hands up.

"She did." I swing my left foot over the back of the horse and its saddle. Fin's hands grip my waist. "But, it took the others years to realize she had essentially adopted a Sirian child. They started to help out when she needed." Fin grips me tightly, easily lowering me to the ground.

Even after my feet are on the ground and I gain my balance, he keeps his hands on me, my body pressing against him.

I close my eyes momentarily. The chilled breeze coming off the ocean is drastically different from the heat radiating off of him. The waves lapping on the rock lull my thoughts.

This is the most peace I've felt in a while.

"There is this really small piece of land right off the coast," Fin whispers, using his hands to maneuver my body toward the ocean. There is a patch of land not too far in the distance, maybe a mile out. "It's small, and there are these trees right off the shore that create a border around the perimeter of the island. Within the perimeter, though, it's just open. We've used it for various training exercises over the years, and I thought it would be a good place for you to expel some of that pent-up power you were talking about."

His voice is quieter when he says power, but I hear him despite said power vibrating in my veins. It senses my anticipation and anxiety around being able to let some of it out.

But only the Light.

"Thank you," I murmur. I twist in his arms, blinking up at those soft, glittering emerald eyes. I place both my hands flat on his solid chest. "Really. This means a lot. You don't realize how much this is going to help."

"I told you, Reva." Fin lowers, brushing his nose against mine. "Anything."

He pulls away, gently grabbing my hand in his to help me into the rowboat. I cautiously step in, lifting my skirt to avoid falling on my face.

After I've sat, Fin heaves us into the water, his boots only going ankle-deep briefly before he gracefully leaps in, taking the oars into his hands.

"So," he sighs, falling into a slow, leisurely speed. "It was just Karasi and you for the early part of your childhood?"

I turn my attention out to the ocean, tightening the cloak I'm glad I brought around my shoulders. The winter is still not ready to pass yet, but I don't believe there will be any snow for what remains of the season.

"I barely remember the years where it was just Karasi and me," I explain, tapping into my firepower to heat my hands, rubbing them along my arms and legs. "Even with Dahlia, Willem, and Remy in my life, there was still a lot of time when it was just Karasi and me at the little hut we lived in."

"And, who are these people?" Fin asks, cocking his head to the side. "If you're willing that is. I don't want you to assume I'm prying."

"It's okay." My heart tugs at another memory of when Remy barely dodged the firepower flowing from my young, adolescent hands, almost setting his clothes on fire. My mouth tilts up. "Remy was the first to learn about me and meet me. He's a Magic and the youngest of that crew. He's got to be 59, now."

"59?" Fin exclaims, his rowing halting momentarily.

I laugh at the shock and incredulity on his face twisted in dismay. I clutch my hand to my stomach. "You have a whole community of Magics in Saros. Didn't you know they don't age like any old human?" I cough, still grinning with crinkled eyes. "That's actually quite young for a Magic."

"Gods," Fin sighs, shaking his head and resuming his rowing. "I thought that was only special ones, not all of them."

I roll my eyes playfully. "Anyways, like I said, he's the youngest. Then, there is Willem and Dahlia, who are 72 and

65, respectively. I don't know if I'd really count Rol as part of this makeshift family, but regardless, he's a Magic who owns The Red Raven right now—has for the last 50-something years—and he's got to be well into his hundreds."

"I hope I get used to this," Fin mutters under his breath. He recovers quickly. "Did they all teach you how to use your powers, then?"

"Well enough." I nod, glancing behind me at the island before continuing, "They did what they could with the resources they had. Eldamain can be a very good place for secrecy and taboo dealings, but even a Sirian isn't safe there. That sort of information could make some people a lot of money or grant immunity.

"They were the only people that knew what I was, except Rol. If they were able to find any books or teachings on how to use my power, it was just basics they pieced together based on tapping into their own knowledge of how they access their powers."

"Which isn't much of anything, right?" Fin asks.

"It's nothing like what the Sirians have." I hold out my hands. "The House of Echidna Magics can see in the dark, and sometimes they have wings, but even that is extremely rare these days. The House of Argo can see underwater and swim longer than a lot of humans, but again, it's nothing like they used to be able to do thousands of years ago."

"So, what really makes Magics these advanced healers? If they're not like what they used to be and have evolved almost to be more mortal-ish, then what makes what they do with potions different than a mortal?"

I pause, inspecting him before handing over that trust with not just my secrets, but an entire community. How much I share doesn't just affect me, now, but a host of people that I don't *actually* belong to.

"I don't know how much of this is public knowledge in the library," I start, cautiously. "So, just in case, this stays between us."

Fin pretends to seal his lips, twisting and throwing an imaginary key into the ocean.

I level him with a glare. "Magics might not be religious in Eldamain, but it doesn't mean they don't believe in the Gods," I repeat, having told Clint something similar. "With the belief that Magics were created by a God, that means they believe their blood is god-touched. Adding their blood to any potion or elixir they create seems to add an extra level of efficiency. It enhances the potion's properties and healing abilities."

"So, anytime I've accepted some sort of tonic or salve.." Fin trails off when all I do is offer him a tight-lipped grin. I almost chuckle at the unease as he averts his gaze, staring over my shoulder. "Got it. And, what about Sirians? Is yours even more enhanced?"

"Not as much as you'd think it'd be." I shrug, pulling my cloak tighter. "It does the same thing, maybe a pinch more. I'd venture the Sirians' gifts for healing come from using the Light."

"So, the rare abilities that some Magics have." Fin raises an eyebrow in interest. "I'm guessing your friends had some of those?"

"Remy has wings, but he only uses them in emergencies. He used them once with me to get us out of a situation after I almost revealed myself." I avoid elaborating because, once again, I almost set an entire forest on fire. "He can see in the dark and has other characteristics like sharp canines. Willem and Dahlia both come from the House of Nemea and have very minimal characteristics. Neither have wings, Willem has sharper canines, and Dahlia has retractable claws."

"You say some of these things like they're nothing," Fin scoffs, looking back at me. "I'm human. I have not a single bit of that. If I were to make any of your potions or concoctions, they would barely hold any of the same weight as yours, let alone your friends and Karasi. I would just be your average medicine man."

"Being human isn't something negative," I remind him. "My friends live in exile so they can have some semblance of a normal life, and I live in secret pretending to be something I'm not. My very existence is a death sentence."

"I don't believe King Darius would kill you for being Sirian," Fin vocalizes, but the mere thought of the King knowing what I am sets me on edge, my power crawling through me to voice itself.

"I don't want to test that," I shut down.

Fin stares at me before nodding once, resuming his rowing. "Should only be a few more minutes."

I peer down at my hands briefly, checking to see if my powers are starting to make themselves known with a glow to my body.

As if knowing what I'm thinking about, Fin interrupts,

"Your eyes flashed that glowing white briefly. It was gone in a blink."

Gazing at him, there is hesitation and caution in his gaze and how he tilts back.

I didn't consider that maybe telling people about this power within me would make them fear me if even just a little.

I shift sideways on the little bench in the boat, watching the shore approach for the last few minutes as we draw closer.

After Fin secures the boat on a similar rocky shore, I follow closely behind him as we encroach a line of trees that spreads as far as the island goes in either direction. The trees sway back and forth in the breeze that whips pieces of my hair out of the braid I tied.

We pass through the first line of trees, approaching the clearing in the middle that Fin mentioned. It spreads out a few miles north of us and on either side, the size of a small field where people would play tournament games. There is barely any grass here and the clearing is mostly made of dried dirt, some rocky spots, and bare areas where the grass is like straw.

"You all have thoroughly wrecked this island," I observe, making a small circle as I survey the surrounding area.

He wasn't lying when he said it was enclosed by the trees, almost like an arena.

He shrugs, sheepishly. "We do a lot practicing hand-to-hand combat within the elements. We've held games, tournaments, wrestling matches—you name it, we've done it."

"Good Gods," I sigh, trying to suppress the smile as I imagine some knights wrestling in the dirt, screaming at each other.

I reach the opposite side of the clearing, just a few yards in front of Fin. After one last glance around me, I take a deep, unsteady breath.

Fin takes an imperceptible step back.

I chuckle darkly. "Trust me, Fin. I have control over it."

I spread my arms out wide in front of me, letting the power rise to the surface. The fire and Light battle for dominance, racing each other to be free.

I lean into the bright, chilled power of the Light. It takes over, muting the hot, molten power of fire. I extend my head to the grey sky, letting the Light flow from me.

The pure white power bleeds from my hands, jumping off me in small bursts of energy like silent fireworks before disappearing into the air as though they never existed. I concentrate, tapping deep enough into my power without touching the bottom where that white power starts to turn a tinge of blue on the corners and transforms into ice cold—too strong for expelling some energy.

The white light stops flashing, dragging out in ethereal tendrils on either side of me and arching over my head to meet. Once the two hands of Light meet above me, they start to steadily rain down in a white-blue veil like an umbrella.

There's a small tug of my lips as the power vibrates around me, making my hair float like I'm underwater. Small, twinkling bits of Light fall from the edges of the umbrella I've created like shooting stars.

A flash of bright, white-blue has me yanking that power too fast, snapping back into me like a boomerang.

I inhale sharply, gasping and stumbling forward. I catch myself with my legs wide in a lunge and one of my fingertips brushing the dirt below me.

"Reva?" Fin asks, cautiously. I whip my head up at him, more hair falling into my face. "Did you bring more salve?"

"Yes," I breathe, closing my eyes against the cold receding from my veins.

Fin takes that as an invitation, rushing to kneel in front of me. He grabs my face in his hands and examines every angle. His eyes linger on my Mark.

"That was," he shakes his head, eyes wide in awe, shock, and a little something that makes me nervous. "I've never seen anything like that. It was like watching a fairytale play out in front of me."

"I would expect that to have been a first," I wince, pressing into his embrace to stand up straight. Once I'm sure I'm balanced, I wipe the dirt off my hand against my cloak. "I try not to tap in too far, but I always struggle when I start to edge that line and need to pull it back in."

"What line?" Fin asks, tilting his head to the side.

"It's like a dam," I try to explain, holding my hands out in front of me to mimic a wall. I keep my fingers separated. "Water can still flow from it, but it's controlled and steady. If you want more water, you have to remove part of that dam."

To demonstrate, I bend my pinky finger into my palm. "But, any time you pull a piece away, you have to be careful how much you open up. Sometimes, it's a little."

I straighten my pinky finger, but this time I bend my pointer finger. "Sometimes it's a lot."

With my pointer finger still bent, I also bend my middle finger and pointer finger. "Sometimes it's too much and it overwhelms me. I'm not used to taking that much power."

"That," Fin pauses, considering, "Actually makes sense to me. Great analogy."

I chuckle, lowering my hands. "Thanks."

"Do you feel better?" He inquires.

I nod, encouraging. "I do," I follow him back to the shoreline. "A lot better. It's quieter and doesn't feel as threatened now. I do appreciate it."

"I'm glad I can help." Fin slings an arm over my shoulder and tugs me under his embrace. "Whatever you need from me to keep it at bay or from revealing itself, I will do what I can."

"It's not an animal." I laugh timidly. "It's just that... I don't know. It's meant to be a defense, I think. I really wish I knew more about the nature of the Sirians and the true story or tales behind their existence."

"We'll figure it out," Fin reassures, squeezing his hand on my shoulder.

I lean into his embrace, allowing his warmth to envelope me so I can put some of the firepower aside.

Even if I can pretend for a moment that what I saw in Fin's gaze wasn't a hint of terror after my little demonstration.

CHAPTER 16

I stand next to Clint's bed, making notes in the journal about the progress he's made from the most recent addition to his medication. I underline the word *temporary* to ensure that not only the king and queen know what to expect, but so I remember what I'm up against.

At least until I can find a way to undoubtedly determine what's going on inside Clint without opening him up and risking his life.

"You have your concentrated face on today," Clint observes, his arm stretched out in front of him with the palm facing up.

My fingers rest against his pulse. It's stronger than it was the other day during his small episode. I press my lips together tightly, writing down the positive results.

"I have a lot of notes to take since we're adding wormwood to your treatment," I admit, removing my fingers from his wrist and shutting the book with a hard clap. "Too much can be toxic to your kidneys, so we need to know how your body is reacting to everything we are doing."

"Yeah," Clint sighs, resting his head against the wooden

frame.

I slip my notebook into my satchel hanging on the chair but glimpse him over my shoulder. His platinum blonde hair hangs in front of his face, grown and brightened since I arrived at the castle. Those eyes that match his sister's and father's are glowing, staring out the open window where the cool breeze swoops in.

"Don't give up on me now, Prince," I call, returning to gather the vials for his next dose.

A few heartbeats pass before my organizing is interrupted by a ruckus outside Clint's window. I pause, placing the vials back down on the small table.

Clint must have also heard it because he's already frowning, his attention to the window.

I tilt my head to the side, focusing on the sounds from outside to discern what's going on. Clint's brow is furrowed as he extends his arms beside him trying to sit up. I hold out a finger to him, grasping my heavy skirt before walking quickly over to the open window.

I peer over the windowsill where the view overlooks the entrance of the Castle of Andromeda. Nothing seems too out of sorts, but I assume the source of the noise has been handled since I arrived at the window.

"Can you see anything?" Clint questions, trying to conceal his concern.

I shake my head, not voicing an answer until I'm certain.

The hinges on Clint's bedroom door protest with the force that swings them open. I swiftly turn on my heel, my heart pounding in my chest.

Elly and I lock eyes just as she slams the door shut behind her, flattening her body against the frame. Her chest rises and falls frantically, straining against the tight vest fastened over her blouse. Panic flashes in her eyes like fireworks.

"Did you hear the commotion?" Elly whispers, shoving a chair under the handle.

My heart doesn't have time to recover, a deep throbbing settling at the bottom of my ribcage.

Once she secures the chair, she leaps toward the same side of Clint's bed I'm standing at. She grips my forearms tightly in her hands, her gaze still fixated on the door.

"Yes, but I wasn't able to see what it was," I explain, allowing her to drag me closer to Clint's mattress. She gingerly sits beside him, reaching for Clint's hand while keeping my arm fastened in the other. I wince at the intensity of her grip tightening. "Elly—"

"Someone broke into the castle," she whispers, barely audible. I hold Clint's worried gaze. "They knew some of the knight entrances, and they're trying to make their way into the various wings. I don't know much more but I was just down the hall when I heard some of our knights rushing from this hallway."

"What do you think they want?" I ask, keeping my voice low as my body presses into hers.

I pray to the Gods that no one can hear our whispering, or my heartbeat that's pounding against my ribcage as if it's trying to escape. Not to mention my power sparking off through my bloodstream as it rushes through my veins.

"I don't know, Reva. I wish I could say…" She trails off

when there is a sudden commotion coming from down the hallway somewhere outside Clint's door.

There is shouting, a few men yelling at each other, but the words are indiscernible. It doesn't take long for their swords being drawn from their sheaths to sing through the door.

There is no escaping if the intruders know where the prince's room is. Without a lock equipped on his door, we are relying solely on the chair jammed precariously underneath the handle.

I desperately scan the room for a weapon, but there isn't even a poker for the fire in this room. I swear softly under my breath, removing my hand from Elly's.

"Reva," she pleads as quietly as she can.

I slip my shoes off to keep from making much more noise than necessary. I check both sides of the fireplace again, but there are no tools. The walls only bear various framed pictures, no decorative swords or spears.

I wring my hands together in front of me, my mind running rampant with ideas and nothing to support them.

Two resounding, simultaneous thumps snap my attention back to the door. My arms zip to my sides, my hands tightly gripping my skirt.

"Reva," Clint warns, just before rushed steps come to a dead stop in front of Clint's door.

My heart stops with them.

I blink at Clint and Elly, both of their gazes locked on me in desperation. I hold up two fingers to them.

Two sets of steps.

What does that mean, though, when we have a princess, a disabled young prince, and an untrained Sirian disguised as a Magic?

The handle on the door jiggles ferociously, wrenching a yelp from Elly. Her hand clamps over her mouth too late, shutting her eyes at the mistake she knows she's made.

I control my breathing, forcing myself to take deep breaths in and out for four counts each. I inch forward, standing between the bed and the door, not daring to take my eyes off it.

A hard thump rattles the door on its hinges, the chair wavering from the impact. My power vibrates through me, and I know I won't be able to control it much longer.

Whoever is trying to get in is on a mission, and I highly doubt it involves letting any of us out of this room alive.

The second thud effectively loosens the chair, which means the next collision will break the door open and allow the intruders in. I collect one last breath of air, facing Elly and Clint for what could possibly be the last time.

Once they know what I am, it's all over.

Both of their eyes bulge out of their heads, nearly identical to each other in their moment of shock. My power tingles at my fingertips, and I know my eyes are already glowing.

Elly confirms that thought when her mouth drops open, her eyes locked onto my forehead despite being under attack.

"I'm sorry," I say, facing the door just in time for it to slam open, one of the hinges flying off the wall.

I don't hesitate.

I yank open that dam and funnel all the Light energy toward the man standing in the doorway. The stream of blaring white light hits his chest, blasting him backward into the hallway.

He collides with the opposite wall, something snapping like a twig. He falls in a limp pile on the floor, and I can't process if I've killed him or not because another man comes running at me, sword raised above him.

I only have time to respond by manipulating the impact. I raise my hand between us. A wall of glowing white-blue light caresses his hand, causing it to hover between us.

Confusion flickers across his features and I recognize him as the knight who tried to assault me weeks ago in the hallway. I frown, tilting my head to the side.

The momentary distraction is enough for him to gather his wits.

His free hand swings underneath the Light wall to punch me in the stomach. The wind rushes out of me, my power snuffing out as Elly's scream echoes in Clint's bedroom.

The sudden absence of the Light holding his arm causes him to drop his sword, but it doesn't stop him from advancing on me, grabbing me by my throat.

The pressure rips a small gasp from me before cutting off my airway.

"You stupid bitch," he sneers, spittle flying onto my face. My brain panics despite trying to keep a level head. I blink quickly to keep my vision. "I knew you couldn't be trusted as a Magic, and here you are, one of *them*."

I claw at his hands around my throat, but it's no use.

Whether or not I'm drawing blood, he doesn't care. My head continues to lighten as the pressure behind my eyes builds, my vision blurring on the edges.

I stay alert and fight the lack of oxygen to my brain, hoping to keep him busy long enough for Elly and Clint to get out.

"I am going to enjoy watching the pathetic *Light* leave your eyes," he chuckles, squeezing a little tighter.

The pressure turns painful, pinching the arteries in my neck. I force my attention to navigate around the pain and haze, opening up the dam to my power but finding it buried at the bottom.

"Then, I'm going to leave a beautiful message for the King so he can see just what this world thinks of Magic and *Sirian* sympathizers—" He howls, releasing his grip from around my throat.

I drop to the ground, landing harshly on my hands and knees. The air rushes into my head like a tidal wave. I lift it despite the searing pain in my neck.

Clint *stands* behind the knight, sword in his hands and blood glistening off one side. With his attention now on Clint, I get a full view of the surface-level gash across the knight's back.

Fighting the pain around my neck and my tilting vision, I painstakingly raise my hand in front of me, my palm facing the knight.

"You're going to regret that, you little shit," the knight growls, lunging for Clint.

I manage to shoot a weakened stream of power that

knocks him to the side instead of tackling Clint.

The prince and I lock eyes, his face turning paler the longer he stands. His eyes roll to the back of his head, and just as he's about to collapse, Elly slides across the floor to catch him in her arms. She tenderly lowers his head into her lap.

"Enough," the knight growls, rising from where he'd landed after I'd thrown him. Blood drips from a laceration on his head, no doubt caused by what he flew into.

I stand nearly to full height, albeit not confidently. My vision totters and I stumble forward.

The knight wipes blood from his eyes, obscuring his vision enough that he doesn't see me grab his sword in my hand where it fell from Clint's grip. I freeze, bent at the waist, waiting for him to get close enough.

"I'm ending this—"

A guttural cry rips through my damaged throat and aching chest. I channel my Light into the sword, giving me the extra strength I need to lift it from the ground and drive it directly through the middle of his torso.

His face contorts into shock as his gaze drops to the sword protruding from his abdomen.

Knowing more about anatomy than swordplay, I let out a hoarse cry as I yank it back out of his body with all I have left.

He falls to his knees in front of me, eyes wide and latched onto me, even as the life flickers out of them. His body topples to the side in a growing puddle of blood, and his sword clatters to the ground with him, my hands warm and sticky with blood.

"Reva," someone says from the door.

But I have nothing left in me. I was never trained to wield for battle, to fight the adrenaline that threatens to burn through me as strong as my power. Being choked nearly unconscious catches up with me.

I'm able to lift my eyes to emerald green ones before gravity collapses on top of me and I'm swallowed by a cold darkness.

★★★

"What if someone sees me," I asked, my hair whipping around me from the storm threatening to wreak havoc.

Karasi stood under the protection of our front porch, her arms crossed over her chest. She raised her eyebrow, bored. "You are safe here, child," Karasi insisted, searching the sky as lightning streaked across, followed by a clap of thunder that shook my bones.

I furrowed my brow, knowing she could sense my annoyance even if she couldn't see me from the porch.

I closed my eyes against the wind and ignored the edges of my hair lashing my cheeks. I held my arms out on either side of me, diving into the pit in my stomach where I envisioned my power. I splashed into that pool of power, wincing as the impact of hitting it too fast sent it burning cold through my veins. I reeled it back, trying to tread.

"Control, aster," Karasi warned, not unkindly. "You don't need that much to conjure kinetic energy."

It was too late, though. My grip slipped on the rope of power I tried to tug on. It lashed out, the tingle turning into sharp pricks at the tips of my fingers. I snarled, trying to battle the well of power that was never ending but could burn me out if wielded too fast.

"Aster," Karasi warned again, her voice booming over the thunder that rattled the earth beneath my feet. "Open your eyes."

I cautiously peeked out from one eye, scanning the world around me.

My hair had stopped spinning in the storm, but so did the rest of my clothes. The sky rained down on the earth around me, but a small circle remained untouched. The raindrops tinkled onto the wall of power I'd created, blocking me from the downpour.

The power strained my muscles, my arms trembling with each additional rain patter. Seconds later, all that power snapped back into me like a lash against my body, sending me to my knees in the dirt. It didn't take long for the rain to soak the ground I'd been protecting, as well as my hair and clothes.

I glance up between wet strands of hair and heavy, wet lashes towards the house.

Karasi no longer stood with her arms crossed, but one braced on a support beam and the other limp at her side.

I knew I had done something incredible, but also something I shouldn't have.

★★★

My sense of sound returns before I can open my eyes. I can't pinpoint where they are, but the not-so-hushed voices gradually become distinguishable words the more my brain recalibrates with reality.

"...said something, Fin," the female's voice—Elly—whispers harshly. "Out of anyone here, I could've been helping."

"She told me in confidence, Elly," Fin pleads, but I can hear the frustration in his voice. "I wasn't going to betray her after she had just revealed herself like that. I can't begin to imagine what she risked telling me."

"She just risked herself to save us." Elly half-laughs, and a warm, smooth hand slips into mine. I realize Elly's voice is closer compared to Fin's. "I know you have feelings there, Fin, but your loyalty lies with us—"

"Don't you pull that bullshit with me—" But he stops mid-sentence, which could only mean that Elly indicated he should stop.

"If you'd let me finish," she drawls, clicking her tongue. "Your loyalty lies with us, and you know if there was anyone who would have kept this secret and *helped* her with this, it would've been me. You know me better than that, Finley Wardson. You've known me your whole life."

"I know," he sighs heavily, a chair creaking somewhere towards my feet. "I didn't know what to do with that knowledge, Elly. I still don't know what we do with this knowledge. Would your dad..."

There is a quiet, uncomfortable pause before Elly answers, "I'm not sure yet. I know he wants to open the community for Magics, but *them*? Is the world ready for that? They're still extremely divided on Magics, apparently."

"You know this went far beyond that. It was Etherea."

"We don't know that yet, Fin, and who knows if we ever will," Elly sighs, her thumb moving along the back of my hand gently. Despite my eyes being shut, tears burn behind my eyelids. "She's powerful, Fin. I could feel it in the room when she…"

"Not here," he whispers. "She was right when she told me we don't know who's listening. We'll need to be discrete."

"I know where we can go," Elly answers, and I envision her head nodding.

I try to swallow the tears threatening to spill, but my throat burns like I'm swallowing a million needles. I jerk from the pain, and Elly's hand instantly tightens in mine.

"Reva," Fin breathes in relief, his footsteps growing closer.

I finally force my eyes open, blinking their blurry images into view.

Elly sits in a chair beside the bed I lay in, studying me with soft, sad eyes. Fin's glow by the blazing fire, concern and panic evident in the downturn of his lips and the puppy eyes, per usual.

I stifle a laugh, but it sends me into one of the most painful coughing fits. I gag at the clogged sharpness there.

"Drink this," Elly urges, placing a mug in my hand. "One of the other Magics here insisted this would help with the pain and ease it at least to the point where it feels like a rough cold."

I already know which concoction she's referring to. I nod, trying to use my other hand to lift myself up in bed—my bed. Elly and Fin are instantly on either side of me, hoisting me against the pillows and headboard.

My heart clenches at their help, twisting. I greedily drink down the tincture, fighting the burn the liquid initiates.

I hand Elly the empty mug, clearing my throat. "Are you okay?"

"Gods, Reva," Elly chuckles, a tear slipping down her cheek. I press my lips into a small pout, grabbing her hand on her lap. She accepts, but guilt and shame rise in me, sour. "You're asking if I'm okay after what you did?"

"Yes," I insist, my voice hoarse as though I'd been inhaling chimney smoke all day. "What I did…"

"Was nothing short of incredible," Elly insists. "You saved mine and Clint's lives. Don't think that isn't going to be forgotten or unnoticed."

My gaze flickers to Fin, who looks like he wants to be anywhere but away from me right now. His eyes soften in knowing.

I sigh, "That's what I'm afraid of."

"We're not going to tell anyone," Elly says, exchanging a confirming nod with Fin before focusing back on me. "Fin has filled me in on what he can, but don't think I won't want to hear it from you. Clint and I have already agreed what truly happened earlier doesn't have to be told."

I frown, pressing my head farther into the headboard. "What do you mean?"

"My father and some of the other knights are going to want to hear our story on what happened for their report," Elly admits, clasping her other hand on top of mine to sandwich it between hers. "But, with your throat being hoarse and healing and, with Clint confined to his bed after his burst of heroism, I will recall the story for the council. They request you be there at least to confirm or deny and maybe fill in any blanks that I miss."

"I can't ask you to lie to the king," I scoff, shifting my eyes back and forth between them. "Let alone officials of this army."

"You forget that one of those higher ranks is standing beside you right now." Fin smiles, one eyebrow raised. "Considering the circumstances, I won't take offense."

"Finley," I warn, narrowing my eyes, but Elly holds up her hand and I know she'll have no more of it.

"I highly encourage you to follow my lead, Reva," she says, quieter than before. "If we move forward with my story, we move forward with all of *this* together. We are your friends, so it's time to treat us that way. Let us help you figure out your powers, because it's clear you still don't know enough about them, and I already have a feeling they can help Clint. No one knows my library better than me."

"There's so much more to it than this, Elly." I stare up at the ceiling, taking a deep breath. "Something else is happening."

"I have a feeling we may have an idea." Elly shrugs.

She looks to Fin, now, sorrow and longing in her eyes.

He offers a tight smile but nods once. "I'll give the King my recommendation," Fin agrees, pausing. "Gods know the minute he reads this report, with or without your father's help, he will come rushing home."

"What are you talking about?" I ask, trying to keep up.

Elly grins wildly, wiggling her eyebrows as she says, "It's time to call my brother back home."

CHAPTER 17

I find myself pacing outside of the throne room—again.

I'm alone.

Fin and Elly are already inside, discussing their points of view from the small attack on the castle yesterday.

Based on what they told me as I rested in my room for the last 24 hours, the knights that harassed me and attacked the castle had joined Mariande's ranks a few months before I arrived.

While it wasn't said directly, the king assumes they're spies for Etherea, who had very strong opinions about Magics. Only one survived to withstand interrogation because he had gone to find Elly elsewhere in the castle and was taken down. The other two did not survive the attack.

Because I killed them.

I fold my trembling hands together in front of me, blinking away the image of the knight's empty eyes.

"Miss Reva," the man at the door calls, pulling me out of my thoughts. I stop mid-stride, looking up at him as I wring my hands together. "Are you ready?"

I take a deep, shuddering breath, unable to control the tremor in my hands. I nod once, taking the first few steps toward the open door. I don't stop walking until I am standing in front of King Darius and Queen Lucia.

To the Queen's left, Elly stands, her face a mask of neutrality, but there is a softness to her eyes as she meets my gaze. A phantom smile flashes briefly across her face.

To the left of the King is Clint, who sits in his wheelchair, paler than usual, but his eyes light up when he spots me. The grin of relief that spreads across his face is heartbreakingly reassuring.

Neither of them appears nervous.

Neither of them acts like they're hiding a secret from everyone else in the room.

I meet Fin's eyes briefly. He offers a tight-lipped grin in encouragement before returning his attention to King Darius.

I mirror him, locking my gaze with the King's amber eyes, identical to his daughter's and son's. Rage boils under the surface, his face taut and shoulders stiffened.

"Reva," King Darius sighs deeply, as if all the weight of the last day's events could be expelled with that breath. "It's truly unfortunate that we keep meeting like this."

"I can assure you it's not intentional, Your Highness," I manage to push out around the soreness in my throat, a small laugh bubbling out of me laced with a little bit of madness.

Queen Lucia raises an eyebrow.

"I'm sure it's not," King Darius mutters, more to himself than to me. He clears his throat. "First and foremost, I want to thank you from the bottom of my heart. If the accounts of my children stand true, you saved both of their lives yesterday. I hope the fact that you nearly sacrificed your life for the Prince and Princess of Mariande is not taken lightly."

"I understand." I nod, keeping my hands folded together in front of me, even if my palms are damp. I refocus on the King as the sweat starts to thicken like blood. "I didn't consider it that way. All I could think about was saving my friends."

Someone clears their throat behind me.

I whip my head around, narrowing my eyes at Pax whose distrust is evident in how he sneers down at me over the top of his nose.

"I would keep your comments short, Sir Pax," King Darius' voice booms across the throne room. Pax responds with a bow to the King.

I turn back to King Darius who is now studying me.

"Eloise," King Darius calls, his attention still locked on me. He extends his hand towards Elly, beckoning with his fingers to come forward.

She steps around the empty wheelchair beside the Queen's throne to stand on the dais in front of her parents.

"Please, recount the story for us so that your brother and Miss Reva can fill in any other important parts."

Elly begins from her own point of view, and how she had been traveling from the library to deliver a book to me personally. She knew I would be in Clint's room then, and she had passed some knights on her way who instructed her to get into a room and barricade herself in because the castle was under attack.

She didn't know the extent of the attack, but all she could

think of was me and Clint in his room, unaware of what could be happening. She rushed to the room where she tried to secure us. She recalls it perfectly, which has me hanging my head anxiously, staring at my hands to ensure my power does not rise in response to the recollection.

"The door flew open after he rammed into it a few times," she continues, her voice steady. "Reva stood between us and him, and it seemed like he recognized her. I knew then that this had to be one of the men who'd been harassing Reva since her arrival. He was instantly upon her, trying to choke her."

I frown to myself but don't dare lift my head, knowing that doing so would implicate Elly in front of the knights and her parents. I wait to hear where she is going with this.

"At some point, he dropped his sword when arguing with her and choking her. Before I could stop him, Clint leaped out of his bed and grabbed the sword, slashing him across the back. This caused him to release his grip on Reva instantly. He turned his attention to Clint, but before he could get to him, Reva reached for the knight's leg and caused him to fall and smack his head on the floor, which subdued him for a moment."

I can't help it when my head snaps to stare at Elly, fighting the urge to widen my eyes. Elly senses me, her gaze momentarily flickering to me.

At this rate, we have completely deterred from the truth.

She has known me for only a few months and is lying to her father—the King of Mariande—to protect me.

"Is there something wrong, Reva?" The King inquires,

slanting forward in his seat.

"No, sir." I clear my throat, recovering with a small shake of my head. "I just think hearing it in the third person is very different from experiencing it. I know the powers of adrenaline, but I never realized…"

"The body can do incredible things when under stress," Queen Lucia says suddenly, her hands clasped in her lap. "And trying to protect those we love."

Love.

Had I truly come to love half the people in this room?

I chance a glance at Fin, who's already watching me intently.

"Continue, Eloise." The King ushers with a wave of his hand.

Elly nods once, finishing her twisted tale. "At this time, Clint had fainted and I held him in my arms. Reva grabbed the knight's sword just as he began to stand. She lifted it up and shoved it through him. After he fell to the floor, Sir Finley arrived at the door just in time to see Reva faint as well."

The king and queen appear to accept that this was how things played out. Despite that, I know Pax's is searing behind me. His suspicion of me is palpable, even without having to acknowledge him.

"My son." King Darius peers at Clint beside him from the corners of his eyes. "Is this true from what you can recall?"

"Yes, Father." Clint nods once, his voice faint. "Reva saved me just like she was hired to do."

A hiccup of a gasp stings the back of my throat, or maybe

it's the tears threatening to spill out of my eyes.

King Darius angles his entire body to face me. He bends at the waist in his seat, resting his forearms on his thighs. His hands hang just in front of his knees.

"And, you?" He asks, not unkindly. "What do you say?"

Elly still stands at the edge of the dais, but her back is now to her father. She's positioned fully flush in front of me. I can't pull away from the softness in her face, the downturn of her eyes, or the slight pout to her lips.

The kindness she extends to me by keeping my secret is a sacrifice she doesn't know she offers. I have a hard time believing that a royal family would produce such a child, an heir who's refused to take the throne and forms a protective bond with a healer who wields forbidden powers.

I want to be angry with her for depriving the world of such a leader, but I have yet to meet her twin who she forfeited the kingdom to.

Our ancestors—centuries ago—stood in this exact spot, except to condemn my kind. Karasi always said that Fate worked in strange ways, that I'd feel it like a soft breeze.

But it's more like static crawling along my skin.

"What she says is true," I declare, that static raising the hairs on my arms, "This is what I can remember as well."

"Very well." King Darius claps and I flinch. He doesn't notice as he rubs his hands together. "You are all dismissed, except Sir Pax and Clint. There are a few things I would like to discuss."

"Do you need me to wait for Clint?" I ask.

"Don't worry, Reva." King Darius shakes his head. "I'll

take my son back. You take another day to rest and recover."

"Thank you." I curtsy before taking my leave.

Quiet steps immediately follow me beside another heavier set as we approach the door. The knight opens it for me and my companions.

"Are you busy, Reva?" Elly asks, drawing up beside me and looping her arm in mine. She's also managed to loop her other arm through the crook of Fin's elbow.

"Not particularly," I admit, allowing her to lead me away to what I can assume is the direction of the library.

"Great!" She grins wildly. "There are some things I would love for us to discuss. I have dismissed my assistants for the day, so we have the library all to ourselves."

Oh, Gods.

I can't shake that this will be an interrogation of sorts.

We approach the grand doors of the library, and Fin steps away from us to hold them open. I pass under the threshold, his hand on my lower back, guiding me towards one of the many tables that Elly is claiming.

I crane my head up to him, narrowing my eyes.

"It's best to just let her ask her questions," Fin chuckles, dimples peeking out from his groomed beard.

"Whatever questions she hasn't already figured out for herself," I grumble, taking the chair Fin pulls out for me.

Elly sits on the opposite end of the table, her hands folded on top of it and her back straight.

"I told you I can figure out many things on my own, Reva," Elly says sweetly, but it drips with suspicion. "When it comes to you... Well, there aren't any books on you, yet."

I scoff, shaking my head in disbelief. "I don't understand. You both have only just met me and not one but two of you keep my secret. I told Fin I didn't want him lying for me, and both of you have now lied to protect me. It's one thing to share the burden of what I am, it's another to ask others to share that. It's out of the question to risk your well-being and your relationships to spin a narrative."

"Oh, Reva," Elly sighs, wrinkling her nose. "Get over yourself. I think we're all about to learn this is bigger than just one person."

My eyebrows draw together and I shove away the shock from her abruptness. "What do you mean?"

"A story for another day," Elly waves away. "All in due time. But, right now, I need to know you, Reva. How did you come to exist?"

"I already told Fin I don't know the specifics." I shake my head. "My father left me with Karasi as a baby and the rest is history."

"How did you learn to wield your powers?" She asks. "Do you know other Sirians?"

"I wish I did," I insist. "But Karasi and some other Magics in my life taught me how to wield power as best as they could with whatever resources they could scrounge up."

"What kind of resources?" Elly narrows her eyes and tilts her head to the side predatorily.

I shrug my shoulders, holding my hands up. "I was really young when they started teaching me, and I never asked," I explain. "No one knows how old Karasi is, so she could have known places to search for books left behind."

"Are you telling me she was alive when the Sirians were on the throne?" Fin gawks, his eyes bulging out of his head.

I press my lips together and Elly gets up from her seat. "I truly don't know," I chuckle, pressing a hand to my forehead and rubbing my temple. "Karasi is complicated, but she knows what she's doing."

"So, you know the bare minimum, enough to protect yourself maybe," Elly ponders, pacing in front of me. "Why did you come here, Reva? Especially considering what you are. Being a *Royal* Healer puts a lot of attention on you, far from the seclusion you're used to in Eldamain. You didn't owe the Crown anything."

Her skirt flows out behind her as she paces twice more in front of me. She stops mid-stride, facing me and tapping her foot. Her bright eyes burn into my soul as if she could unravel me in front of her and dissect me.

The Princess of Mariande, always chasing knowledge and understanding. But why? How could she use what she learns?

I push my chair away from the table, rising. "There were many reasons I came," I say quietly, taking a few steps so we're just mere feet from each other. I'm reminded of the Fate-defining moment in the throne room.

"Karasi is prophetic. How much she actually knows is always vastly different than what she reveals. She hinted that there is something coming for us—for our world. She insists I play an important role in stopping or fighting what's coming.

"She wanted me to come here not just to help Clint but

to take advantage of what she thought was in this library. I've come to believe that it's crucial I came to put into motion whatever is coming, too."

"Destiny and Fate," Fin blurts, hands crossed over his uniformed chest. "You are talking about Gods we barely believe in anymore."

"There are a few of the other continents that still practice their beliefs, Finley," Elly lectures, rolling her eyes. "I know you haven't had the chance to experience them, but I'm sure Tariq will have lots to tell you about when he returns from Riddling."

"The Gods abandoned humanity," I say, motioning to the sky. "When mortals sabotage a God's children and nearly destroy the existence of another, why would they want anything to do with us?"

Elly studies me, the wheels turning in that honey-blond head of hers. She marches over to her desk, grabbing a notebook from a pile next to some writing utensils before joining us back at the table. She positions her pen over the paper.

"We are not writing anything down." I point my finger at her.

She raises an eyebrow. "Do not wag your finger at me." She feigns insult. "Finley knows well enough I have no problems pulling out the princess card. I outrank you, Healer."

"Welcome to my club, Reva," Fin chuckles, plopping down at the table with Elly.

"This is not a band of misfits," I half-yell, throwing my

hands out before me. "These are the Sirians. Power this world hasn't seen in centuries."

"You are not the only Sirian out there, Reva," Elly yells, pointing her pen toward the door. "How many are out there *not* like you? They didn't have the Great Karasi to raise them and teach them. How many are out there in hiding, doing what they can to learn and teach each other? All so that some mysterious, rogue Sirian group wielding the Darkness can come and just annihilate humanity? It's my duty to protect my kingdom, and that's what I intend to do with your help."

"You know more than you're letting on," I realize, joining them to sit again.

Fin and Elly exchange a brief glance of understanding. Fin nods once at her.

"We have been hearing about the Abyss for some time now," Elly explains, fixated on her notebook. "I've done some research, but I know there's more. I just didn't know how seriously to take it. When you brought it up, though, I realized that this was something else.

"I have to be honest, I didn't know if it was possible for Sirians to have the Light still. With how much hiding they've had to do, I thought it would only be the Darkness. But, after what you did, I have to believe there are more like you. And, if the Abyss is living because there are people wielding Darkness… We need more like you, Reva. We need *you.*"

"But I don't know the first thing about wielding the Light enough to fight people who are wielding the Darkness," I explain, sitting beside Fin, across from Elly.

"How am I supposed to learn how to practice it when I have no one to teach me?"

"We will figure that out," Elly sighs, scribbling into her notebook. "I know for a fact there are things hidden in this library that can help us. In order to be discreet, I will have to work around my assistants and search for myself."

"I need you to find books on healing before you go foraging for ones on combat," I say, placing my hands in front of hers on the table. "I found a book not that long ago. It was a journal from a former Royal Healer... He was a *Sirian* Royal Healer. The Sirians must have used their powers as part of the healing."

"How would that work?" Fin asks, but Elly is studying at me with tears brimming in her eyes.

I don't divert from her, holding her stare. "I was employed here to help Clint," I whisper, clearing my throat. "I care about that boy, and he deserves a real life. Something the Sirians did can help him. Then, we can try to save the world, if that's what this is. Part of our power is being able to take the potential energy stored in an object and convert it into charged energy. There has to be something in that."

"I'm inclined to agree," Elly ponders, tapping her pen. "So, we have a plan. First, we figure out how your powers can help Clint. Then, we will try to find a way to teach you combat skills. And find a place to practice."

"Why do I feel like finding her a place to practice is going to be the hardest part," Fin grumbles, scratching his beard.

"Because it is," I clarify. "You guys were lucky that you

were able to spin the story to cover up what I did. But the minute I start wielding the Light, detonating things or setting things on fire—"

"I'm sorry," Elly interrupts, her hand in the air before me. "Did you say *fire?*"

I snap my mouth shut with a click of my teeth, tightening my lips together.

Her eyes are wide and expectant, and Fin's gaze sears into the side of my face.

"You didn't tell me about fire," Fin whispers, the hurt evident in his voice.

I push that away, focusing on the important things and not this poor, beautiful man who I can't seem not to hurt.

"The Light is energy," I drawl. "But we don't know what the fire is. Even Karasi has never told me. Whether she knows and has withheld that information is yet to be seen, but no one has ever been able to find out why I can wield fire."

"How well can you wield it?" Elly lets out a breath of disbelief.

I produce a small flame in my hand, the power burning in my veins.

Where the Light is like a cold burning sensation, the fire is the core of the Earth trying to scorch my insides. The flame flickers precariously as a bit of sweat beads on my forehead from the effort it takes to contort it into a small ball.

Elly's eyes briefly fly from me to the nearest bookshelf. I close my fist, the power snapping back into me as it does.

"You can barely control it," Elly whispers, her eyes wide

in a little bit of discomfort, but no fear.

"I can manipulate existing flames pretty well, or start a fire in a fireplace," I explain, wiping sweat away and being careful not to smear my salve. "When it comes to producing it organically and wielding it like the Light, it's volatile. I feel like I'm being burned from the inside.

"I don't know if it's my lack of training, or there's just not a lot of this foreign power to wield in the first place, or if there's too much that it cannot be contained. I don't know what it means, so we worked on just trying to maintain it. Remy has covered up multiple incidents with my rogue flames."

"Remy?" Elly questions.

"A Magic that helped raise Reva," Fin clarifies for her.

I twist in my seat towards Elly again, gauging the expression on her face. It's a cross between knowing, suspicion, and downright mischief.

Like a child who got away with snatching a cookie from the kitchen.

"What do we do now?" I inquire, slouching into the back of the chair.

"We keep trying to heal Clint," Elly decides, gathering the notebook and pen in her hand. "Otherwise, we wait until Tariq's back."

I gawk, my mouth hanging open. "We are not telling the Crown Prince this," I yell. "No more people need to know."

"People will find out eventually, Reva," Elly argues back, throwing her hand at me. "You can't hide if you want to save the world."

I flare my nostrils, controlling the power running through my veins and threatening to come out to play. I shove it down, swallowing against the burning in my throat. "What if he tells your dad?"

"If there is anything you will learn about my brother and me, it's that we keep far more secrets from the world than anyone could ever dream." Elly smirks, tucking the pen behind her ear. "Not a single soul has ever discovered a secret we didn't want them to know. We are in sync about everything. His sabbatical to Riddling was not just to appease our father. He will react to your Mark the same way I did and the same way Fin did."

"And Pax?" I inquire, pushing.

Something akin to shock and grief flashes across her face.

"He cannot know," Elly whispers, shaking her head slowly. "Not yet."

The three of us observe each other, our pact of secrecy solidifying as we let this comfortable silence and realization settle over us.

Maybe these royals are exactly like I thought they were when it comes to the secrets and ulterior motives driving them to make the decisions they do.

CHAPTER 18

After spending the day working with Clint, I head to the library to meet with Elly and read through some books she found on Sirians and the Black Avalanches.

A few doors from the library, one of them opens on the right and Pax steps out. He spots me, shutting the door behind him and standing at attention, arms folded behind his back.

"Are you incapable of standing any other way?" I glare, gripping the strap of my satchel across my body as an anchor.

He raises an unamused eyebrow. "I am the Lieutenant General of the Mariande Army, so I present myself as such." He pulls one of his hands before him and smoothes it over the patch on his chest. "I protect Mariande and the royal family from threats."

"Sometimes," I correct, cocking my head to the side.

His nostrils flare in irritation, the only sign of emotion on his face. "Do you need escorting somewhere, *Healer?*" He sneers at the title, but there is no curl of his lip to follow, and somehow that's more degrading.

I tighten my grip on the satchel. "I'm perfectly capable

of escorting myself around the castle grounds," I remind, throwing my shoulders back defiantly. "Besides, I'm going just down the hall." I throw my head toward the sealed library doors.

His gaze flickers briefly, his face falling slack. He collects himself quickly, but I already saw the moment of sorrow.

"I have no intentions of harming the royal family," I explain, shaking my head softly. "I don't plan on harming any of your citizens. I came here to heal and find answers to a lot of questions. If the attack on the castle proves anything, Sir Pax, let it be that."

"I was taught never to trust a Magic's intentions," Pax responds, taking two long, slow strides closer. "If you received your position as young as you have, it can only mean you're a powerful Magic. I am well aware of the Houses of the Magics, just as I know that the strength and variations of those abilities can vary greatly."

"You're worried for her." I side-step towards the library, signaling the end of the conversation. "But, you underestimate the princess. Her kindness and compassion will win her favor, and she could easily sit on that throne."

Concern flares in Pax's eyes as he grumbles, "You don't know what you're talking about."

"Maybe I don't." I shrug, twisting my body towards the library and withdrawing.

Just as I'm about to reach the doors, I call out, "Maybe you don't either." His stare seers into my back as I pull the door open and step through it.

The euphoric, clean aroma of the library eases a bit of my

tension, the door quietly sealing shut behind me. Knowing what Elly has planned, I latch the lock in place behind me. Distant feet shuffling resounds shortly before Elly's blonde head pops out from around a nearby aisle.

She smirks, wickedly. "Hello, darling," she greets, carrying three thick books with her.

I wander towards her desk at the same time she does. There are a few more books splayed out across the top of it, all varying from old to archaic, like they just might disintegrate before my eyes.

"Where did you find these?" I graze my fingers gingerly across the cover of one. "A tomb?"

She purses her lips together tightly and places the books in her hands beside the others before sitting in the desk chair.

I grab the other chair and pull it directly across from her.

"I've spent my life trying to make sense of the things in this library," she explains, carefully handling one of the more delicate books. "There are sections I have obviously yet to explore, but there are dark corners I always thought might have enchantments on them. All of my assistants are Magics, so I tasked them with checking the library for any wards. We unlocked one rather quickly, and there were some of these among the collection."

"Elly, these are ancient."

She pets the top of the book. "Considering the history of the Sirians, I anticipated this is what we'd be working with."

With that, she carefully opens the book, delicately peeling the pages back to a section she's bookmarked. It appears to be in an older version of our language and hand-written, like the journal I had found.

"What is this?" I ask, scanning the pages. "Can you read it?"

"I was taught to read many languages, including the various versions of our own," Elly begins, lifting her eyes to me. "This particular book discusses first-hand accounts of the events of the Korbin family… How much do you know about King Alrik and his twelve sons?"

"The very basics," I sigh, nodding. I hold my hands in front of me as I recount, "King Alrik was born to a Sirian royal family, but he was the only one who did not inherit the Mark. Once he rose to power, he began a huge political ploy to gain favor with other countries by marrying off his sons and one daughter to their heirs."

"That's all?" She confirms.

I shrug. "I know of the various political ploys and that King Alrik is single-handedly the reason the Sirians were snubbed out of existence and cast aside. Most of his actions led to that, not to mention his very awkward public opinion of how dangerous they really are.

"But what does this have to do with my powers or the Black Avalanches?"

Elly examines the journal, skimming her fingers across the worn pages. She closes her eyes briefly before staring at me from under her eyelashes. "I have reason to believe the creation of the Abyss is also Alrik's doing."

I recoil, my eyebrows shooting up my forehead and my mouth falling open.

She offers a sheepish grimace but does not back down

from what she said.

I recover enough to frown and ask, "Elly... Alrik's entire argument for why he did what he did was because of the power the Sirians held over the kingdoms. He deemed it a danger to humanity. How could he believe that if he created it? What have you come across that has led you to this epiphany?"

"I'm in the early stages of historical books on the Black Avalanches," she explains, biting at the inside of her cheek. "They predate Alrik's crowning as king. There is no mention of any Abyss. There is nothing of that description until books created *after* King Alrik's reign."

"But how could he do that?" I challenge, my mind entirely blank. "If King Alrik wasn't a Sirian, he had no powers. He was human like you and Fin. The Abyss and the Darkness are directly correlated to Sirians."

"That was my first question, too." Elly holds up a finger, scanning her books.

She pulls one from the collection, flipping to a page. Again, the language is older Etherean. Some words are familiar, but most are written differently than how we write them now.

"King Alrik had a daughter, Tyra, that he married off to the heir of The Clips. The heir murdered Tyra in her sleep after discovering that she not only had the Mark but because she conspired with her Aunt and Uncle to kill the royal family of Eldamain. He said she carried the Darkness."

"Okay," I heed, the wheels slowly moving in my head. "I had heard about the daughter, but I assumed she was human like her brothers. Did they have children before he killed her?"

"Yes." Elly's eyes flit across the page. "But none of them bore the Mark."

I lean back in the chair, studying my hands in my lap. I blink away the ghostly red coating, rubbing them on my skirt.

There was no way that King Alrik didn't know his daughter bore the Mark. With two siblings of his own born Sirian and a wife that finally had herself a girl, he wouldn't have been able to kill her.

If he feared some evil rising in his daughter, he would have forced her to suppress her powers and inadvertently created the Darkness within her. That's if how we presume the Darkness forms is correct.

I stiffen, lurching straight up. "Is there anything that you've found about Alrik's siblings? They were both Sirian," I voice, dread filling my gut because Elly might be onto something.

"From what I've read, their powers manifested like yours." She shrugs. "If they had manifested as the Darkness, they would have been exiled by their Sirian parents who *also* wielded the Light."

"And Tyra had the Darkness," I conclude. "What if King Alrik despised his siblings because they were born Sirian and, as the first-born was not, he had resentment towards his family? What if he hated *all* Sirians?"

Elly gasps, following my train of thought. "He was marrying his sons off already before Tyra was old enough to show her powers, which means he had a plan to ensure that all his sons would take every throne to eliminate the Sirians before she was born."

"He had to create a divide between humans and Sirians," I explain, standing from my seat. I roam between the nearest table and Elly still sitting at the front desk. "But his daughter was born with the Mark, which would have ruined him and all the plans he laid out. So he forced her to suppress her powers."

"No one purposely made a Sirian suppress their powers before?" Elly questions.

I shake my head, strands of hair falling in front of my face. "Never. It was a blessing to be and to have Sirians. Why would anyone want to suppress that?"

"The Darkness was born from that," Elly whispers, her face going slack. "I was right. Alrik created the Abyss."

"He probably held so much anger and hate towards Tyra for being Sirian." I fall back into the seat before Elly. "If he suppressed her powers, they must have exploded one day, which the Black Avalanches responded to... And the Abyss was born."

This could rewrite history as we know it. There is no doubt that, once the Darkness formed in Tyra, he used it to his advantage to exploit the possibility that there could be a bad side to the Sirians. How could he do that?

The Hidden Island was destroyed during that time by the Darkness. What if it was Tyra who destroyed them? They would've never experienced anything like that before, so they'd be helpless.

The perfect military ploy: a sneak attack with a deadly weapon.

"Where does this leave us," I wonder aloud, shaking my head. "Does this help us in any way?"

"Understanding your enemy is vital to war, Reva," Elly says, glancing up from what she is writing. "This will not only help us understand the type of people we're going up against, but it will help us when we need to defend the Sirians who wield the Light to the rest of the world."

I shut my eyes at the thought, shutting out the idea of revealing myself to the world. It goes against everything Karasi taught me.

That, though, is a future problem. Not a *now* problem.

"There's a lot we need to understand before we take that step, Elly," I sigh, taking a deep breath before opening my eyes again.

Elly is eyeing me hesitantly. "Speaking of which," she blurts, reaching for another book and handing it over to me. "I found something I think you'll enjoy."

I take it from her, carefully holding it up to read the title. It's the old Etherean language, but I manage to read it: *Mastering the Light, Level IV.*

"How advanced will a fourth volume be?"

She shrugs, which has me staring at her incredulously. "If you can read enough of it, take it. Let me know how advanced you think it is, and then we can go from there if we find more. All I know is there is no mention of firepower. I'm still searching for that."

"I can't take this with me to my room." I hold the book

in front of me apprehensively, afraid the contents might give me away.

Elly smiles still, shaking her head. She glances at each of the books before her, scanning their titles.

"I have a feeling that you are perfectly capable of hiding that book in a way that people won't recognize it," Elly explains, picking up one and gently flipping the pages. "You're not suspicious enough right now that anyone would allow an unsanctioned search of your room."

"They do that?" I startle, unintentionally slamming the book on the desk.

Elly flinches then glares at me in a warning. A quick once-over lets me know it's unscathed from the outburst.

"Yes, but like I said, it won't happen. Just keep it on you at all times in your satchel or find somewhere to hide it."

I do exactly that, slipping the book into my satchel. She continues to scan the page of the book she's been fiddling with, her eyes roaming slower than before.

Karasi would be appalled if she knew I told not only a knight of Mariande about my Mark but the Princess of Mariande, as well. She'd be skeptical that the Princess of Mariande is using her resources to help me control my powers better, and potentially wield them as a weapon.

All for a cause she insists involves the entire world.

"Not to step on any toes," I project into our comfortable silence. "But are we sure all of your assistants can be trusted? I know they're Magics, but it doesn't mean Magics accept Sirians either. We threaten their existence just as much as the world is convinced Sirians threaten those without power.

They can at least attempt to exist, but with Sirians, it makes things more hostile than it already is."

"I've shared the knowledge of this research with only one of my assistants," Elly explains, placing a bookmark between the pages she'd been reading through. "She is the only one who is removing the wards from different areas of the library. I hired her shortly after you came here and conducted a few tests to see how much she tells the other Magics.

"Lucky for me, she doesn't even talk to them, other than to ask questions about things in the library."

I let out a harsh breath, folding my hands in front of me on the desk. I wring them, fiddling with my fingers. Elly takes notice, reaching out and closing her own hands over mine.

It's one thing to trust the people who raised me, it's another to trust those I've only known for a short few months.

"You have to let us in, Reva," Elly says softly, giving my hands a gentle squeeze in hers. "You know there are good people in the world. Some of them helped raise you. Is it so hard to believe there are more out there? That those people have been placed in your life by Fate or Destiny?"

"My parents died trying to protect me," I blurt, shaking my head and swallowing the tears. "I had yet to live, and they died to protect me. Karasi and the rest of them sacrificed their wild lives to live more secluded existences to help me.

"It's selfish of me to ask this of you, and it's difficult for me to trust anyone's intentions. This isn't a puzzle you solve and leave aside when it's done, Elly. This isn't some party you plan, celebrate, and then move to the next."

Elly's eyes harden briefly before they brighten with determination. "When have I ever given the impression that I am the type of royal that plans parties, Reva? I spent my education studying history and geography so I could be part of the conversations that will change the world. I've been committed to my kingdom since I was young, and I wasn't going to let my choice to give the throne to my brother change that."

Regret and guilt burn in my chest like my firepower, white and hot, for insinuating she was nothing more than a party princess. I swallow against it. "I'm sorry. I'm just terrified."

"We all are." Elly removes her hands from mine. "After opening Mariande to Magics, we started to hear more and more about the Black Avalanches. Reaching adulthood and marrying age, our father knew it was time for us to be more involved in politics and the happenings of the world. He put Tariq and I in charge of finding out exactly what was going on, and said to come to him once we had a strong case on what it could all mean."

"How long have you both been researching this?" I try to recall when I first heard the people of Eldamain speak warily about the mountains.

It'd been stirring for decades, even before I was born according to Dahlia. It'd probably been about 3 years or so ago that it really became the talk of the town.

"I'd say for about a year and a half to two years," Elly confirms, which would make sense for word to start traveling here from Eldamain. "We'd found out enough. Myths and legends talked about the return of Kuk or the Darkness. We knew it had to do with the Sirians, but we didn't know exactly what that meant.

"We'd read as much as we could find and talked to as many people as possible. We befriended the Magics who had any knowledge of the Sirians and were willing to trust us enough to talk. It was enough to learn that the Sirians have the Light and the Darkness. With them disappearing a millennium ago, that was the extent of the knowledge."

"Jorah," I realize. "You befriended Jorah."

"He has insight, and after the Great Karasi, he is probably the next oldest living Magic," Elly explains, sitting back in her chair. "He's over two hundred years old, nearing three hundred, he guesses."

"He could be a bigger asset," I conclude, knowing he can sense things in people's blood. What exactly he can sense is crucial. "So I was like a missing link for you."

"From my point of view, yes," she confirms. "You have convinced me that those with the Light are not power-hungry purely because they have powers. You've learned to control your powers in a positive way and only wish to exist and, whether you realize it or not, do a lot of good. That means that if there are Sirians with the Light, there are those with the Darkness.

"The Magics are right: the Darkness is back, and that can't be good. These Dark Sirians' powers have manifested in fear and anger, which means they are probably furious for the transgressions of our ancestors, and they are what the world fears the Sirians are."

"If we can't reason with Sirians of the Light," I admit. "We can't reason with the Darkness."

"We need to find out the who, what, where, when, and how." Elly rolls her neck, rubbing the back of it. "Tariq went to Riddling as part of our plan."

"Why Riddling?" I ask, the corner of my mouth pulled back.

"Prince Ruhan is the Crown Prince there and is an asset. Difficult to befriend and doesn't hand out trust easily, but he and Tariq have been building a relationship. Tariq's refusal to marry his sister has put a slight wrench in things, but I trust my brother to work his charm. If Prince Ruhan is anything, he's observant. Nothing gets past him."

"So, he may have been already researching if he heard about the Abyss as well," I guess.

"We hope." She nods. "He has studied Law, Order, and History extensively, particularly the evolution of our countries, which could mean he knows more about the Korbin legacy than we do.

"My father has already sent the letter summoning Tariq home, but I sent my own letter to tell him it's time to ask about the Korbins before he leaves. Coded, of course, to sound like a fascinated sister trying to learn more history, but he would know I'm asking because of our research."

I nod, willing to trust the princess and her twin.

I plop my elbow onto the desk and rest my chin in my hand, eyeballing Elly as she fiddles with the necklace around her neck, the same one we picked up from Jorah.

"I think we need to talk to Jorah." I tip my head towards her necklace. "He knew I was Sirian that day. I'm positive about that. *You* also said that day you thought I was a Magic that came from a demi-god. You may be onto something there, and Jorah has to know more."

"I can arrange that." Elly's lips tilt up at the edges, her eyebrows raising ever so slightly. "The hematite in your necklace is looking a little loose."

CHAPTER 19

"*I*t's too hard," I shouted, my voice cracking with the sound of thunder.

I wearily glanced at the sky, where lightning continued to flash in the distance, followed by more thunder.

Remy cleared his throat, pulling my attention back to him. "Lucky for you," he called, that sharp canine tooth peeking out from behind a half smile. "You can keep yourself warm if it rains. I, on the other hand, cannot. So there is a level of urgency here, aster."

I groaned, frustrated that Remy would use my love for him against me. I didn't want him to get cold and wet in the rain, and even if I could keep myself warm with my fire, I still didn't want to get wet.

I placed my hands out in front of me, my elbows locked.

"Don't lock them," Remy lectured, voice stern. "You will hurt yourself again if the power ricochets back into you. Keep a slight bend in the elbows."

I furrowed my brow in concentration and irritation, adjusting my posture so my elbows weren't extended completely. My hands hinged perpendicular to my arms at the wrists, palms flat out in front of me.

I focused on the single tree in front of me and ignored the hundreds that bordered it in the treeline of The Overgrowns.

"Just like you do with the Light," Remy encouraged, but I could tell his patience was dwindling. "Only this time, step into the well. Do not jump in."

Stepping into a well sounded impractical, even to my nine-year-old mind. Besides, when I closed my eyes, I couldn't see a well of fire. I saw a never-ending dark hole in the ground, molten fire churning at the bottom, which seemed like hundreds of feet down. The heat singed my face.

This was how I warmed things—from the heat that radiated from the hole in the ground.

Still, I tried what he said and took a deep breath. I imagined sticking my foot out and stepping into the hole of molten fire.

At first, my stomach floated down, but the closer I got to the heat, the more I panicked. My heart started racing, my hands shaking in my corporeal body. I drew my eyebrows even closer together until they practically touched in the middle.

"Easy, girl," Remy yelled, panic rising in him, too. "You're in control, not the fire."

But there wasn't fire.

The heat was radiating around me, and a strange orange-red liquid was churning below my feet. My breathing increased, my chest rapidly quivering. The liquid was getting closer to me, and my body was heating up.

The panic won.

"Reva, no—" Remy was cut off by the sound of my terrified scream as I tried to crawl out of the hole, but it was too late.

My body had just grazed the surface. Hot and glowing fire

flowed from my hands and fingers toward the tree.

Except it didn't stop there.

The flames exploded into the sky, bark and limbs flying toward the treeline behind where my original target once stood. Multiple trees caught on fire in a series of events, causing a domino effect on every neighboring tree.

In just a few breaths, enough for Remy to realize what had happened, the entire first row of trees on either side of us was engulfed in flames, dancing with smoke into the breaking storm.

"We need to leave," Remy ordered over the roar of the flames mixed with the deafening thunder. "Now."

"But The Overgrowns," I whispered.

Whether he heard me or saw the expression on my face, Remy pinched his lips, exasperated.

"It's about to rain, and someone in town will come anyway to see what the hell is going on," he lectured as he rushed behind me.

I heard the unfurling of his wings before I saw them, like the sound of Karasi shaking out the blankets from the clothesline.

My eyes widened, awestruck.

I gawked at the massive, black, leathery flesh that sprung from his back.

He chuckled, "Don't get used to them, kid. I highly doubt you'll see them again."

Without warning, Remy hooked his arms under my legs and behind my back in a cradle, then launched into the sky. I yelped quietly but then remained silent as we stuck just below the storm clouds and headed back to Karasi's.

That would not be the last time I saw his wings—

A sudden knock on my door startles me awake.

I blink rapidly, adjusting my eyes to the dim light in my room and clearing the image of lifeless eyes out of my view. There is barely any sun coming in from my window, dawn just starting to rise.

I curl my lip, irritation bubbling as I grab the hooded cloak from the chair beside my bed. I wrap it around me and flip up the hood so it pushes some of my hair in front of my Mark to create a shadow.

I unhinge the double lock from the door, cracking it enough to find out who is there.

"Gods, Fin," I sigh, pulling the door open more so he can enter. There's a playful smile plastered on his face and I'm apprehensive of the sheer glee brightening his eyes. "Have you lost your damn mind? Do you know how early it is?"

"Early enough," he shrugs, walking towards one of the chairs positioned in front of the empty fireplace. He plops down, crossing his ankle over his knee.

I shut the door behind me, narrowing my eyes.

He's not in his usual knight uniform, and something entirely different from his day-out garb.

Every article is made of black material, hugging tightly to his body. The tunic is tight on his arms and chest, outlining every swell of muscle. The pants are snug on his waist, but looser around his crotch before they tighten in the thighs and calves. He wears black leather boots that appear lighter and with more give than the ones he wears with his knight uniform.

I finally meet his gaze, raising an eyebrow.

The blush that rushes to his cheeks is charming, distracting me enough from the pile of black fabric he's holding out in his hand. A pair of small leather shoes similar to the ones he's wearing dangles from his other hand.

"What is this?" I ask, glaring as my hand waves between him and the items in his hands before yanking my hood off.

"You need to train," Fin says, letting *your powers* hang silently in the air. "Elly found a place in the castle after scouring through some old maps that were filed away in the library. So we're going to go train."

"You and me?" A harsh laugh escapes and his eyebrow lurches up. "Fin, I bet you're phenomenal at fighting, but you've never trained someone like me before. I could hurt you."

"We're going to do what we can," Fin concludes, leaning forward with the pile of what I can only now assume is training clothes. "Get dressed."

It's my turn to lurch my eyebrows.

Something about the command has me wanting to refuse, just to see what he'd do. Instead, something better comes to mind.

I cautiously eye him as I grab the pile from his hand. I plop it on the end of my bed, surveying him the entire time.

He squints at me.

I force my face into neutrality, letting my cloak inch off my shoulders. His eyes snap back into their normal stare, but they darken in color, despite the sun rising outside.

I unbutton the clasps of my nightgown one by one.

"What are you doing," Fin manages, his voice hoarse as

the blush returns.

I smirk with a shrug. "You said to get dressed and this is my room."

"I could've waited outside," Fin says, almost in a whisper, but he doesn't avert his gaze.

I tilt my head to the side, leisurely bunching the nightgown in my hands. In a swift movement, I lift it up and over my head, momentarily obscuring my view.

When it passes over my head, I find Fin standing with his back to me, facing the other side of the room. His arms are crossed over his chest, but his back is stiff, as though he's restraining himself.

I press my lips together and flare my nostrils in disappointment.

"Let me know when you're done," Fin calls, triumph in his voice, thinking he's won this game.

I sigh heavily, yanking on the very tight clothes.

The shirt is similar to Fin's, but there is an extra piece, like a corset, that I fasten over the top of it. It holds my breasts against my chest, but not to the point of suffocation like a corset usually would.

The pants are tight all the way from my hips to my ankles and made of thicker cotton. I slip a pair of socks on before lacing my boots.

I clear my throat once I'm done.

Fin turns around to face me, his face slacking. He examines unabashedly down my body and back up again.

My stomach flips and my fingers tingle.

When he finds my gaze again, his smile is soft. "You look

like a warrior," he admits, meeting me by the door.

I catch a glimpse of myself in my full-length mirror, snagging a band to secure my hair. Right now, it flows around me in raven-black, soft waves from my braid the day before, brushing along my waist. The dark clothing complements my naturally olive-toned skin, my gold, hazel irises striking.

Fin isn't wrong, either. My Mark stands out against my skin in stark contrast, a few shades paler than my natural skin tone.

I look like a Sirian warrior, if there ever was one.

He opens the door for me, gesturing. I snag my salve before following Fin, rubbing some on my forehead. I hand the tin can over to him and he slides it into a pocket in his pants.

"Well?" He asks, chuckling.

I face forward as we walk down the hallway, not giving him the satisfaction of glimpsing the small excitement rising inside me.

"Oh, shut up."

★★★

Traveling through the castle is an adventure. I wouldn't be able to find this place by myself, and I'm still amazed that Fin was able to navigate without following any sort of map.

It also concerns me that someone else can find us, even if this entrance is buried beneath the castle and hidden in a barely noticeable corridor.

I wait for Fin to finish lighting the intricate sconces, all of which hang from the walls at an angle to better project the light. The floor is dusty and coated in sand, and I'm not sure how deep it goes. It crunches softly beneath my feet like tiny flakes of glass.

The beige stone walls are smooth and covered with faded paint in intricate mandala patterns. The pillars surrounding the circular room reach floor to ceiling with detailed floral carvings, stretching from below the arches to the ceiling above us.

This entire area is roughly the size of the grand dining room, and the ceiling is just as high. I stare up at it, curious about what sits above us in the castle.

Fin places the torch he used in an empty metal bracket on the wall by the corridor that conceals the plethora of stairs we descended to get here.

If the training doesn't make me sore, the journey down and back up will.

"Elly said she gave you a book that might be able to help us gauge where you are on the teaching spectrum for Sirians," Fin begins, transforming into teacher mode.

His hands clasp behind his back as he faces me, feet shoulder-width apart. My eyebrows hike in slight amusement.

He continues, "Have you read it?"

"I was able to skim through it, yes." I cross my arms in front of my chest and tap my foot. "I know how to do a lot of what it says, so I'm more advanced than the fourth level. I'm potentially at the same level as an eighteen-year-old, which puts me behind where I should be by only four years."

"How did you figure that?" Fin questions, studying me.

"One of the journals I have from a previous healer discussed teaching the 'fresh adults', as he put it, which I'm interpreting to mean those who reached eighteen," I explain. "The things he talked about I knew, give or take one or two skills but I could probably teach those to myself."

"So." Fin clicks his tongue against his teeth a few times. "Once they reached adulthood, they probably started teaching them combat or some other specialty. Maybe even medicine practice?"

"That's what I guessed, too."

Fin parades in front of me, one boot in front of the other, the sand crackling underneath him. He thinks aloud, "We can start by teaching you to withhold your powers. It sounds like, from what happened the day of the attack and other times you've mentioned, you have trouble keeping the leash on them and it expends you very quickly."

I'm a little shocked at his ability to translate my power usage. "How can you know that?"

"You described the dam analogy to me on the island that day," he explains, pausing in front of me. "It's the same way thing when you exert yourself physically. Like running, if you sprint the first hundred yards, you're not going to last a whole mile. You have to conserve while still maintaining the advantage."

"So, how do we do that?" I ask, frowning. "I don't even know where to begin."

"We're going to wear you out," Fin sighs. "It's not going

to be fun, but we're going to have to start small."

Fin moves to a dark corner, grabbing a few items that tinkle together. He journeys back with a few empty glass bottles gathered into his arms.

He lines them up in the middle of the room about a dozen or so feet in front of where I stand. Once he's done, he strolls back towards me until he's standing behind me, a few feet to my right.

"I want you to work on tipping each of those over," he commands, not unkindly. "I think you might have a hard time determining the difference between the various uses of your power. You once said you can move things back, project the power, slow an impact, or make something explode. They sound like separate ways you can manipulate energy, and you should view them that way."

"Very observant of you." I hold out my hands in front of me, focusing on the first bottle farthest away.

I imagine the well of power inside me like before, calling the Light into my hands.

My palms and fingers begin to glow bright white-gold. In a slow, gentle stream, the energy shoots from my hand and knocks the bottle over, albeit enough that it rolls away from its brothers.

I face Fin, smiling, but his face is neutral.

"Great," he observes, those damn hands behind his back like Pax. "Faster. Knocking something small like a bottle should be quick." He snaps his fingers to demonstrate.

I clench my jaw, flexing my fists at my side and trying to envision what he says, but all I can see is a body flying across a hall.

My stomach lurches.

His lip twitches at the corner. "So this is a point of contention for you?"

"I have to concentrate," I explain, leaving out the part about trying to maneuver around the flashbacks. "Or it will overtake me like in Clint's room."

"An attacker isn't going to wait for you to figure that out," Fin says. You need to be able to control how much you pull out until it is second nature. Think of it more like... a rope!"

"A rope?" I ask incredulously, one eyebrow raised.

He shrugs. "Like in tug-a-war?" He winces, tilting his head to the side. "Maybe not the best analogy."

I sigh, facing the bottles. "I'll try it."

Instead of a well, I picture my power as a rope. A small tug. That's all I need.

This rope goes taught through my body as my hand runs along it, so responsive to acknowledgment.

This is not going to work.

"Go," Fin commands, and I shoot my power toward the bottle.

It explodes violently, shooting shards of glass everywhere. Some of the pieces make it toward us, skidding across the ground.

Perspiration beads at the nape of my neck and gathers in my palms. I wipe my hands on my pants before the sweat can thicken, like blood dripping down my hands.

I peek at Fin, whose eyes are wide in shock.

"Your rope didn't work."

He glares. "Let's try the next one." Fin waves his hand at the third bottle. "Whatever sort of analogy works for you. But you need to be able to command it quicker. Maybe you need to stop thinking about your power as a separate thing from you..."

"That's not the only issue here," I mutter under my breath, but he doesn't hear me. If I could just stop envisioning the two men I'd killed in Clint's room...

I close my eyes, biting down against the bile rising up my chest when I consider integrating my power as part of me.

My power.

The book Elly gifted me referred to the Light as *your* Light multiple times. I thought maybe I was mistaken in the translation, but Fin saying to stop imagining it as something separate has me thinking I'm right.

Especially as it sings to me in response.

The Light is how mortals have always referred to the powers of the Sirians as a collective, but maybe they never considered it something they shared, like everyone reaching into a combined well.

Maybe viewing it as something that belongs to me is what I've been missing—for both powers—for so long.

This realization also means I will need to adjust the teaching I've learned until this point, not to mention the new memories from using my power triggers during the attack on the castle.

I take a deep breath through my nose, let it leave my

mouth in a controlled exhale, and then nod. "Alright. I know what to do."

"Okay," Fin says, softly, taking another step back.

"Just give me a minute before you yell at me," I mumble, but I know he understands me this time.

I close my eyes and spread my hands wide. The well appears, but I snuff that image from my mind, along with the man standing in Clint's doorway.

Instead, I focus on the power racing through my veins. I imagine that power as vines connecting to me from within and around me, like an aura surrounding my being.

If I can envision this right, I can wield it as an extension of myself.

I pull the power from outside me, into me, fitting it against me until it melts into my skin.

"Are you ready?" Fin asks, a tremor in his voice.

I don't know if he can sense what I've done, but his voice has an element of awe or concern. I ignore it.

"Ready." I snap my eyes open and let my hands fall to my sides.

I wait, my heart pounding against my ribcage.

One heartbeat.

Two…

Three…

"Go," Fin snaps.

In two seconds, I whip my hand up, aim it at the bottle, and unfurl the power from me like a whip. The bottle flies through the air and shatters against the wall.

"Damnit," I swear, digging my boot into the ground.

"Don't beat yourself up," Fin laughs. "It didn't implode on impact. It's just a kick instead of a tap."

I whip my head around, the braid falling over my shoulder. He's doing his best to suppress the grin that's trying to make its way up his cheeks.

"This is going to take practice," Fin reassures. "Besides, you have seven bottles left."

We spend the next however long going from bottle to bottle, the force I deliver to each one softer and softer.

In a way, Fin's trick is working.

I knock the final bottle down with as much force as I had the first one, but in a fraction of the time it took me. My stomach gurgles, alerting me of not only the energy I've used but that I have yet to eat breakfast.

"We should try to organize as much time as we can down here," Fin explains, placing his hands on his hips as he strolls over to me. "I can fit you in the morning before I start my shift, and any days I'm off duty. Which is rare these days."

"Have you picked up more shifts?" I ask, wiping my hands against my pants.

Despite having the tighter band around my midsection, I've never been more comfortable.

"We received word back from Tariq," Fin explains, running a hand through his auburn hair, causing it to go a little awry. "He's asked me to step into Pax's position until he can get back to assess the situation further."

"Pax has been demoted then?" I exclaim, trying and failing to hide my joy.

He inclines his head to me, shaking it in mock disbelief.

"Temporarily, Reva," he laughs, shoving my shoulder. "Don't act so excited."

"He deserved it a little." I shove his shoulder back.

As my hand connects with him, he grabs my wrist firmly and tugs me against his body. A strangled gasp escapes my lips as my entire body presses against his firm body.

Being several inches taller than me, he curls forward and uses his other hand to brace my lower back. I arch into him, allowing my hips to push against him. The muscles in his chest flex.

"Don't think I've forgotten that little stunt in your bedroom, Miss Reva," he says quietly, his voice rumbling against my chest. All the blood rushes between my legs, my core warming at the rough tone of his voice. "You are astonishing in this gear."

"Some would say I look better without it," I counter, breathless.

His nostrils flare, pupils dilating. My heart picks up, hammering against my rib cage and into my throat.

His heart matches my pace, and he hardens against my lower stomach.

"Dangerous, Reva," Fin whispers, his breath brushing against my lips. He angles his head closer to mine. "You are dangerous."

I lose any self-control or sense, smashing my lips against his. We clash like waves against rocks, and I cling to him.

He frees my wrist, so I slide my arms up and around the back of his neck. Tongues dancing, his hands travel from the curves of my waist and down my lower body to cup my ass.

I savor every inch of his touch, from the caress of his lips to his fingers tucked under the curve of my butt.

Still devouring me, he flattens his hands against the back of my thighs and draws me up. I lock my legs around his waist, tangling my fingers into his hair.

He lowers to his knees, using one hand to gently lay me with him on the sandy ground and another to brace himself from collapsing on top of me. He hovers above me, trailing kisses down my jaw and neck.

I curve my back and roll my hips into his, running my hands down his chest and clinging to his shirt. One of his hands roams down my body, leaving a flaming path until it toys with my waistband.

My vagina aches, pulsing in response, and I know I'm already wet from months of only having myself to touch.

His head rears back, but I can't meet those beautiful eyes.

I know what I'll behold in them.

Instead, I kiss him again, urging with another shift of my hips and legs.

He deepens the kiss, his hands slipping under my waistband. He drags his fingers against my clit as his hand travels down, circling steadily and tortuously against my entrance. Finding the slickness there, he groans into my mouth.

Fin presses two fingers in, my breathy moan echoing against his lips. He moves his fingers, gently curling them in. Each time, he trails them perfectly along the most sensitive area, just enough pressure to build the tightening without sending me over the edge too soon.

I glide my hands back up into his hair again, tugging on the strands to bring him closer. I drag my teeth along his bottom lip, nipping. He smirks against my lips, taking that for hunger and picking up the pace with a different movement.

He drags his fingers in and out this time, still pressing against my inner wall. It doesn't take long before I'm clenched around them, the release spreading through me.

I quietly gasp for breath as I ride out my orgasm, quivering even after he relents.

"Reva," he whispers, his voice raspier than I'm used to.

He removes his hand from me and my waistband as rushed steps grow louder, echoing from the corridor we came down.

In multiple, quick movements, Fin yanks himself off of me and I pitch to a seating position. We exchange a quick glance; Fin's face is beat-red, eyes wide with shock but still dark with lust.

Our heads snap back to the corridor in time for Elly to peel around the corner, clutching her skirts in her hands.

She pauses, mouth propped open as if she were going to say something. She shakes her shock away, her shoulders rigid with panic.

She clears her throat, waving a hand. "This can wait. Reva, it's Clint."

I swear, staggering to my feet in tandem with Fin. As I run, I dust the sand off my body, following Elly back to the surface.

During our entire journey back up the stairs and down

the hallways to Clint's room, I caught Fin's swift but longing glances toward me out of the corner of my eye.

Shit.

CHAPTER 20

I sit beside Clint, letting him rest this morning after another bout of vomiting blood yesterday. He lies on his back, one hand resting on his sternum while the other lays limp beside him. His head is angled towards his window, propped open to let some fresh air in.

I also wanted to let out the lingering stench of iron.

I place my hand on top of his, curling my fingers. His pale skin severely contrasts with mine. His head doesn't turn towards me, barely acknowledging me at all.

"I know it's probably pointless to ask," I utter in a low voice that echoes in the eerily silent room. My heart aches for his laughter, for his sarcasm, for his teasing. "I'm not going to ask how you're feeling. So, how about *what* are you feeling?"

Clint blinks and continues to stare out the window. His chest rises with shallow, quivering breaths.

I try again, "You seemed to live through the night."

He slowly pivots his head against the pillow, those dull, distant eyes landing on me.

The amber has been snuffed out, a shadow muting its brilliant color.

Clint clears his throat, but his voice is still raw and

harsh from vomiting and barely holding water down as he challenges, "You call this living, Reva?"

I shut my eyes briefly, the guilt bearing down on me. "Clint—"

"I'm thirteen, Reva." Clint swallows, wincing. "I should be attending classes with others. I should be learning to fight with my brother and Fin. I should be choosing my specialty so I can become a Lord because, even if I get better, there is no kingdom I could ever rule. I would give anything to be a knight, but how am I supposed to do that? How am I supposed to see a life beyond this room and this bed and *this*?"

He lifts his hand from his chest, flicking his wrist over his body. His hair clings to his forehead, stiff from fighting a fever all night.

I bite the inside of my lower lip, fighting the burning in the back of my throat.

"Clint," I plead.

He tries to turn his head back toward the window, but I use my free hand to grip his chin and force him to look at me.

Anger flashes briefly across his face but I squeeze his hand tighter in my other. "You are not allowed to give up on me, do you understand? I am not done with you yet. We are not finished here. I can't do my job if you aren't here to fight the battle with me. I'm going to need every last bit of your strength and mine, whether we find another temporary cure or the real thing."

Tears well in his eyes, lining them with silver and

brightening them.

I lean into him. "You have been fighting for so long, which isn't fair. We both know that but I want you to hold on just a little longer for me. I know the Sirians had a way to fix this. There would be no other reason Karasi sent me instead of another Magic. I'm going to figure it out, and we are going to heal you."

His lower lip wobbles and my body wants to break into a million pieces with him.

I grab both of his shoulders, gently hauling him into me. I wrap both of my arms around his shoulders and back, pinning him there.

After a brief pause, his hands inch up and around me. He buries his face against my collarbone, trembling. I caress the back of his head, sighing as a tear slips down my cheek. I rest my chin on the top of his head.

I had underestimated so much over the last few months. I never expected the prince to be this sick and fighting this hard for his life. I was spoiled when I first arrived and I found a happy kid, despite his ailments.

Not only that, but things were working. I knew deep down this would only be temporary, but so much bliss had been happening around me that I'd got lost in it.

I had friends. I was more accepted than I anticipated. I found someone to share my time with.

I can't help the guilt settling in the pit of my stomach for all the time I could've saved if I'd stopped worrying about my safety and put my trust in Elly. We could've started searching for answers on how to save Clint sooner.

We could've even had the answer by now.

A soft knock on the door startles me, and I have to control my breathing as a flash of the door flying off the wall consumes my mind.

I gently pull away from Clint, helping him lay back down. "Come in," I call out, rising from the bed at the same time the door opens.

King Darius stands at the threshold, silver-streaked hair tousled. His dress shirt has an extra button or two undone at the top, and he doesn't wear a jacket or cloak like he usually does.

To anyone, he could pass for a normal citizen. To see the King of Mariande in distress has my body stiffening.

"Is now a good time to be with my son?" King Darius asks, softly. "Or do you need to examine him?"

"I've administered his medicine for the day," I assure, gathering my skirt in my hand. "This is a perfect time. I don't want to overextend him right now with new treatments."

"Okay," he murmurs, stepping into the room.

I gather my satchel and box of supplies, but I glimpse another man standing just outside the door, peering around the frame.

"Eamon," Clint blurts, noticing him, too.

A ghost of a smile flickers across his face and the man at the door offers a kind, encouraging one back.

"Hey, kiddo," Eamon greets, resting a hand against the door frame. I drift to the door and stand briefly before him, waiting. He offers me a tight-lipped grin before calling out, "I'll find you later, Darius."

Hearing someone refer to King Darius as anything other than his formal title catches me off-guard. I've never heard anyone other than Clint be informal around the King, let alone this man I haven't seen once in the castle.

"Thanks, E," the King responds, sitting beside Clint.

I frown at Eamon as he sidesteps to give me room to pass. He reaches behind me and tugs the handle to shut the door.

"I don't think we've met," I start, facing him head-on. "I'm Reva, the Royal Healer…" My voice fades away as I examine Eamon.

Despite his age—which I would guess is around his 50s like King Darius—there is no mistaking whose father this is. The sharp jawline beneath salt-and-pepper stubble, square face, wave to his nose, and hooded lids of his eyes. Other than his hair being streaked gray amongst the brunette strands, I know this has to be Fin's dad.

Not to mention those same, gem-like emerald eyes.

"I would shake your hand," Eamon smiles, and Gods, if that isn't Fin in 25 years, "But it seems you have your hands full. I'm Eamon Wardson, by the way. I believe you've become acquainted with my son, Finley."

My mind flashes inappropriately to Fin's lips trailing down my jawline.

I nod once, swallowing sharply. "Yes, I have. It's nice to meet you."

"As it is to meet you," he says, head tilting to the side. He extends his hands toward my supply box, studying me. "May I? It wouldn't be very knightly of me if I let you carry that back to wherever it is you're going."

"My room," I reply. He peels the box from my grasp before I can say yes or no. I awkwardly wipe my hands on my skirt before I stretch my arm down the hallway. I lead the way. "You said it wouldn't be knightly of you?"

"Yes! I was a knight for Mariande until Finley was about five years old. These days I'm just a lowly advisor to the King." He chuckles and I find myself smiling. He glances at me, and something unfamiliar flashes across his face. He frowns to himself, shaking his head ever so slightly. "Where is it you're from?"

"I came from Eldamain," I explain, folding my hands in front of me.

He doesn't shy away, his eyes shifting in their sockets as he scans every angle of my face.

I fidget under his scrutiny.

"You look familiar." He still frowns, mumbling his words like he's speaking to himself. He raises his voice more when he says, "What are your parents' names?"

I startle at the question.

He knows I'm acquainted with his son but doesn't know my full story. Either the King and Fin haven't divulged that information to him, or he thinks I still know of my parents or remember them.

"If you find out before I do, I will be indebted to you," I snort, shaking away the strange hollowness in my chest. "I was a baby when Karasi took me in and I'm not sure if she knows who my parents are. All I know is that my father left me with her, and my mother died sometime between my birth and when I showed up on Karasi's doorstep."

He hums, distracted.

We walk in silence for a brief moment before I ask, "So how long have you known the King?"

"Well," Eamon's eyebrows lift as he ponders. "Gods, how long has it been? You're going to reveal my age, Reva."

I shrug, my lips tilting up. "I live amongst Magics. No matter how old or young you are, I guarantee you aren't the oldest person I've ever met."

"Indeed." He narrows his eyes. "For the record, King Darius is older than I am by about a year, but don't tell him I told you that. Alas, it has to be over thirty years at this rate. We met in the Knight School of Mariande and have been close friends ever since. I've been one of his hands since he took the throne when he was nineteen."

"King Darius was nineteen?" I half-yell. I clear my throat, collecting myself, but the brief smile on Eamon's face doesn't go unnoticed. "I did not know that."

"The former king and queen were killed en route to a briefing of sorts," he recalls, and there's a thick sadness to his voice. "He was only nineteen when they passed. He married Lucia, and I married my wife around the same time."

"Gods," I breathe. "That means by my age he'd already had the throne for three years."

"You're the same age as my son." Not a question, but a statement laced with a little bit of apprehensive confusion.

We enter my hallway to find Fin waiting by my door. I pause, gawking at him.

I haven't seen him since we had to usher him and Elly out of Clint's room yesterday so the other Magic healers and I could work on Clint.

We also haven't talked since the moment under the castle.

"Finley!" Eamon shouts from halfway down the hall.

I press my lips together, shaking my head.

Fin grimaces, reeling his head back, studying us. "I never thought I would start my afternoon seeing my father and my—" Fin catches himself, but not soon enough. I falter in my steps, stunned by his claiming of me to anyone, let alone his father. "You and Reva."

"I was with Darius earlier and escorted him to Clint's room, where I was introduced to Reva," Eamon explains, returning my box of items to my arms. He pulls his son into a warm, tight embrace. "You haven't been around the house in a while, Finley. Your mother thinks the worst."

"Of course she does," Fin responds to his dad, but he's watching me over his shoulder.

I level him with a small glare and an arched eyebrow.

I was worried that Fin would run with what happened between us yesterday, and the worst part is I can't even blame him. I've been the queen of mixed signals as of late.

"Do you have a moment?" Eamon asks. "Or are you claimed for lunch already?"

"I was just—" Fin starts but I interrupt with, "Go ahead and take him! I have some things I really need to figure out for Clint right now, anyways."

Fin finally breaks eye contact with me, his shoulders drooping an inch.

Excitement radiates off of Eamon.

How much free time does Fin really have, and how much

of it has been spent with me and this Sirian cause we've formed?

"I'll find you later," Fin says to me as his dad pulls him away, and it sounds a bit like a warning.

***

I hunch over the coffee table in the study, meticulously reading through another journal from a former Sirian Royal Healer, ages ago.

Elly regretfully informed me they still hadn't found any medical books about how Sirians used their powers that differed from just adding their blood to elixirs.

At this point, there was only one thing I was certain about. After reading the journal I'd found over a month ago and the one that Elly had discovered the other day...

Clint's condition must be caused by a cell cluster in his body that is not supposed to be there.

After all the work and potions I'd used so far to help him, an infection should have gone away by now. If it were a permanent deformation internally, then some of the medicine I'd tried would not have worked either, at least for as long as they did.

If there was a cluster of cells in his body, I had to figure out how to stop them from growing or find a way to shrink it.

Ideally, it would be both.

"How did I know I'd find you here?" Fin announces from the doorway. I raise my head, narrowing my eyes. "You look like you're unhappy with me."

I shove my bookmark in the journal, slamming it shut in my lap. After stacking the book on top of the others on the table, I clear my throat and lean back in the oversized chair.

Fin strolls over to the seating area.

"Your father," I begin. "There is a lot that happened I'd like to discuss."

"I could say the same," he agrees, collapsing into the chair across from me.

Our eyes lock, but my brain clears entirely of rational thought, except for a replay of him yanking me up against his body and pulling me into his arms like it was nothing.

I blink away, but he's already noticed the slight flush warming my cheeks.

"Your dad seemed to know about me." I pick at a loose string on the arm of the chair, leaving the statement there for him to confirm, deny, or elaborate.

"He would know about you because of King Darius and a few things I've mentioned," Fin shrugs, nonchalantly. "He asked me about you in the beginning, before I knew much about you. He's also very good at making conversation, whether or not he already knows the answers to what he's asking. There's a reason he's King Darius's right hand."

"I thought it was because they were long-time friends?" I bring my hands into my lap.

"That's partly true," Fin confirms, rubbing at his stubble. "But, it's mostly because he's good at his role. He just so happens to be childhood friends with the King."

"Would you be Prince Tariq's right hand, then?" I ask out

of sheer curiosity.

It doesn't take him long to answer. "If he'll have me, but I won't be disappointed if he doesn't choose me. I have a lot to learn from my dad before then. I also don't think that will be anytime soon."

I bite the inside of my cheek, debating if it's even worth it to bring up his near-claiming of me to his dad. I highly doubt Fin meant anything by it, but how much of our initial conversation on the things I can and cannot give has stuck?

"You dismissed me," Fin says before I can mention my next point.

I startle a little, rocking back.

"It looked like your father wanted to speak with you, and me speaking with you wasn't urgent enough for you to ditch him," I explain. "I didn't mean for it to be malicious."

"I didn't say it was." Fin averts his gaze, surveying something over my shoulder. "But you didn't consider maybe I had plans to speak with you?"

"And what would you like to speak to me about—"

"Yesterday," Fin interrupts, leaning forward. "We hadn't got a chance to speak about it because, well…"

We leave that sentence unfinished, neither of us truly wanting to acknowledge Clint's situation aloud.

I flatten my hands against my skirt, dragging them across it as I wipe the sweat away.

"What would you like to talk about, then?" I ask again, lifting my chin.

He's still leaning forward, his hands folded together. "Are you okay?" He asks, startling me with the question.

"I mean," I pause, scrambling for the right words. "I've done that... It wasn't my first... You didn't break me."

Fin laughs, eyes crinkling at the corners as he throws his head back. I flare my nostrils, suppressing my smile. He shakes his head, still grinning as he clarifies, "I didn't mean physically, Reva. I meant in terms of us and this relationship we have."

"We don't have a relationship," I snap instinctively. Fin flinches, and any traces of laughter snuffed out. I sigh, "I didn't mean it to sound like that."

"I know that I'm not supposed to be expecting anything from you," he quietly defends, eyes scanning my face. "I just don't know what you expect of me."

"I don't expect anything from you, Fin," I clarify, rubbing a hand down the side of my face. "I just don't want things to be complicated. I don't want to hurt you—"

"You've said that before, but I'm a grown-up," he insists. "I can make my own decisions, and I know what I'm getting into."

"But I don't know what I'm getting into."

He hunches further into himself as his gaze falls to his hands.

He's so easy to read, and his disappointment crushes my chest. I throw my head against the back of the chair, shutting my eyes.

He may be a grown-up who makes his own decisions, but it doesn't mean he doesn't feel the pain.

And I have to watch him feel it.

"I know you have a lot on your plate, Reva," Fin quietly

begins. "I don't want to add more unnecessary stress to your life. I understand that even since our initial conversation, things have gotten more complicated for you than they already were. Clint is still sick, and we know things are happening in the world that we are going to be involved in and you will have a big role to play in it. It doesn't help not knowing what that role is.

"But you're not alone in this," Fin reassures, reaching his hand out to rest his fingertips on the coffee table. "I want to be there for you, in whatever capacity you'll have me. It's just that I'm always going to wonder what is going through your head whenever you laugh with me, look at me, kiss me... And you can't fault me for that."

He twists his hand, splaying his palm up. I take in a gentle breath through my nose and release it before angling my head and biting the inside of my cheek.

He's absolutely right, and that's what hurts the most. I can't fault him for how he reads into my actions and reactions. I don't stop his advances; Kuk knows I initiate them, too.

"I know," I agree, remembering what Elly said about Fin not being used to a non-relationship situation.

I didn't anticipate he would need constant reassurance that I'm still somehow in this—whatever it is. The more we are alone together, the more I find us taking it one step further. He's beautiful, kind, compassionate, and patient in his own way, but some part of me is holding back, and I don't know what it is.

His slack expression softens me a little, so I try to ignore my nagging worry about hurting him.

Fin and I could work.

"I still need time," I remind him. "You said so yourself. A lot is going on."

"And, I'll be waiting." His eyes soften.

That's what I'm afraid of.

CHAPTER 21

F in, Elly, and I enter the jewelry store in a single file line, bells tinkling as we pass the threshold. Elly leads us straight down a narrow lane to the back of the store.

Jorah is hunched over his workman's table, a pair of the world's smallest lenses perched at the edge of his pointed nose. He pauses his work, observing us each individually from the opposite side.

"Jorah," Elly says with a smile, hands clasped in front of her. "You sent word that Reva's necklace was repaired."

"Princess," Jorah smirks deviously. "And the Healer."

"Hello, Jorah," I say, scanning his table. "I can't express enough gratitude for repairing my necklace. It's very dear to me."

"I would hope so," he answers, warily.

His hand descends upon the table, raising up with the chain. The hematite pendant dangles from it as he straightens to his full height.

He rests the pendant in his hand, studying it down the length of his nose. "How did you acquire such a necklace?"

"Karasi said it came with me, so she assumed it was a family heirloom from my father or my mother," I explain, unable to tear my gaze from his fingers curled around it, the tips of his pointed nails resting against the palm of his hand.

He holds up his other hand, indicating for us to follow him with a twitch of his finger. I turn to Elly for confirmation, and she tips her head to Jorah.

He leads us to a back wall lined with bookshelves. He drags his finger along the spine of every book on the second shelf.

A soft, barely audible click sounds from behind it. With a breath, it cracks open and away from the wall like a door. Jorah reaches his hand into the small opening, separating the shelf further from the crack, creating enough space for us to enter this secret entrance one person at a time.

Fin enters first, followed by Elly, then me.

The hidden room is small, nearly the size of the living area of my home back in Eldamain. The walls have rows upon rows of shelves full of books and various types of tomes.

In the middle of the room is an old, chipped wooden table with four equally distressed wooden chairs tucked underneath.

The click resounds again behind me, and I peer over my shoulder as Jorah floats from the entrance to the table. He holds out the necklace to the room.

"This is a warded room," Jorah explains, letting Fin take my necklace from his hand. "I say that so you know nothing discussed in this room will be heard by intruders. Anything done in this room stays in this room. All I ask is that you don't harm the tomes I have. They are very important not only to me but also to you, Sirian."

My breath hitches in my throat.

I knew that Jorah could sense in my blood that I was Sirian, I just didn't expect him to willingly and casually refer to me as one.

With that, I call my Light forward and will it to burn away the salve masking the Mark on my forehead. Fin's eyes linger hesitantly while Elly stares in awe, buzzing with amusement. A small, sly smile crawls up Jorah's cheeks.

"You knew I was Sirian the day I came into this shop with Elly," I vocalize. "What else did you learn from reading my blood?"

"I felt the power running through your veins," Jorah admits, pulling out a chair from the table. He waves his hand at us, so we all join him. "Aside from your hematite necklace, I also felt great power far beyond any Sirian I've ever encountered."

"You've encountered other Sirians?" I ask, and at the same time Fin asks, "What kind of power?"

Jorah's eyes flicker to Fin briefly, scrutinizing him. He answers Fin first but addresses me, "I can tell you the power of at least one demi-god runs through your veins. Without knowing what kind of powers you can wield outside of the Light, I cannot tell you which child of the Gods.

"As for Sirians." He levels me with an incredulous expression. "I am old, child. I've traveled the world many times over. Not as old as Karasi, but old enough to have encountered living Sirians. Some are long dead, some are as young as yourself."

"What do they wield?" I whisper, my heart fluttering.

Some of the silver specks in Jorah's eyes flash and he draws his lips into a hard line.

"I can only say the Darkness and the Light are even amongst them." He folds his hands in front of him on the table. "Just as I will not reveal your identity to them, I cannot reveal their identity to you. I expect you will come to know many of them eventually. They are not far from us."

My heart hammers against my chest frantically, begging to be free of this.

Fin shifts uneasily beside me as Elly leans further into what Jorah says with every revelation. I study my hands in my lap, considering the riddles Jorah seems to be talking in.

If the Darkness and Light are even thus far in his travels, does that mean in power or by numbers? Because it can make a difference when discussing a war that may come between the two sides.

"You said you would be able to tell us what demi-god Reva descends from," Elly interrupts my thoughts and the silence in the room. "Do you know the demi-gods that influenced the Sirians?"

Jorah holds up his finger, pushing up from his chair. He strolls over to one of the shelves with his back turned, explaining, "Magics believe that the Gods have abandoned this world. After the Sirians were all but eliminated, including descendants of many of the demi-gods, they left us to fend for ourselves. So, teachings of the Gods dwindled away in many of the countries in our world."

He produces an older book, flipping through it as he

drifts back over to us. He points to the page he finds with his pointed nail, smirking. Elly and I lean over the table at an angle, reading: *The Demi-Gods and Their Reign*.

"How many demi-gods were there?" I question, tearing my attention from the book.

"Three of the Gods reproduced with humans, Magics, and Sirians alike," Jorah explains, sitting back in his seat. Across the three of them, they had nine demi-gods. Three were responsible for the creation of the Houses of the Magics, two belonged to the mortals, and four were Sirians."

"Four?" Elly exclaims, rapidly scanning the pages. She gently reaches out and flips the next page, eyes still frantic.

"Tales suggest the Goddess Danica loved her Sirians." Jorah shrugs, unabashed. "Whether she had four children with one Sirian or four children with multiple Sirians is unknown to history. The bottom line is there are four Sirian power variants. Which do you have, the Great Reva?"

"I really hope that name sticks," Fin mumbles under his breath.

I shoot him a warning glare, raising my finger.

He suppresses his smile, aimlessly studying the books surrounding us.

"Reva," Elly breathes, her eyes glued to a specific point on the page. Her finger slowly lowers, pointing at a bolded word: *Dionne*.

"Who is Dionne?" I ask, annunciating their name.

Jorah's attention jumps from Elly to me, dissecting as he stands over her shoulder.

"Dionne was a son of Danica," Jorah says, his head tilting

to the side. In addition to wielding the Light, he could draw
directly from the core of the Earth."

"It says he could manipulate heat?" Elly inquires,
glancing up at Jorah. He caresses her shoulder before pacing
the room.

"I can generate fire," I correct, placing my hand out in
front of me.

Jorah stops mid-stride, his eyes glowing in the flame that
flares to life in my hand. His face blanches, and he holds his
breath.

I let the fire reel back into me.

"You can barely generate it," Jorah lectures, scratching at
the scaled skin on his neck. "It practically controls you. That
is not fire you are generating."

"You know, I'm getting real sick of people—"

"What do you mean it's not fire?" Fin interrupts,
frowning. "It's a flame."

Jorah shakes his head again, wagging his finger at Fin and
me. "Sirian demi-gods all had the Light, which is the ability
to generate the Energy of All Things. Dionne could draw
from the earth's core, which is molten. It is heat in liquid
form. With his enhanced abilities, he could manipulate that
heat to shape it, create whatever he wanted, and make things
hotter."

"I can warm things," I confirm, rubbing my arms. "I can
warm myself or others if it's cold."

Jorah sucks in a breath. "You are lucky you haven't killed
anyone, child. You can barely control that power and you
are warming others? What if you warmed them too much

and gave them a fever? Boiled their blood, thus boiling them alive?"

In opposition to what he says, my blood runs cold and my entire body freezes.

I had never considered that when wielding this power since I had some control over it.

At least I thought I did, but everyone silently screams "Fire!" anytime I wield it.

He is right, though. I have been lucky.

"Gods, children literally playing with fire," Jorah sighs, rubbing his temples with both hands. "Outside of heat manipulation, Dionne could manipulate existing fire and heat. He could also convert the energy of the Light into heat and fire, creating flames out of essentially nothing."

"So what Reva just did there," Fin verifies, but I can barely hear either of them.

Instead, I'm distracted by all the times I tapped into my firepower like Remy had directed. I could never imagine reaching into a well of fire as he suggested. It was always a dark hole in the ground, full of molten fire.

The core of the earth.

"You are far more powerful than you should be," Jorah interrupts my thoughts, pointing an accusatory finger at me. "The way you wield that power is reckless."

"I didn't have someone to teach me how to use either power growing up," I snap, clenching my fists at my side. "I had Magics raising me. I wasn't taught by any of your *friends* who are Sirians. I had no resources!"

"Reva," Elly soothes, calmly rising from her chair. Her

voice sounds like it's underwater, far from where my mind can reach.

"I will not have anyone judging my abilities to control my power when they don't understand the first thing about what runs through my veins," I yell, swiping my palm across the front of my body.

The surge of my power releases without said control, hitting the table and knocking it onto its side. The room descends into stunned silence, and Jorah observes me intently.

"At least you didn't shatter it," Fin offers, his back pressed against the bookcase.

I snarl at him.

"You need someone to teach you," Jorah says, helping Fin set the table back on its legs again. I slouch into the chair I had been sitting in before.

"We cannot have Magics and mortals trying to teach you to control a power they don't understand, that we can agree on. I will see what I can do to help you. I may know some that are willing and daring enough to help."

"Jorah," Elly interjects. "The Crown could not pay them for their services. Those in this room are the only people who know of Reva's powers."

"I understand," Jorah assures. "You will probably need to employ them somewhere as a cover. Perhaps your library, Princess?"

"I could arrange that," Elly agrees, the wheels already turning in her head.

I exhale deeply, rubbing my forehead just beside my Mark. "There is something else, Jorah," I begin, meeting his gaze. "It has to do with the prince."

"Clint?" Jorah turns to Elly for confirmation. She pauses her reading, closing her eyes as she nods. "Do you know what ails him?"

"I believe there is a mass in his stomach," I explain, rubbing my hands on my skirt. "Something I've been able to keep at bay, but I cannot shrink or stop it from growing. And it has grown."

"I have heard of such illnesses and have some resources I can send you home with. From what I know of them, they require you to use the Light. How, exactly, is beyond my knowledge and I can't begin to understand how you would use it. All I know is that this illness has been impossible to treat since the disappearance of Sirians."

I press my lips, rolling them together. "Will it be enough?" I whisper, meeting Fin's soft gaze. "Will all of it be enough?"

"Don't carry this burden alone, Reva," Elly interjects. "I told you: my brother and I have been involved with all of this since before you came into our lives. This isn't just about you."

"The princess is right, Reva," Jorah joins in, leaning back in his chair. "The Abyss has been growing for nearly three decades now. First, a whisper. Now, a chorus.

"The power that runs in your veins is the strongest I've felt in all my years, even now, with the number of Sirians I have met. When the time comes to fight the Darkness, you will be at the forefront of the battle. The Sirians who join may turn to you to lead."

"Why me?" I splay my hands out in front of me. "Am I the only Sirian that has managed to harness the bloodline of a demi-god? And how does this qualify me to lead?"

"No," Jorah admits, tilting his head side-to-side. "There are others. There may be another who reigns from Dionne, as well. It has been a millennia since the demi-gods' bloodlines have been known. Their descendants are spread far, but you are the only one I have met in my three centuries of existence that has the power of more than one demi-god."

"You are sure I have more than one?" I shake my head. "I have only ever known the Light and the fire—well, not fire, I guess. The *heat*."

"Maybe it has yet to manifest." He shrugs, crossing his arms over his chest. "But it is there. It is not just Dionne, and that is important to the Sirians."

"You know more than you're letting on," Fin jumps in, eyes narrowed at Jorah. He mimics his posture, crossing his arms over his chest as he leans back in the chair and lifts his chin at Jorah. "How many Sirians do you know?"

"I will not reveal my networks," Jorah states, blinking at Fin. "I may trust the princess, but I will still wait to see how things play out for yourself and the Great Reva."

"This is how the Magic trade, Fin," I explain, not nearly as offended by Jorah's lack of trust, no matter who or what I am. "This is the consequence of being shoved aside by others for centuries and centuries. They do not show themselves willingly."

"You did," Fin says quietly, focusing on my Mark.

I swallow the lump in my throat.

"And look what that has gotten her," Jorah exclaims, throwing his hand out. "A princess who has now revealed that secret to others, and a knight who fears what she is."

"I do not fear her," Fin defends, and Elly follows that with an exclamation of her own, "Excuse me, Jorah."

"You may not fear her, but you fear her power. And what you fail to understand, Knight, is that her power will always be with her. That Mark may disappear with salve, but it is still there."

Fin and I part from Elly once we arrive at the castle. She takes the books Jorah lent us to the library, hiding them away for our studies while Fin and I make the journey back to my room.

Neither of us have uttered a word since Jorah spoke aloud what I had been thinking for a few weeks now.

Approaching my door, I pull the key from my satchel and unlock it. I crack it open, throwing Fin a tight-lipped grin over my shoulder as I try to sneak in.

His hand flattens against the frame before I can shut it. "We need to talk about what Jorah said," he finally blurts, lowering his head towards me to whisper, "I need to."

"We've been doing a lot of talking," I mutter under my breath. He purses his lips, inclining his head towards me. I sigh, "Then, come in."

I shut the door behind him after he squeezes past me. The lock clicks into place before he begins.

"I don't fear you, Reva," Fin repeats, trailing me to the edge of my bed. I wrap my arms around myself. "You have to know that. For the love of the Gods, I just let you lock me in a room with you."

"It's not about being alone with me, Fin," I explain, whirling around to face him. "It's my power, and Jorah is right. These abilities will never go away. They will never disappear when all the bad in the world is gone. I get to live with them for the rest of my life, however long or short that is."

"Jorah was right when he said you can barely control them, Reva," Fin half-laughs, throwing his hand out. "Can you blame me for also noticing that and being a little apprehensive when you're wielding a strong force of energy and flames in front of me?"

"A little trust wouldn't hurt," I scoff, but there is truth to his words.

I wouldn't blame him if he were a little worried when I wielded my power, but I know the difference between apprehension and fear.

My family in Eldamain always regarded me with apprehension when I was wielding my power. It was a wince or a press of their lips together.

Never a recoil or wide, glistening eyes.

Fin shortens the distance between us in a few strides, seizing my shoulders in his hands. He pulls me into his arms, trapping my own between our bodies.

He presses his forehead to mine. "I don't care what you are, Reva. I care who you are and what you stand for. The love you have for Clint, a boy you've known for just a few months, and the care you are committed to... That speaks to who you are and your heart. That is what I care about."

I sink into his embrace, his warmth a cocoon to guard every single worry away. I keep my arms pinned between us, my palms flat against his chest.

I know the intent behind his hug, but the tightness in my chest doesn't let up.

I let him hold me and lay with me in my bed if only to pretend for a little while longer than I could ever hold some semblance of a normal relationship.

At least before it's ripped away like everything else I've ever come to know.

CHAPTER 22

F in and Clint play a game of cards together as I examine the prince, pressing around his abdomen at the mass in his stomach.

It's grown since his most recent episode.

My own stomach twists in knots as I press my lips firmly together, biting down on them to suppress the anxiety sitting on my chest.

I snag my notebook from the bedside table to write down the estimated growth and current size of the mass, including a note that my recent concoction is slowing the growth. A small idea pops into my head for a solution I could add to delay it even more. I approach the wooden basket of vials poised on the desk.

"That's cheating," Fin blurts, slamming his hand and cards down on his leg, squinting at Clint. "You can't do that. We've been through this before."

"Are you going to deny a sick prince?" Clint grills in a strained, gravelly voice.

I roll my eyes, but a small, relieved grin tugs at the corners of my lip. As long as we can maintain some semblance of Clint's personality through all of this, I'm going to take it as a win.

"Oh," Fin snickers. "Don't pull that one on me, kid. You are barking up the wrong tree if you think I'm going to let you off the hook because you look like death—"

"Finley!" I whirl around, two vials in both hands.

Clint's chortling morphs into a small cough.

Fin holds up both his hands, palms facing me. "Hey. I made him laugh."

I flare my nostrils, leveling him with a threatening glare before returning to my experiment. I set the vials aside to muddle a few herbs with my mortar and pestle.

A knock on the door rumbles through Clint's chamber just before it creaks on its new hinges.

I shut my eyes against the onslaught of images in my head: a door flying off the wall, a blast of Light, a man slamming into a wall.

Crack.

"Pardon my interruption," a husky voice says. I regard the knight at the door with a single nod, which he returns with his lips pressed together before directing his request to Fin. "Sir Finley, you are needed in the King's office. It's about the return of the Crown Prince."

"Yes," Fin solemnly responds, his back straightening, head inclined an inch higher. "Thank you, Sir Ryder. I will leave promptly. You are dismissed."

Fin hands his cards to Clint with an elaborate bow, pulling another smile from the kid. He strides over to me, the only sound his military boots clicking against the stone floor.

He stands beside me, one hand clasped in a fist behind his back. The other hand lays against my mid-back in a casual caress.

"You're doing great," Fin whispers, leaning closer to my ear. His breath tickles against my neck. "If you didn't know."

"It doesn't feel like I am," I mumble back.

He keeps his hand pressed into my back as his thumb gently traces up and down my spine. My eyes flutter shut, stinging at the corners.

"You're doing better than anyone with what we've got," Fin insists, his cheek brushing against mine. "You've got Elly and I with you, and you're making him comfortable while we figure this out. That's all anyone can ask right now. We are going to figure it out, Reva."

I clear the tears from the back of my throat, nodding.

Fin hugs me quickly from the side, shoulder-to-shoulder, before exiting the bedroom door with a soft click.

I stare at the wooden door for a moment longer before shaking any stray thoughts of Fin's hand on my back from my head.

"Are you and Fin dating?" Clint bursts out.

I startle enough that the liquid in the vials quivers, and I blink up at the ceiling. "Why would you want to know, Clint?"

"I don't know," he grumbles, but there's a smirk in his voice. "I need to know who my competition is."

I spin on my heel, a wide, open-mouthed smile plastered on my face. I let out a short titter, "Is that so? You know I'm nearly ten years your senior."

"To be honest, that's not that bad," Clint argues, shrugging his shoulders. "It may seem so now, but if you wait for me, I promise it'll be worth it."

"Clint!" I scream playfully, but now I'm laughing heartily. I set the vials on the desk, bracing my arms on the edge as my shoulders shake.

I thought I had lost this version of Clint to his illness, but somehow, he has managed to preserve it, and I've never felt more relieved. The tightness in my chest loosens and I inhale without the corset of grief wrapped around my ribcage.

I climb into the bed beside him, our shoulders touching one another and my back propped against the headboard.

I'm still beaming from the inside out as I respond, "I'm flattered, Young Prince, but I don't think anyone would approve of any prince, no matter where he sits in the line of succession, to marry a lowly Royal Healer, especially one with *Marks* like myself."

Clint waves my comment away. "I'm going to change that."

I raise my eyebrows, stunned. "Oh, are you?"

"When you heal me, we'll show the world all the good you can do, and no one will argue the value of Magics or people like you again."

I squeeze his hand, fighting the overwhelming emotions bubbling inside. He bends his neck to the side, setting his head against my shoulder. My entire body warms, and I settle my head delicately on top of his.

"You didn't answer my question, though," he reminds

me.

"If Fin and I are dating?" I repeat, very aware of my avoidance. I huff, "I wouldn't call it that. I'm not sure what we are doing anymore."

"Are you going to attend the Glow Ball with him?" Clint asks, his voice vibrating his body.

I scowl. "What's a Glow Ball?" I ask, lifting my head to glance down at him.

He peels off my shoulder, swiveling his body towards me on the bed and gaping at me like I've offended him.

"It's to celebrate Khonsu," Clint drawls, waiting for me to catch on. I press my lips together, scrunching my nose and shaking my head. "Oh, Reva. You are so lost."

"Excuse me, Prince," I snort, twisting my body so our knees touch. "Then help me understand. You forget I'm a wild animal that was raised by wolves in Eldamain."

"I do sometimes forget." Clint sighs like the weight of the world is on his shoulders.

He rests one elbow on his thigh, the other angled between us as he explains, "Khonsu is our holiday for Khonsa. Teslin and Etherea celebrate it with us, so every year we hold a service where we pray together and watch a reenactment of the Creation of Aveesh. Afterward, there is a Glow Ball where we celebrate outside under the moon. It happens once it's nice enough outside and the spring is fully blooming. We all get to dress up in our best suits and dresses and dance."

I remember learning a little about which countries celebrated which Deities or Gods, but I never considered whether they still held religious celebrations for them anymore.

Most of the main continent had abandoned religion when they believed the Gods abandoned them. Nowadays, the celebration most likely has less to do with honoring Khonsa and more about three countries getting to throw a big party and get along for once.

"I have never attended a grand ball, so I'm sure it's going to be an interesting affair for me," I admit, rubbing the palms of my hands against my skirt.

"So," Clint urges, wagging his eyebrows. "Are you going to go with Fin?"

"I don't know," I exclaim, throwing my hands out. "That would imply we're dating or together, and I'm not sure that's something I want other countries to assume about me."

"So you're not dating then," Clint concludes, raising his chin up and examining me through hooded eyes. "So you're open?"

"Clint," I chuckle again but he continues.

"I'm not talking about me," Clint waves me away again like a fly. "I've got to make it to the Glow Ball first." I gawk at him. "Oh, don't give me that look, Reva, I'm joking. I'm just asking because you are very beautiful and strong and funny and smart. There are people who would admire that."

I narrow my eyes at him before patting him on the knee sympathetically.

★★★

I parade through the aisles to a back table of the library we've designated as our studying area. Within the safety of the library, it's hidden further within the multitude of shelves, giving us more privacy to discuss traitorous topics without being caught by someone while simultaneously positioning us to hear anyone coming in.

"What's on the agenda for today's study session," I call out, effectively announcing my arrival.

I saunter to the table Elly's hunched over, shuffling through the pages of a book we'd inherited from Jorah.

At the table with her is someone I've yet to meet, but she looks strangely familiar. Her facial features tickle at the back of my head, yet I can't quite itch it.

"Reva!" Elly grins, springing straight up from the chair. She gestures her arm towards the other woman bent over another book. "This is Jorah's referral."

The woman lifts her head, smiling softly. She has to be around mine and Elly's age. If I didn't know she was a Magic, let alone a Sirian, I would've been able to guess as much.

Her eyes practically glow against her darker skin, her irises a white and blue iridescent color. Charcoal-grey dreadlocks hang down past her shoulders, which only make her eyes stand out more. Her forehead is bare, though, which means she must also have some sort of salve covering her Mark.

"Lightning," she declares, holding out a delicate hand over the table.

I tilt my head to the side but accept her outstretched hand. My hands have a strange tingle as if they've fallen asleep. It glows in response, a single pulse, startling me. "In power and name."

"Wait," I gawk overtly. "Your name is Lightning? And your power?"

"I was given the nickname at a young age to protect my identity. I've heard it's the old way of the Magics to have a single name, as you're familiar with," she alludes, knowingly.

"Karasi," I nod once. "And myself, inadvertently. So you have the power of a demi-god, too?"

"If Jorah is anything, he's intentional." Lightning exchanges a shrewd glance with Elly. "He knows you need help with the Light and your god-powers. So, why not give you someone who is an expert in both?"

"Expert?" I challenge.

I'm unable to discredit this ethereal radiation from her. It's uncanny how my senses prickle with the anticipation of a storm, like the static in the air is heightened just by her presence.

I also can't shake the feeling I've seen her somewhere before. I can't tell if her facial features or how she holds herself reminds me of Dahlia.

"Lightning has had professional training," Elly notes, folding her hands in front of her. "That is all Jorah said. That, and she knows what she's doing."

"To be honest," Lightning chimes in, sitting in one of the chairs at the table. I follow suit. "We thought I'd be leading this war but after I heard you have the power of *two* demi-gods? Looks like you'll be taking the reins there."

I inhale sharply through my nose. "As you'll learn, I'm in

no condition to lead. I barely have my powers under control, let alone mastered enough to lead others. And war? No one said anything about war."

Elly and Lightning regard one another again.

I know I'm missing something crucial, something that Elly must have just recently learned about. That, or it's of the many secrets she's implied keeping her twin.

Elly sits with us at the table, folding her hands in front of her and twiddling her fingers together.

Lightning clears her throat. "You're aware of the Abyss and how much it's grown in the past few decades," she explains, folding her hands in her lap. "It's not a coincidence. Our intelligence believes a very powerful Darkness wielder has gone unchecked and formed an army to fight against the human kingdoms."

"How have you learned that?" I test, startled by her implication.

My brain has effectively cleared my mind of anything I've ever known or learned, flooding it with questions.

How many Sirians are there if they have intelligence? Who is this *intelligence* that has allowed them to learn this? Why haven't they told anyone?

"We have our ways of obtaining information," Lightning admits, her white-blue eyes intent. "We've come into contact with Sirians wielding Darkness who are part of this movement. Whoever is leading them is very powerful, both in Darkness and in the relationships they keep. They plan to overthrow the mortals and essentially destroy the world as we know it. While I can't argue that this world needs a bit of rearranging, I'm not about to let it be by those who wish to punish people for the acts of their ancestors."

"And you want me to lead it? Why can't you still lead it?" I pivot my body towards her fully. "I am not ready for something like that."

"But, you will be ready," Lightning declares, frowning. "I'll make sure you are. Your royal friends will make sure you are. You have been placed precisely where you need to be."

I don't care whether or not the world presumes leading a Sirian army is where I need to be because I still don't know where that is.

My entire existence has been hidden my whole life, and I'm just now learning about the world. I'm learning about kingdoms, forgotten history, my powers, and glowing balls, and I can't reiterate enough to those around me how *not* meant for this I am.

A heavy emotion clogs my throat, and part of me longs to return to the little house at the edge of a lake where I would work at a pub every night.

But meeting Elly's amber gaze, her eyes soft and caring, I'm reminded of how instantaneously I was thrown under her wing. Now, I can't imagine life without her in it.

I'm reminded of the sick boy who needs me, the one who is like a little brother to me now.

I'm even reminded of Fin, his kindness, compassion, and care, even if he can't acknowledge his deep fear of what I am and what I'm capable of.

I mourn the life I left behind, but this new life makes me feel something...

I've never felt more alive.

Maybe that's what scares me about everything I've encountered: caring for Clint, revealing who I am to my friends, allowing Fin to have pieces of me, and leaning on Elly for help.

Living is much harder than existing, but Gods is it so much better.

"I need to figure out how to help Clint first," I announce, straightening in my seat. I face down Lightning, but out of the corner of my eye, Elly's gaze burns into the side of my head. "He is my priority. Then I will do whatever you need me to do."

Lightning studies my face momentarily, the deafening silence compelling me to fidget in my seat.

After a painstaking minute, she breaks it, "You'll continue your training with me. Elly told me you've been working with a knight to practice in some private area in the castle?"

"Yes." I nod once, releasing a breath I didn't realize I was holding. "Fin is part of this club we have going on, too."

Lightning smirks, amused. "So we're in agreement?"

I shut my eyes, centering myself with four breaths in and four breaths out.

Karasi sent me here to learn about myself, my powers, and even the Abyss, but I can't help wondering how much she meddled with the events she saw unfold in her strange, prophetic mind.

My heart cracks, a few pieces flaking off at the thought of her alone in her hut after sending me away to help save the world. I pray to whatever Gods are left that she continues to live so she can see what we are going to try to do here.

I know I do not have much longer left in this life.

"Okay," I agree.

"Then let's get back to work here. We need to find a passage where a Healer talks about treating infected cells."

We spend the next few hours scouring the more medical-focused Sirian books. We then have dinner together in the library, obeying Elly's rule of eating at a separate table before returning to the one with all the old books on it.

In our search, we uncover different educational and historical books discussing big moments in history that predate King Alrik and his legacy.

His poor daughter, Tyra, crosses my mind more than a few times. A Sirian feared and shoved so far away that she developed a malevolent entity and power that affects us all centuries later.

"Lightning, Reva," Elly startles, jumping out of her seat with a book in her hand. "I think I found something."

Lightning and I exchange wild eyes, shoving our chairs back. The three of us rush together to the side of the table as Elly gently places the book back down, her eyes glued to the page. They frantically peruse the words on the page, her gaze intensifying the further she gets through the text.

Finally, she points her finger at the section that must have initially caught her attention. Lightning and I hunch over the table beside her, all huddling around it like a fire for warmth.

It's an educational book, based on how it's written, but

from the point of view of whoever figured out what they're writing about. It's in better condition than some of the others we've been handling, and it's in modern Etherean, which means someone must have translated the original.

The Sirian who wrote this talks about the Light we wield, but they call it *Energy* instead. They even discuss the importance of making this distinction when it comes to wielding it as a weapon or a medicine.

This Energy exists in everything around us from the air we breathe to the cells in our bodies. They write: *That is why the Goddess Danica belongs to the Sirians, the Goddess of Nature and Energy of All Things.*

They go on to explain one of the many ways Sirians wield Energy is by "charging" it.

Sirians can convert it to charge the object in question with explosive or disruptive results, depending on the amount of force exerted on that item.

The next part doesn't just say Energy stored in objects but stored in *cells*.

"Reva, you've said that this cluster of cells in Clint's body continues to grow?" Elly voices, barely above a whisper.

"Yes," I confirm, and the wheels in my brain start turning. "This means the cluster has an Energy within it that contributes to this excessive growth that has been building and building. If I can disrupt its growth using Energy, I can stop the cells from growing."

"We could do more than that," Lightning adds, her finger still trailing the part she's reading. "Disruption isn't just stopping. That also means altering. We could alter the energy in the cells so that they don't just stop growing, but *shrink.*"

"Shrink to a manageable size and stop it from growing," I finish for her. "Then the illness becomes manageable with medicine again. He might need special Sirian treatment every so often if the manipulation wears off over time, but again... That would be significantly better than feeling like we're battling time to save his life."

"You just have to learn how to do it without blowing him up," Elly cuts in, her finger lingering where it says this charging could have explosive results.

"Well, you know how to wield your Light better than I do," I state, unfolding and turning to Lightning. "Or are we calling it Energy? Either way, you should be the one to do it."

"I can't," Lighting admits, shaking her head fiercely. "You are the Royal Healer. Nobody knows I'm Sirian. I would damage my reputation and put myself in danger, which doesn't do our war or you any good. I can teach you how to do this."

"We don't have time," I yell, throwing my hands out. "It's growing faster every day. The potions I'm coming up with are barely doing anything anymore. I am battling the impossible."

"It's not impossible." Elly smiles through tears. "Not anymore. We can save him, Reva."

I swallow against the pressure building in my throat, my panic subsiding but my anxiety rising to take its place as my heart beats in my head.

Now that Elly knows there is a solution, the stakes are even higher against me. The pressure to master my powers enough to accomplish this without killing the poor kid is overwhelming.

It's not too late to go back to existing...

I shove the thought into oblivion.

I roll my shoulders back and down, straightening.

"How good of a teacher are you?" I confront, clenching my fists at my sides and digging my fingernails into my palms.

Her eyebrow twitches as she folds her arms over her chest, leaning on one leg. "How good of a student are you?" She counters. "I don't know where you are skill-wise, but Jorah hinted toward novice. You're going to need to control your Light so we don't blow up the prince. Doing that would put a wrench in a few plans."

Elly wheezes in disbelief, but I don't break Lightning's gaze as I say, "There will be no blowing up of any young boys. We know the solution now, so I'll spend all my time training with you instead of researching. I hope you're ready to teach a teenage-level Sirian how to wield Light at the level of an experienced, professional Healer. I'm not going to let this boy die."

"The clock starts now." Lightning nods once, those striking blue eyes flashing.

The cool breeze of Fate prickles the back of my neck, echoing, *The clock starts now.*

CHAPTER 23

F in leads Lightning and me down to the hidden chamber where he and I had practiced my powers before.

And did some other things, too...

I'm sure my Sirian ancestors frowned upon me using this perfect space for something it was not intended for.

When we enter the open chamber, Fin and I light the sconces along the walls. Lightning moseys towards the middle of the room, casually studying the walls.

"Why aren't you using your powers to do that?" Lightning scrutinizes, her voice reflecting off the stone walls.

"I don't want to risk that," I confess, lighting the final sconce on my end of the room. I meet her in the center with Fin, handing him my torch. "We're not here to teach me to wield that anyway."

"Not yet." Lightning wags her finger at me, circling the center. "But you will be soon. Our current focus is definitely your Light, but with the right guidance, we'll be able to fix some of the kinks you have had in your firepower teaching. Through all of this, I'm hoping we get you to manifest your other hidden god-power at some point. Until then, we can get you at least comfortable with Dionne's gift."

"I don't know if I'd call wielding the core of the Earth a gift," Fin mutters, peeking at me from the corner of his eyes.

Lightning twists angrily, her jaw set. "You don't know anything about being a Magic or a Sirian," she lectures, holding her hand out in front of her.

My heart flutters as the Light appears, hovering in her hand. Where mine manifests in a concentrated ball, hers is like a white flame, waving and dancing with the air. A string in my stomach connects to that power in her hands, urging me towards it.

"Any power given by a God is a gift. Having a god-power in a time where an army that wields Darkness grows underneath your royal noses is a *gift*. You can't win without Sirians, and you won't win without the god-powered."

Fin averts his gaze, straightening like a commander scolding a knight. I ignore him, more impressed by Lightning.

When she said she was meant to lead the Sirians, I thought she just meant in power, but this isn't the first time she's displayed strong leadership skills. Remaining level-headed with me in the library while I battled an identity crisis was the first time.

"We'll be good here, Fin," I assure, placing a tender hand on his shoulder.

He directs his attention to me, pursing his lips. His eyes roam over my face, scanning for something.

But he quickly turns on his heel and stalks away, leaving

us behind without saying a word.

"You and Elly recruited him for this cause?" Lightning questions, shrugging off the cloak she wears.

Underneath is the same fighting gear Fin had made for me, the same gear I'm wearing under my own cloak.

No one was shocked when I wore them last time; Fin crafted a very good lie about learning self-defense after the incident with the rebel knights. Having another perceived Magic walking around in gear would cause others to raise questions we don't want to answer.

Not yet, at least.

"I wouldn't say recruited is the right word," I chuckle, setting my own cloak aside. I roll my shoulders back. "He was one of the first people to really earn my trust here. I told him about being a Sirian first, and it just so happened that he's been working with Elly and the Crown Prince on the mysteries of the Abyss, too."

"I noticed the badge he wears." She points toward the doorway, wagging her finger. "He's higher ranking than most knights I have encountered, but I can tell he's new to being a leader. He can't hide his emotions, and he's battling his authority versus the seeming authority of others. He easily could have defended against me, talked about how you may not have experienced power being a gift, that I don't know or understand the life you live. But he didn't. He folded."

I startle, surprised she was able to gather that from one interaction.

And she's entirely correct. Fin and I have been in these

scenarios many times. "You were testing him?"

"Anyone getting involved in this war will be tested by me and others." Lightning shrugs. "I need to know where people stand and what they still need to learn. He may be compassionate and willing to accept Sirians, but he doesn't know the first thing about being a Magic or Sirian. He needs to learn, and that's easy to teach.

"Like Princess Eloise, who knows far more than you think. She is a scholar and a politician, as much as she pretends she's not."

"I would say you're pretty spot on," I agree, flexing my arms in front of me. "And me?"

Lightning smiles coyly, lowering her head to peer at me through her eyelashes. "Oh, honey. You could be a queen if only you let yourself."

The Light comes to her so quickly, radiating out from every pore of her body. It pulses like an aura around her but doesn't extend beyond her by less than a foot.

She embraces the Light she's generating like she's welcoming the caress of a lover. I'm transfixed by her ability to *own* the Light and Energy.

Without warning, she arches her arm out in front of her and the Light shoves my chest like two hands, hurling me to my back.

The wind rushes out of my lungs in a woosh, leaving me gasping for air on the ground like a fish out of water. My hand clenches my chest, expecting my clothes to be burned or marked, but there is nothing there.

Her boots crunch against the sand and dust on the

ground. Lightning looms over me, bent at the waist with her hands resting on her knees.

She tilts her head to the side. "That didn't look like it felt too good," she winces, but there's a ghost of a smile behind her mocking mask. I growl at her. "That's it? No rebuttal?"

"The last two people I used my power on I killed," I cough, still trying to catch my breath.

"If that's supposed to impress me," Lightning shrugs.

I clench my jaw, biting down against the rising panic in my chest that threatens to wash over me at the thought of flinging any power at her.

She must detect my internal battle because her face becomes apologetic. "We've all had to do what we've needed to survive. What would impress me was if you hadn't killed them with one sweep of your hand, showed a little restraint. If I had wanted to, I could have sent you flying against that back wall and probably broken a few bones. But I kind of need you in one piece, so I only took a little bit of the Energy."

"Took?" I question, swallowing against the taste of vinegar in my mouth.

She extends her hand out, and I accept. In one quick swoop, she yanks me to my feet and helps steady me before taking up the place she'd been standing before.

"This is where Sirians and Magics differ," Lightning begins. "Magics' powers are pockets within them. When they want to access one of their abilities, they have to open a door to let them out. Think of the House of Echidna and their wings. They have to open themselves up to let the wings out. So, that's how they view power."

Remy crosses my mind, the memory of him fresh from when he revealed his wings to me. I remember the sound they made, like shaking out a blanket or a rug.

"Our power is different. We take what we want to use. Like a knight getting ready for battle, he can decide to use a dagger or a sword. And, like they teach warriors and fighters, that weapon becomes an extension of you.

"Thus the Light becomes an extension of you. You take it, and you control it."

"Fin had me imagine using it as an extension of me," I explain, conjuring my power in my hand. I'm definitely faster at it than I used to be, but I still view it as opening up to let it out. "I've had to change how I regard it recently."

"That's okay," Lightning promises. "Everything gets much easier once you embrace it as something you can take. It's all about control, and that's how it's going to be for your god-power."

That dark pit of molten fire pops into my head.

"The difference is like riding a horse versus a bull. You can control a horse a lot easier, but when you take the power of a God, it tries to control you and wants to fight you every step of the way."

I close my hand into a fist, snuffing out the Light. I exhale slowly in an attempt to relax my nerves.

Lightning chuckles, arms outstretched. "You can't hurt me! Not only can I match your power, but I have been trained to fight with mine. I know how to counter you in case you try to blast me to the moon."

"How is this going to help me control my Light with Clint?" I challenge, folding my arms across my chest.

"It's easier to learn how to be big, then get smaller and smaller until we're learning how to take enough power to disrupt a clump of cells the size of a small ball. Now, take the Energy, Reva."

I recall how the Healer described Energy in the book we read, how it's in everything around us, even the air we breathe. Instead of trying to imagine a wall, I stretch out my senses around me.

A small, nonpainful prickling sensation presses against the very top layer of my skin, expanding beyond me and surrounding every minuscule bit of space. It pulses—no, *breathes*.

Like lungs shifting the chest muscles in and out, so does the Energy breathe in the world around me. It's the brush of fingertips against your body, a taste of what you could have and own.

I imagine absorbing that Energy into me and breathing it in. I breathe out, allowing the amount I took to leave through my hand directly at Lightning.

A blaring burst of Light erupts from my hand, and just before it can hit her, she drops to the ground and braces on her hands like dropping from a pushup.

My stomach drops.

If this amount of power has caught her off-guard, I don't want to find out what it's going to do to the chamber walls it's headed for.

I fling my hand out, concentrating on that stream of

Light hurtling through the air. I spread my fingers wide, reaching for the pulse of this manifested Energy.

It belongs to me, so I command it back.

It stops mid-course to the wall, just inches away from colliding. The force, suddenly stopping, creates a gust of wind that sends the sand below scattering like frightened mice.

As quickly as it stopped, it changes course, heading right back to me.

It slams into my body, throwing me back onto the ground. The Energy snaps back into me like it usually does, but I swear I can *hear* the crack like a whip this time.

I gape at the ceiling, white stars dancing in my vision. A single breath of disbelief escapes me.

"What," Lightning hollers from the other side of the room, "in the *hell*. Was that."

I peel myself off the floor and back onto my feet, albeit not as gracefully as I initially planned. I brush off my slacks before hesitantly meeting Lightning's squinting eyes, a mix of suspicion and confusion.

"I told you I produce a lot of power when it's big—"

"No, not the amount of Energy you projected," Lighting shakes her hand in a line, cutting me off. "I knew you'd be powerful because Jorah warned me. We should probably have practiced somewhere else where your power blast can't be felt throughout the castle on impact, but I digress.

"I meant when you *stopped* it and *pulled* it back into you, not to mention how you channeled the Energy."

"Well, I didn't want people to know," I shout back. "I

couldn't let it hit the wall. I didn't even know I could do that. Why didn't you?"

Lightning stares at me, her eyes wide in incredulity. She fixes her hands on her hips, taps her foot, and extends her head forward.

She throws a hand towards where I had stopped my power from blasting the wall. "I can't do that."

"What do you mean?" I whisper. "Sirians can't—"

"No, Reva," Lightning guffaws, a little hysterically. "Sirians can deliver the Energy impact, generate and project, make *physical* objects stop, and charge objects. We cannot stop Energy power, let alone call it back to us like that. Once it's out there, it's out."

"Dionne?" I question, thinking of my god-power. "How would that relate to heat manipulation?"

"It doesn't." Lightning shakes her head. She scoffs, examining me from head to toe. "I've also never seen someone channel the way you did."

"What do you mean?" I press, wringing my hands together.

"I don't know if you took Energy like I said or how you envisioned it, but when you did, I *saw* it. The air around you *quivered*, and if I tried to look past your shoulders, it was distorted. Like when you look through the heat radiating from a fire. Except you weren't generating heat."

"And, let me guess," I scoff. "Other Sirians don't do that."

Lightning's eye twitches once before they flutter rapidly. "I thought the old man was crazy. Jorah's right, though. You have two god-powers."

"Who's the other one then?" I ask, frowning.

I survey my hands, like a small child again, who doesn't know anything about what I am.

"Just with those two things alone, I'm not sure," Lightning admits, hands outstretched. "To be honest, other than my own, I don't know much about the others off the top of my head. Jorah told me you have Dionne's gift, and I know I have Taranis' gift of lightning. But, I don't know who *that* belongs to."

Her hand waves up and down in the air between us.

I clench my fists at my side. "So, what does it mean?"

"It means that, if we can get you working with your power," Lightning shakes her head, smiling, "And now I have a glimpse into how powerful you might be… The Fates may have just tipped the scales in our favor on this one."

"The Fates can honestly kiss my ass," I blurt, power building inside of me. I shove it away, but Lightning senses it.

"Whatever god-power it is, it's also what you keep shoving away when emotions rise," she says, pointing her finger at me. "That is not average Sirian Energy manipulation. I want to learn what else you can do."

"We need to focus on what I can do to help Clint first," I remind her firmly. "I won't leave until I can minimize this power a little more."

"That's what I hoped you'd say." Lightning smirks mischievously.

★★★

"Okay, well, can you float?" Fin asks, perusing over the notes Elly has made.

I whirl on him, splaying my hands out in front of me. "I don't *know*, Finley," I exclaim for the hundredth time since he started asking me if I can do anything else from either of the two god-powers I might have.

Elly presses a hand to her temple, sighing. "Well, now she's using full names, so you've managed to piss her off," Elly concludes, reclining in her seat and balancing on the back two legs. "Again."

Fin, Elly, and I have been in the library for over an hour now debating whether or not my other god-power is from Phoebe or Asteria.

After a grueling session with Lightning—who definitely left some bruises behind—I came straight to Elly and told her to find the book where we had read about Dionne. Fin joined us shortly into our book scrubbing to help us find the right one since they're all nearly identical.

Both descendants of Danica and a Sirian male, Phoebe and Asteria have powers that channel from the sky. Phoebe channels from our moon while Asteria channels from the stars and galaxy.

With the moon, Phoebe can manipulate gravitational energy. The argument that I'm her descendant is that I was able to manipulate the gravitational movement of the Energy I cast, sending it back into me. If we're reading this right, this would also explain why I was able to send so much power at a high speed towards Lightning.

On the other hand, Asteria is like an amplified Sirian.

She could ignore the laws of Energy, change things between a solid and fluid state, and create or destroy energy with impact.

She could also generate shields that absorb energy, negate it, redirect it, or double it and send it back. That last bit is what we think I might have done with Lightning.

But it also says that she could create clones of anything.

And Phoebe could float.

"I just haven't done anything else really," I exclaim, exasperated. "There was this one time I made the rain go around me, but again, it could have been a shield or gravitational manipulation. Nothing else that I'm aware of can possibly indicate one over the other."

"I don't think we're going to find out yet," Elly admits, rising from her chair. "We need to see you wield more of the Light to find out. I have a feeling when I give these notes over to Lightning or maybe Jorah, one of them will be able to help us figure it out. If anything, giving them to Lightning will help her watch you for any signs as she's training you."

"Is her name really Lightning?" Fin blurts, glancing up from the notes.

He hands them over to Elly to file into the little journal she carries, and she shovels all her books into her satchel.

"As far as we know," Elly shrugs, organizing her satchel.

"It's a Magic thing," I explain, cleaning up the other books with Fin to put back in Elly's locked desk. "Magics would change their names or only take on a first name to protect themselves and their families from any sort of persecution from others. Her real name could reveal where she comes from or her family, and maybe she doesn't want people to know."

"Did Karasi change her name?" Fin speculates. "Is that why you're just Reva?"

"Your guess is as good as mine." I tag along with Elly over to the desk, handing her the stack. "I'm just Reva because we don't know my parents, Fin, remember?"

He presses his lips together, bobbing his head as if he actually forgot I'm an orphan.

Elly finishes filing the books into various drawers before locking them with the set of keys she keeps on her. We vacate the library one after the other and start our journey toward the dining area for some much-needed food.

"Isn't this all so exciting?" Elly giggles gleefully, gripping her thin, pale blue journal. "Clint is going to be healed, we walk amongst demi-gods—"

"You have become way too comfortable with the things we know." Fin places a hand on either of our shoulders, walking between us. "We shouldn't discuss any of this while we strut about the castle like we own the place."

"You're too young to be this concerned, Finley," Elly lectures, filing her book into her satchel. "We're talking about Reva's job, what she was hired here to do. There is nothing wrong with that. We could also be speaking metaphorically when I say demi-god. No one will assume otherwise."

I relate to Fin's concern, but Elly is right. No one will question the princess discussing the job of the Healer she's obviously befriended or what people may presume are fantasies of a girl who gave up her chance to take the throne. "Besides," Elly clicks her tongue, inclining her head. "I do own the place."

As we approach the door to the courtyard, a large mass interrupts our path. Elly and I stumble to a halt before running into it as Fin tenses up a foot behind us.

I meet Pax's skeptical glare. "Princess Eloise," Pax addresses Elly formally. "I have come to inform you the Crown Prince has arrived home from his sabbatical in Riddling. He's waiting in the courtyard."

"Pax," Elly whines, suddenly fidgeting. "Why are you standing in the way, then? Let me see my brother!"

Pax pauses before moving, focusing on me.

I raise an eyebrow, daring him to challenge me. By now, we all know that Fin ranks above him as directed by said Crown Prince.

Fin speaks up, "Sir Pax. The Royal Healer will not harm Prince Tariq. You need to stand down, Sir. It's appropriate for Prince Tariq to meet Reva, and there are plenty of knights in the courtyard."

Pax doesn't answer or budge from his place before us, ignoring Fin's official command.

Elly places a timid hand on Pax's bicep and gently pulls him away from the door. She whispers loud enough for the four of us to hear, "Don't make this any harder than it needs to be, Pax."

He finally tears his gaze from me, shifting it to Elly. It transforms from what once could be interpreted as utter loathing to deep regret.

I can't hate him entirely, knowing what I do about him as Elly and Clint explained to me. It's clear how much he cares for her because I continue to catch glimpses of how he falters in his formalities or the shadows of emotion that pass over him.

What exactly did his father do or say to change him from the man Elly clearly fell in love with to this harsh knight?

Elly and Pax exchange a tight-lipped grin with each other before he side-steps out of our way.

Elly takes off in a sprint without so much as a bye to Pax. Fin isn't far behind her.

That leaves Pax and me.

"I'm not the enemy," I remind him, taking a few steps through the doorway.

Elly's squeals of delight bounce off the stone walls of the courtyard. Fin's laugh is echoed by an equally thunderous one.

"We'll see," Pax responds, stalking away from me.

I take a few breaths to regain my footing before meeting the Crown Prince of Mariande, whom I have only heard about for the last few months. I step out into the sun lighting up the courtyard, the taste of spring in the air.

"Tariq," Elly gasps, slightly out of breath. "You know most of everything by now, but this is our new Royal Healer, Reva. She fits perfectly into our little club, as she puts it. I think you'll like her a lot."

Right when she finishes her sentence, I lock eyes with Tariq.

Even from across the courtyard, you can't miss him.

While he's about an inch or two shorter than Fin, he makes up for it with his broad, muscular shoulders and the overall virility and power radiating off him. His white tunic and cloth pants are not the same garb of Mariande, so I can only assume they're the customs of Riddling.

Either way, they hug him in all the right places, showing off bulky muscle underneath. Dirty-blond hair flows around his face and hangs above his shoulders, cut in layers that graze the nape of his neck, jawline, and groomed beard. High cheekbones lead to set-back eyes, the same beautiful amber shade as his siblings and father.

Oh, Gods.

I don't know how long passes, us staring at each other from across the courtyard, before Elly clears her throat.

Tariq's eyes sever from mine, an intoxicating smile spreading across his face when he looks at his sister again.

"I see you've grown attached already, Elly." His deep voice reverberates through me as his gaze swings back to me. "It's nice to finally meet you, Reva."

The End... for now.

Bonus Chapter

Fin

I waited outside the throne room, Darius's indistinct voice rumbling through the large wooden doors. I stood beside one of the guards, rocking back and forth from the balls of my feet to the edges of the heels on my boot.

"Sir Finley," the older guard interjected, followed by a deep chuckle. My gaze flickered to him, but he continued to stare at the wall across from the door. "A Lieutenant Colonel waits at attention when summoned by the king."

I halted any movement, straightening my back and keeping my hands clasped behind me. I pressed my lips together tightly, eyeing the guard out of my peripheral.

He fought a battle against his smirk and lost.

The large wooden door swung open aggressively, startling both myself and the guards.

Pax's face was drawn tight, his jaw clenched so tightly that it shifted on its hinges. His dark eyes seethed as they met mine.

He shook his head stiffly before storming down the

corridor towards the library.

I met the guard's eyes, frowning with a curl of my lip.

What in the Gods' names was that about?

"Sir Finley?" Darius's voice sang from within the throne me, not a trace of negative emotion indicating what had just happened in the room with Pax.

The guard flourished his arm out in front of him, directing me toward the still-open door.

Once I passed under the threshold, the guard shut the door behind me, a soft thud reverberating off the throne room's stone floor and walls. I crossed the distance between the entryway and the dais, keeping my decorum as my hands stayed clasped behind my back.

A small smirk played at the corner of Darius's lips in amusement.

"We're alone, Fin," Darius said, his voice gravelly. He cleared his throat, propping his elbow onto the arm of his grand throne and plopping his head into his palm. "We can lose the act between us, even if this is somewhat of official business."

"Thank Gods," I sighed, my hands unfurling from behind me and my shoulders slouching forward casually. I took a few steps closer, throwing my thumb over my shoulder. "What was with Pax?"

Darius waved away my question with the hand that'd been resting on his knee, rubbing his head on the other. "Another time, although I'm sure he or Elly will have something to tell you after we're finished here."

The frown returned to my face, but I just left the

comment alone for now. "What was it you needed me for, by the way?"

Darius stared at me intently for a moment, his amber eyes studying my face enough to make me shift on my feet. He took a deep breath that rose his shoulders, releasing it carefully.

"As you know," he finally said, looking to the corner of the room. "Clint is not getting better. Nurse Isla is having a difficult time battling his ailment, and she is concerned she no longer knows what ails him."

My mouth went dry at the thought of Clint not improving, his wide, bright grin flashing in my mind. My heart cracked down the middle, seizing in my chest at the implication behind that.

"We worried this day would come, that we would need to bring in stronger reinforcements to find a cure." Darius paused, his eyes slowly skimming the room before latching onto mine, narrowing. "I need you to retrieve the Great Karasi to offer her the position of Royal Healer."

I startled, my eyes snapping open as my head twitched to the side. Question after question barreled through my mind, each beginning with the word *why*. I rubbed my hand across my trimmed beard, the coarse hair scratching against my calluses.

I was entirely bewildered and taken aback, not expecting this to be what I was summoned here for. Not in my wildest imagination. "Darius…"

He interrupted me by rising from the throne and stepping down the dais. "I need you to leave in a few days and take two knights who you think would be up for the task and who don't have the worst history with Magics."

Given his apprehension about the Magic communities lately, I wondered if this was part of why Pax stormed out of this room, but I still couldn't begin to guess what would've set him off that much.

He looked ready to fight.

Darius strolled toward the mural of Magics painted on the throne room walls, studying the one that depicted the different Houses—well, at least I'd been told that's what this particular one was about.

I shook my head, clearing out the hazy confusion. "I mean this as no insult to your ability at persuasion, but why would the Great Karasi, an *ancient* Magic if tales are to be believed, accept a position as a *Royal Healer*? She's lived in Eldamain as long as anyone has ever known."

Darius didn't answer for a long moment, fixated on the paintings. I took a few steps toward him following his line of sight. When I looked back at him, I doubted he was actually studying the figures on the wall.

He twisted his head to me, a small, closed-mouth grin tugging at the corners of his lips. It's the same look I've seen on Tariq's face multiple times in the last few weeks as he battled whether or not to travel to Riddling as Clint declined.

"Karasi may decline." Darius shrugged, blinking with the movement. "When she was here to help after Clint's birth, she told me that this day would come. Of course, she never said when just that I'd know and would need to retrieve her."

He twirled on his heel, marching back and forth from the front of the dais and back toward me and the wall. "Karasi speaks in nothing but half-truths and riddles, either out of choice or necessity for her power the world may never know. What I do know is that I will not continue to play these games with her and go back and forth from Mariande to Eldamain every time Clint needs saving. Maybe an offer of money, protection, and housing will entice her."

To be honest, my entire mind was void of reasoning beyond the questions racing around my brain. I couldn't formulate a thought past the information Darius presented to me.

I had known that the Great Karasi assisted with Clint after his birth, but few were privy to exactly what had been wrong with Clint when he was born to keep our enemies from ever using it against us.

We couldn't hide that she delivered the devastating news about the damage Lucia had suffered to her back, how it was irreparable.

The Queen was still confined to a wheelchair to this day.

I followed Darius's path to the dais, sitting on the stone steps that led to the throne. I shook my head slowly, raising my eyebrows incredulously. "So you want me to retrieve the Great Karasi. From what I understand, that's not exactly an easy feat. She's supposed to be damn-near impossible to find."

"Oh my boy," Darius chuckled, sitting beside me with a classic fatherly groan. "How do you think your father was able to retrieve Karasi the first time thirteen years ago?"

"Wait." I scanned his face as I leaned back, a mischievous smile curling up his cheeks. "My father went and got her for Clint?"

"It's funny how these things come full circle." He stared off toward the door, the previous roguish grin turning serene. "There is a code to retrieve her that Eamon knows. You'll have to ask him, but I know you need to go to a pub called The Red Raven."

"I can ask him," I assured Darius quietly, considering not for the first time how perfectly some things always seemed to work out for the King of Mariande.

Like sending me to retrieve a powerful Magic thirteen years after my father had, both times to save his youngest son.

"I know you think that she might accept an offer so grand as a Royal Healer." I couldn't help the snort that tumbled out of me, earning me a sidelong look from Darius. "But hypothetically, let's say she refuses. What sort of liberties am I granted to persuade her?"

Darius rose again from the dais steps, using his knees to extend his upper body. He shoved his hand in his pockets as he climbed the step, towering above me from the top.

"If she refuses to be the Healer—" Darius pauses, tilting his head like a feline, a strand of his graying blond hair falling to the side. "Then you better not leave until you have an answer for a cure or until she tells you how to fix Clint so he doesn't die."

The lethal rage that leaked from Darius, dripping from his lips like venom as his eyes flashed in the dimly lit room, sent chills rising up my spine. "When you are traveling, Finley, there is never one path. There are many journeys you can take to arrive at your destination. Some may take longer than others and some may be treacherous. Nonetheless, you get to where you're going.

"We always have a choice to make on what paths we take." His eyes grew distant, maybe lost in a memory of all the various choices he'd made in his lifetime. "The prophecies Karasi gives are always her choice on which one will come true. She knows many outcomes. She will choose the more advantageous for our world to protect the greater good."

Darius returned to his throne, his head turned down while he lowered back into the seat. He folded his hands in between his legs, resting his forearms on his thighs as he bent forward.

He slowly lifted his eyes to me, peering up through his lashes, and what he said next portrayed the man hidden under the golden exterior of his crown. "I don't care what happens to the world, what the consequence will be, so long as my boy lives."

"Yes, Your Highness," was all I managed to say as he continued to stare me down.

He nodded once, casually reclining back on his throne as he waved his hand to dismiss me. "Choose your men and prepare for your journey. Oh!" He holds up a finger. "And when you find my daughter, send her here. We have something urgent to discuss."

After leaving the throne room, I went straight to the library because where else would Elly be? I was also shocked to find Tariq there, Elly's head buried in his chest as he whispered something to her, his chin propped on her head.

The library door shutting behind me had them snapping their heads to me, their dismay at my frazzled state bringing out their identical traits.

"I just spoke with Darius," I managed, frowning at both of them. "He wants to see Elly, but what's wrong with you two?"

I studied Elly's face, stricken and pale with red-rimmed eyes.

She'd been crying.

And I already knew it had to be about Pax.

"What were you doing with our father?" Tariq asked, not unkindly, a crease settling between his eyebrows.

Elly slowly unpeeled from her brother's embrace, accepting the handkerchief from him as I explained, "Well, he requested my assistance with a task. A task that entails me retrieving the Great Karasi."

Both stiffened, Elly pausing with the handkerchief poised underneath her eyelid. Tariq crossed his arms over his chest, tilting his head to the side, which eerily reminded me of Darius in the throne room.

I dove into the specifics of the conversation between the king and me, not skipping a single detail. I explained how Darius acted, as smug as usual, to how quickly he became angered at the end of the conversation when talking about the paths of life.

Elly even snorted at that, shaking her head at her father's dramatics.

"This is a *huge* power move," Tariq vocalized, shaking his head as he rested his hips against the desk. "Appointing a Royal Healer? That hasn't been done in centuries. Since the..."

The proper name hung in the air between us, taunting us to reach out and grab it.

Sirians.

And Tariq was right. There hadn't been an officially appointed Royal Healer in any kingdom since the Sirians used to hold those positions.

"To appoint one again and appoint a Magic..." Elly shook her head, still baffled.

I couldn't blame her because I had also considered whether this was intentional on Darius's part or if this was truly a last-minute, desperate grab of a grieving father.

"I really shouldn't be going to Riddling," Tariq sighed, rolling his fingers on both sides of his temples. "There are too many things happening here. Clint is sicker, and there's going to be a new, very powerful, and ancient Magic entering these walls—"

"It's going to happen whether you're here or not," Elly exclaimed, her arms tightening around her waist. "Clearly Pax is going to keep a harsh eye on her, and I know Fin will also be here to help. There's nothing more we can do about Clint without the help of Magics anyway."

She paced in front of Tariq and me, slowly shaking her pretty blond head as those wheels turned. She stopped in front of Tariq with a grim smile. "It's crucial that we strengthen this relationship with Ruhan and Riddling. They could know about this Abyss and Darkness we keep hearing about, not to mention how relentless Keiran and his father have been about an alliance between us and Etherea."

"You mean your hand in marriage," I interrupted. "We're not going to let that happen, Elly."

"Even if it means I have to accept that marriage to Naja." Tariq closed the short distance between him and Elly, grabbing her shoulders in his hands as he forced her to look at him. "If I need to do that to secure this—"

"I don't want you sacrificing a chance at real love." Elly smiled softly. "Don't force something if you're not feeling it. There have to be other ways to win Riddling than a betrothal."

"You know they love their betrothals," I muttered under my breath, earning a glare from the siblings. I splayed my hands out in front of me, begging them to prove otherwise.

"No." Elly nodded once as if convincing herself. "You need to go to Riddling. Fin will try and retrieve the Great Karasi. We'll be okay here. You know I'll write to you constantly."

"By raven." Tariq removed one of his hands from her shoulders to point it in her face.

She scowled at him, fighting the smile underneath, as she swatted his hand away.

I couldn't help but wince as my heart clenched in my

chest, a strange foreboding pressing into me that things were about to change—for all of us—forever.

We stood a few yards from the porch in front of the hut, staring at the door, apprehension simmering off of the knights with me. I gave them each a glance with a raised eyebrow, daring them to challenge what we were about to do.

"Fin," Jace grumbled beside me, the scar on his face deepening with the frown. "I'm not sure about this. We don't know what she'll do. What if she says no, and you push, and she retaliates—"

"Do not," I held my hand up between us, shutting my eyes for emphasis. "Do *not* do anything to make her feel like she needs to be on the defense. Even as she refuses, we remain calm and reasonable. We do not insinuate or insist anything."

I exchanged another glance with Jace and Maurice before sighing heavily. "Just let me do the talking."

They flanked either side of me as we carefully marched up the rickety wooden steps. My hand hovered momentarily in front of the molded wooden door, concerned a knock would send it flying in on its hinges.

I took a steadying final breath and rapped once.

A strange, heavy silence penetrated through the door, followed by shuffling feet. Near the door was a soft creak of some cabinet or door opening and shutting. More steps echoed closer afterward.

A heartbeat later, the door steadily opened wide,

revealing the woman I'd met at The Red Raven.

And *Gods* if my heart didn't stop for the second time upon seeing her, those glowing hazel eyes piercing into my heart like a dagger, her full lips pursing slightly.

She blinked up at me, scrutinizing me, and something about her effectively cleared my mind of rational thought.

Gods, she was painfully beautiful, even as she propped one hand on her hip and drank all three of us in.

"We meet again," she said, narrowing those eyes at me.

And then I remembered we were here because this was supposed to be the house of the Great Karasi. I knew Magics could age slower than others, but I thought she'd at least look like she was old...

"Wait." I frowned, aghast. "*You're* Karasi?"

"For the sake of both of our troubles," she chuckled, the sultry sound sending a bolt of electricity through every nerve ending. "I wish I was. Please come in."

"My apologies," I managed to make out, bowing and smirking up.

I caught her eye lingering on the corner of my mouth. She took a deliberate breath as she sidestepped from the entryway, inviting me into her home.

The moment I stepped through the threshold, it felt like stepping through a thin sheet, a strange resistance pushing against my skin. A cool breeze tickled at the base of my neck, and I took a cautious glance at the woman again, pretending to scan the area for threats.

Those eyes stayed locked onto me, stealing my breath as I passed over her, that sensation prickling me again.

"What do you need, boy?" An old woman with gray locks piled on her head and beady yellow eyes demanded as she hobbled across the room.

"Madam." I nodded my head in acknowledgment. "My name is Sir Finley Wardson, and I come from the royal family of Mariande…"

OFFICAL SNEAK PEEK OF

FATE DEMANDS SACRIFICE

THE SIRIANS SERIES
BOOK TWO

CHAPTER 1

The orb of Light hovers between my hands, thrumming with the beat of my heart, quivering and buzzing like a fly as I struggle to hold it in this position. Barely bigger than a melon and as bright as a fire its size, the contained Energy threatens to expand, grow, and jerk around the room.

My jaw clenches, a bead of sweat cascading down my hairline and tickling the side of my face. I blink, trying to open my vision beyond the tunnel that's narrowing by the second. Even my arms tremble in front of me from my fingers up to my shoulders.

You'd think I'd been doing pushups for *hours*.

"Hold it there, Reva," Lightning warns, her tone throwing me back into memories of training to control the Light with Remy.

The orb pulses, growing an inch in diameter.

"You have to learn how to maintain control with distractions," Lightning lectures, her voice dropping low. I train my eyes on the ball between me, but her boots crunch against the sand, growing closer. "When you're in the middle of a battlefield, others will be fighting alongside you. You can't get distracted and lose control. The enemy will always try to distract your focus."

"I'm not learning how to battle," I force out from between clamped teeth. "I'm learning to help Clint."

"One and the same, Healer," Lightning whispers, her breath tickling my neck, startling me. Despite the ball blaring briefly, I'm able to reel the Energy back to a steady glow.

Her boots crunch again and she stands in my peripheral with her arms crossed over her chest.

"Good save." Lightning nods her head once. "Let's snuff that out, but don't let it snap back into you like you usually do. Just let it go... whatever that means for you."

We've been working on both generating and releasing the Light for the last week since the first time we trained together. Maintaining control with distractions is my weakness, as well as releasing the Light without it cracking back into my body like a whip against my skin.

I press my eyebrows together, breathing.

I know I need to speed up my powers, but I want to master them before I start flinging things around underneath a castle, which is completely unaware that there are two Sirians training below.

I've been trying to imagine the power absorbing back into my skin, but that never seems to diminish the strength of the recall.

I try something new this time.

Just like I absorb the power *into* me from all around, I try to give it back to nature. I refrain from closing my eyes, watching the orb slowly dim as I do exactly as I picture.

It breaks apart into smaller orbs like little stars scattered in the night sky and, like daylight rising, they fade out into existence.

I've never felt lighter after extinguishing my power. There was no snap or aggressive recall to make me stumble on my feet.

"That was—"

Lightning is cut off by a deep, velvet voice from near the doorway as it calls out, "Whimsical."

Lightning and I spin on our heels to the archway, my heartbeat rising.

Tariq rests against the wall, casually leaning his weight on one leg with his arms crossed over his chest. Fin stands underneath the doorway, feet planted shoulder-width apart and his arms mimicking Tariq.

My heartbeat doesn't slow, now hammering in my chest for an entirely different reason.

"Like a puff of glitter," Tariq continues, demonstrating his metaphor by splaying his fingers out in front of him, letting his arms arch away from him.

I pull my upper lip between my teeth, biting.

"Jesus," Lightning sighs, her hand flying to her chest. "You can't just sneak up on us during practice."

"In theory," Tariq begins, pushing himself off the wall with his back. The movement makes his chest flex, stretching against his black dress shirt. "I can do whatever I want."

He struts across the floor until he stands in front of Lightning and me. He slides his hands into his pockets and bends at the waist, putting his burning amber eyes directly in line with mine. Two strands of dirty blond hair fall from his half-bun.

"But I understand." An inviting smirk tugs at the corners of his lips. "I didn't mean to startle you *too* much."

"I could've hurled Energy at you," I warn him, the threat not coming out as confidently as I would've liked.

He instantly catches that, which only brightens his smile. "I think you have more control than you give yourself credit for."

"You've figured that out in one week of knowing me and less than a handful of sessions you've snuck into?" I question, crossing my hands over my chest and tilting my head to the side.

Tariq's smile minimizes, but his eyes are still alight with excitement. He straightens, shrugging, and purses his lips. "What can I say? I'm a fan."

My gaze flickers to Fin, who's still lingering in the archway but has switched up his posture, now standing like a knight with his hands clasped behind his back. Our eyes lock, and his shoulders lift slightly as if to say: *What are you gonna do?*

"Well, I hope you enjoyed the show," I sneer, stepping into Tariq so there's only an inch between us.

At this proximity, his scent engulfs me so I hold my breath. I made the mistake of inhaling a few days ago, and *Gods,* it was intoxicating.

It was like being submerged in a hot spring during the dead of winter, the warmth seeping into my bones while an icy breeze still kissed my skin.

"I have a younger prince that needs my attention," I finally manage, sidestepping him to walk past. His arm reaches out and his hand wraps around my forearm, halting me.

Both of our heads tilt down at where his skin brandishes mine. We simultaneously raise our gazes at each other, and I can't imagine what he sees in mine as every sense narrows in on the firmness of his grasp.

His face is a perfectly trained mask with a touch of amusement as he says, "I came to let you know that my father requests your presence at dinner with us this evening."

"Just me?" I clear my throat around the slight grumble, averting my gaze.

"I'll be there, too," Fin announces from the archway, still standing at attention.

Tariq removes his hand from my arm, shoves it back into his pocket, and adds, now facing Fin, "We'll all be there."

I walk across the room towards Fin, using all my willpower not to look over my shoulder and check if Tariq—or Lightning—is following behind me. I keep my focus leveled on Fin, whose dimple is slowly peeking out from underneath his auburn-tinted stubble.

By the time I'm standing in front of him, those emerald eyes are twinkling.

"He's not wrong," Fin tilts his head to the side, wincing. "That was whimsical, and you had way more control than you had when you first expelled Energy with me."

I give him a sidelong look, falling in step beside him as

we journey up the stairs.

"I need to get faster," I sigh, extra feet shuffling behind us. "Today was the first time I've been able to release the power like that."

"Reva," Fin chuckles, shaking his head. "It's been just barely over a week since you started training with Lightning. You said so yourself: you have a lot to rethink in your head on how to wield the Light and firepower."

"I am not touching *that* yet." I point my finger at him. "I don't want to risk it popping up when I'm trying to work on that mass for Clint."

"Don't you think it would be a little helpful to at least be familiar with it?" He twists his head to look down at me. "You want to have control to dampen it, too. Not practicing with it doesn't make it any less there."

I steadily inhale through my nose, rolling my eyes. "I hate it when you're right."

Fin laughs a little then, his eyes crinkling at the corners. I can't help the small smirk that sneaks onto my lips.

Fin's laugh has always brought me joy, no matter what's going on around us.

Or between us.

We emerge from the hidden stairwell one after the other, and we're lucky there is no one to see the four of us appear in the hallway. It's less suspicious the fewer there are of us, and we don't want to draw unnecessary attention to our secret training room, considering we're wielding the forbidden Light.

"I'm going to head to the library," Lightning announces,

adjusting the strap on her shoulder. "I'll see you at the same time tomorrow, Reva."

"Ass-crack of dawn," I grumble under my breath, but Lightning narrows her eyes at me with a ghost of a grin.

"I'm going to take my leave as well, unfortunately," Fin sighs. His hand extends towards my arm, but his eyes flicker to Tariq, standing perfectly beside us with a closed-mouth grin, and stops himself.

My heart cracks, swelling around itself.

"I have some rumblings I need to check on in town, but I'll see you both at dinner." Fin makes eye contact with Tariq.

I frown. "Rumblings?"

"We'll debrief you and Elly sometime tomorrow," Fin assures me, returning his attention to me. His smile barely reaches his downturned and soft eyes.

I nod, waiting for him to make it down the hallway before I twist on my heel and start towards my room to prepare for another day with Clint...

Steps follow behind me, and my heart races.

I press my lips together to keep myself from doing a multitude of stupid things. Fin's sad, puppy-dog face flashes in my mind, and that tends to encourage me.

"You know, Reva," Tariq begins, walking in time beside me with those damn hands shoved into his pockets. "I'm a very observant individual—"

"You and your sister both," I mutter, staring straight ahead of me.

He lets out a breath of a laugh. "We are twins, after all. But as I was saying before you interrupted, I'm very observant, and a week of knowing you has allowed me to observe quite a bit about you."

"Oh, Gods," I groan, shaking my head. My stomach twists in a knot, anxiety rising into my chest.

I can't imagine what he's getting at since he already knows I'm a Sirian, but I truthfully don't want to know.

"I know you're dying to know," he says, reflecting the opposite of what I'm thinking. "So I'm going to tell you."

"I figured you would." I twirl my head towards him, squinting.

He's smiling like a fool, and my heart flutters like a bird's wings in my chest.

"The first matter of business is Finley," he starts, clicking his tongue against his teeth. "I'm well aware of his—"

"Don't go there," I snap, balling my hands into fists at my side.

"Calm down, Reva." Tariq chuckles to himself. "I mean no harm by it. It's just I know how smitten he is by you, and I was just going to say that you—"

"There is nothing to discuss about me and Fin," I explain, staring straight ahead, hoping he can't read how complicated it is on my face. I clear my throat. "We have been friendly since I got here, and all of this has only made us closer."

"I hear a *but* at the end of that," Tariq pushes, his voice low.

"But nothing." I shrug and guilt crushes my chest. "That's where we are and that's what we can be."

"And why is that?" He questions, and I silently thank the

Gods as my door grows larger down the hall.

"You stick your nose in places it doesn't belong, don't you?" I divert, allowing myself a glance at him.

He's staring at me intently, void of emotion with that Crown Prince mask perfectly over his face.

"I'm just a curious man." A mischievous grin creeps up the side of his mouth. "See if there's a spot for me to play the game you're playing with Fin."

I stumble in my stride, nearly choking on my own spit.

He walks for a moment longer before realizing I'm not beside him anymore. He straightens, twisting to the side and waiting with an eyebrow raised.

"Something I said?" He asks with a small smirk, eyebrows slightly lifted.

I resume my pace, continuing right past him and not waiting to see if he follows. "There is no game to be played, Prince."

"How many times…" He sighs, exasperated. "You can call me Tariq. I've heard you refer to my brother as Clint and my sister as Elly, so why am I still *Prince?*"

"You're different." I shrug, fumbling with my key.

I stand in front of my door and Tariq leans against the wall beside the frame, his shoulder pressing against it, his hands *still* in his pockets. I pause with the key in the lock, turning my head toward him with an eyebrow raised.

"I'm different," Tariq repeats slowly, tilting his head to the ceiling. "Is it because you're trying to maintain a level of professionalism between us to keep that distance my sister mentioned or because you like taunting me?"

Both.

Without another word, I twist the key in the lock and step through my door.

I wait with my back pressed against it, taking four deep breaths in and out.

It takes nearly a minute of my breathing focus before Tariq's footsteps retreat from the other side.

ACKNOWLEDGEMENTS

I grappled with the acknowledgments for some time, thinking about whether or not it should be over a page. But, you know what… If I'm anything, it's *not* brief. So this is for those who love to read the acknowledgments.

First and foremost, I want to thank those who have been following me since I first made my Instagram account, where I shared little snippets of my journey to publish this book. Thank you for your continued faith in me. You made writing, editing, and crying over this so much more fun. There were so many times I wanted to stop and go back to when writing for my eyes only was easier. You made every last moment worth it. So, thank you from the bottom of my heart.

To my cousin, Rory: you've been my number one fan since childhood. Thank you for always rooting me on and reading every book I've ever written, including this one. To my unofficial editor, my mom: you have always encouraged my love for reading and writing, so thank you for reading Harry Potter to me until I could do it myself. Who knows where where I would be without it? To my Gran: you have never doubted my dream and always believed we would be here one day. Here's to the days when you downloaded Wattpad on your iPod to read my books.

To Cortney Winn: your friendship is one of the best things to have come out of Bookstagram. I can't thank you enough for your honest feedback and fun comments as you read with the Alpha group.

To my cover creator, Brian: thank you for getting just as hyped about creating the cover as I was to receive it. You have been an amazing friend. To my official editor, Sophie: thank you for believing in me despite some of my more embarrassing mistakes. Your love for my story and Fin fan club only gave me more confidence, so you're the real MVP.

To my Beta and ARC Readers: Your enthusiasm, unhinged comments, and love for my characters helped my confidence in my story when I was doubting myself. You have pushed this story forward in a special way, and I hope you will stick around for the rest of the series.

To my Cait: I can never express my gratitude for the things you've stood by me for; this journey is one of them. Thank you for reading my book, being my hype person, and accepting me—Marks and all. To my family: there are too many of you to count. Thank you for reading and supporting me, and I'm sorry/not sorry for Chapter 19.

Last (but never least) thank you to my husband–for so many things, but most importantly, for reading my smut. I'm gonna love you 'til my lungs give out. We'll get those fan club t-shirts made soon.

About the Author

K.M. "Katie" Davidson is an adult fantasy author. Her authorial journey began as a young writer creating YA fantasy novels in composition notebooks and publishing them on Wattpad. After getting her Bachelor's in Creative Writing and Master's in English Literature—and abandoning 20+ book ideas—she finally sat down in 2023 and finished her debut novel, *Darkness Comes Again*.

Outside of writing and reading, Katie is a Content Marketer. She loves dance parties with her husband and dog, hiking, traveling, entertaining conspiracy theories (none more than aliens), collecting more rocks, and buying old copies of books published over 100 years ago.

For exclusive sneak peeks, character aesthetics, and more news, follow K.M. Davidson on social media: @kmdavidsonbooks